SOPHIA BENOIT is the author of *Well, This Is Exhausting*, writes regular columns for *GQ* and Bustle, and has written for *WSJ*, *The Guardian*, The Cut, Fatherly, Insider, Refinery29, *Allure*, PS, and more. Sophia doesn't have an MFA from anywhere, and probably isn't ever going to, much to the chagrin of her father. She is the host of the sex-and-relationships Ringer podcast *None of My Business*. Originally from St. Louis, she now lives in Los Angeles with her dog and her boyfriend (but usually only spouses make it into bios, so don't worry about him).

The Very Definition of Love

Sophia Benoit

PIATKUS

PIATKUS

First published in the US in 2026 by Slowburn,
An imprint of Zando
Published in Great Britain in 2026 by Piatkus

1 3 5 7 9 10 8 6 4 2

Copyright © 2026 by Sophia Benoit

The moral right of the author has been asserted.

A CIP catalogue record for this book
is available from the British Library.

ISBN 978-0-349-45021-6

Printed and bound in Great Britain by Clays Ltd, Elcograf S.p.A.

Papers used by Piatkus are from well-managed forests
and other responsible sources.

Piatkus
An imprint of
Little, Brown Book Group
Carmelite House
50 Victoria Embankment
London EC4Y 0DZ

The authorised representative
in the EEA is
Hachette Ireland
8 Castlecourt Centre
Dublin 15, D15 XTP3, Ireland
(email: info@hbgi.ie)

An Hachette UK Company
www.hachette.co.uk

www.littlebrown.co.uk

This one's for my sister Lena, who introduced me to
romance novels. I'm sorry I snuck into your closet
and stole your books all the time. I owe you
way more than a book dedication.

The Very Definition of Love

1816 – London

Chapter One

Harriet loathed dancing. More accurately, she loathed watching people dance. Which is what she normally did at balls. There were so many better uses of her time, like reading, or sending words to Mr. Dawkins, or keeping her sisters away from their father, or their father away from the gambling tables. Normally, the prospect of leaving for a ball within the half hour would have her filled with dread.

The few times she had danced, mostly during her debut season, had proved disastrous. Unfortunately, as the eldest unmarried daughter of the Earl of Tidewell, dancing—or observing dances—was to be her lot in life for a little while longer. It was as unspoken as it was obvious that Harriet was not likely to marry after five unsuccessful seasons, but no one had any definitive answers for when she might be allowed to beg off the charade.

Harriet would have gladly married the nearest available man simply to get out of attending balls; however, this was not an option available to her. Her elder sister, Philippa, had already strained the bounds of propriety with her marriage six years ago, and was now, as a widow, further testing society's limits. Any damage Philippa hadn't done to the Bancroft family's reputation, their father had taken care of.

Of course, this overlooked the chief reason Harriet didn't just marry the first man she brushed past at a ball: Gentlemen always seemed to have better options about, and those options were so often her own sisters. When coerced into attendance, Harriet spent balls holding wineglasses and eyeglasses, lending a hairpin or mending a hem, watching as Philippa and Caroline danced with and dazzled haute society.

But tonight was going to be different. Oh god, she hoped it would be different. According to his latest letter, Mr. Dawkins had arrived from Oxford last week and was to be at the Dunley ball. Lady Dunley took pride in just how full her ballroom could get and didn't mind inviting a few non-peers if it meant that the season started with a crush. Tonight was about one thing, and one thing only:

"Your breasts," Philippa said.

"My what?" Harriet sputtered, stiffening in her seat at Philippa's—rarely used—davenport desk. She had arrived at her sister's house dressed in her best gown, ready to leave for the ball, only to find that Philippa had not even begun her preparations. *Typical.* Caroline, already too beautiful for anyone's own good, was taking advantage of Philippa's well-trained lady's maids and her large stock of hair ribbons and baubles.

"Oh, I do beg your pardon, would you prefer another term?" Philippa drawled, as she was being helped into a pair of silk stockings—a task which Harriet felt didn't necessitate assistance. "What other words are there for them?"

Harriet almost answered—*bosom* was not unheard of, *décolletage* if you were feeling French, *booby* if you were being naughty, and apparently *dairy*, although that felt quite vulgar indeed; *globes*, *apples*, *paps*—but most people, including her sisters, weren't actually interested in words.

Mr. Dawkins was, though. Whatever time was left over after running the household for their father—begging servants not to leave, writing them glowing letters of recommendation in her father's hand, learning to mend and sweep and wash and cook in their stead, bargaining with the butcher and flattering the fishmonger—Harriet devoted to the dictionary. The dictionary of slang and cant words she and Mr. Dawkins had been working on for months, though they'd never met.

"Well, what about them?" Harriet grumbled, trying not to sound as irritable or as interested as she was. Her sister did know something about enticing men.

"Like me, you have been blessed." From the floor, where she knelt smoothing skirts, one of Philippa's maids, Gertie, snorted. Philippa continued, ignoring her. "Yet you keep them completely hidden!" Harriet fought back an unladylike groan. This again. Another lecture from her sister about her appearance.

"She's right, you know." This came quietly from Caroline, who sat across the room having her hair expertly curled by another maid in Philippa's employ.

"Not you too," Harriet moaned.

Philippa twisted her entire body toward Harriet, thwarting Gertie's attempts to fasten a string of pearls around her neck. "Harriet! I'm quite serious!"

Caroline continued without moving an inch, ever the embodiment of grace. "Harriet, you know how rare it is that I agree with Philippa, but if you are to garner any attention at all tonight from your Mr. Dawkins—"

From Philippa's bed, where she was reading outdated scandal sheets, their youngest sister, Frances, sat bolt upright. "Mr. Dawkins will be there? This is the first ball I've ever been sorry to miss!"

"I don't think Mr. Dawkins is interested in my . . . breasts," Harriet informed the room, reaching up to pat at her modest low bun. Still pinned in place. Still simple.

Everyone grew silent. Harriet finally looked around. "What?"

Philippa and Gertie screamed with laughter. Frances looked at her like she was the biggest cabbagehead imaginable. Even Caroline's lips twitched with mirth.

"My dear," Philippa said sagely, as if she were thirteen years rather than thirteen months older than Harriet, "I can assure you Mr. Dawkins is *most* interested in your breasts."

"He doesn't know they exist," Frances said from the bed, not looking up from her periodical. "Did you know that the Duke of Waverly has fathered a child with an opera singer?"

"Frances, that sheet is from January, we all know, and of course Mr. Dawkins knows she has breasts!"

"Can we all stop talking about this? Please?" Harriet begged. Everyone ignored her, as usual.

"Father doesn't allow us to buy scandal sheets, Philippa! So how would I know? You get to have all the fun!" Frances continued. "And Harriet signs all her letters to Mr. Dawkins as H. M. Bancroft. He has no idea that the person who has been writing to him has breasts. Or that she's been pining after him."

"I have not been pining—" Harriet began.

"Yes, you have." Philippa cut her off, sizing up her appearance in the mirror. It was, as ever, to her satisfaction.

"Does he really not know that you're a woman?" Caroline asked. There was something so sweet, so pure about Caroline that Harriet felt she must always give her the truth.

It was damned inconvenient.

"No, he doesn't know I'm a woman. I did not think it relevant to my work. He is interested in me for my mind, not my breasts. And besides—" She was cut off by everyone's shrieking and squabbling. Philippa and Gertie were laughing again, no doubt at her. Harriet bit her lip in embarrassment. How did her sisters seem to know so much about men? How could they anticipate what men thought? What they liked? What lesson had Harriet missed?

"Well, tonight we are going to change that," Philippa announced, and when Harriet looked up, she noticed that her sister was looking quite shrewdly at her.

"Philippa," Harriet warned, knowing that an idea was taking root in her sister's mind. Ideas were a dangerous thing for Philippa to be in possession of. The only person more dangerous with an idea was Frances.

"A splendid idea," said Caroline, in full agreement with Philippa. Heavens, the ideas were spreading across the room. Frances looked back and forth between Caroline and Philippa, and Harriet fought the urge to stand and block her view, as if perhaps that would keep Frances from joining in.

"Oh, *yes!*" Frances's eyes gleamed, which was the most dangerous portent of all. Everything—everyone—started moving at once, and all the activity seemed to coalesce around Harriet herself.

"You'll wear this," Philippa insisted, sorting through a haphazard pile of dresses that lay on the bed. She pulled out a low-cut white gown, not dissimilar to Philippa's own, save for the detailing. It was, if you had to choose one word, *exquisite*. And if you had to choose another, *wanton*. "You can borrow stays."

"And Clothilde can do your hair too. She's almost finished with mine," Caroline insisted, referring to Philippa's French and rather rude lady's maid, who, it must be said, did a lovely job with hair if you could put up with her vexing attitude. Caroline could put up with anyone. Harriet wondered if Caroline even knew Clothilde was mean.

"Wear some of Philippa's rouge! And the perfume she has, the one that smells of lilies!" Everyone turned to Frances. Frances, who wore trousers as often as skirts; who usually tracked dirt to the dinner table; who thought women who rode sidesaddle were cowards.

"What? Just because I can't go to balls yet doesn't mean I don't understand all this frippery. I'm not an idiot, you know. I read all the same issues of *La Belle Assemblée* as you do. I daresay I dance better than the lot of you, as well." This reveal stunned Harriet, conveniently giving Philippa enough time to pull Harriet up from her chair. Just as quickly, Gertie started flicking open the buttons running down the back of Harriet's admittedly plain gown.

Caroline sprang into action next and after that, there was really nothing to be done. For as much responsibility as Harriet had when it came to her sisters, she had little control, which is precisely how she ended up in a corset instead of her normal unrestricted short stays, and slippers not a little too small for her, with rouged cheeks and her hair actually styled, smelling of lilies. Despite the discomfort and her better judgment, when Philippa's carriage arrived at Lady Dunley's ball, she had to admit to feeling at least a little bit beautiful.

And worse: a little bit hopeful.

Alexander loved dancing. He had discovered a natural talent for it early on and his skill only improved with practice. Besides, it gave one something to do at parties that wasn't so dull as talking about pheasant hunting.

Alexander had found himself genuinely enjoying dancing after a few balls his first season; his lack of reluctance—indeed his apparent pleasure in the activity—endeared him to women of all stations.

Above all else, Alexander loved dancing because ladies loved dancing and Alexander loved ladies. What was there not to like about a physical activity that brought another person gratification? Alexander happened to adore activities that fell into that category, of which there were quite a few.

He was rarely without a partner, despite being a second son, and a rumored bastard at that. Although one didn't need rumors to tell them what their eyes could plainly see: Lord Alexander Stirling was not the product of marital relations between his mother and the Duke of Belhaven any more than a lion could be the product of a chicken and a rooster.

Alexander's jet-black hair and substantial height would have been enough to convince anyone that a minor Venetian prince was his true father, but it was his languid confidence and easy charm that separated him the most from his parents. Not that anyone remembered much about his mother, who was rumored to be in the Americas now, or India, or even Cornwall, depending on whom you went to for gossip.

All anyone really remembered was that a flighty blonde had been the catch of the season some thirty years past, and that the ill-tempered Duke of Belhaven had been friendly enough with her money-chasing father to ensure a match. She'd given him a natural heir and a bastard spare, whom he'd been forced to claim as his own. What people didn't remember, or more precisely didn't know, was that at the sight of the bastard's ink-black hair, the duke had sent his wife—the mother of his children—away.

Thus, as a child, Alexander knew few women outside of his household staff, all of whom were far too afraid of the duke's wrath to coddle or comfort the young bastard. At sixteen, he'd sneaked out of Harrow School over Christmas holiday with a few mates and found his way into the arms of a young gap-toothed woman who charged him a shilling for an hour, then let him have a second hour for free when he didn't try anything. After his fourth visit, she explained the purpose of women in her profession. Then she demonstrated. After that, he visited her thrice more, paid her a pound each time, asked her to teach him everything he needed to know, and then made up his mind never to go too long without female company again.

And he hadn't.

Tonight, like many nights before, he found himself preparing for yet another ball. What many of his male peers overlooked was that balls were a fabulous arena at which to meet female company, even if one did not intend to offer marriage. One could tease a spinster, enchant a dowager, captivate a debutante, provoke a chaperone, embrace a widow, and tempt a hostess, only to end the evening in bed with a Cyprian who wouldn't have been let in the doors.

While his male peers often spent balls comparing livestock and complaining about Parliament, Alexander forwent such topics. For him, economic matters were reserved for clubs and coffeehouses. Balls were for dancing and drinking. And above all else: women.

This evening he was forced, unfortunately, to break his personal rule. He planned to use Lady Dunley's ball to meet with the heavenly— and widowed—Philippa Fanshawe, Baroness Ellerton, holder of vast swaths of land in the Lake District. Land he intended to purchase. It did chafe him a bit to sully such an evening with talk of money, but he hoped to balance the faux pas with the promise of pleasure.

Alexander wasn't actively in the market for a new paramour, having a quite expensive and experienced mistress currently perched in a townhome in St. John's Wood. His and Giuliana's agreement was not explicitly exclusive; she often sported jewels Alexander was most certain he hadn't purchased for her. He liked that she was not overly reliant upon him, or interested in his general whereabouts. While her indifference wasn't false, he suspected she played it up a bit, correctly sensing that he was the sort to be alarmed rather than aroused by displays of devotion.

While discreet, Alexander had never been one to limit himself. That way lay stagnation and dissatisfaction. He wasn't the sort to grow lovesick or possessive over his partners, and he never, ever offered promises of fidelity. He might meet with an opera singer on Thursday and an unhappily married marchioness on Friday.

And one would be a fool to turn down Lady Ellerton's company in any form; she was one of the most beautiful women of the *ton*, and one of the few who could match his seductive capabilities. While he did not feel desperate for her affection, he was undeniably interested.

Tonight, if Lady Ellerton found herself inclined to join him in bed, after they discussed the land she held in Applethwaite, Alexander would count himself all the luckier. They'd been circling each other for months now; it was only a matter of time.

Chapter Two

Lady Dunley was unduly proud of having stairs down to her ballroom, a feature she claimed put every entrance on display.

It was at the top of those very stairs that Harriet discovered an unfortunate truth. Not only had she expected tonight to be different, she'd expected *herself* to be different. And for others to take note. Until she experienced the distinct lack of reaction, she didn't realize she'd been anticipating one.

No one looked up. No one dropped a champagne glass. No one pointed or even whispered. What would they have even said? "The third Bancroft sister—what's her name again? Looks a little better tonight. A tad unfortunate to have to stand beside the other two, but good for her."

God, she was a muttonhead. Three ladies entering a ball—no matter how lovely they were—was common, arguably the very point of the event. She felt her face flame with the embarrassment of her own vanity and the disappointment of discovering that even with a corset, she was still herself.

And her sisters were still her sisters.

Philippa had recently finished the half-mourning period for her late husband Reginald, the 14th Baron Ellerton, and was thrilled to be back in the world as a widow. Caroline was, by virtually all accounts, the loveliest creature to ever grace a London ballroom and thus—despite being four years younger than Harriet—was the Bancroft daughter next in line to marry. She was positively swarmed with suitors, something no chaperone had had to contend with while watching Harriet.

As a widow—and a young, beautiful one at that—Philippa tended to abdicate her protective duties for more important things like champagne and sexually frustrated marquesses, leaving Harriet to watch their younger sister in her stead. Thus, Harriet often ended up alone at balls. A genuine wallflower. Although the flower part always seemed a little generous: She felt more like a wall-potted plant. There for ambience but not adding any particular beauty to a ballroom. Harriet let out a rueful snort of laughter at her fanciful ideas of the evening.

"Are you all right?" Caroline asked, ever concerned with how people around her were faring. She gripped tightly onto Harriet's arm as they descended the steps.

"Certainly, just sharing a private joke of sorts with myself." Harriet focused on not letting Caroline falter. Philippa was rather occupied with swanning down the stairs herself, likely garnering the precise reaction Harriet had imagined for herself. If she did, Harriet missed it in favor of steadying Caroline.

"Do you need your eyeglasses?" Harriet whispered as Caroline stumbled a bit.

"No, no, I simply haven't worn these slippers in ages. I'm not used to them." The two of them continued down the steps in Philippa's wake. At the bottom, Caroline relaxed. Philippa turned back to them, thrumming with the excitement of being among so many people.

"Shall I fetch us some ratafia?" Harriet asked, ready to be useful.

"Harriet, darling, that's practically the only thing a man's good for," Philippa replied, scanning the room.

"I'm perfectly capable of carrying three glasses."

"Yes, but a man likes to do little tasks for women. It makes him feel ever so good. Why rob him of that? I'll go find us one." Philippa left them alone. Nothing like a ball to remind Harriet that male attention was both a game and a certainty for her elder sister.

"If you have to go off and get a gentleman, isn't it just as easy to go off and get a refreshment yourself?" Harriet muttered.

Caroline smiled pleasantly at the exchange, as she gazed out on the dance floor, making a clear effort not to squint. Harriet noticed this because she watched her sisters quite closely and also because she had no interest in looking around the ballroom herself. What was there to see? The entire *ton* staring in awe at Caroline's beauty? A man walking toward her only to dip away when he realized she was Harriet and *not* Philippa?

"Would you like to take a peek, Caroline?" Harriet whispered. Caroline started, having been lost in a daze of her own. After a moment of reluctance, she nodded.

Harriet led them over to a tall houseplant and then turned back to face the ballroom. Behind her, halfway in the foliage, Caroline fished her eyeglasses out of her reticule. The entire charade was silly, as no one ever looked Harriet's way very long. Her invisibility was her greatest gift when it came to ballrooms. This reality was incomprehensible to her dear sister, however, no matter how many times Harriet tried to assure her.

"Is anyone looking at us?" Caroline asked.

"Yes, rather, I think I've caught the eye of the Duke of Grange. Oh dear. He's walking this way. Our fortune is changing! I think he's quite taken with me. Imagine, I'll have forty thousand a year or more!"

Caroline gave her a small pinch. "You devil!"

"No one is looking," Harriet reassured her.

Caroline slipped her eyeglasses on and gazed around the ballroom. From behind her, Harriet could hear a small, contented sigh.

"You could wear them all the time, you know."

"Yes, but sometimes it's nice not to see things, isn't it?" This was Caroline's standard response to Harriet's standard suggestion.

"It only decreases your beauty by about half, and I think you rather have more than enough, don't you?" Harriet teased, knowing full well that the eyeglasses wouldn't decrease her sister's beauty even an ounce.

Caroline stepped out from behind her and folded up her eyeglasses again most carefully. "Half, you say? Last time it was a quarter."

"I suppose it's your new hairstyle. Really unbecoming. You—" Harriet's teasing was cut off by the return of Philippa and the arrival of her entourage. Before she married, Philippa had always been flanked by a large group of friends and admirers. Widowhood had taken her popularity to new heights. Though her behavior was sufficiently scandalous to make a lady persona non grata, Philippa was smart enough to matchmake between the awestruck debutantes and the unseasoned young bucks who followed her around, which quite endeared her to the matchmaking mamas. Besides, her presence at your rout or musicale ensured at least a two-fold increase in male attendance.

"Excellent news! We've found just the man for our arduous task!" Philippa exclaimed to them, as if finding a man for beverage-fetching had been a group endeavor, rather than her own undertaking.

"Lord Hartford, may I present my sisters, Lady Harriet and Lady Caroline. They're ever so parched. Would it be possible for you to deliver us some ratafia?" Harriet looked up out of politeness at the introduction—her third to Lord Hartford—which is when she noticed that Philippa, who believed ratafia was beneath her, was already carrying a glass of champagne. Harriet wondered absently which man had won the chance to deliver the drink. Lord Hartford looked sick to leave Philippa's side but dashed off regardless.

"There!" Philippa said. Having satisfied her sisterly duty, she looped her arms through two gentlemen's and sailed off. Harriet didn't know enough about men or balls to guess their destination. Another young lord—Lord Pendleton, Harriet believed—took the whittled-down competition as his chance.

"Lady Caroline, would you care to dance with me for this set?"

"Yes, of course, my lord," Caroline answered, beaming. And then she hesitated. A small moment that only a sister would notice.

Caroline shot her hand behind her back and Harriet seamlessly took her eyeglasses. With that, she was off, leaving Harriet in the circle of Philippa's friends without protection.

Despite her misgivings, and her previous experience attempting to converse with gentlemen, Harriet drew from her deep well of social graces and turned to the man next to her.

"Good evening, Lord Cockburn," Harriet intoned.

"Good evening?" he replied, phrasing it as a question. Harriet knew what the question was: *Why is this woman speaking to me?* A lifetime in this role allowed Harriet the patience to offer up an explanation for her existence.

"I'm Lady Ellerton's sister. We met two weeks ago at the Dunforth musicale. And a week before that in Hyde Park. Your new horse's name is Kratos. You said you didn't know why, and I told you Kratos is the Greek god of strength."

"Oh yes, I remember you. Her sister. Well, the other sister. There's another, isn't there?"

"We have two other sisters, yes," Harriet said with a tight smile. "One is not yet out, and the other is on the dance floor now with Lord Pendleton."

Lord Cockburn's neck nearly snapped from his effort to look.

"*She's* your sister too?" he asked, wondrously, not taking his eyes from Caroline.

"Yes."

"She wasn't in Hyde Park."

"No, she wasn't. Excellent memory," Harriet replied, though the man entirely missed her sarcasm.

"Does she have dances after this?"

"You know, Lord Cockburn, I'm not certain. As she is an entirely separate being from myself."

The poor man was thoroughly confused, which was quite all right with Harriet. Men were often confused in her presence, and she did nothing to disabuse them of the feeling. Still, it stung a bit when he turned to the man next to him and took the conversation back up without even excusing himself from the one he and Harriet had been having.

"Lady Ellerton has a sister," he informed his companion, rather loudly. "She's with Pendy now, take a look."

Harriet hadn't even realized how much she'd been hoping for the interaction to go differently until it went precisely as it always did. Suddenly the low-cut bodice felt foolish. What was a wallflower doing in this gown? Why was she trying to look like Philippa at all? The more they looked alike the clearer it was that what set Harriet and Philippa apart was not their appearance, but something more ephemeral than that, an unnamable *something* within Philippa that drew people to her, made people want to talk to her, know her, choose her.

Harriet preferred when she'd thought she was simply lacking Philippa's good looks. She felt rather disheartened to discover that she lacked something much more fundamental.

Philippa returned then, as if summoned by Harriet's maudlin thoughts. Next to her, one of the men she'd left with was juggling oranges and being ignored by everyone else in the group. Harriet felt badly for him, although what would give someone the notion that Philippa would be impressed with orange juggling?

To her credit as a sister, despite the gaggle around her, Philippa focused most of her attention on Harriet. The rest would pair up or dissipate soon enough without Philippa's special attentions.

"Is there someone *you'd* like to dance with?"

"I'm not sure that's the order of things, Philippa—picking men like bonnet ribbons. Although I appreciate the compliment of you believing it to be within my power."

"Oh, of course it is! I'll introduce you to any man of your choosing, just point him out."

"I prefer watching to dancing."

Philippa leaned in close. "Any gentleman would count himself blessed indeed to be in such proximity to your . . . abundant assets . . . tonight. I hardly think he'd notice if you tread on a toe or two."

Before Harriet could admonish her sister, Philippa abruptly straightened and focused her gaze across the dance floor.

"Is Father here?" Harriet asked, searching the ballroom, trying to find the source of Philippa's regard.

"No, no. I'm sorry. It's just, well. *He's* here. He's been trying to get an audience with me for ages. It's become almost tiresome." Harriet did not believe that Philippa had any idea how often she spoke about men wanting her or throwing themselves at her feet, or if she did, how these blasé announcements felt like pinpricks to Harriet. Philippa complaining about a man wanting her was as common as using a handkerchief.

Except that when Harriet's eyes followed Philippa's across the ballroom, she found herself staring at the least common man she'd ever beheld: Lord Alexander Stirling.

"*He* wants you?" Harriet choked, quite rudely.

"Desperately," Philippa groaned, as if it were an inconvenience to be desired by Lord Alexander. Harriet suspected this was at least partly for show. Her sister enjoyed toying with men, and if rumors were to be believed, Lord Alexander was a formidable playfellow.

Philippa languidly turned her body away from the man. Harriet surmised this to be a calculated move, one that made men even more interested in approaching her.

The attention of Lord Alexander was a boon, even if Philippa acted otherwise. To be sure, he was a duke's second son. But a duke's son is a duke's son, even without the rumors of his brother's ill-health. Even if he was known to be an obdurate bachelor—with rumors that he debased himself by dealing in matters of commerce—Lord Alexander Stirling was one of the most striking men to grace a London ballroom since at least before the war. He was, undeniably, the most beautiful man Harriet had ever seen. It was embarrassing, for some peculiar reason.

Philippa turned her eyes up to Harriet over the rim of her champagne glass. "Is he coming this way?"

Harriet dreaded having to look over her sister's shoulder again, dreaded having to watch him with any level of attention, or being in his path at all. But sisterly duty snapped her head back up to see Lord Alexander striding elegantly and leisurely toward them. Out of nowhere, her mind formed a distinct image of him walking just as calmly out of a house on fire, and for some reason the scene made her shiver.

"Well? Is he coming?"

Oh, right. Philippa.

"Quite" was all Harriet could manage, for Lord Alexander was only a few yards away at this point.

Philippa adjusted her posture, dabbed carefully at her lips, and glanced down at her bodice to make sure it was sufficiently in danger of exposing her nipples. Then she turned to him, thankfully blocking Harriet from view.

"Lady Ellerton."

"Lord Alexander, may I in—"

"I have a request of my own first." Harriet swallowed a laugh. No one interrupted Philippa, least of all a man. Harriet couldn't wait to hear Philippa's retort.

"Yes, my lord?"

Yes, my lord? Philippa did not "Yes, my lord" any man!

"This dance. Then you may ask of me whatever you wish." Harriet rolled her eyes behind her sister's back. Surely Philippa was not persuaded by this flummery.

"Gladly, my lord." Harriet took a sharp breath. She'd heard stories of Lord Alexander's charm before, and certainly the man was handsome, but his ploy struck her as unimpressive. Perhaps his words held more sway when he was actually looking at you.

"Harriet, do you mind?" Philippa turned and held out her half-full champagne glass reluctantly. It was the apology in her eyes that removed the sting of her action. Harriet simply reached for the glass and forced the smile up to her eyes as Philippa was led to the dance floor.

Harriet supposed she ought to take advantage of her solitude to seek out Mr. Dawkins. No one was even keeping up the pretense that she required a chaperone, and so Harriet wove her way through the ball with ease. She tried to search the room methodically, but people kept *moving*, as they were wont to do at balls, she supposed. She decided to stake out a spot with a good view of the stairway, in case he hadn't yet arrived.

Seeking out a man so desperately made her feel more than a little doltish. But she pushed the self-recrimination away. He was, after all, the raison d'être for her attendance. Harriet was giddy at the idea of finally getting to speak with him in person, and not having to wait days or even weeks for his correspondence. Never had she felt so connected, so understood by someone as she did by Mr. Dawkins. And so, she returned to her almost pathetic search.

All she had to go off of was a likeness of him she'd seen drawn in a periodical a few years back, her only image of the man she'd been corresponding with for so long. Of course, she had no idea how accurate the depiction was. And though she'd hinted she'd be in attendance this evening, he still presumed her to be a man.

Harriet stationed herself against a column. Nearby was a rather sizable group of men—although, Harriet thought to herself, any more than one man felt like a sizable group to her—only a few of whom she recognized. She settled in to shamelessly eavesdrop and took a few sips of Philippa's champagne; listening to men, after all, was usually quite boring. They were horrible sources of gossip, preferring to prattle on about horseflesh, land, and their deuced clubs. But occasionally someone used a word Harriet hadn't heard before; men were allowed so many more words.

"She isn't your type at all, I'm afraid," Lord Wexler, a handsome young buck, proclaimed.

"And what is my type, Wex? Pray tell," rejoined Lord Trenton, a man Philippa had warned Caroline away from at their last ball.

"Well, for one thing, she's not like your usual dirty puzzles. She's quite the tease, in fact."

A what?

Another man, one Harriet didn't know, chimed in then. "'Tis true. No one's seen that monosyllable. Her sister is very protective too; doesn't let her out of her sight."

"You, Trenton, will not be the first to ride that quim."

Harriet inched closer, her mind racing as she tried to keep up with their words. Alas, the men had moved on to talking about this mystery woman riding something. Harriet was quite confused about the jump to horsemanship.

Dirty puzzle? Is that what he had called the woman? Monosyllable? Quim? She briefly considered smashing her reputation on the cold, hard, terrazzo floor, marching up to Lord Wexler—to whom she had never been introduced—and demanding he repeat himself and explain every word he'd just said. Groups of men were allowed such fun, vulgar phrases, phrases that were so difficult to find again, certainly not in the books Father kept in his library. Harriet's hand again itched for a pencil or quill. Surely somewhere in this house—

The library! Yes, of course. The library. Even a couple such as the Dunleys had one, Harriet supposed. A house without a library? No one was that tasteless. The search for Mr. Dawkins could wait; in fact, when she met him, she would share her new words. *Dirty puzzle. Monosyllable. Quim.* Harriet tossed back the rest of Philippa's abandoned champagne in what would have been deemed an unladylike manner if anyone had noticed her enough to find her manner unladylike; then she set off across the ballroom once more, this time in search of something much more interesting than a man.

"I'm eager to hear what you believe you can offer me," Lady Ellerton teased as they met up mid-dance, only to be separated again. Alexander bided his time, happy to let her wait; women seemed to like it when you moved very, very slowly. Patience was the simplest part of seduction, although not always the easiest.

The dance ended. They applauded politely and then, when Philippa turned her gorgeous eyes up to him, Alexander finally responded.

"While I am happy to discuss such matters on the dance floor, it would be far easier and far more pleasurable for me to demonstrate. Meet me in the library in ten minutes."

"I'm afraid I have a dance with Lord Crowley next. I simply can't miss it; he's promised to take me to see John Julius Angerstein's private art collection later this week." Alexander had a strong suspicion that she'd agreed to nothing of the sort with the man, that this was some tactic intended to heighten his interest in her. What she didn't understand was that he was already interested and had no desire to compete for her time. He spied Lord Crowley a short distance away.

"Follow me," he instructed. Philippa obeyed, which did not surprise him at all. Women like her grew tired of the milksops and namby-pambies who trailed them and tended to appreciate a more direct gentleman.

"Lord Crowley," he said, upon approaching the man. "If you were to receive a banknote from me for two hundred and fifty pounds, would that be sufficient to keep your appointment at Angerstein's with this lovely lady, even should she cry off your dance?"

Lord Crowley looked around, shocked at being addressed by Alexander, who did not, as a rule, mention money in front of women. He nodded and let out a stunned "That would be . . . all right."

Alexander inclined his head, both to thank the man and to take his leave. A few feet away, he turned back to Lady Ellerton, who seemed to be trying not to appear as impressed as she was. "The library, then?"

"The library," Philippa said, a little breathlessly. He tried not to watch her ample chest rise and fall, but there was something about the cut of that dress. The modiste who had made it was quite wicked. To make a dress in white, so common a color, and then cut it so? Devilish indeed.

"Ten minutes," he reminded her. If the land negotiations took as long as he thought they might, he'd find out how effective his advances were in about fourteen minutes.

Chapter Three

Harriet crossed the cavernous room, searching for a writing desk, or at least a quill. The Dunleys' library saddened her, woefully overstocked for its underuse. You'd be hard pressed to find a book that wasn't wrapped in a blanket of dust. Harriet couldn't help herself; she trailed her fingertips along titles she would have paid handsomely to hold. Father's money was rarely around long enough to purchase anything as useful or enjoyable as a book, busy as it was at the gambling tables.

Unfortunately, Harriet couldn't dawdle. While she was frequently unchaperoned, that didn't mean she was immune from ruin or censure. She moved reluctantly to a forgotten escritoire in a back corner of the room, likely last used under the reign of George II, certainly there now merely for show. Harriet gingerly opened the desk drawer and was rewarded with a blunt quill and a pot of old ink. No paper.

Not unused to this predicament, Harriet rolled down her left glove and dipped the quill into the ink. She began to roughly scratch the word *quim* onto her wrist, although the quill hurt and the ink was too old to work well. The letters were ugly, and her wrist was rather red. She began next on *monosyllable* but only got to *monos* before giving up on the endeavor. She'd have to remember *dirty puzzle* on her own later. She shoved the quill and ink back in the drawer and blew softly on the skin at her wrist to dry the ink, shivering ever so slightly.

"Cold?" came a man's voice right at her ear. An unladylike shout escaped Harriet's lips before she could stop it. The strange man had wrapped his arms around her! In the time it took for her to turn and shove her knee upward—she had read once this was the best course of action when being abducted by a man—Harriet also registered that this was the first time she'd ever been in a man's arms.

The man in question let out a loud groan, dropping his arms and crumpling in on himself.

Harriet turned to escape the madman, when he gritted out a muffled "Lady Ellerton—"

Oh.

Not mad, then. Simply confused.

Harriet turned back to face him. Lord Alexander. *Of course* her sister had secured the private attentions of the most handsome man of the *ton*. A man who seemed entirely shocked at his current situation—whether that being her attack or her identity or both, Harriet wasn't sure.

"Lord Alexander, I'm afraid you have the wrong Bancroft sister. I am Lady Harriet. I do apologize for . . . well . . . for kneeing you in the bollocks."

Lord Alexander, still doubled over, let out a loud crack of a laugh.

How puzzling.

"What?" she spit out.

"Well," he said finally, straightening with a grimace, "I don't think I've ever heard a lady say *bollocks* before. Rather I have, but not . . ."

"An innocent?" Harriet supplied. His eyes sparked, as if he'd intended to say something else. Harriet wished dearly she'd held her tongue and found out.

"Did I use it correctly?" she asked.

"Your knee? Yes, your aim was rather perfect."

"*Bollocks*. Did I use the word correctly?"

Lord Alexander looked behind him, as if to confirm that someone else was a party to, and just as confused by, this mystifying conversation. Alas, he and the girl were completely alone—something he was about to rectify, since ruining innocents was not for him. As he went to excuse himself, however, he found something else coming out of his mouth.

"Yes, you used *bollocks* with great mastery."

"It was my first time saying it aloud."

"Quite?"

"Yes. Well, again, I beg your forgiveness for the bollocks incident. I read once that it was the best course of action in an abduction. I am glad to discover the maneuver's success, and sorry it came at your expense. I do hope it recovers."

"An abduction?" Alexander found himself hiding a smirk.

"Yes. Why else would a man come up behind me?" The smirk quickly morphed into a cough as Alexander choked on absolutely nothing. There were many reasons he could conceive of that a man might want to come up behind her.

"The apology is mine to make. I am afraid I mistook you for your sister, whom I was supposed to meet here." Now that he saw her face, he had a rather difficult time imagining that anyone could confuse the two. This girl—Lady Harriet, was it?—had a rounder face and a less prominent nose. They had the same coloring: chestnut hair; dark, dominating eyebrows; gray eyes; less fair skin than was strictly fashionable. But Lady Harriet had a fuller mouth. Lush lips, one of which she was biting now, apparently because of nerves. Lady Ellerton, on the other hand, did not seem the sort to fall prey to nerves. The woman before him had none of her sister's sultriness. Yet something about her struck him as far more dangerous.

"I'm sorry to have interrupted your assignation," she said, bowing to him as she took her leave.

"Lady Harriet," he called after her. Once again, he was unsure why he felt the desire to stretch the time he was alone with an unwed woman. "You used it incorrectly."

"Pardon?"

"You said you hope 'it' recovers, but *bollocks* is plural. *They* recover." Harriet's eyes widened and he immediately regretted having spoken up. What kind of gentleman—not that he usually identified as such—said such a thing in the presence of a lady, let alone *to* her? And when was the last time he'd overthought a remark to a woman?

Christ, but this was why he avoided innocents. He was about to apologize again—surely this was a record number of apologies in one evening for him—when he noticed her smile.

"That's ever so useful to know! Thank you!" She looked so genuinely pleased with him that something in his chest twinged.

"Happy to help you with any filthy words you might encounter," Alexander nobly offered, in jest.

"Truly? There is one, actually," Harriet eagerly replied, glancing down at her wrist. Alexander followed her eyes to her ungloved wrist, which was red. He stepped toward her, closing the distance between them and reaching for her hand. Harriet flinched at the touch, trying to draw her arm back, but not before he saw the word *quim* quite clearly written upon her skin.

"What is this?" he demanded, hating how high-handed he sounded. Had he ever scolded a woman before?

"*Quim*," Harriet explained, squinting at her own handwriting, then up at him as if concerned for his literacy. "Do you know the word?"

Alexander felt himself in danger of blushing. He had done or witnessed just about every possible act that might call for embarrassment, yet he could not remember a single previous instance of blushing. Never had a woman—nay, any person—made him feel so off-balance. It was as if *he* were the innocent. He gathered himself to his full height, straightened his posture, and cleared his throat, as if to start the whole interaction over.

"I do."

Christ. That was not *starting over.*

"And? Its meaning?" she asked, her large gray eyes gazing up at him expectantly. A rather attractive move, he had to admit. Although, was it a move? She hardly seemed the type to employ seductive stratagems.

"I can hardly—" Alexander began.

"We've already spoken of bollocks, I hardly imagine this is worse."

She was correct: *Quim* was far better than *bollocks*, although not at all in the sense she meant.

"All right, only if you promise not to tell your mother I told you."

"Worried I'll ruin your reputation?"

"Worried I'll ruin *yours*."

Something heated flashed between them then, a familiar jolt of shared attraction. This was not the sort of woman with whom one could share such a thing, Alexander knew. But it had been ages since an interaction with anyone had proven this captivating.

"It means . . . it's a woman's . . . parts," he explained inelegantly, entirely unused to striving for propriety or circumspection. At her look of confusion he continued, "Her commodity. Her money. Her . . ." Alexander nodded downward, and the lady's eyes widened even further.

"Oh! Oh my! This is wonderful," she said, almost breathlessly.

What on earth was he still doing in the library with this woman? Why was he still holding her wrist? Surely, there must be a logical explanation for this, one he would discover imminently—for

Alexander, like most men, believed himself to be ruled by logic above all else. Logic felt very, very far away at the moment.

"You cannot leave this room with that written on your wrist. It's indecent!" he insisted sharply, taking on a tone he had never employed before with a woman, a tone he was borrowing from his father.

An unwed woman of the *ton* simply could not walk around with the word *quim* branded on her. Was this Bancroft sister mad? More to the point, was *he* mad? Why did he care? His brain tried desperately to contrive a reason why he minded so much what happened to this woman.

"Indecency requires an audience. I don't plan on anyone seeing my wrist. That's what gloves are for."

"There are plenty of indecent things you can do alone, I assure you. And someone *has* seen it."

"Tell me what *monosyllable* means and I'll gladly erase it," Harriet goaded.

Lord Alexander groaned. If he heard one more body part come out of her mouth! He took his handkerchief from his pocket, wet it with the only thing he could think of—his own tongue—and started rubbing Harriet's wrist. She let out a loud, affronted gasp.

A gasp that, as it turned out, covered the sound of the library door opening. It could not, however, cover the shriek that came next.

Alexander and Harriet whirled together toward the sound, more graceful than any dance step Harriet had ever attempted.

At the entry stood a very concerned Philippa and an equally over-whelmed dowager, the Marchioness of Neddlesby. Lady Neddlesby was not the biggest gossip of the *ton* by any means. No, that distinction belonged to her dearest sister, Lady Swindon, a woman who treated private information like tea—something a good hostess would offer anyone who stopped by. Lady Neddlesby was a lonely woman whose great loves were her rose garden and finding someone to entrap into conversation about her rose garden. And long visits with her sister.

∾

Most ruination happens gradually, but every once in a while, something goes catastrophically wrong in an instant. In those cases, the most acute pain comes in the first few seconds after disaster occurs, when "before" feels so close, so reachable. In these early moments the new order of things seems quite literally unacceptable.

Why, I am in the same dress, the same slippers, the same room, the very same spot on the very same Axminster as I was before this happened, you might think to yourself. At least, that was what Harriet was thinking to herself when her life ended.

No, that was rather dramatic. In fact, being caught alone in a compromising position with Lord Alexander *wasn't* going to end her life. Unfortunately. Death would have been the simpler outcome: Her sisters could have gone into mourning for a year and reemerged woeful, tragic, but not altogether objectionable misses. This, however? This was ruination. Obliteration.

"Oh dear," Lady Neddlesby squeaked, rather unhelpfully, although Harriet gave her credit for being the first one to find her voice.

Harriet, who never before had frozen during a crisis, found herself utterly incapable of reply. Perhaps this was the experience of being the one to have *caused* said crisis. Interesting. Other people's calamities were so much easier to iron out, she was rapidly discovering.

"Well, then!" Philippa exclaimed, thawing into her usual self and regaining her voice. "Lady Neddlesby, I'm ever so sorry we were unable to continue our chat about your hothouse. I should dearly love to see it someday!"

Lady Neddlesby stood rooted to the spot.

"Oh dear," she repeated, just as unhelpfully as before. Philippa ratcheted her charm up even higher.

"I suppose their secret is out, then. I *told* Father we'd have to share the happy news sooner rather than later. It's ever so difficult for young couples to keep a long engagement quiet. Young love is—"

Harriet didn't wait to discover what young love was; she stopped listening after the word *engagement*. Or maybe she'd simply stopped hearing due to the ringing in her ears.

She had the twin urges to glance at Lord Alexander's face to see if it betrayed any emotion and to never look at the man's face again, for she feared she knew exactly what she would find: Contempt. Disgust. Regret.

Someone whispered, "I didn't intend—" and midway through the utterance Harriet realized it was her mouth doing the talking. What had been her mouth's plan for ending the sentence? *I didn't intend to be caught in a library with you with your hands on me? I didn't intend for Lady Neddlesby to intrude? I didn't intend for us to be shackled together for all eternity?* Clearly, her mouth was not to be trusted.

Her eyes were next to betray her as they wandered up, quite of their own volition, to Lord Alexander's. There they discovered that "Oh dear" was actually quite an apt reaction, all apologies to Lady Neddlesby.

Lord Alexander had turned to stone. Unyielding, cold, immobile. If Harriet had hoped to gain some insight into his mental state, she was sorely disappointed. The worst of it was that his face was no less handsome for having shuttered. Harriet truly *understood* the word *stunning* for the first time. She felt as if she'd never regain full consciousness.

Perhaps noticing that neither half of the happy couple intended to address the situation at hand, Philippa decided to usher Lady Neddlesby from the room. "I do apologize for this small impropriety. Again, you must know how long engagements chafe young people."

At this, Harriet became *un*stunned enough to let out a snort of laughter. She'd been out five seasons already with a sixth in mourning for Philippa's husband, and surely Lord Alexander was eight and twenty if he was a day.

His head whipped to hers, the first movement he'd made since they'd been discovered. Harriet avoided his glare, fearful that what she might see would be worse than stone.

Lady Neddlesby was still at the threshold. Lord, but the woman was slow-moving. Philippa persisted: "I want to thank you for the privacy and discretion you're affording our family. We're all truly elated, but we still need to discuss the engagement announcement and some other . . . minor details."

Even as Philippa began to close the door on her, Lady Neddlesby's eyes remained on the "elated" young couple, who did not seem to be aware that they were still touching one another.

"Lord Alexander, I had no idea that *this* was why you requested my presence in the library. I must give you credit: It has been ever so long since a man has surprised me!" Philippa crowed, somehow having fun with the situation.

Harriet, whose gaze was firmly and bravely on the carpet, let out a strangled, "Philippa."

"An engagement? To my sister? I was unaware that you two had spoken. Or had even been introduced!" Philippa trilled, gaining momentum.

"*Philippa*," Harriet implored.

"And, Harriet? How could you keep such a thing from me?"

"Lady Ellerton!" Lord Alexander growled, finally cutting into her rant. Something about his voice warmed Harriet from the inside, even as it terrified her. Which was absolutely not the thing to be fixating on right now. Her apparently impending nuptials to the son of a duke ought to have been her sole focus.

As if his own outburst snapped him back to reality, Alexander dropped Harriet's wrist, pocketed his handkerchief, and abruptly left the room, with a simple bow of his head.

Harriet remained planted where she was. As soon as she moved, she knew the situation would become permanent. It would have happen*ed* in the past tense, and the past tense was dangerous; there was no changing things that had already happened, only things that were still happen*ing*. And as long as she stood in the same spot on the carpet, she felt as if all of this was still happen*ing*.

"I think perhaps it's time to go, my dear," Philippa gently implored. "Why don't we head out from the garden, then I'll return to the ballroom to gather Caroline and meet you in the carriage?"

Harriet nodded and slid her glove back over her wrist, determined to ignore what was on it and how *words* had led to this. For the first time in at least an hour she remembered something.

"Mr. Dawkins didn't happen to show up tonight, did he?" she asked Philippa as her sister led her down a blessedly empty corridor. The look that Philippa gave her was full of pity. "I suppose it doesn't much matter now, does it?"

Philippa shook her head, agreeing with the sentiment. They walked the rest of the way to the carriage in silence. Harriet climbed inside in silence. Then she waited in silence for her sisters to return.

She felt thoroughly done with silence by the time they arrived.

The feeling lasted only a moment.

"You're engaged? To Lord Alexander?" Caroline asked, uncharacteristically upfront. Silence clearly had its benefits.

"I don't rather know, do I?" Harriet responded, suddenly more exhausted than she'd ever been in her life. "The blasted man left the blasted room before I could bloody well talk to him! And don't say 'language,' please don't say 'language,' Caroline. I will wring your neck and then I'll wring my own neck."

"He left the room?" Caroline asked.

"He left the room," Harriet confirmed. Then she leaned back against the seat and closed her eyes.

"What does that mean?"

"Caroline, dear, let's give Harriet some time." Her two sisters had, in the face of this crisis, seemingly switched roles—Caroline becoming blunt and Philippa softening into an almost comforting figure. Even more bizarrely, Harriet herself was the one *causing* said crisis. Surreal. No one was playing their correct part in their usual family play.

"Does she *have* time?"

Harriet's eyes snapped open. "What do you mean by *that*?"

"Well, just that—" Caroline demurred at the trained attention of her elder sisters, one warning, one murderous.

"Let's talk of something else until we arrive home. How was the ball for you, Caroline? Anyone of interest?"

Harriet did not want to hear about anyone of interest. She didn't want to hear about balls for the rest of her life and certainly nothing about this particular ball. She leaned back against the squab again, eyes closed, and allowed herself to think of the only comforting thing her brain had the capacity to think about: She knew a new word.

Chapter Four

"I ruined an innocent tonight," Alexander announced, settling in the sitting room of his mistress's town house, a glass of brandy in hand. He hadn't known precisely where he intended to go until the direction to his driver was leaving his mouth. Tonight wasn't their usual weekly appointment, but things were rather dire.

Giuliana thought about this a moment, before answering, "That doesn't sound like you."

"I do have quite the reputation as a debauchee."

"Yet not as a despoiler of virgins."

"I didn't despoil her."

"If you would prefer me to spend the next hour teasing this tale out of you, I'm more than happy to do so. You pay me handsomely enough to be perfectly amenable to any sort of evening you wish. However, if you'd rather forget the topic and get to fucking, I'm equally acquiescent."

"Yes, yes, let's," Alexander said, although he didn't move from the armchair.

Knowing better than to try to converse with a distracted Alexander, Giuliana stood from her own chair, crossed the room, and took the brandy out of his hand, setting it on the side table. She leaned in close, loosened his cravat, and pushed off his chair to stand before him. Then she began leisurely unbuttoning her dress. Alexander's eyes skittered by habit to her hands, but he found himself unable to focus.

"We were simply together in a library. It was the oddest thing . . . on her wrist she had written . . ."

Giuliana shrugged the dress off her shoulders, exposing inches of flawless skin. Skin designed to tantalize the most stoic of men. Alexander had pressed many a kiss to the very décolletage now on display.

"What had she written?" Giuliana asked, smirking just enough to entice him. Then she let her gown fall to the floor with a simple *whoosh*.

"*Quim*," Alexander answered, rather dazed. Giuliana was no longer in focus for him. "*Monosyllable*."

As his mistress, she'd heard him say much filthier things over the past two years, but never outside the context of sex. And despite her best efforts, they were not on the path to having sex. Giuliana grabbed his brandy glass off the side table, took a sip, and then crossed the room to sit in a chair of her own, understanding that, unprecedentedly, Alexander wanted to talk *first*.

"She didn't know what the words meant."

"I suppose you offered to show her?" His eyes, which had been absently watching his discarded cravat weave through his hands, snapped up to her.

"I did nothing of the sort."

"Not your usual course with women."

"With unmarried women it is."

"Interesting. I don't recall ever marrying, and you swived me quite senseless just the day before yesterday."

For the second time that evening, Alexander found himself in the presence of a woman who made him want to growl, who made his head hurt and the bridge of his nose beg for a pinch. He groaned instead, imploring her with his eyes to take this situation seriously.

"She is a lady, then?"

At Alexander's nod, Giuliana finished off his brandy and stood to refill the glass. On her way back, she stopped to sit on the arm of his chair.

"Are you going to marry her?" she asked, handing him back his drink.

"I can't."

"Oh dear, I'm afraid I'm going to hear quite a silly belief a man has about himself. I do so adore when this happens!"

"I'm a bastard," he answered, draining the glass.

"I'm plenty aware, my lord." Giuliana took back the glass and went to refill it once more at the sideboard. "You always fuck like you have something to prove."

Alexander groaned again. It was quite clear that she wasn't taking this crisis seriously at all. She probably believed there was a simple solution.

"You know, there is a simple solution."

"Women always think that."

"Men would be much more attractive if they didn't view my sex as a monolith, but I suppose that might be too much to ask."

"What's the simple solution, then?"

"Break whatever silly little promise you made to yourself about marriage—all men of your status have lofty, self-important ideas about evading the parson's mousetrap—and marry the girl."

Alexander leaned back in the chair and closed his eyes. His voice was barely audible when he said, "I didn't make the promise to myself. I made it to my brother."

Across town, Harriet sat in a similar fashion, although she'd brought a pillow to her face to muffle a scream. On the opposite sofa, Philippa waited patiently for her sister's episode to finish. All things considered, shouting into a divan cushion seemed like a reasonable reaction.

"Well said," she commented, attempting to draw Harriet out. "Now, are you ready to make a plan?"

Harriet tossed the pillow aside and tried to shuffle herself up into a more polite posture. The ball gown—which she felt bore some responsibility for the evening's events—limited her range of motion. "No!"

"All right then, let's to bed. Tomorrow we can put a notice in the paper that you two are to be engaged. Force his hand."

"He won't be forced! The man is far too high in the instep and roguish for that! He'll simply ignore the announcement and then I'll be even *more* than a pariah! I'll be pathetic!"

"You're being horribly disagreeable, which is usually my thing, or really Frances's."

"Yes, well, I don't *usually* end up engaged to an ill-favored rake."

"I don't think anyone could claim the man is ill-favored. And you two *aren't* engaged."

Harriet picked up the pillow once more and let out a long, low groan.

"Yes, that does seem rather concerning. We can discuss it at length tomorrow morning. For now, I think it best that you either get some rest, or—" Philippa already knew that this suggestion would be rejected out of hand, which is why she headed to the sideboard to pour herself a glass of sherry.

"Rest?!" Harriet sat fully up, which took quite a lot of work—blast the dress! "Philippa, this won't be solved in the morning. If anything, the problem will have gotten worse!"

"Indeed. Then back to my earlier suggestion: Shall we make a plan?"

"I don't see a way at this. I have nothing to entice Lord Alexander. I'm a passed-over wallflower with no dowry and a family on the edge of scandal—don't argue!" Harriet warned as Philippa opened her mouth to speak. "It's not just Father, you know! Your little . . . assignations . . . draw attention!"

"I wasn't going to disagree with that part," Philippa said, rather solemnly. "Only, it's not true that you have *nothing* to offer."

"Please, let us forgo the homily on how lovely you find me. I'm not sure Lord Alexander will be persuaded into marriage with the promise of giggling over needlework or creative accounting to hide Father's debts."

"I wasn't going to do that *either*. Will you listen for once, instead of guessing what everyone else is going to say?"

Harriet closed her mouth.

"There is a reason Lord Alexander wanted to meet with me in the library tonight."

"I'm well aware of the reasons," Harriet said, gesturing with her hand up and down the entirety of Philippa's being.

Philippa shot her a look and continued. "He's after Hardwicke."

"Is that a euphemism for something only married women know about?"

"Harriet!"

"No, then?"

"Hardwicke is part of the land Reginald left me when he died, up north, near Applethwaite."

"Why does Lord Alexander want that?"

"It abuts his property, or a property he's trying to purchase, or something. My steward explained it in a long, boring letter that kept me quite warm when I threw it on the fire. Either way, Lord Alexander has been a beast about the whole thing apparently. Dying to buy from me."

"And you won't sell?"

"I don't care one whit about the land, frankly. However, I can't sell anything entailed or otherwise until Reginald's infernal long-lost cousin arrives to claim the barony. I'm not to touch a teaspoon until we get the estate settled."

"I don't see how this helps me if you can't sell the land."

"*He* doesn't know that, does he? For all Lord Alexander knows, I'm holding on to Hardwicke for good reason. And maybe I will. I do wonder why he wants the land so desperately, but we needn't bother finding that out now. All you must convey to him is that, if he *doesn't* marry you, I won't ever sell."

Harriet mulled this over for a moment, heart sinking. "I didn't imagine I'd have to threaten a man into an engagement."

"How else do you think marriage comes about?" Philippa stood then and walked over to refill her glass with sherry. Becoming a widow had erased any desire she previously had, small though it was, to conform to decorum.

"Fondness, courtship . . . love . . . ?" Harriet murmured.

Philippa returned to the settee and frowned. "Unfortunately, I don't think Lord Alexander will offer much of those. Fondness, perhaps. He's said to be quite enthusiastic in"—Philippa paused for a moment—"his interactions with women."

"I've read as much, and I'm well aware that I am not the sort to entice him."

Philippa's mouth tugged into a frown, as it did whenever Harriet trended toward self-deprecation. "For all his reputation as a rake, he seems to be rather generous with women. He's had a mistress for a while who is said to live quite well in St. John's Wood."

"Splendid! Shall I head over there now and get some lessons in how he likes to be swived?" Harriet felt frenzied.

Philippa choked on her sherry.

"Harriet! I didn't even know you knew the word!"

"I'll admit, I've never used it before. I heard one of the Thompson boys say it a few months back and I've been anxious to employ it." Harriet chewed on her lip then, thinking.

"I understand he's not your first choice—"

"He's not my 4,485th choice," Harriet interjected, which Philippa ignored.

"Nevertheless, you must marry him."

"I agree." There was no other option; she had to put sentimentality aside. "The question is *how*."

"Blackmail, seduction, putting his name in the paper. Hell! Knowing your skill, you might be able to talk the man into it! I haven't won an argument with you since you were six years old. No one has."

"You suggest I knock on his door, hand my card to his butler, and hope he's accepting callers?"

"Well, I don't think he'll be coming to you any time soon. And with Father out of town until Lord knows when, it's not as if anyone else is going to track the man down and force him to the altar."

Harriet got rather silent then. Philippa was so disturbed by her lack of talking that she went around the rarely used sitting room straightening any little knickknack she could find and dusting off a chair no one had sat in since the 1700s, which had surely been dusted the day before by one of her maids. Finally, Harriet spoke up again.

"Let's head to bed. Ideas had after midnight aren't to be trusted."

"Oh see, those are the only ones I listen to."

"I know," Harriet said, with a weary smile. She let Philippa lead her up to one of the many guest rooms kept at the ready. At the threshold, Philippa pulled her into an embrace and kissed the top of her head.

"It will sort itself out, Harriet. I promise."

Harriet nodded, afraid that if she opened her mouth, she'd tell Philippa precisely what she planned to do.

Chapter Five

If life had taught Harriet anything, it was that problems did not sort themselves out. As her family's resident problem sorter, she did not have the luxury of believing such nonsense. Problems demanded action, not patience or hope. Certainly not sleeping soundly assuming someone else would step in and solve them.

Harriet left a note for her sister before slipping out the servants' entrance and hailing a hackney carriage. She had never been in a carriage alone before, and never alone in the city at this hour; each passing moment brought more doubt. Doubt was replaced with panic as the hack rolled to a stop in front of a dark, imposing townhome. As she alighted, a shiver ran down her spine, only partially from the cool night air. The driver looked at her and then up at the house.

"You sure this is the right address, miss?"

Harriet gathered herself. "Yes, thank you, sir."

"Should you like me to wait here for you? I'll charge you a shilling for four hours." Harriet wanted to snort, both at his assumption that she had the money and that she might be the type of woman who would stay at this address for that long.

"No, thank you, sir. Good night." With that, Harriet began her walk to the grim front doors. Perhaps it was the darkness of the evening and the task at hand that made them appear so foreboding. Surely during the day, they were ordinary doors. At least, that's what Harriet told herself. She reached her hand up to knock softly, the sound frightening her even as she made it. She bit her lip and rocked back on her heels, hoping she wouldn't have to knock any louder. Hoping someone had heard. Certainly the butler of a rakehell such as Lord Alexander was up at this hour. Indeed, men who weren't half as promiscuous as he stayed out all hours of the night.

Just as she was about to give in and knock again, the door swung open, and a shockingly affable old man inclined his head. "Apologies for the delay, miss, I didn't expect you at this door. I'll take you right up to his room. He's not in yet, but I will send a message along to apprise him of your presence."

Harriet's eyes grew wide as the butler led the way up a grand staircase.

"Oh, I'm—I'm sorry—" Harriet began, quite rooted to the spot. The butler turned then, a twinkle in his eye.

"Yes?"

"I'm not—I'm not here to—Well, I'm not—" Harriet wasn't ready to use the word *swive* with a butler, no matter her practice earlier tonight. The butler's confusion barely registered before his eyes widened in surprise. His gaze swept over her, and he paused, chuckling to himself.

"No, I don't suppose you are. Tell me then, what is a lady such as yourself doing here to see Lord Alexander? You seem too guileless to be a widow and too shrewd to be unhappily married, if you don't mind me saying. Either way, those sorts of ladies do so rarely use the front door."

Harriet found herself smiling at his impropriety. Something about the warmth this stranger exuded steeled her, making her feel as if he was on her side.

"I must talk to your . . . uh, well, to Lord Alexander. I'm afraid he and I ended up in a bit of a situation this evening. An entanglement, if you will." The butler's eyes narrowed with concern, in a way that made Harriet's heart catch.

"I assure you, he's all right."

"I'm not worried about him, my lady."

It took Harriet a moment before she could reply with an "Oh. Well—" although she had no idea where the sentence was going. Luckily for her, Lord Alexander's butler didn't mind taking control of a situation.

"I can have you wait in the sitting room, if you'd like. I'll bring you tea while you wait, although I must warn you, he will be a while."

Harriet didn't have a while. If Philippa found the letter she'd left, she'd be here within minutes. Now that she thought of it, she hadn't even given herself much time to convince the man; blast the part of her that felt compelled to inform at least one of her sisters precisely where she was at all times.

"There is an exceedingly urgent matter I must discuss with him this evening. Could you perhaps tell me where he is?"

The butler thought for a moment, clearly weighing his options.

"I can do you one better, my lady. I'll send you there. Although I do hope you're not one to scandalize easily. He's a bit of a git, he is. Too handsome for his own good, I've always said." He chuckled, as if they were sharing a joke, although Harriet couldn't tell who it was on. He cleared his throat and turned graver. "He's with company is what I mean."

What an odd butler, Harriet thought. She liked him immensely.

"His mistress?" she asked, trying to keep the shakiness out of her voice. To make it seem as if she frequently spoke of such things to gentlemen's butlers.

"I'm afraid so. Lovely woman, she is. I have a strong suspicion you two would get on." Harriet smiled. "It's that or wait till morning, I'm afraid. And morning for my lord starts around noon."

"I suppose I have no choice, then." Harriet and the butler shared a look, as if they were in league together, which she supposed they were. He simply nodded and left the room, his absence bringing back the chill of the evening.

"What the bloody hell am I doing?" Harriet whispered to herself, allowing herself a few curses as the situation seemed to call for them.

As if in response, a nearby clock chimed two.

Time's running out.

After decades of dealing with both her father and Philippa, Harriet had been virtually certain that nothing could shock her. Her first thought upon entering Lord Alexander's mistress's sitting room was not shock per se, but rather an honest reappraisal of her own naivety.

She charged in, ready to spar once again with the indomitable Lord Alexander, only to be greeted by a roaring fire illuminating two people in shocking states of undress. One—the most gorgeous woman Harriet had ever seen—was entirely nude and sitting casually on a loveseat reading a book. The other, Lord Alexander himself, was sitting—or rather sleeping—in a nearby chair, snoring softly. His jacket and waistcoat had been removed, his shirt unbuttoned, and his cravat discarded. His feet were appallingly bare, though most egregious of all was that his breeches appeared to be unfastened— that was the last detail Harriet observed before she threw her gaze elsewhere and tried to blink away the image.

To her credit, the nude woman barely flinched at Harriet's presence. She simply snapped her book closed and smiled, as if she'd been expecting her. "Good evening," she said, standing. "I trust Sanderson let you in?" The woman—Lord Alexander's mistress, presumably— was tall and lean, with a mass of light-brown hair that cascaded down her back as she stood.

Harriet nodded and turned her face toward the wall a bit, doing her best not to notice anything else about the nude woman, but then wondered perhaps if that was rude. She didn't want to appear as if she *wasn't* looking out of distaste or disgust. Where *did* one look when presented with someone's nipples?

"I hope I didn't—Won't you forget what page you're on?" Harriet said to the wall. She knew it was a silly thing to ask, and she winced, waiting for the woman to laugh at her.

And she did. It was, however, a warm laugh. A shared laugh. "Page 265. Not to worry. I have an excellent memory for such things." As she said this, the woman picked up a blanket thrown over the settee and tucked it around herself with practiced ease, looking even more like a goddess than before, which Harriet would not have thought possible.

With an ease Harriet envied, she extended an arm and dipped into a small curtsy. "You must be the woman from the library. I'm Miss Hightower, but you may call me Giuliana." Harriet had no idea what the etiquette books said about being shown into a gentleman's mistress's house by said gentleman's mistress's butler to arrange a marriage after an incident of public compromise only to find both the gentleman and the mistress in states of undress. Giuliana, however, behaved as if she'd experienced this many times before.

"Please, have a seat. Would you like me to ring for tea? Otherwise, you can join me in drinking his good brandy." Harriet took the seat across from Giuliana, still dazed by the sheer ordinariness of their conversation.

"No, thank you. I'm actually here to—" Harriet gestured vaguely toward Lord Alexander's body.

"Yes, I assumed so. I heard you two had quite the *meeting* at the Dunley ball this evening." Giuliana peered up over the rim of her brandy glass in a way that sent a thrill through Harriet. The woman was clearly good at her job. The word *meeting* sounded positively filthy coming from her mouth.

"No, no, we didn't—we just . . . His arms, mostly . . . And, well, my wrist. Someone saw, you see? Well, they didn't see. But they thought they saw. Something. But nothing happened. So then he . . . Well, he didn't offer, which I understand, but I have sisters. Younger ones. So, I'm here because my father is missing. Well, not missing. But gone. He gambles a lot. And goes off for months on end. So we have to marry, you understand . . ."

Despite her frenzied and nonsensical monologue, Giuliana nodded. "I do, in fact, although you're going to have a devil of a time discussing such things with him tonight. He's quite drunk, I'm afraid."

"Typical, I suppose," Harriet muttered. Giuliana seemed about to say something, but she held back. The weight of the evening's events chose precisely then to settle on Harriet, and she felt suddenly on the verge of crying. Crying wasn't an act Harriet was opposed to, but she didn't particularly relish the idea of doing so in front of this goddess.

"So, what's our plan, then?" Giuliana asked, a glint in her eye. For such a vexing, vain man, Alexander certainly surrounded himself with warm and welcoming people.

"Plan?"

"Certainly, you didn't come all the way here to the house of a known Cyprian without a plan?"

"My plan got incapacitated," Harriet said, gesturing vaguely once again in the direction of Lord Alexander, who she assumed was still slumped and softly snoring in his chair. No doubt his breeches were still unfastened and halfway down his lap, but Harriet had been studiously avoiding checking on that.

"Your plan was to get him to agree, yes?"

"Yes . . . ?" Harriet had no idea where this was going.

"Agree to what?"

". . . To marriage," Harriet said, wondering which of the two of them was the dimwit.

"Of course, dear, but what then? Was it to be a special license? Or banns to be read in hopes your father returned in time? Or an elopement? Come now, what did you have in mind?"

"Ideally . . . Well, I can't wait for the banns to be read. My father is unlikely to return for an age. I certainly can't procure a special license myself. Even if he were amenable, we'd need him awake for that. I supposed I hoped for, well, an elopement." Harriet winced.

"Marvelous!" Giuliana said, clapping her hands together. The woman had a lot of faith in the blanket stretched across her bosom, petite though she was. "I must admit, I'm a sap when it comes to elopements! So romantic!" Every time Harriet felt she was getting somewhere in this conversation, it turned, and she was left wondering which of the two of them didn't understand things. Nothing about this situation was romantic.

"He's . . . well, he's asleep, Miss Hightower," she gingerly reminded the woman.

"I insist you call me Giuliana, and I fear he's a little past asleep. The poor fellow has had enough brandy to kill every man in the House of Lords."

"Even worse!" Harriet exclaimed, throwing up her hands and trying not to lose patience.

"Even *better*," Giuliana smirked, leaning back against the velvet divan, looking more regal, more divine than ever. Had Harriet any ounce of artistic ability she would have wanted to paint the scene. "Now, you needn't waste your time getting Alexander to agree. You'll find he's quite *agreeable* as he is."

Harriet's throat caught a bit at her casual use of his given name.

"Convenient, that," Giuliana continued, "since he's a stubborn bugger when awake; can't convince the poor sod of anything unless he's made to think it's his idea."

"I know the type well," Harriet answered.

"Now that we have everything sorted, would you like any tea before you go?" Harriet wasn't sure they had *anything* sorted, or where she was meant to go, but Giuliana appeared entirely serene as she rang a small brass bell sitting on her occasional table.

Within seconds, the doors to the sitting room opened and a strikingly handsome footman appeared. Harriet noted idly that she was in the presence of the three most beautiful people she'd ever seen. Not that she was looking at Lord Alexander; she was in fact studiously *not* looking.

"Richard, darling, please tell Charleston to ready my carriage, and then pack a few of Lord Alexander's things into a trunk. Pack warmly. He'll be taking a short journey north. When you're finished, do find Sanderson and have him help you assist Lord Alexander to my carriage. Oh, and tell Miss Temple to pack some food in a basket."

The man nodded and left the room without comment or question; either these types of requests came frequently, or Miss Hightower took the training of her servants seriously. She turned back to Harriet, still with a gleeful energy about her as if *she* were the one kidnapping a peer and riding into the night with his body. And as if the idea were a thrilling one.

"Now then," Giuliana said, standing. "What do *you* need? I can't imagine you want to stop at home before leaving. Time is not your friend tonight. I was not gifted with your . . . ample blessings . . ." Giuliana gestured to Harriet's breasts, still overexposed in Philippa's gown. "So I don't have much to share. But a comb? Hairpins? Tooth powder? I don't wear night rails, but I have a chemise or two that might fit."

Harriet had never met someone who took care of things like she herself did—someone who was prepared, uncowed, ready for action. It was rather surreal to be on the other side of the equation. For the first time in her life, Harriet let herself relax into the feeling of being managed by someone else. She followed Giuliana upstairs like a little duckling, ignoring as best as possible what would inevitably come after she left the woman's care.

Once *he* was her only company.

Chapter Six

Alexander's head was pounding, which would have been his chief concern if not for the fact that he also was moving. He didn't remember getting into a carriage at any point, although he was rather crapulous. Still drunk even, perhaps. He decided to prise an eye open in case that cleared things up.

Bloody hell.

Sitting across from him was a woman. Not just any woman either. *The* woman. The woman with the wrists. From the library. The woman who wanted to marry him. Good Lord, where were they? Where had they gone? When had they gone? *Why* had they gone?

None of those pressing questions, however, escaped his lips. Instead, the first question that formed was: "What are you doing?"

Harriet startled at the sound of his voice. She looked down at the book in her lap and then up at him. She took only a second to collect herself, then pertly replied: "You do know about reading, don't you?"

Alexander tried to work out whether she was teasing him or if she really thought maybe he didn't know about reading, but the puzzling required too much effort in his current state. As he closed his eyes again, he thought he saw her smirk. Yes, closed eyes were much better.

"Why are you reading in my carriage, Lady . . ." What was her name?

"Harriet. Lady Harriet. Strictly speaking, it's not *your* carriage. Well, you know, it may be. I don't *actually* know if you purchased it for Miss Hightower as a gift, or if she purchased it with her earnings, or if it is more of a loan. I admit I'm unfamiliar with how those sorts of . . . arrangements . . . work."

Despite the continued ache in his head and the ever more desperate desire he had to stop the carriage, Alexander found himself smiling.

"You've never kept a mistress? A mister? . . . Is there a word for that? Well, whatever it is."

"Not yet."

That had to be the smallest number of words she'd spoken to him. He peeled one eye open again for a moment only to find her mouth on the verge of continuing, which oddly made him smile *again*. Alexander was quite used to smiling at women. Smiling, he'd found, was at least a third of charming a lady. Another third was dancing and the last third mostly involved other things with mouths. But these present smiles were unusual. They were for his own benefit.

"Do you have something to say?" he asked, certain he would regret it.

"You haven't asked why I'm here, my lord."

"I try not to question when a woman is in my carriage." Before she could correct him again—for he knew she was itching to do so—he added, "I did indeed loan this carriage to Miss Hightower. Although should our arrangement ever end, I would not ask for it back, so perhaps your point stands."

Harriet made a quiet *hmm* and didn't continue the conversation. Alexander opened both eyes this time, slowly accepting that despite her silence, he was not going to be resting. She was reading quickly, occasionally pausing to scribble something in the book on her lap, with a short stub of a pencil. Just watching her read was making him feel sick. He glanced at the slivers of early-morning light coming in from the curtains, just enough for her to read, he supposed. He peeled one back just a little. Greenery whirred past and despite being in an incredibly well-sprung carriage—one didn't want their mistress to be jostled when her mouth was on their most valuable parts—the road was quite rough. Alexander assumed they were outside of London, a place he tried to be as little as possible.

"You seem quite undisturbed, so I assume this is your doing."

Harriet didn't look up from her book to answer. "I would argue that this entire affair is *your* doing; I had no desire to be compromised in a library. Compromised at all, even."

"I find that rather difficult to believe."

Harriet's gaze finally lifted. "My lord?" she repeated, although this time, the words were dripping with disdain.

"Please stop with this infernal 'my lord.' Call me Alexander."

"As you wish, my lord." Her gaze dropped back to the book, the casualness of her tone belied by her clenched jaw. Alexander stretched and spread himself across the seat further, taking up as much space as possible. He felt—hoped—doing so would irk her.

"So, you did *not* come to the ball intent on ruin by a very wealthy—and might I add handsome—son of a duke?"

"That was indeed my aim. Unfortunately, I met you instead." She seemed pleased with herself for this retort.

Alexander chuckled lightly. "Come now, you must find me at least a little enticing."

"I find you inconvenient, arrogant, and morally bankrupt." He started to counter that before she cut him off. "I also find you necessary, seeing as Lady Neddlesby is mere hours away from trading her version of last night's events in for a small dose of the attention ordinarily lavished upon her dear sister. Try to set aside your high opinion of yourself for a moment's time and understand that I have absolutely no wish to marry you."

"Sharing a carriage with me seems a poor way to avoid that fate."

"You mistake intent for desire. I am no happier about it than you are, I assure you. I came to Miss Hightower's house last night to discuss an elopement with a rational, conscious man. Alas, none was to be found. This seemed the best course of action."

"Naturally. Kidnapping is rather more convenient than waiting until morning when I might call on your father and clear this whole mess up," Alexander tossed out, sarcastically. He couldn't recall a more aggravating female companion in his past. Truly, a wasp's nest would have been more welcome in the carriage than she.

Harriet paused for a moment before she answered. "Yes, in fact."

He breathed deeply to regulate himself. "Why don't we simply turn this carriage around, announce our whirlwind engagement, and then, after a passionate month, you might jilt me and we'll be unscathed?"

"A month of you courting me?" Harriet replied with a sharp, humorless laugh.

"Well, yes . . . ?" Alexander said, his rum-soaked brain admittedly a little puzzled as to why it wasn't a perfect solution.

"You couldn't even be bothered to remember my name. No one will believe it."

"One hates to be crass, but I am known to be rather skilled at seduction."

"You and I both know I am not the sort of woman you seek out. The rest of the *ton* knows it too."

"Except I did." Alexander clasped his hands together as if that ended the argument. He was quite hopeful it had. He could barely keep up with this woman's mad rantings while sober; in his current state, he felt hopeless.

God, he wished he could undo it all: the library, the touching her, most certainly the gallons of brandy that had come afterward.

She was blessedly quiet for a moment. Alexander believed he'd had the last word when she all but whispered, "Because you thought I was Philippa."

Good God! Alexander took a deep breath in and decided to be done with this.

"How insulting of me to mistake you for another gorgeous woman, one whom I was to meet in the very room you were in—one you happen to look remarkably like! Especially from behind! That must really sting!"

"You seem to be under the mistaken impression I suffer from the lack of your attention. I was merely pointing out the incredulity of you courting me!"

"You're correct, I would not go after you—I will readily admit that. Not because you're lacking something, or because you're a wall-flower—believe me, the quiet ones often hold the best surprises—but because you're an unmarried innocent and I don't make a habit of entertaining *those* types of women."

His little speech made him feel more nauseated than before.

Harriet was silent for a moment, although not still. Truly the sound of her fidgeting was irritating beyond belief, and her move-ments seemed to send the erotic scent of sweet oranges throughout the entire carriage, which Alexander promised his cock he'd think about later.

"Cicisbeo. Cavalier servente. Paramour. Gallant."

Oh god, how much had *he drunk? What was she saying?*

"It's just that . . . earlier you . . . well, you asked if there was a word for a 'mister' and there are a few, just not very good ones. No one uses them. Though I believe that's the fault of society rather than language."

Alexander stared at her in wonder. She bit her full, lush lip and blushed with embarrassment, which was really quite a shame because he'd have preferred her to do those things for a whole different reason entirely.

He was, unprecedentedly, too hungover to be fully aroused, or to do anything about it even if he were. Instead, he closed his eyes once more and tried to fall back asleep. He could reason with this clever termagant later.

Blessedly, the carriage began to slow as they approached The Red Lion, a small but busy posting inn. Alexander exited the carriage, his stomach grateful to be on terra firma again. He reached to help Lady Harriet down, but she ignored his outstretched hand. Their driver, Charleston, was already down and talking to the stable boy about fresh horses, but Alexander had no intention of continuing to Gretna Green. He was here to freshen up, perhaps cast up his accounts, and then convince the chit to go back to London with him.

Harriet knew she ought to be thinking of how to convince the man to elope to Gretna Green now that he was awake. Only, she was alone in a room with a man for the second time in her life. In an inn! She'd never been to an inn. Alexander himself did not seem to be similarly affected by the situation. In fact, he was still quite cross. Since casting up his accounts behind the stables—something she wasn't supposed to know he'd done—he appeared noticeably haler, if not happier with her presence.

"Tell me you did not kidnap me without a change of clothing." It was an order, no question in sight. "You haul along a trunk no doubt full of bits and bobs and baubles, and I'm to endure this endeavor in a singular pair of small clothes?"

Harriet willed herself not to blush at the mention of undergarments. Blushing every time the man spoke of something indecorous was as inconvenient as it was embarrassing.

"That is *your* trunk, my lord," she bit out. Alexander raised an eyebrow at her.

"I didn't exactly have access to your full wardrobe and accouterments, did I? Your, er . . . Miss Hightower . . . was kind enough to have her footman pack some clothing that you keep at her house, presumably for . . . reasons." Why had she even begun to speculate about the conditions under which a gentleman might require spare clothes at his mistress's house?

He bent and rifled through the trunk with a frown.

"She said those were your clothes—is something wrong? If so, I'm deeply sorry."

"Your manners are a credit to kidnappers everywhere," Alexander retorted. "They are my clothes, yes, but they're *business* clothes. Hardly fit for travel." He grabbed them anyway. Privately, Harriet thought he was being quite the petulant child. His sour mood went a long way to assuage her lust for him.

"I had to make do. Surely you can purchase something more suitable in Gretna Green."

"Ah, the first mention of our mysterious destination!"

"Come now, where did you think we were going to elope, my lord?"

"Will you cease with the 'my lord'? It makes me itch. I give you leave to use my Christian name."

"No, thank you." Harriet liked the distance the title provided. Best to remember exactly whom she was dealing with at all times. "My lord," she added a moment later, just to watch the muscles of his jaw clench.

Just then, the door opened, and a servant girl entered with a bottle of gin and two glasses. She looked up at Alexander adoringly. *He's not so special as all that*, Harriet wanted to tell her.

"We didn't have any brandy, sir, only gin. I'll return with your meal soon." She curtsied then, her eyes lingering on him. Harriet rolled her own eyes; no wonder the man was so insufferable.

"Thank you kindly . . ."

"Miss Evans."

"Thank you kindly, Miss Evans. Gin will do just fine." He set the bottle and glasses down on the small table beside Harriet, then fished a coin from his pocket and pressed it into Miss Evans's hand. As if buoyed by the female attention, his mood changed entirely. Harriet could feel the air shift; she wanted to hurl her book at his head.

He plucked a shirt out of his trunk and tossed it onto the bed.

"Right then," Alexander began, as he started to undo his shirt buttons, "where are your things? Shall we call back Miss Evans to assist you with that delightful dress? Or would you rather your *husband* do it for you? Quite scandalous. I approve, of course." He winked, which Harriet supposed was meant to do something to a lady. As it stood, she was too vexed by him to feel anything.

"I told the innkeeper we were husband and wife to *avoid* scandal," she rejoined. "I'm not one of your many lovesick admirers; I won't have you painting me as a wanton fool who loses her senses at the sight of your hands."

"It's my hands for you, then? I get eyes more often. Shoulders even. One woman went mad for my calves, but she was French."

The man was at least half devil. The best thing to do with misbehaving little boys was to ignore them.

"Personally, I think my best feature is my—"

"I don't have other clothes," she cut him off. "This is the only dress I have."

"And what a *lovely* carriage dress it is." Alexander's mouth tilted into an appreciative smile, which heated Harriet's cheeks again. Calling what she was wearing a carriage dress was like calling a handkerchief a picnic blanket. "My abduction just became a fair bit more endurable."

He kept his smile—his *practiced smile*, Harriet reminded herself—pasted on his face as he finished unbuttoning his shirt, pulling it over his head. Unfortunately, as soon as he stopped talking, the attraction returned.

Those ladies were right. His deep brown eyes, yes. His broad shoulders, absolutely. His calves were hidden by the bed between them at the moment, but likely those too. It was only a surprise they didn't mention his thick, dark hair, his distinguished nose, his surprisingly perfect teeth, the lines near his eyes from all his flirtatious smiles, the way his . . .

His shirt was off. Gone. It might be floating in the Nile for all she knew.

Harriet had gotten used to breathing while looking at his exposed neck, but when Lord Alexander removed his shirt to reveal the entirety of his bare chest, that did her poor respiratory system in. She inhaled sharply, promptly choked on the air she'd inhaled, and spun around quickly to have a coughing fit facing the wall, which seemed approximately one percent less embarrassing than continuing to face him.

Behind her, Alexander laughed warmly, clearly enjoying himself. "Normally, I'd ask if you were all right, but it really wouldn't do to save my captor."

Harriet ignored this and tried to get her mortifying cough under control.

"I must say," he continued, relishing every excruciating second of her ordeal, "I don't believe I've ever had that precise reaction from a lady upon seeing my chest."

In the future, Harriet decided, it would be best to remain in circumstances in which she didn't have to hear him name any body parts. She cleared her throat, trying to behave as if everything was under control. She turned a quarter of the way back to him, unwilling to be confronted with the whole of him again.

"Apologies, my lord." She tried to keep some bite in the honorific, some hint of the sting his title was supposed to deliver. But even to her own ears, it sounded meek and missish. "It was my first."

"Your first?" She could tell—even from across the room, with her eyes trained on a small knot in the beam of the wall—that he was once again smirking.

"My first . . . chest." Harriet winced at the word. She had never disliked a word before, ever. Every word had a point, a purpose. As it turned out, the word *chest* was designed to humiliate her as deeply as possible.

"I can only pray it lived up to your expectations."

She turned to him fully then, finding his lips quirked in precisely the manner she'd predicted.

Until now, she would not have thought she *had* expectations about men's chests. But apparently, she did, for Alexander's soared high above anything she'd ever imagined.

"What else have you yet to see, I wonder," Alexander mused, reaching down to undo the buttons of his fall.

The question snapped her out of her reverie. She spun abruptly back toward the wall. The wall, with its *fascinating* wooden beams and uneven plaster.

"Oh, come now, you might enjoy the next part even more than my chest."

"I'm sorry I stared."

"I'm not," Alexander said simply. There wasn't an ounce of flirtation in his voice, which turned out to be much more affecting than anything else he'd said. The rest of his teasing she could dismiss, but this? A woman could almost believe he was telling the truth.

He truly seemed unbothered by her having seen him disrobe. Harriet couldn't imagine how she'd feel if he saw her in her chemise. Then suddenly she *was* imagining it, and her face heated another degree. This had to be the warmest inn in the entire country, and there wasn't even a fire in the bloody room.

From behind her, she heard Alexander's footsteps getting closer, felt her entire body clench in anticipation of . . . anticipation of . . . something. Was he going to touch her? Her back tingled. Her insides clenched. She felt his breath against her ear.

"Are you still blushing?"

"No!" she snapped, whirling back to face him, conscious this time to keep her eyes no farther south than his hairline.

"If we were to marry, you'd see a lot more than that."

"*If?*" She knew she sounded shrill, but she found it difficult to keep the panic out of her voice. The *ton* wasn't very forgiving if a lady was found embracing a man in a library; but being found alone in a coaching inn, again with the same man? Was there a word beyond *ruination*? *Annihilation*, perhaps?

"There is nothing you can offer me that I want, I'm afraid." Lord Alexander paused and then grinned at her, sliding one arm into the clean shirt. "At least, nothing that requires matrimony," he teased.

"You don't bed innocents, my lord."

"Oh, but you've been recently ruined. Regardless, one must always enforce one's own rules rather liberally. There's nothing so dull as a man with good discipline."

"Why, my lord, you must be the most diverting man in England, then!"

"You have no idea." He shot Harriet a smoldering look, one that might entice a woman to do just about any foolish thing he suggested. A look he'd probably spent years of his life perfecting.

Thankfully, Harriet had learned well to ignore the caprices of a man. Although Alexander's dark, fiery eyes were much more tempting to give in to than the rheumy, drunk eyes of her father.

"My sister will never sell you her land if you don't marry me."

Chapter Seven

ALEXANDER STILLED. HE WANTED THE LAND; MORE PRECISELY, HE wanted his father not to have it. He'd spent most of the last decade buying land out from under his father, usually using other gentlemen's names so that the duke wouldn't notice the pattern and put a stop to it.

Recently, he'd formed a tenuous partnership with the unfortunately pious Lord Holden; the only thing the man cared for more than land was God. He had connections in the Lake District and knew the local magistrate from the summers he'd spent in Portinscale as a boy. Lord Holden had made it clear to Alexander that he did not approve of his lifestyle, and Alexander had attempted to be a little more discreet as of late to appease him. If he wanted Hardwicke, he needed Lord Holden's help.

"It's why you wanted to meet my sister in the library, was it not?"

"Among other things," Alexander said, readopting an impassive tone—a mask for how out of control he felt. "I still have no desire to be wed."

"This might prove difficult for you to believe, but I assure you I have little interest in marrying you." Alexander felt that was a little discourteous—he had not specified that he didn't want to marry *her*. He opened his mouth to interject, but Harriet rushed ahead. "I am aware I'm not the . . . caliber . . . of woman you likely imagined for matrimony; however, when one ruins a woman, one offers for her. That is the way things are done."

"I did *not* ruin you." Harriet shot him a withering look, but he felt like provoking the harridan. "What we did was as close to ruination as a carriage is to a cabbage. Believe me."

She ignored the flirtation entirely, but her cheeks seemed to heat a bit. *Interesting.*

"My only intention is to protect my sisters from scandal. Rather, *more* scandal. Our father is already quite the stain on our reputation, and certainly Philippa isn't helping much in the respectability department. I fear even the hint of another transgression would prove fatal for Caroline's season, and poor Frances isn't even out yet. I am—as you can tell from the kidnapping—quite desperate. I will be honest, I—"

Alexander decided to cut her off. He was shocked at how many words had just come out of her and how quickly. Before now, he'd assumed wallflowers to be reticent.

"Why don't you want to marry me?" He tried to hide how desperate he was to know the answer. He may not have desired matrimony, but a woman not wanting him . . . well, it was odd, to say the least.

"It isn't obvious?"

"Not to me, although I suppose I don't possess the brilliant mind of Lady Harriet Bancroft," he drawled, stepping closer to her. Her breath picked up even more. *Thrilling*. He hoped she wasn't the type to swoon; she didn't seem it.

"We don't suit, my lord," Harriet choked out, taking a step backward to account for his advance.

"Why is that?"

"To begin with, you're, well . . . you're . . ."

"I'm?" he asked, lips quirked into a smile as he continued to advance toward her. She was, as most women were, positively heaven to bedevil.

"Yes! Precisely!" she exclaimed, inching backward farther until she knocked into the table.

"I'm what, Lady Harriet? What is it about me that is so far beneath you?" Her hand reached out to steady herself, clinging to the table's edge.

"Beneath me?" She laughed harshly, and her grip relaxed. Alexander noticed because he'd been staring at her long, delicate fingers. Fingers! What on earth was he doing watching a woman's fingers? He instructed his eyes to go back to a normal position: her bosom. There was plenty for them to see there, and less trouble for them to get into than on a lady's hands. Under no circumstances were they to travel up toward her lips and, God forbid, her gray eyes. Breasts were safe.

When he turned his attention back to Harriet, he found she was in the middle of another one of her long speeches.

"—sure I am not *your* first choice. I'm not even your first choice among my sisters! You have money and property and probably belong to a club and own two carriages and a phaeton and employ a chef with regularity if not permanence and know fourteen ways to tie a cravat—"

"My valet does that for me, I must admit."

"You're titled and wealthy and can have any woman you choose. If the rumors are true, you *do* have all the women you choose. I do not intend to burden you with marriage. I vow I did not have any designs on entrapment when I entered the library. *Please* believe me. I wouldn't marry you unless it were very dire indeed." He reached around her, bringing them within inches of one another, a distance which made Harriet's breath audibly hitch.

"Yes, you keep saying that," he said, grabbing the bottle of gin behind her.

"It's simply true. I have no more interest in this marriage than you do. But we both require it."

"I assure you I do not." He removed the bottle and put a small, safe distance between them.

"I hardly think your reputation can withstand absconding with a daughter of a peer—and we both know that's how this will be written up—especially since you're already known to be a . . ." She cut herself off and bit her lip.

Ahh.

There it was. Because he was a bastard. For some in society it was quite the knock against his character. Although really, he'd had nothing to do with the whole ordeal—that had been his parents' doing.

He hadn't expected her to care about it for some reason. He took a drink straight out of the bottle.

It now seemed rather foolish that he had ever worried a lady might try to trap him for his money or his title, when this woman, this bluestocking with no dowry and a scandalous family, had made it clear that she was marrying him only out of desperation.

Perhaps all the ladies of the *ton* had always felt that way. Perhaps the courtesans and mistresses and actresses—and yes, the bored wives before he realized that was too messy—were as good as he could get. He had believed he'd been holding the *ton* at arm's length, avoiding a match, avoiding the climbers and the desperate mamas. Maybe they'd been avoiding him. The thought stung for about four seconds before he discarded it.

She was correct about one thing: He couldn't afford scandal if he wanted Lord Holden to continue to do business with him. Which he did.

"Ah yes, I suppose that does rather contaminate a person, doesn't it?" he sneered, feeling rather venomous. Any fun he'd been having vexing her evaporated. His mind sharpened in defensive fury, and he took another drink of the warm, and not very good, gin.

"I don't know why you're upset with *me* about it! I do not dictate societal morals. In fact, I fancy it's been rather *noble* of you to keep all the widows of the *ton* such nice company over the years! And think of the opera singers! They'd be bored out of their minds if it weren't for you!"

Oh.

She had meant a rake, not a bastard. Her words from earlier came back to him: *I find you inconvenient, arrogant, and morally bankrupt.* He let out a half laugh and scrubbed a hand down his face, his beard already growing in from a day and a half without a shave.

She quieted at the sound of his laughter, her ire deflating with his. He thought for a moment. Her argument was not unfounded. A compromising position at a ballroom might be overlooked eventually. Or chalked up to the type of roguish behavior befitting a bastard second son. But leaving the city with the daughter of an earl? No, the minx had done well forcing his hand. It had been years since someone managed him so deftly, and he felt something akin to admiration.

He reached around her casually for the glasses. His arm brushed against hers, their chests inches apart. When he stood back, her eyes were wide, and her breathing unsteady. He was delighted that she seemed at least a little affected by his touch. Although he reminded himself that it might simply be fear, rather than sensual excitement. He ignored that his breathing matched her own.

He poured two glasses and held one out to her.

"It's midday, my lord."

"Excellent point; we are behind." He nudged the glass out to her again and this time she took it. He placed the bottle on the floor— he didn't need to keep brushing up against her—and then backed away to give his brain some space to think. He always thought better while pacing.

Alexander was forced to admit she was making some sense. At this sobering thought, he sat down on the edge of the bed and took another, longer drink.

"All right," he said with a swallow, "I suppose I'll go to your father, then." She laughed and again it was harsh and joyless. He lost himself for a moment imagining her real laugh. One that wasn't bitter. He raised an eyebrow at her.

She squeezed her eyes shut and took a large swill of gin to steel herself for what came next. Unfortunately, what came next was a coughing fit. Alexander let out his own very real laugh, although he tried to cover it up when her eyes shot to him mid-cough.

"The trick is to breathe out after the *sip*," he explained.

"There won't be another '*sip*'!" she exclaimed. "That was dreadful! I used to resent men for keeping this from us. They've just risen in my esteem quite a bit now."

"Except me." Alexander found himself pushing the issue of her dislike for him yet again. He wasn't sure why it disturbed him so for this woman not to like him—perhaps because it was a rather novel experience for him.

Everything she had listed—his money, his servants, his carriages, of which there were actually four—seemed like an asset. Some perverse part of him wanted her to admit that she looked down on him because he was a bastard, no matter how sickly his older brother might be. Despite her own family's ill repute, she surely thought herself to be above an illegitimate second son.

Or was it something else? Even if he was not her desired partner in matrimony, surely some small part of her was enamored of him?

"Sadly, you have dropped even further in my esteem, my lord, as you were the one to finally *provide* me with the drink. Thus, I must lay all blame squarely at your feet." Her eyes were twinkling a little; Alexander had the strangest feeling that she might be flirting with him. He ignored the small bell that pealed inside of his chest, warning him.

"Your father won't acquiesce to you marrying me? I assure you I'm quite persuasive."

"That I believe."

Alexander found himself quietly thrilled by that statement, for some reason.

"Why, may I ask, do you assume he'd refuse my suit? *If* I were to offer, which—although the end of last evening is a little fuzzy—I do not recall doing. I'll remind you that I am the son of a duke." Alexander braced himself to hear that his bastard blood was too dirty for Lord Tidewell's pure, sweet princess of a daughter.

"Regardless of your parentage, you'll have a difficult time getting permission for my hand from my father—" Here it came, the truth of the matter: His parentage *was* an issue for her, and her father as well. "—as he is . . . well . . . *in absentia.*"

Alexander's attention returned to her a little late.

"In absentia?"

"Yes, he's . . . well, he's gone."

"Gone where?"

"I haven't a clue. I'm afraid he's missing."

"Your father is *missing?*"

"Is there something I'm not explaining well? I'm normally quite good with words." He had no doubt about that, the woman clearly enjoyed talking.

"And your mother?"

"I presume she's still in the parish cemetery." Harriet said it casually, but her entire body stiffened.

A knock on the door interrupted Alexander's lack of response.

"Come in," Harriet called out and Miss Evans entered again with a tray laden with food.

She lingered for much longer than it should have taken to deposit a tray, making sheep's eyes at Alexander. Harriet pursed her lips in poorly concealed annoyance, and Alexander allowed himself to feel warmed by that. Perhaps she was more interested in him than she let on.

As soon as Miss Evans left, Harriet tucked into their breakfast. He was never so grateful for coddled eggs; the interruption in her speech gave him time to think. And to finish dressing. Even if the clothing she provided wasn't meant to be traveled in, at least it didn't smell of perspiration and liquor. He felt sorry Harriet didn't have her own change of clothes, but he didn't mind the sight of her in that white dress.

He turned his mind back to their elopement-abduction. "We could annul," he suggested, grabbing a cravat and trying his best to tie it without the aid of a valet or a looking glass.

"No," she said simply. He waited for her to continue, which of course she did. "If we were to annul, I'd be ruined, which is precisely what I'm trying to avoid. Besides, you can annul a marriage only in instances of fraud, incompetence, and impotence."

"Surely a kidnapping counts as fraud."

"I don't believe it does, as we were in *your* carriage and you haven't stopped our journey. Who would believe that I overpowered both you and your driver?"

Alexander had enough experience with women to know that the correct answer was not: "Anyone who'd spent seven minutes in your company."

"Charleston is on my side of things anyway, I'm afraid; he's quite the romantic. You *could* claim fraud if I didn't come with the dowry you expected; however, you already know I don't have one, and more to the point, the entire *ton* does too. So then, *I* must be the one to find fault in you. You would have to claim to own something that you do not, which is rather difficult as you own half the country, and furthermore leads us back to issues of reputation." She paused for breath. "Neither of us can claim incompetence. Which leaves us with impotence!" Harriet had picked up her pace throughout the speech and by the end clearly felt rather delighted with herself. *Bloody hell.*

"Shall we testify that you are impotent?"

"No," he grumbled, not quite as delighted as she was with her lecture.

"It's a relatively simple process. We stay together for three years, and so long as we don't consummate the marriage, and I remain . . . *intact* . . . then we can apply for it. Of course, you'd have to go in front of the court-appointed courtesans and make clear that you cannot . . ."

Her hesitancy amused Alexander. He gave up on tying the cravat well and simply knotted it.

"That I cannot what?" He hoped he sounded both casual and ignorant enough for her to continue her spiel.

"Well, I don't know what it means precisely but"—Harriet gulped—"from what I read . . ."

"Yes?" He turned to watch her face.

"A man must prove that he can't . . . function . . . when presented with . . . stimulus." Harriet blushed an enticing shade of pink.

"I suppose that rules out an annulment. I'm afraid I'm quite *functional*, my dear." Harriet shivered slightly at his use of a pet name, and he smirked.

"You could act as if you aren't."

"I'm really not sure that I could. Beyond that, I have quite a licentious reputation, as you have pointed out. I fail to see how it would benefit me to be separated from you yet publicly known to be impotent. Rather defeats the point of being unwed, doesn't it?"

"Well then, we're to be wed." Harriet clapped her hands together once again, as if she'd settled the matter to her satisfaction. Only the tightness of her mouth spoke to any trepidation she felt.

"All right," Alexander conceded. The dratted woman seemed to have won. Now that he'd ostensibly removed her from London in his carriage, there was no possibility of salvaging either of their reputations without a wedding. "But it will be a marriage in name only," Alexander clarified. The church and the newspapers and society could recognize the marriage; it didn't mean the two of them had to. It wasn't the ideal solution, but it was the best at hand. And his years in business had taught him that taking action was better than waiting for perfection.

"I'm hardly the type of woman to lower herself to begging for your affections," Harriet retorted, and Alexander did his best to ignore the sting of her words. He was not enjoying this portion of their banter; Alexander liked being on good terms with women.

"It's only, I do not intend for any sort of romantic attachment to form between us. Ever." He knew this was a harsh directive, but better to set expectations from the start. God forbid she enter this arrangement expecting flowers or letters or love. Or worse, poems.

"I truly had not considered the possibility," Harriet said, looking almost bored with the topic. "I'll do my best to bear an heir as expediently as possible and then we may remove ourselves from each other's lives."

"There will be no heir."

Harriet's face looked as if she'd been slapped. Admittedly, his tone could have been a degree less absolute. Only, he didn't want to leave any room for negotiation. There was none. Emotions passed across her face that he did his best not to read.

Harriet paused before speaking again. "No heir?" was all she came up with.

"*I* will have no children, which means, I'm afraid, *you* will have no children. Unless I die, of course, in which case you are freed of this contract and may procreate at will."

"How generous of you," Harriet said, tersely. Despite his efforts not to notice, he could tell she was unhappy with these rules.

He couldn't linger too long on robbing her of children, though. Nor could he promise to raise her bastard. Least of all could he bend his principles and entertain having children with her. The image of such came unbidden to his mind: babies with sticky hands, children with wild energy like he and John had had as boys, their eyes gray and their minds precocious from their mother.

"Additionally—" he began, cutting the fantasy off at its knees.

"Are you incapable?" At his no doubt evident confusion, she clarified: "Are you incapable of producing children?"

Allow me to demonstrate just how capable I am. The thought came immediately, perhaps born from years of innuendo, but there was also something heavy and appealing about the idea. Being in a bedroom with this woman for this long was not good for him.

Alexander cleared his throat. "Not that I'm aware of. Everything . . . works as it should."

"Rather a miracle then that you haven't yet sired a child," she tossed back at him. "Unless you have?"

"I have not. There are many methods to ensure a child is not conceived and I make use of most of them. I am exceedingly careful with all my . . . attachments that no child is created and I shall continue to be, for both of our sakes."

"Continue?" Harriet looked a little pale now, although Alexander was still trying his best not to notice her emotions overmuch. This was the only way he would marry, and she'd have to accept it.

"I have no interest in forcing a child to be raised a bastard. It was rather miserable for me, and I will not damn someone else to that existence. As such, I also ask that you take care in your own affairs."

And then she laughed. *What about this was humorous?*

"I'm sorry, I wasn't meaning to . . . I just . . . I feel rather silly I suppose, but I didn't realize you meant to . . . continue. Or that you meant for me to . . . Though of course you do. You're . . ." Harriet gestured toward his entire being with a smile that didn't entirely reach her eyes.

It took Alexander a moment to retrace the conversation and understand her. *Of course* he meant to continue seeing women. It had not occurred to him that she might assume otherwise. Resentment bubbled up in him—society was forcing this on both of them; he had no desire to offend her or cause her misery. He simply wanted to be left alone, to do as he always had.

Alexander took a deep, steadying breath. "I *am* sorry. I should have been more delicate about the topic. Or perhaps less honest. Since the marriage is in name only, I figured that, upon return to London, we might both resume our lives."

"I agree entirely, my lord. And I appreciate your honesty."

Alexander had the distinct impression that, despite her words of concurrence, she was still upset. Her mouth was getting tight again. She didn't speak for a while, which he was learning was quite a bad sign with Harriet.

"Well then," she said, standing from the table and heading over to the water ewer to wash up, "I see no reason to engage in amorous congress at all."

He did. He saw many reasons. Every atom in his body stilled, as if that might alter what she had said.

"I beg your pardon?" he asked, carefully.

"As I understand, you have many willing partners. I cannot fathom you having a need to bed *me.*"

"Don't be absurd! Of course I intend to bed my wife."

"Whatever for? You have no desire for children, to do so would only increase the risk of begetting an heir." She dried her hands on a small piece of toweling, and then reached up to adjust the pins in her hair. Her efforts did little to help rein in the mass of rich mahogany hair.

"We must at least consummate our marriage." Indeed, the promise of a wedding night was perhaps the *only* upside to the custom of matrimony.

"As long as we don't plan to annul—which we both agreed would be antithetical to our interests—there isn't any reason. Certainly not a legal one."

"A great oversight on the part of Parliament," Alexander retorted. *Antithetical to our interests?* Bedding her perfectly aligned with his interests. He was famous for those very interests!

"Is this about your pride?" she asked, hairpin between her teeth. He hadn't been condescended to by a woman in ages. In fact, *ever*, if recollection served.

"I shouldn't like to think myself a prisoner of my ego; however, I can't imagine there's another man in England who hasn't tupped his wife!" This entire conversation was perplexing. He felt as if he'd been repeatedly thrown in the Thames with his limbs bound. And every time he scrambled to shore, he got tossed in again. One of them was going mad and he wasn't certain it wasn't him.

"Perhaps it will be a balm to recall how many other men's wives *you've* tupped," Harriet offered, and the oddest part was that she seemed almost sincere in her attempt to soothe him. "No one need know. I hardly plan to go about announcing that I've been . . . overlooked . . . by my own husband."

"Any man who would overlook you is a fool, and I don't plan on being a fool."

Harriet smiled then, and Alexander returned it. *Thank goodness.* Perhaps their conversation could return to more agreeable avenues— like what she thought of his bare chest and where they planned to stop for the night.

"You really are incredibly practiced at your little coquetries, aren't you, my lord?" she said, patting his arm as she swished past him, still in that bewitching ball gown.

Oh, hell. She hadn't been smiling; she'd been laughing at him. She thought his compliment false. Alexander wasn't used to his flirtation being so easily dismissed.

"I'll wait for you in the carriage," she called after herself, sailing out of the room, leaving a bewildered Alexander and the strong scent of hothouse citrus in her wake.

Worse, she'd finished off the entire breakfast tray, leaving him nothing but kippers.

Christ, this was going to be a long marriage.

Chapter Eight

Lord, this was going to be a long elopement. Harriet's neck was stiff and her toes, still clad in slippers meant for a ballroom, were growing ever more frigid as they made their way north to Scotland, with its harsh climate and lenient marriage laws. Another blanket would have been more than welcome; unfortunately, one doesn't always know what to pack when kidnapping a peer of the realm.

Harriet's greatest tribulation, however, was Alexander's presence. The man was awfully, woefully, horrifically handsome. Not that she would admit it out loud. She'd rather have her ears removed with a paring knife. She'd just spent an hour at a coaching inn having one of the most frustrating and insulting conversations of her life, and it had done very little to temper her ardor. The man was a blighter. Unfortunately, objectively, he was a quite gorgeous blighter.

She did her best to focus on the book she'd brought along, uninteresting as it was; Philippa's house was not the best source for last-minute, engrossing reading material. Still, she ought to be circling words she didn't know and *not* stealing glances at a man's jaw.

She'd never been so close to such a good-looking man. Harriet tried to talk herself out of any feelings of inferiority, but really, his beauty bordered on absurdity. He was just so . . . large. And strong. And still. He moved slowly and deliberately, which Harriet couldn't really explain her excitement over. So much of her attraction to him was confounding.

To be sure, she knew why she liked certain parts of him. He had thick, black hair that seemed in danger of growing out of fashion within the week. And thick, black eyebrows to match; were eyebrows meant to be such a dominating feature? And such an attractive one? He had a wide mouth that she couldn't stop her eyes from returning to again and again—her fingers burned to trace his lips. How could one describe a man's lips without sounding brainsick? All of this was to say nothing of the chest she'd seen earlier, fit and broad and dusted with hair. Lord knows where he had his breeches made, but she dearly hoped the tailor who fitted them knew the effect his work had on women. Byron would have wept to have his creations affect people so deeply. No wonder Miss Evans had lingered so.

No matter how she cataloged the pieces, there was something about the whole of Lord Alexander that made one *want*. Desperately. Something that made books—books!—fail to hold focus. He was a danger to her.

Thus, her decision *not* to engage in intercourse with the man. So much as a quarter of an hour in his bed was bound to inspire feelings of love—which she was certain would not be reciprocated. And the last thing she intended was to become a twitterpated birdbrain over Lord Alexander like so many others did in his presence. *For good reason*, she added mentally, not wanting to denigrate anyone who might have fallen for his charms. Every heady glimpse at the man reinforced her decision.

"What are you doing?" he asked, tipping one side of his mouth up into a smirk.

"Reading," Harriet replied, her heart racing at being caught.

"Does your reading ordinarily involve so much . . ." *Mooning over men? No.* "Circling?"

Harriet tore her gaze away from him and down, bashfully, to the pages in her lap, where she had circled the words *farmer* and *landscape* as if they were unknown to her. God, but she was cork-brained.

"Oh. That." Harriet swallowed thickly, her throat full of nerves and some odd, unfamiliar cousin of hunger. Her eyes went back to the feast at hand—*his* throat. Why on earth would a man's neck be erotic? Only, it was. He hadn't shaved at the inn and stubble was beginning to show. It was oddly intimate to see an unshaven man.

Erotic! That's what his lips were.

Alexander smiled at her, as if he knew precisely what she'd been thinking. Harriet flinched. "I'm circling words I don't recognize. Of course, often I understand them due to context, but I haven't recorded them before."

Alexander reached across the carriage and lazily tipped up the spine of her book.

"You read about . . . agricultural precast of Welsh farmers in 1764 frequently, do you?" Words. Words were solid. This was solid ground. With the conversation returning to her dictionary, Alexander ceased to be an object of desire and became instead an audience for her passion.

"Oh, no no! Well, sometimes. But no, I aim to document everything I can find. I'm creating a dictionary of sorts, particularly of slang words, cant terms, idiomatic expressions of our time. That makes it sound like I'm doing it all, when really it's Mr. Dawkins's book; I'm only aiding him. I've been sending him words for years now. Anyway, I grabbed this book rather haphazardly; it's not proving very fruitful. However, I'm hopeful I'll be able to send something to Mr. Dawkins soon. I was going to—" *Marry him.* She was going to marry him.

"You write letters to a man? Isn't that a bit scandalous for an unmarried woman?"

"All the more reason to hurry to Gretna Green, isn't it?"

"You'll continue to send this man letters? Once we're . . ." He waved his hand around to indicate the full weight of holy matrimony.

Harriet dithered. What was one's obligation when it came to telling one's intended about letters they had been sending another man? Under a false identity? Especially considering the erstwhile hope that one day those letters would turn into something romantic.

"He doesn't actually know . . . me."

"You haven't met him?" Alexander tried to keep the shock out of his voice, to no avail.

"Sadly, no. I read of his work and wrote to him. He lives in Oxford. He's a brilliant professor, you see. I read a pamphlet he'd worked on, and I wrote a letter correcting him on the origins of a certain word. He claimed the origin to be unknown; however, I knew it to be from seamen."

Alexander let out a snort that he tried to disguise as a cough. Clearly, he thought her a fool. Men frequently dismissed women's knowledge, and she was rather disappointed he'd joined their ranks. Mr. Dawkins never had, but he hadn't known her to be a woman.

"Anyway, we began writing to one another, and I began submitting words to him. He's promised me twenty-five percent of the profits of his dictionary when it's published this fall." There. That ought to shut him up.

Harriet adjusted her posture smugly, but he did not respond. The man positively adored smirking in silence. Was this how he acquired female company? Was this his winning strategy? Just stay quiet while they blather on, creating an image of him that suited their needs?

"I was supposed to meet him at the ball. His father is a cousin of Lady Dunley's. I was going to reveal to him that I'm . . . well . . ."

"An unwed society miss and not an academic?"

"Yes, I had a mind that we'd—well . . . never mind, I guess . . ." Harriet muttered something under her breath that sounded like "Foolish anyway."

Alexander's brows pinched with confusion before springing back up with understanding. "You were hoping he'd propose?!"

"No! Well. No. That is, I thought we might start . . . courting."

Alexander let out a sharp crack of laughter at the admission, which went through Harriet like a hatchet. At the look on her face, no doubt one of pathetic pain, he stopped. God, she was making a cake of herself, just like she'd always assumed she would do in the presence of a man. Marvelous.

Instead, he cleared his throat. "I apologize sincerely," he said solemnly. Harriet held her breath for a moment, anticipating a continuation of his teasing. However, his eyes held hers, and he seemed to be trying to convey sincerity.

"If you weren't such a . . . louche . . . man, I would have made it out of the library quite intact and perhaps my plan might have gone . . . well . . . according to plan."

"So the ambush in the library was intended for him?"

"I hardly *ambushed* you!"

"How do you know him to be good marriageable material? Do you know him to be unattached? Relatively young? In decent health—unless, perhaps, you had a mind to take his Oxford fortune? Does one make a comfortable living as a professor?"

"Not everyone builds their life around the pursuit of wealth. Some of us seek more important things," she sniffed.

"Your message would be better delivered outside of the carriage where you've abducted a duke's son."

"Will you cease with the bloody kidnapping nonsense? You agreed at the last inn to go forward with me. I no longer have you here under duress. Had you offered for my hand like an honorable man, I would never have been in the position to kidnap you at all." Harriet got the feeling she did when she and Philippa used to race down the hill by their old house, before Mama died. She was gaining momentum. "As for Mr. Dawkins, I know him to be an amiable and intelligent man, and whatever else he may be, I should think it falls after that in significance."

"What if his likeness didn't suit you? Perhaps he has a weak chin or sparse hair? A dastardly scar across his face?"

"I should like a scar, I think," Harriet rejoined. Alexander's eyes flashed with something that Harriet wished were envy, though she discarded the thought as quickly as it came and continued, "but his likeness is acceptable."

"You've seen a portrait of him?"

Harriet squirmed the tiniest amount in her seat, realizing the mistake she'd made. Of course, this failed to escape Alexander's hawklike notice. No wonder the man did so well in business. Something about his piercing eyes made one want to come undone, to unburden oneself, to beg for approval. Beg for something. At that last thought, Harriet clenched her legs tightly together. Why did her body keep *clenching* around him? Drat.

"Ahh, so there *is* a portrait. A picture somewhere? Did you cut it out of a newspaper? Paste it in a locket? Is it buried in your trousseau?"

"I don't have a trousseau."

"Back to the photo of our dear Mr. Drexel . . ."

"Dawkins!"

Alexander waved away her correction and suddenly his eyes lit up, wolfishly. Harriet feared what might come out of his mouth next.

"Don't tell me you have it on your person?" *Oh dear.*

Harriet couldn't keep up with how quickly he was jumping from embarrassing inquiry to awful assumption. She didn't have time to school her face into a believable expression of denial. No, her traitorous eyes had already glanced down at her reticule, giving her away. Alexander snatched up the bag, and within seconds held the small, creased pamphlet, which had, until a fateful library meeting, contained her entire plan for the future.

He held it up dramatically. "Let's see the man of the hour. The paragon of intellect who captured the affections of our dear Lady Harriet Bancroft!" Alexander turned the paper over and then flipped it back to the front, as if dissatisfied with what he'd seen.

"This is him?" he asked, holding up the pamphlet with the back facing Harriet.

"Yes," she admitted, reluctantly.

"Hmm."

"What?"

"His nose is a bit . . . squidgy, but perhaps that's owed to the artist's interpretation. His eyes are lacking in expression and his hair looks . . . well, *unfortunate* is the word that comes to mind. His valet should be let go. Or hanged."

"He doesn't have a valet, my lord. He's an academician. And that's not what the word *squidgy* means."

"What does it mean?"

"Damp, wet, or clammy."

"How do you know that is not precisely what I meant?"

Harriet rolled her eyes. It bothered her to hear words used without precision. "His nose is—"

"Unfavorable, infelicitous, feeble?"

"His nose is fine!"

Alexander grimaced. "Hardly what one wants to hear about such a dominating feature."

Harriet reached out to grab the pamphlet back, but he pulled it out of her reach. He held it aloft and took one last disdainful look at the man, and then handed it back over, along with her reticule.

She sighed with gratitude.

"Need something to help you at night?" he asked, with a wink.

Alexander expected her to be horrified. Instead, Harriet looked confused at the remark, which made him altogether more intrigued than he ought to be. He was saved from deciding where to take the scintillating topic when the carriage hit a rut, sending her book, pencil, and reticule flying. The contents of the purse scattered across the floor; hairpins, hard candies, and dozens of scraps of paper littered the carriage.

Harriet bent to collect her scattered possessions, wedging herself on the floor of the carriage on her hands and knees to reach under her seat.

Alexander doubted she had any idea how enticing her bottom looked in that position. He lazily reached under his own bench to retrieve some of her errant papers, his eyes remaining faithfully glued to her arse. He was to marry the chit, after all. This might be the *most* appropriate gander he'd leveled at a woman's backside, all things considered.

Alexander brought his arm back up from its fishing expedition under the bench. He rather felt he'd been playing a parlor game. He set his goods on the bench next to him and began sorting them out.

"Look! I have won . . ." He picked up the scraps of paper and began reading out loud. "'*Shag*'!" He flipped over another. "'*Lady-bird*'?" And then: "*Bloody hell*!"

"*Bloody hell* is *not* one of my words," she responded in a muffled voice, still reaching for something under her own seat.

"No, this is far worse."

"They're *words*. They're not bad," she muttered. She seemed offended at what he'd said, although he had no idea why. The word he'd just read was far filthier than anything he'd said. "A word can't be bad! It simply exists!"

He smiled. She was defending the words.

"I assure you, Miss Bancroft, that this word is very bad indeed."

"Which is it?" She sat back up on her knees and reached over, trying to grab the paper out of his hand even as Alexander tucked it into his lapel pocket, betting she wasn't bold enough to risk touching him there. The bet paid off and he found himself smirking again.

It had been ages since he'd smiled so much outside of a bedroom or ballroom. Then again, he couldn't think of the last time he'd been around a woman for this long. Women were like brandy—dangerous after a couple hours or a couple helpings.

She brushed the loose strands of her chestnut hair out of her face in frustration and returned to her unknowingly lewd position. Alexander reached his arm under the seat again, in case something was still underneath or, if he were honest, in case the position afforded him an even better view of her.

His half-hearted search proved fruitful when his fingers grazed a pair of spectacles. He'd never seen her with them on. Or if he had, he hadn't noticed. Was she vain about her appearance? Did she only need them for reading? Had she been teased? His heart gave a peculiar squeeze imagining that.

As Harriet finally returned to her seat after doing the lion's share of the cleanup, Alexander leaned over to gently place the glasses on her face. She flinched as he did, ducking out of his reach. He pulled back, frowning.

"You can wear them in front of me, you know."

"No, I—"

"Spectacles can be quite attractive, I've always thought," he ventured. "Are they for reading?"

"They're for objects farther in the distance, my lord," she said, smiling slyly. Why did he feel she was trying not to laugh at him?

"Would they not help you, say, see out the carriage, then?" Why was she being so stubborn? She was missing the world outside. Not that this was a particularly scenic road, but nevertheless, she ought to be able to see it all.

"They would *not*," she said, her lips twitching, "as they are not mine." Alexander felt more puzzled than ever.

"They're my sister Caroline's. She's forever losing them, and one's own spectacles are naturally the hardest thing to find. I keep an extra pair on me; I often end up wearing them on my head just to keep track of them. And I've found something marvelous when I do: They make you even *more* invisible." *Why did she want that?*

Harriet reached over to pat his knee. "Thank you for that . . . chivalrous assault. I'm elated to know you find spectacles attractive." She drew her hand back quickly, as if touching him had burned her.

Alexander was simultaneously embarrassed and full of wonder. He couldn't remember the last time he had experienced such humiliation. He suspected he was flushed bright red.

A giggle escaped her.

Seeing Alexander's mortification, she tried to rein herself in, which only made her laughter turn into hiccoughs, which then made her laugh *more*. And then she let it out—her real, full laugh. It was loud and rich and involved her entire body. *Bloody hell, indeed.*

He leveled as much of a glare at her as he could manage while still feeling utterly unmoored.

"I'm so sorry," she sniffled, trying unsuccessfully to hide her continued delight at his gaffe, "it's just, well—you were so sincere!" That sent her into further peals of laughter.

Alexander placed the spectacles on the bench next to her and leaned back against the squab, stunned into silence.

Lady Harriet was to be his undoing. Women didn't laugh at him. Women fawned over him. He ought to have hated it, yet some obviously ill part of his mind whispered that he'd gladly make a fool of himself to get to hear her laugh like that again.

Chapter Nine

Alexander had never been one for complaining. From an early age, he'd learned that no one around him cared much if he was uncomfortable. As a grown man with a great deal of control over his circumstances, he found the act both unnecessary and unbecoming.

But this carriage ride was testing the bounds of his patience. He could not be in this damned vehicle with her a moment longer. Not in that dress—or any other she owned, he suspected. Not with those breasts. Not with the scent of oranges and hothouse flowers emanating off her. Her laughing at him hadn't diminished his arousal a whit. In fact, it had done the opposite.

He virtually bolted out of the carriage upon arrival at another small inn. Tomorrow, he planned to spend the entire day on horseback.

Harriet followed him, shivering in the cold night air. He might have offered her his coat, but he didn't think getting close to her in his current state would be wise. Thankfully, the inn itself was quite warm. Lively as well. The sound of bad singing and even worse piano playing filled the downstairs. Alexander cut an easy swath across the hall to the innkeeper. Despite his general distaste for the aristocracy, it did have its uses when one wanted to cross a room.

"Two rooms, please. We'll take our suppers there, and a bath as well, please," Alexander informed the man, laying a few too many coins on the counter in hopes of expediency. A bath sounded like heaven.

"Sorry, milord," answered the innkeeper, sounding not very sorry at all. "Don't have two rooms. We're full, really, but I can kick Eddie out to the barn and give you his. He don't mind." There was no hint as to who Eddie was, and Alexander didn't care to ask.

"Excellent. We'll take it."

"Oh, we don't want to be a bother. We're happy to—" came Harriet's voice behind him. Alexander whipped around.

"We are *not* sleeping in a barn. There aren't any more inns for miles, so unless you want to spend the night in a shared room with a fifth of the crowd you see here, Eddie's room it is."

Harriet snapped her mouth shut and glared at him. The innkeeper didn't seem to have heard any of their conversation and was already around the bar leading them up the stairs.

Alexander swept out his hand in a gesture for her to follow the man while he brought up the rear. One bloody room. With her one bloody dress. And one bloody bed. An entire day in a carriage with her had been agony. A night in bed with her? Hell, she probably knew a perfect word for what lay beyond torture.

"It's Tuesday, is it not?" he asked her as they climbed the steps, her arse precisely at eye level. If there were a god, he enjoyed suffering. Harriet glanced over her shoulder with a quizzical expression.

"It is," she replied, clearly expecting him to elaborate. Silence was much safer.

Tuesday. Tuesdays were for boxing at Jackson's, drinking at White's, then—should he still feel unsettled—sinking his cock into an opera singer until he forgot all else. Tuesday meant he hadn't spent in three days. Bollocks. Bollocks indeed. *His* poor bollocks in particular, trapped in one room with Harriet.

He swept into the room and began undressing himself, doing his best to ignore Harriet. A bath had been a terrible, terrible idea. One of his worst, and he'd once wagered his townhome that he could catch a knife by the blade while drunk. He hadn't lost the townhome, and he wasn't going to lose control tonight.

A knock on the door signaled a pair of girls, one with supper, the other with hot water. Harriet let out a moan of delight at the sight of food and he quickly began buttoning his waistcoat again.

"You may bathe first," he muttered gruffly.

"Oh, thank you, my lord," she said, almost timidly. She didn't sound any keener on his staying in the room while she bathed than he was. Although that was a lie, wasn't it? He was quite keen indeed to be present, which was precisely the issue. "Would you mind helping me with my dress?"

"Yes."

"Yes, you mind?" Harriet looked at him rather oddly, which was warranted.

"No. Yes. Never mind. Turn around." He knew he sounded terse, but he was merely attempting to survive the interaction. Weren't there maids to do this sort of thing? Why had the blasted girl with the blasted food tray left? The buttons down Harriet's back taunted him, more seeming to appear before his fingers every time he unbuttoned another. "There," he said, an interminable amount of time later. She could need no more assistance than that. Surely. He hastily retied his cravat and stuffed his arms back into his tailcoat. Someone in the room needed to be dressed.

"Aren't you hungry?" she inquired over her shoulder, glancing at the meal that had been left for them.

Ravenous.

"No, thank you," he intoned before quitting the room. He'd find food below. And perhaps a tankard of ale to drown himself in while she soaked in the damned tub.

Harriet wasn't sure precisely what had transpired that afternoon to make Alexander so taciturn, and she was doubly unsure how much she was meant to worry over it. Ever since the spectacle incident, he'd been quite withdrawn. Perhaps she shouldn't have laughed at him. Men did seem to have quite fragile egos about such things. Or perhaps the man was predisposed to such fits of reticence.

Maybe it was not a particular event so much as the entire situation. Being forced to marry a plump bluestocking might do this to a celebrated rake, she supposed. The very idea of the two of them together twisted her mouth into a wry smile.

The Thompson boys had an old, fat donkey they called Barrel and the donkey's dearest friend was their father's stallion, Claudius.

(Privately, Harriet thought it ridiculous to name your prized horse after an emperor who apparently had trouble walking, but Mr. Thompson wasn't exactly the scholarly type.) Harriet imagined she and Alexander made a similar pair.

She shook her head and continued eating her much-needed but mediocre meat pie as the two maids returned to finish filling the bath. They left and she was, for the first time in days, alone. This was the farthest she'd ever traveled, the longest she'd gone without seeing one of her sisters, and the most danger she'd ever been in.

All to marry a man who didn't want her.

Despite her best efforts, she wanted him plenty—in ways she didn't fully understand or have words for. She'd have to ask Philippa when she got home.

The thought of her sister brought an uncomfortable truth to mind: Alexander wanted someone like Philippa. Philippa specifically, in fact.

Alas. There were things one could control and things one could not. Harriet could not become Philippa any more than Barrel the donkey could become Pegasus. Perhaps Alexander *did* want a woman like Philippa. He could have as many of them as he wished when they returned to London. He could be having one now. Alexander was not hers, nor would he be; he'd made that clear. Their lives were to be separate.

There was nothing to attend, no one to manage—she might as well enjoy herself. She leaned her head back and closed her eyes, sighing at the warmth of the tub. Normally, she'd hurry through a bath so her sisters could get hot water, but Alexander seemed in no rush to return to her company.

Harriet woke with a splash sometime later when the door opened. She startled and covered herself, which was unrequired as the bath was behind a screen.

"Sorry!" she blurted, entirely disoriented. "I mean—I'm not . . . You didn't. Oh gosh, sorry . . ."

He let out a soft, low half laugh from the other side of the screen. Harriet did her best to keep her gaze trained straight ahead of her, not wanting to find out how much might be seen through the flimsy separation. Thank heavens for the wall of the tub.

"I don't know why I'm apologizing. I just—you startled me. I'm afraid I fell asleep. Probably not very safe. I won't be long, I promise. I just need to finish . . . uh, well, washing up," Harriet called out nervously. She went about the task rather more loudly than was altogether necessary. Somehow making noise helped to cut through the awkwardness of being nude while he was in the room. "Won't be but a moment. I hope the water isn't too cold for you. It still feels somewhat warm. I really didn't mean to take so long! I do apologize for that. Oh dear, I'm nattering on again, aren't I?"

"You are," he replied plainly, although not unkindly. Harriet heard a chair scraping across the floor, and the metal clink of utensils, which sounded like him sitting down at the small table to his undoubtedly frigid meat pie. Her face burned from being naked so near to such a man. From what she could hear, he seemed terribly unaffected by the situation, however. And he was still being frustrat-ingly laconic.

"I am sorry, too, about your dinner. I hope it hasn't gone too cold; if it's any comfort, it wasn't very good warm." Why was her voice getting more and more high-pitched? "Sorry, too, about the prattling. My sisters are always telling me not to get started. With talking, that is. I just have a hard time stopping. It's worse when I'm nervous."

He let out a low chuckle again, which made Harriet's heart leap a bit for unknown reasons.

"I make you nervous?" he asked after a moment. His speech had slowed, and he seemed plainspoken—artless, even—which was far more seductive than his ordinary attempts to charm.

Conceding this felt like a loss, but still she answered: "When you aren't making me furious, yes."

He laughed again, the sound halfway between honey and gravel. Harriet swallowed thickly and rewashed her left leg for perhaps the eleventh time. A towel and a robe sat on a stool a few feet from the bath and Harriet scrunched her nose at the distance. Perhaps after he finished his meal, she could ask him to leave again.

"Either way, I *am* sorry for all the nattering; I'm always talking nineteen to the dozen. I'm aware it's entirely unladylike," she responded, hoping she sounded prim enough to balance out the rest of their conversation.

"Some of my favorite women haven't been very ladylike," Alexander replied. He picked up his drink then and quickly drained it, before settling the mug back down with a heavy thud. Which

Harriet should not have seen as she was *not* looking through the screen. "Besides, I've come to like your prattling."

"Have you been drinking gin?" Harriet inquired, rather meekly. Alexander didn't answer for a moment, as if puzzling over a tough question. Harriet's heart dropped. Her father had taught her well how men lie about drinking; here poor Alexander wasn't even very good at it.

"Only a bit."

"I see," Harriet answered. The bath suddenly seemed colder than ever, and she was eager to escape its frigid waters. "Can you see through the screen, my lord?"

"Not very well, I'm afraid." Harriet rolled her eyes at his practiced and no doubt drunken flirtation. The blandishments had returned.

"Do you mind averting your eyes so that I may dress for bed?" she asked haughtily, putting her hands on the sides of the tub to stand. Then she realized her folly. "That is . . . if you were actually . . . I don't want to assume you were looking. At me. I apologize for the implication."

"I was," he answered simply. At her silence he continued, "And I will. Avert my eyes, that is. No need to make you more nervous. I'll only get a monologue on the origins of the word *bath* or a lecture about how I'm using an adverb incorrectly."

Harriet was so heated at his admission that he'd been watching, she barely registered his jest. She clamored out of the tub quickly and dried off with her back to him. Facing him seemed much too wanton, screens and averted eyes be damned. She donned Giuliana's too-small chemise and peeked from behind the screen to see him at the table simply swiping his thumb around the lip of his glass, staring off into the far corner of the room, where no bathing or nudity had taken place.

She tiptoed to the bed and climbed in. Only once she was under the covers did he blow out the candle on her nightstand, plunging them further into darkness. Harriet couldn't help but listen to the sounds of him undressing. She felt embarrassed to be overhearing something so intimate, although certainly he didn't consider the act private, if one were to go by his boldness in disrobing in daylight in front of her that very day. At the *thunk* of his boots hitting the ground and the sound of his trousers following, Harriet felt herself start to heat again. She tried her hardest to stay still, in hopes he'd believe her to be asleep, although her legs felt particularly restless. She felt a desperate need to squirm, to rub them together when she heard him get into the tub. Christ, but this was inappropriate.

As she fell asleep, she found herself wondering at the fact that his speech hadn't been slurred at all when he spoke. Nor had he had trouble undressing or bathing. And he certainly didn't smell as her father did after a night of drunkenness. Perhaps he had been telling the truth.

∽

Harriet was disturbed from her sleep a short while later by movement in the bed next to her. Alexander was lying down, but he seemed to be tossing and turning. Or not turning, but moving. It was as though he was having a nightmare, except he was silent and still, other than for his arm. He lay facing away from her and his arm was working. Quickly too. This wasn't the action of someone asleep. It seemed purposeful, intentional. Harriet shut her eyes tightly; then, with effort, relaxed them and slowed her breathing, so he might believe her truly asleep should he turn over. Whatever was he doing?

With her own breath quieted, she was better able to overhear his, which was growing heavier and more rapid in time with whatever he was doing with his hand. She dearly hoped he was all right. After a few moments, he let out a low groan, which would have been quiet if not for the silence of the room and the fact that every cell in Harriet's body was attuned to him. Seconds later came an exhausted sigh, the contented, tired sound one made when finished with a difficult task.

Harriet's tongue stung with the impulse to ask him if he was well, but an even stronger one compelled her to continue to feign sleep. After a few moments of heavy breathing, he got up out of the bed, crossed the room to the washstand, and then came back and lay down again as if nothing had occurred.

What had he been doing? Surely, he could have done this when he was downstairs if it weren't private? Or in the bath if it were? Was this something men normally did at night? To be sure, Harriet would not know about it if that were the case. Was this a particular habit of Lord Alexander's? An old injury? She kept turning the event over in her mind. Was he hurt, or satisfied? It sounded as if he'd gotten relief—at least at the end. And most of all, why was she so certain that if he'd known she was awake, he wouldn't have continued?

Chapter Ten

For the past hour, Alexander had been trying in vain to ignore the rain.

The first mile of the day's ride, he'd spent on Harriet's lips. The second on her breasts. The third on her blue-gray eyes, which flashed with humor and intelligence. He then spent the next five miles attempting to forget that he knew this woman's eye color. For the sake of sanity, he'd tried to think of the eye color of every woman he'd ever met in his life. All he could remember was that his mother's were bright blue and distinctly not his.

The incessant return of his mind to her was proof that he ought to continue riding out. It was only a drizzle, he told himself. Which was true enough, though it was also—as usual in England—relentless. Unyielding. Freezing. And though it was more appealing than an enclosed space with her, enduring such frigid conditions on horseback was only possible for so long.

Finally, he signaled for the driver to stop. He dismounted and, with a sense of defeat, reentered the carriage.

The scent of oranges hit him immediately. How did she smell so heavenly after hours of travel? How did she look so lovely? He had intended for last night to slake his needs and therefore dull the attraction he felt toward her. Normally, he'd have had a woman by now, and if not, he'd at least have other appropriate outlets for his lust. Taking himself in hand had been his only option and so he'd taken the risk.

Upon waking this morning, he'd understood his miscalculation. Lying next to the woman imagining all sorts of filthy things they might do had, in retrospect, been woodenheaded. Harriet splayed on a bed, wearing nothing, chestnut hair unbound. Her on her knees, gazing up at him with desire. Tracing his hands up her bare legs, which he had no idea of, but had pictured quite distinctly. And repeatedly.

Thus, this morning, he'd feigned carriage sickness and declared the need to ride out. Only to be thwarted by the damned weather of this damned country.

"You're positively drenched," she exclaimed, before realizing how familiarly she'd spoken to him. She cleared her throat and began again: "Are you all right, my lord?"

He really wished she wouldn't call him that; he didn't relish any part of his title.

"I'm perfectly fine," he answered, removing his greatcoat. She held out her hand to trade him the blanket that had been across her lap. Had he been even a degree less chilled, he would have refused. She carefully draped the wet coat over the bench next to her and returned to circling in her book. Alexander luxuriated in the warmth of the blanket and did his level best to avoid watching her. There were only so many places one could look in a carriage, and he intended to exhaust them all before resorting to looking at her.

He must have run out of them quite quickly, for only a moment later he watched as her lips curled into a mischievous smile. Despite his best efforts, he gave in to his instinct to charm a woman.

"Something particularly humorous about agricultural practices? Personally, I've always found crop rotation highly amusing."

"I was thinking, actually," she said with a guileless look, "about how much *quim* has shaped my life. Strange, isn't it? We have that in common now."

∽

Alexander was silent for a moment before letting out a loud crack of laughter at the jest. Unconsciously, she joined him, their laughter looping around each other's. It felt so good to laugh this hard. Doing so made her miss her sisters sharply but also gave her some small hope that there might be more laughter in their future. Matrimony might not be a dour and formal affair after all; perhaps the two of them could find a sort of friendship with one another.

But suddenly Alexander's face stilled, and he turned distant, as though remembering something.

"Are you going to become unwell from the carriage?"

Alexander looked at her curiously. "No. I'm fine."

"Shall I open a window? The air helps carriage sickness, does it not?"

"I'm quite all right, thank you." His eyes returned to the window.

They sat in silence for a moment before Harriet decided to take advantage of her captive audience.

"What does *monosyllable* mean?"

He groaned and reached up, removing his hat and scrubbing a hand through his dark hair. Was everything the man did meant to be erotic? Did he *know* the act made Harriet want to run *her* hands through his hair? Surely he must.

"Harriet," he complained, but she did not intend to be moved. After a few moments of pointed silence, Alexander seemed to realize this. "Oh, very well, you hellcat. It's the same thing as *quim*. There."

"Honest?"

"Yes. It's just another word for it."

"Your lot do have quite a few words for that part."

"Yes, well, it's of utmost importance—shapes one's life, as you pointed out."

"Why *monosyllable*, though? An odd name, no?" Alexander laughed.

"It's in reference to another, *more* inappropriate word for a woman's . . ."

"Quim."

"Yes."

Harriet held his gaze steadily; he *would* tell her the word. If she was going to give up having children for him, surely he could give up propriety for her. Alexander realized the meaning behind her stare and laughed again.

"All right. All right," he said, throwing his hands up. "The word is *cunt*. Are you satisfied?" Harriet hurried to scribble the word in the margin of her book.

"Hardly! Do you know other words for *swive*?" Harriet had her pencil at the ready. The man was a veritable font of knowledge; she didn't know why she hadn't thought to quiz him earlier.

"Please, no more." He reached his hand under the blanket and shifted, rearranging himself across the seat. No doubt he was uncomfortable from a day of riding out in the rain. "I'm not going to list off filthy words for your Mr. Deacon."

"Oh, these aren't for Mr. Dawkins. I presume he knows quite a lot of them; men always know words. They're likely already in his dictionary—unless you know something *really* vulgar. They're for me. I don't see when I might have the opportunity to learn them organically. I ought not to be robbed of words simply because I'm to forgo . . . amorous congress, don't you think?"

"You . . . you plan to never . . . have intercourse? In your entire life?" He looked horrified at the prospect, but Harriet wasn't certain what he'd expected if she wasn't to consummate the wedding with him.

∽

Alexander felt certain he'd misunderstood her. But then she said blithely, "I have lived this long without engaging in fornication. I don't suspect I'll miss it overmuch."

"I assure you that it's precisely because you haven't done it before that you say that." Alexander assumed that, as usual, Harriet would fight him on this point.

Instead, she replied, sagely, "I presume you're correct. Hence, my intent to abstain. I am not aware of what I'm missing and therefore there's little to miss." His heart pinched pathetically at the thought of her never getting to experience a good bedding. Although surely it was better than her announcing her intent to have relations with all and sundry.

And then, because conversation with Harriet often felt as smooth as being thrown from a horse, she continued: "I suppose the only thing I'd really miss is kissing. As I have seen it done before, I'm somewhat aware of what I'm lacking. I shouldn't like to die without a proper kiss."

Seen? *Seen?* She'd never even been kissed? The very idea undid something in Alexander. Had he been capable of forming thoughts, he might have had ones like: *Lady Harriet Bancroft going to her grave unkissed would be a tragedy. And who would I be if I didn't prevent such a thing?*

In the name of something like chivalry—certainly not unbridled lust—he leaned across the carriage, took her lovely face in his hands, and met her mouth with his own.

It wasn't the longest or most passionate kiss of his life. In fact, by all measures it was rather restrained. This was her first experience after all; he wanted to tempt her, not overwhelm her. He hadn't allowed his tongue to sweep over her full lower lip, or—more enticingly—dive into her mouth. The kiss was simple and sweet. But God, did it thrill.

Heat coursed through his body, and he had to make a concerted effort not to draw her into his lap.

In faith, he'd wanted to kiss her ever since the library, and while this kiss did little to sate his desires, he was glad to know just how she tasted, even if only to add accuracy to his fantasies. He let go of her after a moment of catching his breath, aware he'd likely shocked her with his advance.

At least she wouldn't die without a proper kiss. Sadly, he might die *because of* it. His heart was racing, and he felt all the more indignant that she might never lie with a man. Specifically, himself.

Alternatively, Harriet appeared . . . unmoved. *Peculiar*. The only signs to the contrary were her swollen, red lips and a slightly dazed look in her eyes. She gathered her wits quickly—one of her most particular skills—and went back to the action her mouth knew best: talking.

"Thank you," she offered politely. "However, that was *not* a proper kiss."

"The best kisses aren't."

"I don't mean it was scandalous; I mean it was . . . unfulfilling."

That was like a dull kick to the chest.

"Unfulfilling?" Alexander growled, trying hard to keep himself in check.

"Oh dear, is this about your ego again?"

"I have never had a kiss described as 'unfulfilling' before."

"I believe you," she offered, like a governess to a lad of four or five. "Although, let us keep at the forefront of our minds that many of the kisses you've given have gone to women whom you've also been plying with jewels and town houses, have they not?"

"I'm quite certain I have left very, very many ladies quite fulfilled."

"Yes, but you see, that's part of the problem. You've gone around giving such kisses to everyone. Your kiss is rather devalued in the marketplace of such intimacies, is it not?" She reached out then and patted his knee. "But a nice kiss, nevertheless. Your expertise is appreciated. It was quite educational."

"Educational?" he repeated flatly.

She nodded kindly. *She meant it!*

"As I said, I don't intend to seek out intercourse. However, I cannot promise I'll turn down an opportunity for a proper kiss from someone. Someone who *means* it."

Alexander had absolutely *meant it.* He would gladly demonstrate just how much he'd bloody meant it.

Harriet was fidgeting. Alexander was coming to understand that she hated silence.

"Shall we be friends then?"

"I beg your pardon?"

"It's just that I'd been wondering what this marriage might look like after we return to London. I know we're to recommence our previous lives, but we'll be expected to interact on occasion. You haven't been entirely intolerable company, thus it occurred to me just now that you might become a friend."

"I don't believe I've ever had a female friend before." Alexander was bewildered. He was drifting, spinning, floating far above himself.

"What abject poverty you live in!" Harriet replied.

"And you? Do you have many friends of the opposite sex?" he challenged.

"Naturally! Our neighbor Mr. Hammons has poor eyesight, and I read to him on Thursdays. He's the nicest man one could imagine, and uncommonly droll. And Garrett, his stable boy, I've been teaching him his letters, even though he's almost sixteen. He's most eager to learn."

"I'm quite sure he is," Alexander rejoined. Harriet paused then and studied his face.

"Not *everything* is about intercourse, you know."

"When you're a sixteen-year-old boy it is."

Harriet rolled her eyes, although a quite becoming blush spread down from her cheeks to her neck. Alexander blinked as she continued. "The Thompson boys down the road, although they're closer in age to Caroline and Frances. And, of course, Mr. Dawkins."

"Yes, our inimitable Mr. Dawkins, how can we forget him?" Alexander grumbled. He knew he was being surly, but really. He'd just kissed the woman, and she was listing other men.

"Oh! Giuliana! There—you have a female friend!" She looked delighted for some reason.

"I do not view Giuliana in that capacity."

"Do you enjoy her company?"

"In ways you can't imagine," he gritted out.

"Do you attend to one another?"

"Yes," Alexander replied, although he was rather certain the type of attending he was thinking of bore little relation to what Harriet spoke of.

"And do you value her opinion?"

"Certainly."

"Well, there's a friend of yours!" Harriet replied smugly as if she'd settled a matter in his life that needed sorting.

Alexander couldn't help but want to wipe the look off her face, which is perhaps why he replied: "One doesn't usually want to fuck one's friend."

"On the contrary, I imagine that the desire to fuck one's friend occurs quite frequently. You mustn't let such a silly thing interfere with friendship!" The carriage was rolling to a stop, and Harriet alighted without any help from him or a groom, clearly quite pleased with her exit.

Alexander stayed seated in the carriage for a moment, until his driver, confused, peered around the door.

"Do you, uh, require assistance, sir?" Charleston asked, shyly.

"No, no." Alexander brushed him off and gathered his hat and gloves from the seat beside him.

As he stepped out of the carriage, he was hit with a wave of bracing cold, which was welcome. The temperature was something to think about that wasn't, well, *her*.

The respite was brief, however. As soon as he walked into the tavern, his eyes found Harriet once again, this time sidled up to the bar chatting with a female barkeep, a woman good-looking enough to appear out of place in such an establishment. A woman whose undeniable beauty would, under normal circumstances, inform Alexander's evening plans. Surely decency was the reason for his uncharacteristic lack of interest; it was not the done thing to bed a barmaid while eloping with one's fiancée. Why had his attention snagged so on Harriet? Because she was under his protection? Because he was to marry her?

He shook off that line of thinking and made his way over to the pair, where Harriet was already unfathomably deep in conversation. Damn, but the woman loved talking. Her status as a wallflower was baffling. How anyone had gotten her to stop speaking long enough to stand on the wall was a mystery.

"There you are! Sarah, this is . . ." Harriet began, spinning toward him, her cheeks flushed from either the cold or the delight of having a new conversation partner. Beside her, a rough-looking man sat, nursing an ale.

"Lord Alexander Stirling. Her husband," Alexander cut in, gruffly, neglecting to give the false name they'd agreed upon. It was a little possessive, but he didn't particularly like the way the man was eyeing the two women.

Harriet casually looped her arm through Alexander's without her eyes ever leaving Sarah's face. Next to them, the drunken man let out a loud belch before humming something to himself. Harriet didn't seem to notice. "My lord, this is Sarah. Sarah owns this place—how magnificent is that? A female innkeeper?"

He nodded to Sarah. "Lovely to make your acquaintance, and congratulations on the inn."

Something about the offhanded touch mere minutes after he'd heard the word *fuck* come out of her mouth set Alexander on edge. Or perhaps it was the knowledge that Harriet had no intention of ever touching him beyond these moments of playacting. And certainly, no intention of fucking him.

"Sorry to interrupt this"—Alexander swept a hand between the newly minted friends—"but do we have a room secured, *darling*? I'd like to dry off if that's all right." He wasn't sure why, but he needed distance from her good mood. His undue sullenness would surely puncture her happiness.

"Of course, my lord," Sarah responded, "you are upstairs, the third door on the left. I had Ruthie make it up for you, she should be almost done. Would you like to take your dinner upstairs?"

"Yes, thank you," Alexander replied, just as Harriet said, "No, we'll eat down here!"

Alexander loathed the idea of acting cheerful right now, although he couldn't have said why he felt the need to perform for her at all. Surely a man could enjoy a bout of disagreeableness from time to time. However, he knew Harriet well enough to know she wouldn't be moved, and he didn't relish the idea of her eating downstairs without him, so he nodded his acquiescence before heading to the room to freshen up.

Alexander washed himself in the basin and then sat gingerly on the end of the bed in the small though well-appointed room. He was not a slight man, and inns always made him feel even larger. He scrubbed his hands through his hair, no doubt messing it up further; his valet would be quite put out seeing him now. Alexander laughed, imagining explaining himself to the man. "Coleson, I know I seem in a state right now. As it happens, I can't stop thinking about my wife, which might sound perfectly acceptable, only I've found out I'm never to bed her. Ever."

Damn if he wasn't a bit disappointed that telling the truth had cost him having her, even just once. It shouldn't have felt such a great loss; he hadn't even noticed the lass before the Dunley ball—fool that he was. Even if he *had* noticed her then, it wouldn't have done him any good, he reminded himself. He didn't court unmarried ladies or dally with innocents.

He was noticing her just fine now, as his cock was eager to point out. Indeed, for the next week he was to be tormented by her lips, which never stopped moving, and the citrusy scent of her, and her massive pile of chestnut hair, which was always escaping her terrible coiffures.

God, but he needed to get this wedding over with so he could go back to London, back to a place with women he actually *could* swive, back to drinking at White's on Tuesdays, back to courting widows at balls. Back to who he was.

Chapter Eleven

Harriet was in heaven. The dinner was hearty and simple, and the room buzzed with people talking and laughing. The few balls she'd attended paled in comparison to this inn. Everyone here seemed happy, lively. The citizens of Mayfair prided themselves on their affected boredom; with this one evening, Harriet became certain she'd never see the elegance in that again. The smiles in this pub made a fool of every stiff upper lip in London.

In the corner a man played country songs on a fiddle, and as the night wore on and more ale flowed, someone took up the old piano in the corner, out of tune though it was. This, of course, led to dancing. One could hardly be in such a convivial space and be expected to sit still. Tables were pushed to the walls, and the floor was cleared as a few young couples began a country dance. Harriet clapped along, gleefully. Sarah stopped by and dropped off two pints of ale.

"You ought to have the full experience," she said, winking. Harriet's eyes widened and she glanced at Alexander, before deciding she didn't need his permission. This man might be her husband for the evening, and for the future, but he'd made it clear theirs was to be a marriage in name only. She wasn't going to curb his appetite for women, why should he be allowed to curb hers for spirits? Harriet hadn't had ale before, and she wanted to try it—and she *would*. If he had something to say, he could talk to an opera singer about it.

She glanced at him over the rim of the pint. He didn't look disapproving at all; in fact, he simply looked surprised. She lowered the glass a bit and looked at him. "Is it as bad as gin?"

He smiled. An easy, open smile. One she hadn't seen before.

"No, not so strong as that. Although I still do recommend you sip first. It's a bit of an acquired taste."

Harriet set the drink down, untried. "I never understood that. How does someone acquire a taste? More to the point: *why*? If it's bad to begin with, simply don't drink it!"

"Yes, but ale comes with other benefits. Such as making it much easier to speak to women."

"So *that's* your secret, then?"

"I don't require ale for that, personally."

"Well," Harriet said, glancing down at the glass again, "I don't need much help talking to women."

"You don't need help talking at all."

Harriet snorted. Unlike her father, Alexander didn't seem to be insulting her. He said it like a plain, neutral observation of her character. "Anything else ale can do?"

"Outside of making even the most mundane situations more diverting, it tends to make one slightly less clever, a touch more agreeable, and a much better dancer."

Harriet looked at him and without saying another word she took a large swig of ale. She winced a little at the taste, but he hadn't lied—it wasn't at all like gin. She took another large swill. Alexander sent her a questioning look.

Harriet shrugged and simply said, "It's always been my dearest wish to be half as clever and twice as good at dancing."

He tipped his head back and let out a loud, full laugh. The sound of it shot directly and deeply inside of Harriet, filling her with a strange warmth.

"Harriet, all the ale in this tavern won't change the fact that even half as clever, you're twice as brilliant as most of us in this room. As for the dancing, I can help with that." He pushed his chair back with a scrape and stood, holding out his hand. She took a deep breath and another bracing drink, then took his hand.

Alexander was not used to being wrong. But he could not, as it turned out, make Harriet a good dancer. She was, for all her sins, hopeless.

Her movements were awkward and jerky. She resembled nothing so much as a newborn horse, lurching around the room, stepping on his toes, turning the wrong direction. But Lord, was she having fun. She hadn't stopped laughing since they stood up, likely aided by the reinforcements of ale she kept sneaking in between songs. After dancing four or five sets, Alexander left her at the table to get another couple pints, and when he returned, she was in the arms of an old, half-toothless man, and yelling over her shoulder to Sarah, who was dancing with a woman who had been behind the bar earlier.

Spotting Alexander, Harriet's smile grew even wider, which hadn't seemed possible. Alexander stumbled, sloshing the ale over the tankards in his hands. He couldn't remember the last time someone had been so genuinely happy to see him, although at this point, she may have been simply happy to see more ale.

He sat and watched her dance with the old man, sipping his drink and enjoying the music. When the song ended, Harriet came back to the table, blowing loose tendrils of hair out of her face. She took a swig of her freshly delivered ale and then reached out her hand to him.

"Come on now, I've learned a lot from Mr. Gibbons over there. I can teach you a thing or two." He smiled and shot to his feet, eager to have her back in his arms. They danced together and apart and together again and wheeled around the room, Harriet barely avoiding catastrophic crashes into other couples and errant bar tables.

"Shall we head upstairs, wife?" Alexander asked at the end of another disastrous reel, leaning in quite close to her, as if what he asked was indecent. He supposed in some ways it was. They were still unwed until tomorrow.

Harriet was breathing heavily from the exertion of her twirling and looping and stomping on his toes. She was still flushed and giddy, as she had been since entering the inn. It was after midnight, though there was something about the night that felt separate from time, apart from the rest of life. She put her hands on her hips and nodded, her chest rising and falling heavily, making Alexander think of dangerous things. Things she'd vowed not to do with him.

"Good night, Sarah!" Harriet called over her shoulder as she left the crowd, waving her hand like a princess in a passing carriage. Her energy was not at all diminished by the evening ending. She lifted her skirts to ascend the stairs faster; Alexander didn't bother averting his gaze from the flashes of ankles she exposed. As soon as the door closed behind them to their room, she collapsed against the door, giggling. Alexander hoped she hadn't had too much ale.

"I haven't had this much fun in ages," she said, her hands over her face. She was heaven to watch like this. A shiver ran down her back, and she whined, "It's quite nippy up here!" but she was still smiling. She didn't seem to be drunk, but she certainly was happy.

"Yes, well, dancing keeps one rather warm. As does ale," he replied, matching her smile with his own. He couldn't have stopped himself if he wanted to. He hadn't had as much fun in perhaps . . . forever.

"Do you mind?" she asked, turning her back to him for help with her dress.

He minded. Oh god, he minded helping her undress yet again with no relief in sight. He braced himself and tried to think of curricle accidents and typhoid fever. As soon as he undid the last button, he backed away from her and began on his own clothing. He couldn't trust himself. Besides, it *was* rather cold in the room, and the bed was calling, even if it meant the torture of her proximity.

"I'm going to die from the cold!" Harriet complained again, still laughing. She was rubbing her arms and bouncing herself to keep warm. Alexander fought the urge, strong as it was, to cross the room and help warm her up. Instead, he turned and finished undressing looking at the wall. He soon heard her gown fall to the floor, and then the soft *thud* of each of her shoes. Something light then—stockings perhaps? He did not turn to look. Surely by the end of this trip, walls would be the most erotic sight in the world to him. Inconvenient, that.

She was still hopping about making small sounds of complaint about the cold as Alexander finished undressing and crawled into their warm bed. It was a grave tactical error. The only natural view from the bed was Harriet, and the sight was . . . unbearable.

She wore only a thin night shift—although *thin* was not the most distinct attribute of the slip of fabric she was in. No, the poor scrap of fabric clinging to Harriet was, above all else, too small. Although, even across the room, Alexander could tell the garment could *not* be described as poor. For one, it was fine cream-colored silk, with expensive lace around the edges designed specifically to taunt a man. But more importantly, it was touching Harriet in many places Alexander would like to be. Alexander knew then why the French called them *negligées*—to neglect, to disregard, to treat carelessly. He wasn't sure who was being more mistreated, himself or the chemise.

"Where the devil did you get that?" he asked, unable to help himself.

"Pardon?" Harriet said, looking around, unsure what he was referring to and still rubbing her arms for warmth. The posture did miraculous things to her breasts.

"That . . ." Alexander gestured to the clothing in question, truly unable to refer to the piece as a night shift. The shifts he had experienced in his time on earth—which had been quite a few—had nothing in common with what Harriet was wearing. The modiste who made it would herself have fainted upon seeing it on Harriet's body. The word *obscene* came to mind.

Harriet caught his meaning and looked down, dropping her arms. And hell, the thing was see-through! She didn't seem to recognize just how indecent she looked in the garment.

"Is it so bad? Giuliana was kind enough to lend it to me. She didn't have anything else that fit, though." He wasn't sure whether to punish Giuliana for her wicked gift when he arrived back in London or to lie prostrate at her feet, ever in her debt.

At Harriet's searching look, he realized he'd never answered her question. He cleared his throat and did his best to keep his voice steady. "No, no, it's fine. I just—" *Want to rip it off with my teeth? Will never again be able to see a chemise without getting aroused?* "I just worried you were cold."

"I am! I'm fairly freezing!" she exclaimed, shocked back into action. She rushed through her nightly ablutions at the wash basin— which Alexander forced himself not to watch—and scurried into bed on her tiptoes, moaning when she finally made it under the sheets. God, that was not the sound he wanted to hear. Or perhaps it was the only sound he'd ever like to hear again. Lord above, someone had sent her to punish him. Alexander scrubbed a hand over his eyes for what felt like the thousandth time in the past three days and groaned.

Harriet blew out her candle, plunging them into darkness. Then she turned on her side, propped herself up on an elbow as best as the tight chemise allowed, and studied him. He did his best to ignore how her perusal inflamed him. Did she like what she saw?

"Is something wrong?" she asked, her voice still merry and light-hearted.

Alexander let out a huff that was almost laughter. Everything was so clearly wrong.

He shook his head and closed his eyes. "No, nothing's wrong."

Undeterred, she nudged his shin with her ice-cold foot, which by all rights should have killed his burgeoning cockstand, not encouraged it.

"Tell me! You said we were to be friends." Alexander bit back a groan and opened his eyes, training them on the ceiling.

"*You* said that. I never acquiesced."

"You don't want to be friends with me?" she asked, in a pouty voice he'd never heard from her. It was so distinctly out of character for this capable, headstrong woman, it sounded as if she were . . . flirting. The possibility warmed Alexander's chest and then spread. Southward.

He chanced a glance at her, which he'd always remember as his most fatal mistake. She pursed her lovely, biteable lips, pretending to sulk. But at his look, she collapsed into a fit of laughter, turning over onto her stomach and burying her face in the pillow. He couldn't help the smile that sneaked out the side of his mouth.

Finished laughing, Harriet pushed herself up on her elbows. She glanced over at him with a moony smile, which was presumably why he said what he did next.

"All right, I'll be your friend."

She beamed and kicked her feet in a fit of glee.

"Your second female friend!"

Alexander rolled his eyes. Giuliana was most certainly not a friend. "My first."

"All right. I'll be your first," she said, solemnly. As if she didn't know what else the words could mean. She paused for a beat and then asked, "How is it going so far?"

"There's more staying up late talking in bed than I expected," he conceded.

"That's a cornerstone of friendship."

Alexander turned on his side toward her, trying his best to appear unaffected.

"So, you often stay up talking in bed with men?"

"Oh no! I suppose I don't. Just with my sisters, and sometimes when we used to get snowed in at the Yardsleys' at Christmas. Never with a man. I'll have to make an exception for you."

A knot that had been in Alexander's chest loosened a bit, and he felt his face heat at its ever having been there. He was a fool.

"What does one talk about in bed then, with . . . ahem . . . female friends?" he asked as a gesture of goodwill.

"All sorts of things. Ribbons, how Mrs. Tatters flirts with her carriage driver, which of the butcher's sons we'd like to marry, what books we've been reading."

"Which of the butcher's sons?"

"The obvious choice is Malcolm, for he's the most handsome. But I confess I'm more partial to Edmund, as he's the eldest and most responsible. Jasper is too . . . Jaspery. Frances always goes for Benjamin, though he's far too young for me to take him seriously. And a horrible singer." Alexander laughed.

"How practical of you."

"Now, *you* must tell me a secret."

"Pardon?" The secrets he had—and he had plenty—were not the sort to be whispered in bed to an innocent. He may not have female friends, but he knew that.

"You must share something with me! That's how these late-night talks go." She nudged him with her foot, and again his body responded. It was as if his cock had no idea they were practicing friendship.

"Does the butcher have any daughters?" he deadpanned. Harriet laughed loudly, her entire body shaking and her head dropping between her hands.

She turned back on her side to face him, and they both grew quiet at their closeness. After a moment, Harriet flipped onto her back, pulling her hands out of the tightly tucked covers. If he didn't know her so well, he'd have thought she was settling into sleep. Alexander knew she wasn't going to miss a chance to talk. She kept her gaze on the ceiling, worrying her bottom lip and fidgeting her hands. Alexander's heart clenched in preparation for what came next. If Harriet was shy to say something, it must be grave indeed.

"What were you doing last night?" she inquired, in a soft voice, so soft he wasn't sure he'd heard her correctly. Blood rushed through his ears, and his heart began racing. Surely, she didn't mean—

"In bed," she clarified, removing any hope that she might have been referencing something else.

He groaned and sat up, the bedsheet falling around his waist. Some part of his brain registered Harriet's eager eyes on his chest, which stirred him, even as a cold panic set in.

"I was—It is—What I was—" Alexander was making an ass of himself. He never should have taken himself in hand in the same room, in the same bed as her. And why was he even considering explaining himself?

Her eyes. Her eyes were why. She let out a soft laugh, a friendly one, as she drew circles on the coverlet with her finger.

"Not often you're at a loss for words in bed with a woman, is it?" She hitched up half of her mouth wryly. Something about the look made him think she was embarrassed, self-conscious, as if she was the problem. *Hell.* Now he had to tell her.

"No, although most of the women I've been with know about tossing off."

Harriet's brow furrowed in confusion. Alexander took a deep breath and began. Might as well be honest with her—how else was she to learn? And what a pity it would be to live without knowing how to bring oneself pleasure.

She scooted and sat up in bed, her back against the headboard, ever the eager pupil.

"Do you know anything of intercourse? What happens between a man and woman?" Alexander almost amended that it could happen between any number of people of any sex but felt that was getting off topic. Besides, Harriet was already blushing madly.

"Not really," she whispered, the blush having traveled from her cheeks down her neck and across her chest. He would dearly like to see where else it spread.

"I see. Well, there's a . . . point . . . at the end of intercourse. A crisis."

"A crisis?" Harriet looked concerned again. *Blast it.*

"Or, rather, a peak. A culmination." Harriet nodded along with him, waiting for more.

Dear God, was he really going to explain self-gratification to a blushing innocent? Apparently so. "This, uh—"

"Apotheosis?" she provided, hurrying him along adorably.

"This *apotheosis*," he said, trying desperately not to laugh at the suggestion, "well, it feels . . . blissful. Heavenly. It's the reason men do half of what they do."

"Half?"

"True, it's vastly more than half, come to think of it. We'd hardly be managing land or fighting duels or racing curricles or wearing skin-tight breeches if coming didn't feel so damned good."

"But last night—" Harriet began, clearly unsure of how to ask what she wanted to know. "You believed me to be asleep."

"I did not intend to subject you to my actions; I am sorry."

"I see," she said. "Is it always that way? With the woman asleep?" And then Alexander *did* let out a laugh.

"No, no, the woman isn't asleep for intercourse at all."

"I don't understand."

"I'm not explaining it well, I fear. This climax, you can produce it on your own, outside of intercourse. You don't need a partner for it. That's what I was doing last night."

"Oh," Harriet said, looking down at her lap. Alexander waited, knowing there was more. She was far too curious for the discussion to end there. "So why wear tight breeches then? Or race curricles? Or . . . enjoy . . . women at all? If men can do that themselves?"

"It's far, far more pleasurable with someone else, I promise you," Alexander responded, knowing he was tiptoeing into quite dangerous territory, but unable to stop himself. It wasn't the ale or the dancing or even the damned shift, but the feeling he had that the two of them were entirely removed from the rest of the world in that tiny, cold room, which compelled him to add, "It's not just men who can do so themselves."

He willed Harriet to ask the next question, even as he knew he should end this conversation. For all his rakehell ways, he knew he should not be discussing frigging habits with an innocent. And yet. He could tell she wanted to know. Harriet *always* wanted to know things. And he wanted to be the one to teach her.

"Women can toss themselves off, then?"

He laughed, a full laugh. Harriet startled, which made him feel like the worst sort of person. He unthinkingly reached over and placed a hand on her arm to stay her.

"They can. It's only, I'm not certain it's called 'tossing off' for a woman." Harriet looked down at her arm where his hand lay and then up at him. Even in the dim moonlight, he could see her gray eyes widen with desire. Desire to learn a vocabulary word, yes, but desire all the same.

"What is it, then?"

He brought his arm back to his lap, which felt safer. Nothing in all his years had prepared him for this interaction.

"I'm not certain I know the phrase for women."

"You don't know?" She sounded affronted.

"I'm afraid I don't. Bring oneself off? That may apply to either sex. Self-pollute surely does, although that seems to carry a negative connotation I shouldn't like to associate with the act. I'll admit, I'm not very studied in this."

"I am appalled to hear that you don't know about female pleasure. I felt certain, based on your reputation, that it was your specialty."

Alexander turned his entire body to face her, insulted. "I will not have you discredit me. I simply don't know the *words* a lady might use for touching herself. I assure you, I know *plenty* about female pleasure. Indeed, I have forgotten more about bringing a lady to her peak than many men have ever learned." He could feel himself breathing more heavily and was glad to see that she was too. Dancing wasn't to blame this time. She was silent for a moment before she parted her lips, darting her tongue out to wet them before she began.

"So, you *do* know how it's done?"

"Of course I know how intercourse is done. I'd hardly be worthy of my title as London's Most Notorious Rake if I didn't, would I?"

Harriet held his gaze for a moment, and he couldn't look away. From the edge of his vision, he saw her throat swallow thickly. She was gathering her nerves. He was doomed.

"I meant touching myself," she corrected, quietly.

Chapter Twelve

As soon as the words left her mouth, Harriet regretted them. Her entire body felt prickly and hot, her skin too small. Her chemise, which already *was* too small, felt even tighter. Her father had always been disappointed with her curiosity, had told her it wouldn't serve her, that it would get her in trouble. He'd been right, apparently.

Compared to her heat, Alexander seemed frozen in place—likely from shame. No doubt ladies were not meant to ask such things. Harriet flinched, a remnant of living so long with her father. She scrambled to apologize, to smooth things over.

"I beg your pardon! I shouldn't have—I'm—Oh, I'm—" She buried her face in her hands. It was useless.

Alexander reached out to lower her arms, and Harriet realized just how wrong she'd been.

He wasn't cold at all.

"Harriet," he whispered, his voice low and deep.

How many levels of blushing were possible? Harriet felt sure she'd experienced every single one of them. She kept her eyes trained on the coverlet; if she met his gaze, the inn would ignite.

"Harriet," he repeated, his thumb stroking up her arm seductively. No wonder the man didn't care about words as she did. If he could achieve this much with his hands, he had no need for a mouth.

His touch traveled up to her shoulder, then he traced his fingers across her collarbone. A bone she'd never felt anything for previously. If you'd asked yesterday, Harriet would have been virtually certain seduction shouldn't have anything to do with clavicles.

"Is this it?" Harriet asked, her eyes meeting his, the flammability of the inn be damned. She heard herself practically panting. It would have been quite embarrassing if she weren't so desperate. She had no capacity for shame; she needed more. More . . . something. "Is this how women touch themselves?"

The question seemed to snap Alexander back to himself. He pulled his hand away and rubbed his eyes. "I feel certain you're trying to kill me," he groaned.

Harriet crawled out from beneath the covers and sat up on her knees to force him to meet her gaze. The chill of the room was now welcome against her hot skin.

"Will you teach me? If you know—and it seems likely you do— will you teach me?"

"Harriet," he repeated, although this time it sounded like a warning.

"Yes, my lord?" Harriet replied, feeling suddenly quite mischievous. Alexander let out another deep groan.

Despite his displays of annoyance, she knew he wasn't like her father; he wouldn't strike her for being brazen or curious. He wouldn't hurt her at all. So she pressed.

"It's only fair, wouldn't you concede? If you are to have a mistress, who I suspect helps you with those . . . peaks . . . that I should get to have them as well?" Alexander's hands fisted in the sheets, which made Harriet grin. If there was one thing she was good at, it was talking someone into seeing her way of things. And she was getting close. "Come now, you wouldn't want a wife who had no outlets for such things, would you? Surely that way lies danger? A wife who might go asking someone *else* for . . . assistance?"

Alexander's eyes snapped to hers, flashing with something that made Harriet's heart skip or race or . . . do something which hearts weren't meant to do. Tonight was an education in how little she knew of anatomy.

"Harriet, you've survived until now without having this particular experience. I think you should be quite well without it." When she opened her mouth to argue, Alexander cut her off. "Alternatively, you can ask your sister when we arrive back in London; I'm certain she's informed on this topic."

"I couldn't possibly ask my sister! Firstly, what if she doesn't . . . do it? I don't, after all, so we must assume some women don't. Secondly, what should she think of my husband, unable to satisfy me? That's a rumor she'd be only too glad to spread around, I'm sure." Alexander didn't look convinced by either of these arguments, and so Harriet played her last card.

"Please? Please teach me to touch myself?" She drew in a breath and looked right into his obsidian eyes. "*Please*, Alexander?"

He only took a moment before giving her a simple nod. "Lie back," he instructed. Alexander's voice was direct and even. He wasn't being playful or charming. Harriet's insides thrilled; her entire body was molten. She somehow still managed to do as he bid, sliding back under the covers.

"To begin with, simply touch yourself wherever feels good."

Harriet frowned. This wasn't inspired instruction, she felt. Before she could open her mouth to voice said complaint, he cut her off.

"Don't question me. If you want my help, follow my orders."

"I didn't realize they were orders," she teased, giddy at his commanding tone.

"They are now, you impertinent little chit." Alexander straightened his posture, seeming to take his role seriously, which made Harriet want to laugh even more. "Touch your arm as I was before," he instructed. "Easy . . . lighter. That's it. All right."

Harriet swallowed, not wanting to admit she wasn't feeling much.

"Where did it feel best when I touched you?" Evidently, any ounce of embarrassment he had earlier was gone.

"Ummm . . ." Harriet trailed her hand up to her collarbone. "Here, I think . . ." She knew.

"All right. From there you might want to travel lower."

"Lower?" Harriet still felt confused about this whole process. It was like when Frances attempted to explain the rules of a game to her but didn't tell her the aim. She huffed out a breath. "Can you please just tell me what I'm supposed to be doing?"

"I'm trying, aren't I?"

"Well, I'm not certain I'm going to reach any kind of 'crisis' from my collarbone, as nice as this feels."

Alexander tossed his hands up in frustration. "You're the most impatient—! Look, you need to touch your quim. That's where the spot is if you're a woman. I was *attempting*—foolishly, apparently— to get you into the right mindset for what comes next! If you want to start in between your legs, by all means!" He spread his hands wide as if inviting her to dance.

"My quim?"

"Yes."

"Interesting. I suppose that makes sense, if for men it's their . . ."

"Cock?"

Harriet nodded and a rare silence stretched between them. Her hands had stilled on her chest, and she wasn't certain what she ought to do next. Alexander studied her from his side of the bed; since she'd insisted on this, she felt she must forge on.

She reached down under the coverlet and up the skirt of her shift. She traced her hands along herself, unsure precisely what she was meant to be doing. When they arrived at her quim, she trailed her fingers up and down her seam as she'd done with her clavicle. While it felt nice enough, she couldn't say it was blissful.

"I'm—I'm not sure I'm doing this correctly," she said, wincing in embarrassment. She chanced a glance at Alexander, whose eyes held in them an emotion she'd never seen before. He was staring so intently at her that her hand stilled.

He cleared his throat. "It's different for everyone, but there are a few places on a woman that rather reliably feel good." At her silence, he continued, "I was trying to direct you there earlier, but for many women their breasts feel nice to touch." As he said this, his gaze dipped to her chest, and she felt an unfamiliar throb between her legs. Maybe breasts *were* the key. She took her left hand and placed it on her breast over the chemise, running her hand along herself, in plain sight of Alexander.

The look it elicited from him inflamed her more than any touch of her own had.

He spoke again, his voice somehow even deeper than before. "You don't have to just be gentle. You can do all sorts of things. Pinch, grab, rub. Whatever feels nice."

Harriet felt certain she should have died from this conversation. Perhaps she had. Perhaps she'd died on the dance floor, and everything afterward was the afterlife.

Feeling desperate, she pinched one nipple lightly. *Christ.* Before she could stop herself, she let out a loud moan. Both her hands fled their stations and clapped over her mouth in horror.

"No, that's good. That's a sign it's working."

"You didn't do that! Last night, you didn't make a sound!" she protested, the heat suffusing her body now with embarrassment as well as arousal.

"I've had lots of practice at keeping silent while I do that. I assure you, I make sounds when I can." The thought of him moaning sent something surging through her. Something that caused her hands to report back to their positions. Her left hand played with her breast again—pleasing, but ultimately not enough.

Her right hand, however, was the problem. She tried to be a little bolder, taking a cue from what he'd instructed about her breasts. But . . . nothing. She might as well have been touching her knee. "I have no idea what I'm supposed to do . . . down there," she groused after a minute of fumbling.

"I don't—I don't know how to explain," he said, looking a little stricken. "There's, well, there's a nub of pleasure down there, and when you touch that—you should feel quite good. I can't see what you're doing, so I can't be sure, but that's how it's worked with every woman I've been with."

Harriet didn't want to think of the women he'd been with before. "A nub?"

"A button, a—I don't know! You're the wordsmith! It's at the top of your cunt, but not inside. I don't know how to explain it, I just know how to do it!" He sounded exasperated.

Harriet decided right then that she was already far too deep into the experience to back out now. She shoved the covers off herself and kicked them to the end of the bed. Alexander got very still again.

"Show me."

There was no way he hadn't heard her. Even if blood was rushing in his ears as it was in hers, they were the only two people in the quiet room. There wasn't even a fire crackling. The noise from below had died out a little while ago. He'd heard her. Yet still, he asked, "Pardon?"

"Show me. If you know how to do it—and I believe you do—show me."

He waited one more moment, breathing heavily. Harriet was just about to retreat under the coverlet in shame, convinced he wasn't going to, when he gathered her right hand in his own. He guided her back under her chemise, between her legs, and used her middle finger—perhaps that was the key!—in between her slick folds. She felt her body jolt at the contact. He shuddered next to her. She had the distinct desire to close her legs tightly around his hand and rub them together.

Something was most certainly happening.

"Here," he instructed. His voice was low as he positioned her hand and rubbed his own finger on top of hers in a steady rhythm. "Like this." He slowly withdrew his hand and let her try on her own.

The feeling was . . . sin. It was galvanic. She bit her lip hard to keep another desperate sound from coming out. He might enjoy making sounds, but Harriet felt mortified by them.

She could feel his intense stare on her as she tried to concentrate on the task. As she continued, however, the desperation she'd felt only moments ago dissipated. And with it, her boldness. She slowed her ministrations and risked a glance back at Alexander, whose pupils had overtaken nearly all of his eyes.

"I'm not . . . It's not . . ." She wasn't certain how to explain that this wasn't going anywhere.

"You have to experiment. Find out what feels best for *you*. It's not the same for everyone," he explained. Despite his even delivery, something about him seemed tense. Harriet didn't have the time or the patience to try forty different ways to touch herself. She wanted relief *now*.

"Then how do you know what to do for the women you're with?" she asked, in frustration. "Or do you usually not touch their . . . quims?"

"I've touched every quim I've gotten the chance to." That ought not to have given Harriet the idea it did.

"Well, all right then. What's one more?" She gestured down at herself, praying he would not humiliate her.

His lips twisted as if he were about to decline; instead, he muttered something that sounded like "Oh, hell" and moved over her, grabbing her hands and pinning them above her head even as his mouth crashed against hers.

It was nothing like their not-proper kiss in the carriage. It was desperate and punishing. As if he were trying to prove something. He swept his tongue over Harriet's lips, and she heard herself moan again. She didn't have time to feel ashamed of the sound before his tongue sailed over her own, tasting her, having her, demanding something of her. And while his mouth kept hers occupied, one of his hands left hers and snaked down the side of her chemise, brushing against her breast and ribs, then grasped her hip as if he was claiming her.

Harriet giggled at the thought, foolish as it was. She sounded almost poetic. "Something amusing?" he asked, leaning back for a moment, then leaning in and grazing his lips along her jaw, his stubble an erotic contrast to her own soft skin.

"Just . . . well . . ." She rubbed her legs together, entirely too overcome to speak coherently. Alexander rolled off her and over to his side again. He loosened his grip on her hips and swept his fingers across her stomach, which shut off all thoughts of humor. And then he bit her lightly on the shoulder and she lost the ability to think completely.

"I wouldn't want to miss out on a good joke," he said into her neck, giving her a short respite from having his mouth on her.

"It's . . ." She shook her head, unable to think of a single other word she could add to the sentence.

"Should I show you then, how I know what to do? With quims and the like?"

Harriet nodded. Or she thought she did. Or perhaps she spoke clearly and coherently and asked him to positively ruin her. She had no idea. All she knew was his hand was finally—*finally*—reaching the curls above her quim again.

"Spread your legs," he bid her; the sentence hit her squarely in the chest. Was she supposed to be aroused by indifferent instruction?

How much warmer could her body flush? For her own sake, she rushed to obey the command.

"Good," he replied.

Oh. Oh, that's how much hotter a body could heat.

He—betraying none of her own undone-ness—slipped his hand farther down, parting her and settling where her own hand had just been. And then he demonstrated precisely where and how he'd intended for her to touch herself.

"Is there . . . a word . . . for that . . . ?" Harriet panted, desperately trying to commit this all to memory.

He laughed, which should have embarrassed her, except she couldn't summon the energy. "*Clitoris*," he answered, still smiling as he stroked her.

"Oh," Harriet choked out, "remind me again tomorrow." Alexander nodded at her, clearly biting back a grin. She knew other ladies weren't asking about words in his company; however, this might be her only chance in bed with a man and by God she wasn't going to miss a single thing.

"You're quite wet," he said in a tone Harriet couldn't read. The word made her clamp her legs together, trapping his hand. It broke any sort of spell she'd just been under. Her heart began racing with uncertainty instead of arousal.

"Sorry. Am I? I'm—"

He brought his other hand to her mouth and traced her lips, quieting her. Why did lips feel so sensitive? Had her lips always felt so much? Then her mind jumped back to her mortification at being . . . wet. Wet? *Wet?*

"It's good, Harriet. It's . . . it's more than good. It's necessary." Harriet glanced down to where his hand was. A mistake. Having him touch her was enough without *seeing* it. She leaned her head back and closed her eyes tightly. This was humiliating on so many levels.

". . . it is?" she gritted out.

"Yes, it means you're ready."

"For?"

"Relax your legs again," he instructed, and Harriet did. "For this," he said, slipping a finger farther back and then slowly *inside* her. Her entire body tensed. Her hand shot out and gripped Alexander's forearm.

Was he . . . ? That was . . . ? Was this . . . ?

What came out of her mouth, however, was simply "Alexander"— only it came out in a pitch she was certain she'd never used before. It came out as a sob. A plea.

"It's all right," he said, his voice deeper and rougher than she'd ever heard. "Let yourself go. Let me in."

She wanted to. God, she wanted to, but she couldn't. She couldn't relax. His finger was working its way inside her. And his palm was still pressing on her clitoris. And God, she felt so . . . so full. And then when she couldn't imagine a single other sensation, he began to remove his finger. She opened her mouth to beg him not to, only for him to thrust it back inside. Her legs writhed in pleasure, in agony. She needed . . . more.

"*Alexander*," she pleaded.

"Yes?" he teased.

"*Please*," she begged, although she had no earthly idea what she was begging for.

But he did. He seemed to know precisely what she was asking for. His mouth met hers again just as his hand found a perfect rhythm. She ground herself wantonly against him, distantly aware that she'd be embarrassed later, only it felt far too good in the moment to stop.

He broke the kiss to look down and watch her, which only made her feel more exposed, lewder. Then he looked back at her, and she saw his eyes were fiery and hungry and his breath matched hers. He wasn't unaffected. He wasn't doing her a favor. He whispered "Harriet" as a plea of his own, then kissed her again and she was utterly lost.

The base of her spine tingled, and her toes curled, and every single muscle in her body seemed to clench at once and then what followed was . . . ecstasy. Hot liquid pouring through her veins. Something . . . oh god, they didn't make words for it. Because how could you ever tell someone about this?

"Oh god. Oh my god. I had . . . I had no idea," Harriet panted out, when her mind returned. Her body hadn't moved an inch since she'd reached her peak. She wasn't sure how he'd found the energy to remove his hand, draw down her chemise, pull up the covers, and roll over. "No wonder men wear tight breeches."

Alexander laughed lightly but said nothing. He was looking at her in a way she'd never seen before.

"Thank you" was all she could eke out before her eyes closed. Before she drifted off, she heard one last thing from him.

"Happy to be of service."

She was asleep by the end of his sentence. He was awake for most of the night.

Chapter Thirteen

Having realized sleep was not to come, Alexander rose before sunrise and dressed. He gave instructions to a maid to wake Harriet in an hour. It was less than a half day's ride to the border; the sooner they got there and were married the better. The rain continued, but it was light enough to ride out. He rode ahead to Gretna Green, informing his driver where to meet upon arrival. He had an errand to run.

Gretna Green was a small town, the first over the border to Scotland, and thus the most common destination for eloping couples. An enterprising man, understanding his town's function, had opened a jewelry store only a few doors down from the blacksmith's shop. Alexander entered to find an older gentleman puttering about, polishing the many rings on display. Heaven forbid someone in this town want a coral necklace for his wife or a simple bracelet for his daughter, Alexander mused.

"Good mornin' to ye," the man said, warmly. His burr wasn't as thick as some of the Scottish people Alexander had known, no doubt the result of living so close to the border. "After a ring?"

"I am."

"What sort?" At Alexander's pause, the man smiled and then shuffled over to a large case. "What cooler ur 'er eyes?"

"Gray." That Alexander knew the answer to.

"Och. Dinnae ken if I hev a gray stone."

"Need it match her eyes?" *Was that some kind of wedding-ring rule?*

"Nae, just tha sort of poetic shite toffs like ye normally go fer." Alexander let out a huff of laughter.

"I'll just take the nicest ring you have."

"Hold an a moment noo. Caitriona. Iona. Finella!" the man shouted, not even bothering to turn his head toward the back of the store. From a small door came, in short order, three young women, all with the same fair skin and generous splash of freckles. The first woman had deep, dark-brown hair, followed by a redhead holding a bucket of water who looked aggrieved to be there, and finally a younger girl with light brown, almost blonde hair who was reading a book. "Ma dochters," the jeweler explained. "Any of them favor yer gal?"

Despite little resemblance—Harriet's hair was darker, richer, warmer, her skin wasn't as pale and was absent of freckles, and her eyes were lighter—Alexander nodded at the last girl, the one with the book. "What ring would you choose?"

"Me?" the girl asked, startled at being addressed directly.

"Yes. If you were to have a ring, any ring here, what would it be?" The girl glanced over at her father, who shrugged and nodded. The redhead sighed and headed through the door, back to whatever work she'd been doing. The other sister crossed her arms and waited. The bookish girl rounded the counter and walked right over to a small display.

"That un," she said, pointing to a simple emerald ring. It wasn't the largest stone in the store, but it was undeniably beautiful.

"I'll take it."

All told, there was nothing extraordinary about their wedding. Thousands of couples had married across the border in a blacksmith's shop and thousands more would after them. Perhaps the only thing of note was the slightly rumpled evening gown worn by the bride. Of course, the blacksmith took little notice of what couples wore, or what they were running from. That was their business. They were married within minutes with no fanfare. The groom gave the bride a kiss and a ring and the blacksmith struck the anvil, and they were on their way.

Both the kiss and the ring shocked the living daylights out of Harriet. Yes, they were part of the ceremony, she knew as much, even if she'd never attended a wedding before. But some part of her had assumed those customs wouldn't apply to Lord Alexander Stirling.

She felt inclined to apologize to him, as if *she* were the one who had asked for their inclusion in the ceremony. "Oh, sir, you don't understand, we aren't having a real marriage. He needn't kiss me, and he surely doesn't have a ring," she imagined replying when the blacksmith directed Alexander. Only he *did* have a ring. And he didn't hesitate to kiss her at all. True, it was her third kiss in her entire life and likely his thirty thousandth; no doubt, he was beyond the point in life where a kiss could *mean something*.

Still, it didn't *feel* perfunctory to Harriet. Or perhaps that was the very skill of a rake—to make each woman feel she was, if not the first, the only.

After they were pronounced husband and wife, Harriet tried to discern if she felt any different than she had before. *You are now married to Lord Alexander. You are now Lady Alexander Stirling*, she repeated to herself. But she felt nothing. She sneaked glances down at the exquisite ring he'd given her. She didn't want him to think her a silly woman, captivated with jewels like a crow. It was the nicest gift anyone had ever given her.

Climbing back in the carriage after the hasty ceremony, Harriet was hit with a sudden wave of exhaustion. Alexander was silent, which was usual, and Harriet joined him, which was unusual; however, every time she tried to think of something, anything to say, the words died quickly in her throat. Alexander looked as weary as she felt. They'd stayed up late last night, but it was as if the wedding itself had dispirited both of them. The purpose of their journey was complete.

They were married.

What came next? And did last night signify? Was their marriage to be a nonce? The idea of asking him, of bringing up any topic at all, felt like carrying a trunk of cannonballs up four flights of stairs.

Instead, she leaned back against the squabs and closed her eyes. Unbidden, her mind returned to the kiss at the altar. And the ones the night before. Everything from the night before. Surely it meant very little to him, another in a long line of romantic evenings. He probably had more singular memories of tying neckties than he did of being in bed with a woman. But Harriet could privately cherish it, even if he never gave it another thought.

He regretted that kiss. He regretted all their kisses, for entirely different reasons. This one had been far too chaste but alas. The blacksmith was no vicar; regardless, one could not ravish one's wife at the altar. Or at the anvil. Alexander wished the kiss had lasted longer, that he'd tasted her more, that he'd lingered. He wasn't certain when he'd kiss her again. If at all. There was no reason to kiss her again after this.

A knot of feeling low in his stomach protested: *Of course there is reason to kiss her again.* Simply because if he didn't, he would spend eternity dreaming about it. Although he supposed he'd probably do that either way.

He was quite obviously going daft.

He watched Harriet, her head tilted back against the squab, her eyes closed. He was certain she wasn't sleeping. Her arms were crossed, her spine rigid, her breath shallow, her lips pursed in annoyance. Perhaps at him. The thought made his mouth twitch with pleasure. Would he ever stop delighting in bedeviling her?

His smile was tossed over quickly as her tongue darted out to wet her lips. He watched as the long, bare column of her throat swallowed. She let out a small sigh and shifted in her seat.

She seemed . . . No.

Alexander shook off the notion. The woman was *not* sitting across the carriage fantasizing about anything. Other than perhaps gerunds.

At the next stop he'd hire another horse; he needed to ride out again. This was unbearable. He cleared his throat, hoping to wake her from her spurious slumber. His plan worked in that her eyes fluttered open, but her dazed, glassy look was just as bad, if not worse, than when she'd been pretending to sleep.

She didn't take the opportunity to talk, which was stunningly out of character. He missed her chatter. Even her circling things in her book. It was bizarre to see her so relatively idle.

The only part of her that moved was her thumb, spinning the emerald ring on her hand around and around. Some tiny, jealous part of him liked her having it on. A ring that signified that she was his. The thought was so foolish as to be embarrassing.

Harriet glanced up and then followed his eyes down to the ring. Her hand stilled immediately; the spinning stopped.

"It's lovely, by the way. I don't know if I said that already. But it's . . . it's the nicest thing I've ever owned. Not that I own it. You do. Of course . . . You understand me."

Alexander was gladder to have her rambling again than he could say.

"It's yours. You own it."

"Not in the eyes of the law."

"The eyes of the law see the Duke of Belhaven as my father. I'm not certain you can trust their vision."

She laughed, a softer, kinder laugh than he'd heard before. *He was cataloging a woman's laughter?! God help him.* The monotony of riding in a carriage for this many days in a row was obviously getting to him. He was restless and desperate.

He knocked abruptly on the roof of the carriage, rolling it to a stop. By way of explanation he simply said, "Please excuse me for being indecorous, but I fear the carriage is making me rather unwell. I will ride out again today." Then he tipped his hat and climbed up front with his driver. At the next stop, he'd saddle a horse. Anything to be out of this blasted carriage with her blasted sighs. And her blasted lips. And that blasted wedding ring. On her blasted gorgeous hands that just last night had been . . .

Air. He needed air.

∽

They stopped earlier in the evening than Harriet expected. The weather was still frigid, and she could hardly understand Alexander's ability to ride out all day when the walk across the inn's courtyard left her eyes tearing up, her cheeks raw, and her nose sniffling.

Alexander asked for a single room for the two of them, which confounded her, but she was doing everything in her power to stop obsessing over his actions. Before this week her brain had never spent so much time on so unimportant a topic as a man.

For the sake of not losing the ability—which she feared she might, based on how much space in her thoughts Alexander occupied—she went over the Greek alphabet in her head and then, as they climbed the stairs to their room, she did a few sums. Math had never been her strong suit, but she feared for the state of her mind. She'd spent a good quarter of an hour earlier today just thinking of his chest hair!

As if summoned by her thoughts, Alexander began unbuttoning his wet shirt. He re-dressed as Harriet sat glumly on the bed, doing her level best to ignore his proximity.

"You can order a bath or food or anything else you'd like. I'll be back later," he announced. Presuming he was going downstairs to drink, Harriet nodded and said nothing. He seemed to have little to say to her, and she felt silly for having expected otherwise. She wouldn't worry he regretted last night. She wouldn't worry about him at all.

For a while, Harriet attempted to read, but after going over the same paragraph for a fourth time, she gave up. Eventually her eyes dropped to his discarded clothing and without her wishing for it, the image of him shirtless returned.

She left the bed and sneaked over to the pile, as if she might not be allowed to touch her husband's clothing.

Husband. That was odd.

She reached for his jacket and found the lapel pocket, hoping dearly to find what she was looking for. Her fingers brushed on a piece of foolscap and she fished it out. *Godemiche.*

That was the word he was scandalized by?

Footsteps up the stairs startled her back over to her bed, and she tucked the slip of paper into her book. A knock on the door brought a maid with a tray of dinner.

"Your husband said you might like to eat up here?" she said, phrasing it as a question.

Harriet nodded and thanked the woman, who brought the tray directly to the bed. A luxury she'd never enjoyed before in her life. She owned that it was rather enjoyable. After the hearty stew and warm bread, Harriet cleared the tray to the floor and unpinned her hair, sighing with the satisfaction of letting it down. Then she leaned back with the dreadfully dull book on agriculture and nodded off within minutes.

She woke again an indeterminate time later when the door creaked open. It was much darker now; almost no light was coming in through the windows.

"Sorry to wake you," Alexander whispered.

"It's quite all right. I can't believe I fell asleep so early."

He sat to remove his boots. "Would you like help out of your dress?"

Harriet looked down at herself as if remembering the fact of the garment. "Oh yes, I suppose I should."

She tossed the quilt off and stood groggily. He met her by the bed, and she turned, facing her back to him. He swept her hair out of the way and the momentary touch sent tingles along her spine. Her breasts drew into stiff peaks, although she told herself that it must have been the cold.

Alexander began unbuttoning. She shivered as his knuckles brushed along her bare neck as he went. "Cold?"

A lifetime of being trained not to complain had her answer: "I'm fine."

"You have gooseflesh," he said, over her shoulder. Harriet whirled around.

"I beg your pardon?!" He was insulting her! On their wedding night?

She registered a small moment of shock in his eyes before they crinkled with his laughter. His whole body shook. She'd never seen him laugh so hard. He could barely speak. Surely he wasn't this cruel?

"Harriet! Harriet, no. It's . . . it's a word for . . . Harriet," he tried to explain, gathering himself together. "It's a word for when your skin gets like this." He reached out for her arm and traced a finger along it. "You see? How the hair stands up and there are little bumps? It's like a plucked goose, I suppose. You haven't heard the term before?"

Harriet could hardly think. She looked from where his thumb was still tracing the skin on her arm up to his eyes, which were warm and kind. Although still full of mirth at her expense.

"I promise you, it's a real word! You can add it to your dictionary!"

Normally, she felt certain that handsomeness was a blight on trustworthiness. But the mirth in his dark eyes and his breathtaking smile easily overcame her reservations. She decided to believe him.

She turned back around and let him finish unbuttoning her. On the final button, his knuckle grazed her spine, and she shivered again.

"Get under the covers, you fool!" he teased, releasing her dress and guiding her toward the bed. Whatever tension had stretched between them today seemed to have melted away. Harriet scrambled out of her open dress and pulled Giuliana's tight chemise over her head. Only once she was in bed did she realize she hadn't asked him to face away while she changed.

He followed quickly after in only his shirt. Harriet made little effort to avert her gaze from his muscled calves and bare feet. Would it always be such a shock to see a man in this state?

A chill swept over her as Alexander peeled back the covers and climbed in. She rubbed her feet together to warm herself.

"Put them on me," he offered.

"What?"

"Your feet, you can warm them on me. On my legs," he added at her look of confusion.

Harriet was not in the position to decline any offer of warmth. She pressed her ice-cold toes to his legs and he let out a hiss. She yelped in surprise and snatched them away.

"It's fine; put them back. Just a little cold."

"Really?" Harriet squinted at him in suspicion.

"Positive."

He reached down under the covers and grabbed one of her thighs, pulling her leg over toward him.

Though he'd touched her quim the night before, the casualness of this contact felt more intimate.

"Come on now, use me. Get warm."

"Thank you," she said, unable to keep a grin off her face. He was willing to warm her up at the cost of his comfort. A thrill shot through her: She'd inconvenienced a man, and he hadn't laughed or yelled at her.

It was no wonder women of the *ton* threw themselves at him. He was so bloody nice. And at ease. Something about him invited you to be at ease in his presence too. To enjoy yourself.

"You're staring at me."

"Your eyes are closed!" she squealed. God, he made her feel positively girlish. For perhaps the first time in her entire life.

"I can feel it."

"You cannot!"

"I can. You little minx, you're imagining me naked, aren't you?" Harriet shrieked a laugh, and he finally pried his eyes open.

The laughter died in her throat. His dark eyes were molten and hungry. He looked like he might positively devour her. Ten thousand dictionaries wouldn't hold words enough to express herself; she hardly knew what she wanted.

She swallowed thickly as his hand came up to her face, his thumb tracing her lip.

"I like your hair down" was all he said before crawling over her and claiming her mouth in a searing kiss.

Her mind was still thinking of the comment about her hair; meanwhile her body was in some kind of exquisite agony under him.

He licked the seam of her lips and when she opened her mouth, he slid his tongue along hers, tasting of spice and . . . brandy.

Brandy. He'd been drinking. *Oh.*

Did he need drink to steel his courage for this? Would he always drink before he kissed her? Or was it like her father, where drinking was simply a daily requirement?

God, his tongue felt so good. As one of his hands made its way up her ribs again, she had a feeling its destination was her breasts, her breasts that ached for him. Why did her breasts want her to get involved in swiving? Swiving! Bloody hell! She couldn't swive him. She couldn't let him swive her. He'd think her quite the pitiable wanton if she went back on her promise the very first—*oh god, his hands.*

Hands that would be on another woman just as soon as they returned to London.

"I—" Harriet muttered, deeply regretting what she was going to say next. "I—we shouldn't. I'm sorry." To his credit, Alexander pulled back immediately, putting the greatest possible distance between them that the small bed allowed.

"Right. Yes."

"I am sorry, it's only . . ." God, but she didn't want to explain herself. What was the not-pathetic version of "I think I might fall madly in love with you if we do this and it won't even register for you as any different than any other night"? She was saved from having to elaborate.

"I remember. No need to explain yourself. Got carried away . . . being a rake and all that." He tried to say the last part casually, but Harriet could hear the falseness in it. He sounded . . . spurned. Although she couldn't imagine he felt rejected by *her*.

More likely she was hearing his embarrassment at the situation. Women didn't turn down Lord Alexander Stirling. Some part of Harriet assumed it would be a thrill to deny him, to be the one woman who wasn't enraptured by him. It felt much more like a loss.

After a few moments of awkward silence, where Alexander retreated under the covers and turned away from her to face the wall, she decided to speak up. Who knew how many more nights they'd have together? Since she'd declined his affections, he'd likely insist on separate rooms from here out. And they weren't going to share a room back in London. That was more than certain. Besides, they were meant to be friends. Friends could not-swive one another and still be cordial. Friends could talk.

"I do have a question."

"I feel certain I will loathe it, but go ahead," Alexander grumbled, still facing the wall.

"Earlier, I looked in your lapel pocket . . ."

"Yes?"

"And I found my word"—she reached over to her book, opened the page she'd marked, and took out the slip of paper she'd stolen back—"*godemiche*."

Still facing away from her, he let out a whispered curse.

"Please? I'll never ask for another definition again."

"I highly doubt that."

"All right, I will continue to ask for definitions. But that's even *more* reason to tell me. I won't stop! Surely, there is some limit to the number of filthy words out there."

"I should hope," he gritted out.

She wasn't ready to let it go, however. Staring up at the ceiling, she thought of Philippa and what she would do in this scenario. Harriet was good at persuasion, and Philippa at men. Combining their powers had always proven successful when dealing with unwanted creditors and callers. Philippa insisted that the key to men was to behave entirely in opposition to one's aims.

"I'm sorry to have asked. You've already taught me so much. I'll simply ask Mr. Dawkins when I return to town." Harriet gave herself credit for how even she kept her voice. She'd played the part with flawless offhanded indifference.

Alexander fell right into her trap.

"You will not," he growled, rolling to face her. She adored how deep and gravelly his voice became at night.

"Whyever not?" she asked, feigning innocence.

"I won't have my wife asking another man what a bloody *godemiche* is."

"My, how utterly imperious you sound!" Harriet goaded.

He said nothing, clearly stewing in whatever emotion made a man start a sentence with "I won't have."

"Do you think Mr. Dawkins knows its meaning? Or is it more esoteric?" Harriet asked, trying to keep the delight out of her voice. She knew she was close to getting what she wanted.

"Fine! Fine! I'll tell you what it means."

"Wonderful!"

"Don't you dare celebrate your victory. It's in poor taste."

"I was under the impression you liked women in poor taste," she teased, gleeful at his defeat.

He ignored the comment, breathing deeply through his nose a few times before speaking. "A *godemiche* is . . . It's . . ."

"Yes?" Alexander shot her a sharp look at her impatience.

"It's another word for dildo."

"Right." This was rather upsetting as Harriet had no idea what *that* word meant. Although the pause he took before uttering it made her certain she'd like to know. She wasn't sure how to play her hand to get *another* definition out of him. Harriet bit her lip, considering her next move.

"God above!" he exclaimed after glancing over at her. "A dildo is a toy that resembles a . . . Oh hell, why do I care? It resembles a cock. And ladies, and I suppose certain gentlemen, use it to pleasure themselves."

"Oh, Alexander, this is *fascinating*! You don't happen to know the origin of either word, do you? No, never mind, of course you don't. One uses a *godemiche* alone?"

"Not, uh . . . not necessarily. A partner *could* use one with you."

"Does it feel the same? As a real cock?"

Alexander choked a bit and then coughed, though he recovered quickly. "I don't rightfully know."

"Of course."

"Are we finished?"

"I'm sorry if I've embarrassed you."

"Believe me, you didn't."

"Annoyed you."

"You. Didn't."

"Angered you?"

"Frustrated," he bit out. "You *frustrated* me. You *are* frustrating me. Present tense. I'm ever so weary of ending up in situations with you where my cock is so hard it hurts."

"Oh."

"Yes, rather!" His voice was barely restrained. She felt rather badly for the poor man. "You can toss yourself off if you'd like. I don't mind at all."

"Harriet!" he roared, clearly no longer concerned with the other guests at the inn.

"Sorry! Sorry!"

"Please, I am begging you, go to sleep." He rolled back over to face the wall while Harriet played the night over again in her mind. She was certain she'd been correct to keep her promise not to consummate their vows. They had only a few short evenings left together before returning to London. She wished for that not to feel like a tragedy.

Alexander woke so early the next day it would have been generous to call it morning. Sleeping chastely next to her had been painful. Talking to her last night had been torture. Riding in a carriage with her would be hell.

Alexander couldn't stand another night in another inn in another bed with her. He simply would not make it. He could not be expected to lie next to her heavy curtain of hair and those lush lips and those breasts in that too-tight chemise—a woman who in the farthest corners of England still smelled like an orange grove—and not *want*.

Alexander needed respite. He needed distance. In faith, Alexander was a little concerned that distance wouldn't ameliorate the issue. Riding out had barely helped. He'd still thought of her at least every other moment. How wet she'd been for him. The sounds she'd made as she came. Her lips when she held that damned pencil in her mouth—a sight certainly not intended to be erotic.

He could barely remember what he used to think of on long rides. Land acquisition? Tenant concerns? Drainage ditches? How could one spare thoughts for plots and parcels when her mouth existed?

He tried to convince himself that the only reason he felt this way was because he *wasn't* able to bed her. If they'd fucked, he wouldn't be fixated on her so. He'd never been the type to obsess over a woman, even as a lad. Oh, he had favorites—like Giuliana—partners who were particularly attractive or adventurous in bed, partners who knew what he offered and didn't ask for more. But he'd never felt consumed by someone. Here he was pining over a woman who'd forced him to the altar, who couldn't stop talking to save her life.

He needed to get home. To return to his normal life. To White's and ballrooms, to Giuliana and meetings with his man of business. He would simply ride to London and leave her the carriage. Having made up his mind, he rose and dressed expediently and silently. Remaining with her was out of the question.

Unfortunately, his thoughts for most of the days-long journey home stayed in the warm bed with Harriet. He dearly hoped it was guilt at his leaving her and not something worse. Something like true affection.

Chapter Fourteen

Upon rising, it took Harriet a moment to realize something was different. Wrong. The room was empty of Alexander's effects. Confused, she got out of bed and wandered to the table and chairs, where a small breakfast waited for her, still mostly warm. And a scrap of paper, folded in half. She'd never seen his handwriting before, and she traced her finger over her name in his hand.

> *Harriet,*
>
> *I've ridden ahead to London. I left instructions and*
> *sufficient funds with Charleston. There should be a day*
> *dress for you, if the innkeeper was able to procure one.*
> *I hope your travel is agreeable.*
> *—Lord Alexander Stirling*

Agreeable? He had *left* her? With nary a hint of contrition. A chasm opened in her chest, and she felt tears welling up in her eyes.

This was the cost of refusing him, apparently.

Harriet felt like the world's biggest fool for having believed he'd grown to like her company. Yes, they'd laughed in bed. And she'd given him a cockstand, if her understanding of such things was correct. However, there was no shortage of either in Alexander's life.

Their marriage was to be in name only. Anyone with a decently functional brain could have predicted how this would go. The rake did not fall for the wallflower. He wasn't pining over her simply because she wouldn't lie with him. He had moved on.

And so should she. She allowed herself a maudlin breakfast, hardly aware of what she ate. It was good to allow oneself a quarter of an hour to wallow. When her time was up, she gave herself a stern talking-to. Only a week ago, the man had been a stranger, and she'd been perfectly happy, hadn't she? *Hadn't she?*

Lord Alexander wasn't sparing her a thought, and thus, even if solely for prideful reasons, she ought not to give him another.

Her eyes traveled around the room and landed on a dress that was draped over the footboard of the bed, the ball gown that she had been wearing for days under it. The dress was plain, and rather worn, and Harriet almost wept with excitement.

She stepped into the dress, grateful for its simple design that did not require a lady's maid. It did not fit well—too large for her in most places, oddly tight in others—but she couldn't have named a dress she loved more.

She decided to grant Alexander one more small, short, *non-amorous* thought: *thank you*. Then she pinned up her hair, washed her face, gathered her book, and shoved Philippa's soiled gown into her valise. She wished she could have left the reminder of this week—of *him*—behind. She looked around the room, and at the last minute decided to take Alexander's note with her.

Charleston was waiting downstairs, cap in hand, shyly shuffling from foot to foot. At Harriet's arrival, he stood at attention. Harriet felt glad to see the driver. It was always much easier to put on a happy face for the sake of others.

"Charleston, good morning."

Charleston blushed at her direct attention. "My lady, should you like to break your fast before we leave?"

"I already have, thank you. I'm ready if you are."

"I'll pull the carriage around, my lady," Charleston said, taking her valise and handing over a heavy leather pouch. "Won't be but a moment."

"Thank you, Charleston," she said, bewildered by the exchange. But he was already out the door, buzzing with frantic, nervous energy. Confused, Harriet opened the bag. Then swiftly closed it and tucked it against her. Inside was at least thirty pounds. Maybe fifty. It was more coin than Harriet had ever seen. It would have changed her and her sisters' lives. And Lord Alexander left it in a purse with a driver.

Harriet stepped out of the inn and Charleston—seeming far less nervous now, perhaps because he was around horses or not in possession of the moneybag—deftly handed her into the carriage. Then she was alone.

Truly alone.

As they pulled away from the inn, Harriet had the peculiar feeling that she had left something behind.

∽

Upon his arrival in London, Alexander was hit with a sense of unfamiliarity. Obviously, the city hadn't been altered by his weeklong absence; the change must lie within himself. The notion was probably worth examining, and therefore, like any reasonable man, Alexander quickly dismissed it.

Nothing was changing. Not him, not his ways, not the company he kept. That was the agreement he'd made with Harriet. Theirs was not a love match. Life would continue as it had been. Those were *his* conditions.

He grunted as he passed his hat and gloves to Presley, hoping it seemed like a greeting and didn't betray his inner turmoil.

"Ahh, Lady Harriet found you then, did she?" Presley intoned in a singsong voice, the one he used when he was filled to the brim with satisfaction. Alexander gritted his teeth and spun to face his butler. He was about to explain something—why he was back without said lady, how the marriage came to be, the proper deference to be shown to one's employer—although the effort would be lost on Presley, who knew things about people before they knew them about themselves.

"She was here?" Alexander asked, the implication of Presley's words dawning on him.

"Indeed. I almost sent her up to your room, my lord. I assumed she was one of your appointments."

"Good Lord, Presley, she's a lady!"

"I shouldn't send the ladies up to you in the future, then? Why, the widows of London will wear black!"

"Presley."

"Only trying to learn my place, my lord."

"You have absolutely no interest in your place and we both know it."

"Yes, but one always must pretend for the sake of one's employer," Presley said, bowing his head solemnly.

Alexander settled a warning look on the butler and stormed off to his study. He spent the rest of the day with his man of business, Hawthorne, going over everything he'd missed.

Hawthorne was small and twitchy and had the terrible habit of starting sentences with "Yes, yes" or—when he was really excited—"Yes, yes, yes." Still, Alexander trusted him implicitly.

After a few quick hours of minor crises about sheep and some vital decision-making about crops, Hawthorne began fiddling with his mustache, a sign Alexander understood to mean there was a topic he wanted to broach.

"What is it, Hawthorne? Something wrong?" Alexander sighed, even as he found their familiarity comforting.

"Yes, yes, oh no. No. Nothing, nothing of concern."

"Better to tell me what you're thinking."

"Yes, yes, it's about the land . . . up near Applethwaite."

"What about it?"

"I dine with Lord Holden's man of business from time to time. Nothing too extravagant, Mr. Pottingale is uncommonly dyspeptic.

He revealed to me, however, that Lord Holden has some reservations about working with you . . . as you are . . ."

"A reprobate? A degenerate?" Hawthorne's mustache was twitching with nerves. "This has been known for quite some time about me, Hawthorne."

"Yes, yes, yes." A third yes. Oh dear. "Only now, you've gone and ruined an innocent and kidnapped her and dragged her to Gretna Green. Which is a rather precipitous deterioration in your reputation."

Alexander couldn't argue with that. In fact, that's precisely why he'd married Harriet. To avoid this.

"I *did* marry her."

"Yes, yes. Good, good. I did assure Mr. Pottingale that you had made things right. Still . . . one does worry."

"And we can't get the land without Lord Holden?"

"No. Well. No, no. It's unlikely. He holds the lands on the other side. Besides, there's the matter of the magistrate."

"I know, devil take it!"

"Yes, yes. Perhaps you could . . ."

Alexander stared at Hawthorne, daring the man to finish his sentence. He knew he wasn't going to like Hawthorne's proposal. Nothing that made Hawthorne *this* nervous was going to be pleasant.

". . . a man doesn't like to meddle in another's business."

"Hawthorne, you are, unless I'm mistaken, my man of business, are you not?"

"Yes, yes, quite right. Excellent point, sir." Alexander held the man's gaze until he relented. "I thought perhaps you could make a show of it."

"Of . . . what?"

"Your marriage. I thought you might . . . make a gesture at reformation. Take her around with you. Act besotted, devoted. Act *changed*. That sort of thing."

Alexander thought for a moment. He had been doing his level best *not* to think of her. The sooner they were permanently apart, the better for both of them. Still, Hawthorne had a point. Certainly, a display of affection would aid Harriet's reputation as well.

"All right. When she arrives, we'll gad about for a short while. At least until the land is purchased."

They finished their meeting and Alexander sent Hawthorne off with instructions for his various properties and investments. The man was positively quivering with excitement at the prospect of having tasks.

Alexander poured himself a brandy and considered Hawthorne's advice. If he were to do this, he couldn't exactly return to his ordinary activities. It wouldn't do to go to a ball or the opera without his new wife. In fact, going anywhere on his own might raise questions about her whereabouts, and it didn't seem at all the thing to say, "Oh yes, she's in a carriage alone somewhere near Doncaster. Left a bit of coin for her with the driver." He'd better stay at home until she arrived.

Chapter Fifteen

When they got closer to London, Charleston stopped and inquired where Harriet might like to be left off. A more difficult question than the driver intended to ask, no doubt. Not knowing where she was meant to go, Harriet simply gave the address to her father's house and spent the last hour of her journey praying he wasn't home.

Harriet handed Charleston a few pounds for all his trouble and headed to the door. Charleston lingered for a bit before Harriet was able to convince him that she was quite all right and he could return to Giuliana with the woman's belongings. Harriet had tucked a note of thanks and a few more pounds inside the valise. Etiquette hadn't taught her how to address a thank-you note to one's in-name-only husband's mistress, but she muddled through.

She slipped inside the house, which was rather quiet. She saw no signs of her father. Her prayers were either answered or, more likely, unnecessary.

Eventually, she made her way to the small back garden, where she found Caroline and Frances. Happiness overwhelmed her. Upon seeing Harriet, Caroline stood from the tub where she was washing linens and Frances stopped chasing one of the many stray cats she fed. All three sisters screeched in excitement over being reunited.

"Harriet, you beast! You wanton!" Frances crowed. "Tell us everything! Are you married?"

"Of course she's married," Caroline said.

"Well, he didn't seem all that eager to wed her," Frances bluntly pointed out. Harriet smiled.

"No, he wasn't."

"But you convinced him?" Frances asked, ever letting her curiosity overtake her manners. "How?" Frances waggled her eyebrows suggestively.

"Frances!" both sisters chided. It was difficult not to be scolding when speaking with Frances.

"What? Men are known to be quite carnal creatures. Which is the case for many species."

Both sisters unspokenly agreed that it was best to ignore this comment.

"Why are you here?" Caroline asked, wiping her hands off on her apron and pulling her spectacles out of her pocket.

"Oh, that reminds me! I have your other pair of spectacles." Harriet fished the eyeglasses out of her reticule. "I'm so sorry to have kept them for so long." Caroline closed her fingers around them, but it didn't work as a distraction.

"Why are you here, Harriet? Are you intending to stay?"

"Of course I am. It's my home."

"But you're married," Frances helpfully reminded her. Harriet fidgeted under her sisters' shrewd gazes.

"Come, let's go inside and I'll make us something. I know you can't have fared well with Caroline's cooking. Frances, leave the cat outside and wash up." Neither sister moved. Nor did they deny that Caroline's skills in the kitchen were substandard. Harriet was forced to relent. "You can pester me inside! I'll explain everything!"

And she did. As she prepared a simple meal—all she was capable of, really—she told them everything.

Well, not everything. Some things one didn't tell one's unmarried sisters.

∽

After dinner, the three girls sat in the small parlor, the warmest room of the house, while Harriet read aloud from *A Sicilian Romance*. She'd read it to her sisters at least four times before. She tried, studiously, not to imagine Alexander's face when she envisioned Hippolytus.

Eventually, she sent Frances up to bed and turned to Caroline to speak more freely.

"Has Father been back?"

"Not yet," Caroline answered softly. They both knew that the longer their father stayed away, the worse his returns tended to be. Long absences meant he'd found money to spend or a man to swindle or a woman to lure with false promises. Harriet nodded.

"You ought to head to bed yourself," she told Caroline, though her sister hardly needed instruction. Ever obliging, Caroline went.

"Aren't you coming?" Caroline asked from the stairs.

"I'll only be a moment."

Instead, Harriet stayed awake another two hours, poring over household accounts and searching the house for anything that might need to be hidden from her father should he return soon. She found a few gin bottles in his library, which she moved behind the woodpile. The vial of laudanum in his desk drawer she wrapped in cloth and stashed in the linen chest. The cash book she hid behind the family's untouched Bible—seeing what little money he had tended to send the Earl of Tidewell into fits of rage. When she finally slipped into her and her sisters' room, she tucked the pouch with what was left of her coin into her walking boots and put her ring in a small wooden jewelry box that had been their mother's. Currently it held a few acorn caps Frances had saved so she could whistle with them and a seashell Caroline had found years ago.

Harriet fell into bed tired but content. Mostly content. This was where she was meant to be. Caring for her sisters. Running the household. And so what if she didn't have children of her own? She had raised her younger sisters. Surely, she had enough to manage without the trouble.

Maybe, once she got them married off, and if her father . . . well . . . if he didn't present too many obstacles, perhaps she'd find a companion of sorts. A friend with whom she might share intimate conversations. Or even, on occasion, a proper kiss. Oh, how she wished she had remained ignorant of that experience. Once you drank from that well, you only became thirstier.

∽

It had been four days since Alexander had returned to London. Surely, Harriet would be arriving soon. He was becoming restless and irritable. Obviously, this was a symptom of not being allowed out in society and *not*, as he occasionally worried, an indication that he was besotted with a woman.

Lost for something to do, he headed to the library and decided to take a frank assessment of its inventory. Both the books and the brandy. This would be a fantastic use of his time.

After nearly emptying a decanter and fully emptying four entire bookcases, Alexander could say with certainty that his library was, in a word, shit. He'd been about an inch deep into the decanter when he had the bright idea to sort his books into stacks.

He started a pile of books *he'd* enjoyed, which then spilled over into the largest pile—books Harriet might like to read. Of course, he had no earthly idea what she actually enjoyed in a book. Surely, she didn't only read agricultural tomes?

Thus, almost everything ended up in Harriet's pile. The only books that escaped that designation were those in poor condition or those in the wrong section of the library, based on its loose organization some ten years prior.

A few hours into his undertaking, he happened upon a shelf he'd forgotten about, one filled with dusty tomes of sermons and pamphlets on morality, behind which a much younger Alexander had stashed a trove of erotic literature. He smiled stupidly at the discovery, and at his younger self, so randy yet so embarrassed to enjoy such material. Scooping up the hidden books, their pages dusty and yellowed, as untouched as the pious protectors who shielded them, he settled into an armchair and began reading.

Early the next morning, he awoke feeling sick as a horse. Again. He hadn't been so irresponsibly lush in ages. In faith, he had never been entirely abstemious, but before Harriet he had not been so immoderate.

A quite tawdry book rested spine-up on his thigh, and he was happy to see that the brandy had taken him out before he'd taken out his cock. At least he hadn't fully reverted into a randy, green lad. Marriage did not seem to be maturing him, despite conventional wisdom.

He sat up and surveyed the mess he'd made of the library, wincing. To be sure, the room was due for updating, but there had to be thousands more efficient ways to go about it. He stretched his back, aching from the night spent in a hard chair, and stood to find Presley.

Before he left, he gathered the stack of erotic novels he'd unearthed. Wouldn't want someone to be scandalized. Better to just take them up to his chambers until the organizing was done. Then he could move them back to the library.

Or give them to Harriet, wherever she might be.

Chapter Sixteen

ACROSS TOWN, HARRIET STOOD FROZEN IN THE SMALL KITCHEN, wishing she could somehow communicate with her mind to her sisters, warning them to remain outdoors.

"What in God's name are *you* doing here?!" the Earl of Tidewell spat. They were the first words out of his mouth upon returning to his daughters two days later. His luck had run out and with it, theirs as well.

"Father, how are you?" Harriet asked, her voice syrupy, head bowed. Overtures of submission were historically safest when dealing with their father, Hamish, especially when he'd been drinking. And if he'd run out of money, surely he had been.

"I asked why *you* were here. In *my* house," he thundered. "I thought you'd gotten yourself leg shackled. Though it is difficult to credit a duke's son going after my Harriet, isn't it?"

"I couldn't argue otherwise, Father. Though we did marry."

"What are you doing in my house, then?"

"I only thought—"

"You only thought I'd pay for your comforts? Save that duke of yours some coin, eh? Does he want to board his horses here in my mews as well?" They hadn't been able to keep a horse in years, but Harriet ignored that. "I'll be damned before I take in another man's wife!" Hamish Bancroft was growing more and more livid. Of course, her mind-communication hadn't worked, because at that moment, Frances and Caroline returned from their walk to the cheesemonger. *Stuff and bother!*

"Oh, Father, you're here," Caroline muttered. The sisters shared glances with one another to assess his mood. Harriet's eyes told her sisters just how dire the situation was.

"You sound surprised to see me in my own house!" Hamish bellowed, turning and advancing on her.

"I'm not, Father, only . . ." Caroline, more than the rest of them, grew meek at their father's rages. Philippa had always shouted back, defiant in the face of his violence. Frances brushed it off, staying quiet and removed in his presence and laughing about it later.

Harriet, of course, tried to talk him down.

"She's delighted, Father. We all are." Harriet rushed over and laid her hand on his arm to calm him. Only it seemed to do the opposite.

He stopped, looking down at her in disgust and then up at her.

"You think to lay a hand on me?" he sneered. Harriet quickly pulled back. "When I can no longer lay a hand on you?"

"No, no . . . of course not, Father . . ." But Hamish was far past the point of listening.

"I can no longer strike you, can I? You'll just go tattling to that duke of yours." He reached out and grabbed Harriet's arm, gripping hard enough to bruise. "And you *are* his property now, aren't you?

I can't very well damage a duke's property, can I?" he taunted, tightening his grip. Harriet refrained from correcting that Alexander was a duke's son. And a second son at that. And not at all interested in her or her well-being.

"Father, please, let me—"

"Let you what? Run my accounts into the ground again? You were meant to be the intelligent one, yet once again, I haven't a sixpence to scratch with. I wonder what it is you do with all my blunt. Is that how you attracted the duke? Heaven knows it wasn't a love match. That was never in the cards for you. And I'm to believe a duke would pick *you* of all my daughters? The man would have to be blinder than Caroline and deafer than Beethoven!" He laughed heartily at his barbs, gleeful at getting to belittle two daughters at once.

Unfortunately, none of his daughters shared his amusement at his gibes.

That, as it turned out, was an insult too large to be borne. He dropped Harriet's arm and crossed the room in a few short seconds, grabbing Caroline next, who let out a yelp that seemed to satisfy him. The man *loved* inspiring fear in others.

With all the care one might use to swat a fly, he struck Caroline across the face. All three girls tried their best not to let their reactions show; they had been here many times before. Caroline's eyes teared up. Frances balled her hands into fists, clearly stewing in anger. Harriet swallowed nervously.

"Father, please let her go, I—" Harriet scrambled, trying to think of what she could do. "I'll leave. I promise I'll leave."

"I changed my mind." He grinned at her. "You can stay. You can *watch* me manage those daughters that still *are* mine. There's no need to strike you at all, is there?" He reached up again, ready to hit Caroline once more.

"Wait!" Harriet yelled, louder than she'd ever spoken to him. She wasn't certain she'd ever given him a command in her life. "I have money. Thirty-four pounds. You can have it—if you'll leave."

He crossed back to Harriet now, his prey forgotten at the mention of money.

"Ahh, so you *did* take my money, then, did you? Thought to filch from your own father?" The idea of the Earl of Tidewell having thirty-four pounds to steal was laughable. Harriet wasn't certain how to play this hand, but she took a risk, bypassing his accusation.

"Will you leave immediately? If I give it to you?"

The earl mulled it over for a bit, weighing whether forgoing the money was worth it for the sake of antagonizing his daughters.

"You can't tell me what to do," he tried, puffing his chest out.

"I would never dare to, Father. I only thought to prevent you from having to stay here; you always say how we drain you. I figured you might use the money to recoup some funds. You've always been so proficient at providing for your family at the tables. Few men have your skill at wagering." There was some truth to that. At one point, the earl had made himself quite wealthy through betting. Unfortunately, his skill was eclipsed by his inability to quit while ahead.

"You are correct that time in the company of three such stupid girls is quite a waste for a mind such as mine. I've been damned to atrophy every time I enter my own home. A man isn't meant to live as such!"

"Quite right, let me go and get the funds now, and I'll be back in a trice!" Harriet hastened from the room and galloped up the stairs, hoping he wouldn't harm either sister in her short absence. She retrieved the bag, but not before shoving three coins back into the boot. One for each sister at home.

Harriet raced downstairs and sneaked outside to find a hack. She offered the driver a coin if he'd wait a few moments. She returned to the kitchen to find her father at the table, eating the cheese the girls had just brought home.

"There is a hack outside for you. I've paid the man to wait. Once you get in the vehicle, I will give you the money." Harriet prayed this plan would work.

"You're quite the manipulative bitch, aren't you?" Hamish asked, although with an odd touch of fondness. "If you'd been a son, you might have been worth something."

He tucked his hat under his arm, grabbed the small bag he'd brought in with him, and the rest of the cheese, then stood. As much as he loathed to be managed by a woman, staying at home with his daughters had always been a last resort for him. And now he didn't need to.

Harriet followed him and, as agreed, handed the money through the hack's door, closing it and tapping twice to let the driver know to embark.

There was one thing taken care of. Now she simply had to figure out how to make three pounds last her sisters as long as thirty-four pounds lasted her father. She hadn't spoken with Alexander about an allowance, and she didn't know when she might see him again to ask for one. Would asking paint her as a fortune hunter? Certainly, no one with even half a mind would mistake her for one. Before Alexander, she'd aimed to marry an academic!

Mr. Dawkins! Harriet had quite forgotten him in the shuffle of arriving home. Once the dictionary was finished, she might have a small bit of income. That decided it: She'd pay a call to him tomorrow and reveal herself.

It had been six days since he'd arrived home. She should have been here by now. Charleston would have sent word if anything happened. The man had a folding flintlock, no doubt they were safe. The carriage was not marked with his seal. What the devil had waylaid them? Had she discovered a new phrase? Another filthy word? Had she found a new person to talk to?

He shouldn't have left her alone. It was unforgivable. What sort of man *abandoned* his wife?

The sort that was going to ravish her if he didn't.

Alexander paced around his study, doing his best to refocus his concern on his carriage and driver. And *not* on Harriet. He hadn't wanted a wife! Ever. Definitely not a bluestocking wallflower who kept slips of paper with filthy words in her reticule, whose mouth drove him to distraction. Who did not want to fuck him.

He wanted to drink and dance and fence and philander at will; he wanted not to feel as if he was being monitored. More, he wanted to *want* to return to the beds and the balls of high society.

In faith, if she did not return to London, his problem would be solved. So why was he so uninterested in that outcome?

Not knowing what else to do, he marched to the door and grabbed his hat and gloves, mostly as an overture toward decorum. He arrived at Giuliana's no less troubled.

He nodded to the butler as he entered, handed over his effects, and showed himself to the sitting room. Like any mistress worth her salt, Giuliana sailed into the room within minutes.

"I'm surprised to see you so soon," she purred. Only a man who knew her as well as he did would hear the dismissal in her sultry greeting.

"First of all, I'm going to make you pay dearly for the chemise you lent my wife." Giuliana bit back a smile. "I'm married, by the way," he added.

"Good. I had hoped she'd pull it off. I liked her."

"She's quite . . . persuasive."

"Yes, I know. Charleston told me."

"What the devil did she persuade *him* to—" Alexander began, before realizing something. "Charleston told you? He's back? Back here?"

"He arrived four days ago."

Alexander leapt to his feet.

"Where is she?" he bit out, frothing with worry, which—like many men—he masked with anger.

"I assumed she returned to your house."

"She did not. Where is Charleston?" he demanded, feeling crazed.

"I'll fetch him; wait here," Giuliana instructed, not seeming to grasp the magnitude of the situation. Alexander tried his best to regain his composure before they returned, to little avail.

Before Charleston was able to cross the threshold into the room, Alexander barked out, "Where did you leave her?"

"The lady gave me an address near Soho Square. I can find the place again for you, if you'd like, sir."

"Take me there at once." Alexander had no idea what he intended to say to her upon his arrival, but he could consider that on the ride over.

∾

While she might not have enjoyed all, or even most, of the benefits of matrimony, Harriet was delighted to discover one very special perquisite: unchaperoned travel. She hadn't been able to avail herself of the privilege yet as she'd been traveling with a driver. But now, she could gad about town at will. And there was one place she needed to go first.

Mr. Dawkins had mentioned in his last letter that he was taking rooms at a lodging house near Bond Street. The next morning, Harriet sneaked out of her father's house before either of her sisters woke, left a note assuring them of her safety, and walked over to meet him. She did her best not to think *too* much of what it might be like to meet the man she'd been writing to for so long. Or to worry about how he might receive an unexpected visitor. Nevertheless, she hadn't much of a choice.

When she arrived, a spry older landlady let her in, fizzing with energy. She happily led Harriet to a small sitting room on the main floor where she could wait for Mr. Dawkins. Harriet sat and tried not to fidget or fret, only she could feel herself starting to perspire a little. The room was stuffy and overwarm after her walk.

Eventually, she heard footsteps on the stairs and the landlady's singsong tones, and she stood as a man rounded the corner.

It is always difficult to recall what precisely one has imagined once one is presented with reality. Though, upon laying eyes on Mr. Dawkins for the first time, Harriet felt something akin to what she felt when she opened the cupboard only to discover that Frances had eaten her entire stash of nonpareils. A small fit of disenchantment.

He was looking at her oddly, which made sense.

Harriet, gather yourself, she scolded herself.

"Good morning, sir, I'm—I'm Lady Alexander Stirling, although I've been . . . Well, you're perhaps in for a bit of a surprise here: I'm the one who has been writing to you. As H. M. Bancroft." For the first time since she'd begun speaking, a flicker of expression crossed the man's face, though he didn't say anything. "I presume you're Mr. Dawkins?"

"I am," he said simply. His voice was rather . . . ordinary. Indeed, everything about the man was rather ordinary. His dress was simple, his hair halfway between fair and dark. His eyes between green and blue. His shoes brown. His shirt nice but worn. Harriet had the fleeting thought that the portrait of him had in some ways done him favors in making him appear more distinct than he actually was. His nose was entirely unremarkable.

"I've come here to introduce myself. Which, of course, I've done. And to see how I might be of assistance with the dictionary. I had intended to meet you at Lady Dunley's ball the other evening, only, I was . . . waylaid and I . . . Well, I ended up getting married, although that's neither here nor there."

"You were married at a ball?" he asked. The lack of inflection in his voice, and the absence of a smile or a twinkle in his eye made it unclear whether he was teasing or not. Surely the question was in jest. Although most men were not Alexander. They were not usually teasing, were they?

"Well, no. Not at the ball. Right afterward. Er, shortly afterward. Anyway, I've come to introduce myself now that my marriage is . . . settled. To see about the dictionary."

"I see." What did he see? What did that mean? Was he disappointed to find out her gender? He didn't appear to possess any emotions whatsoever. If he did, he kept them quite in check.

Oh heavens! Why was she getting tied in knots over this man and his lack of signals? Wasn't marriage supposed to end forever the need to know what men thought of you? At least non-husband men?

"I thought—I thought we might work on it together. However much is left. I know it's due to the publisher soon. And I have quite a few entries with me that I was unable to send to you. Due to . . . well . . . travel. Plus revisions of a few phrases from my earlier letters."

Mr. Dawkins seemed to be taking this all in very slowly. He studied her for a moment, then nodded.

"All right. I could use another set of eyes on the manuscript before it is to go off."

"Oh, really?" Harriet said, surprised he'd acquiesced to her offer.

Mr. Dawkins raised an eyebrow. Harriet presumed it was at her, but nothing about the man felt knowable. Her insides were knotted with nerves. "I'm to go to an appointment soon, but why don't you bring your words back tomorrow and we can start then?"

"Would you—I hope this isn't too forward of me, only I have a study we could avail ourselves of. It might be a bit . . . more private than the rooms here. It's not far. If you'd like, I can give you the address." Anything would be better than poring over words in this stuffy, cramped sitting room. Unless he meant for her to go up to his rooms? Surely not. She was being crackbrained. Why was this man making her feel so stupid?

"That would be appreciated."

Harriet reached into her reticule and pulled out a pencil and a scrap of paper. After checking that it wasn't one with a word on it— especially not *godemiche*—Harriet wrote down her father's address and handed it over with a shy smile.

Mr. Dawkins took it then and offered, for the first time, a small smile of his own. There was something almost handsome about the man when he did so. Harriet knocked the thought over as soon as she had it. His handsomeness did not signify.

Still, she left the lodging rooms feeling as if she were floating. The dictionary was due soon, and now she'd gotten in touch with Mr. Dawkins. And he hadn't minded that she was a woman! She had not ascertained when they might receive payment for the book, but surely they were close. Her problems were not in the past, but the solutions were on the horizon. She walked back home feeling peaceful for the first time since before Lady Dunley's ball.

After a brief confrontation at the front door—and numerable assurances that he was Harriet's husband—Alexander had been let into an unadorned sitting room in the Earl of Tidewell's home. He hadn't been formally introduced to Harriet's youngest sister, but he had the impression that she was quite formidable. She stood watch over him, eyeing him with suspicion; since she did not sit, he did not, which left them both standing awkwardly in the small room. Had he not already known the man lacked funds, the house would have informed him. The earl was obviously cleaned out based on the sparse and worn furniture.

Nearly a quarter of an hour later, the sister finally sat. Apparently, that was sufficient time to surmise that he was not a threat.

"I'm Frances," she offered.

"Lord Alexander, although you may call me Alexander as we are family now."

"You didn't offer for Harriet," she said, making clear her feelings on the matter. Alexander winced. Like Harriet, she seemed both unafraid of and unimpressed by him. Why hadn't they sent the Bancroft sisters after Napoleon? He would have been taken care of in weeks.

Alexander decided a white lie wouldn't be out of place here. "I am remiss to say that I did not that evening; however, I intended to the next morning."

Frances looked him over with discernment.

"Balderdash." *Oh hell.* He opened his mouth to defend himself further when the door swung open and Harriet entered, looking flustered. Then stunned.

"My lord? What are you doing here?"

"Being interrogated, it would seem."

"Frances, where is Caroline?"

"She is helping Mr. Hammons, I believe."

"Why did you let him in?" Harriet still hadn't looked his way.

"He claims to be your husband. Is that untrue?" Frances, despite her treatment of him, seemed generally unbothered by the idea of letting a man into the house, regardless of his identity.

"He is! But you're alone."

"I have a penknife on me." Frances shrugged, standing and moseying out of the room, clearly bored with the direction of the conversation.

They were alone. Together. And if Harriet closed the door, they could—

"Good day. Do you require something?"

"Good day to you. I'm glad to see you have returned safely to London, a fact I might have been made aware of days ago."

"What for?"

"So that I may know my *wife* is safe."

"Ahhh, this is an issue of property. Your valuables are accounted for, my lord," Harriet replied sarcastically. He knew from his vast experience with women that this was a poor place to be indeed. He needed to change tack.

"I only thought you might return to my house. That is, our house. Now that we are married." Harriet looked at him oddly, as if he had suggested they might move in together to Buckingham Palace.

"I had assumed that would not be necessary based on our agreement. You desire no children, nor do you require me to run your household. I did not think you might like to be apprised of my whereabouts. And I felt *certain* you did not wish me to be apprised of yours."

She did, he supposed, have a point.

"It would seem rather odd to elope only to live apart, would it not?"

"I had not thought so. Hence my residing here." She was being quite difficult.

"Our marriage is supposedly a love match, no?"

"Perhaps we fought," she gritted out.

"Much as I adore the image of us as a passionately tempestuous couple, perhaps you might consider removing to my town house? You may run it as you see fit. My housekeeper, Mrs. Tanning, will be delighted. She's been trying to get me to choose new curtains for the dining room for ages now." Harriet bit her lip, mulling over his request. He thought once again of the door and how it might be closed, even for a brief interval, so he could attend to some matters with her. Matters he'd been imagining over and over and over. "Please?" he added.

"Why do you want me there?"

"Besides the issue of curtains, I think it would be rather . . . beneficial . . . for us to be together."

"Your letter suggested otherwise." His letter. So, she *was* upset he had left her. That *had* been rather badly done of him, he admitted.

"I do apologize, I had business in town that could not be put off." He did not like lying to her, but he felt it was the kindest course of action. "I would like you to come live with me, at least for a little while, for the sake of both of our reputations. That *was* the point of our marrying, was it not? Though we won't be producing heirs, the illusion of attempting to beget them would go far for us both, I believe. We aren't to have a traditional marriage, of course, but as you previously suggested, I hoped we might be . . . friends." Nothing about seeing her again brought friendship to mind, but Alexander ignored that impulse. He also ignored the small voice inside that questioned why he was so invested in her coming to live with him.

"I have conditions." Alexander smiled, despite himself, and nodded for her to continue. "I have just met with Mr. Dawkins." *Hell.* His stomach twisted.

"I understand. You want to keep seeing him?"

"I do." That was not precisely what Alexander wanted to hear, but he would be a hypocrite of the highest order if he were to stop her. If stopping Harriet from doing something she wanted were even possible.

"As I said, as long as you're discreet and do not conceive a child, I do not mind." That wasn't precisely true—he did mind. Although he felt assured that this unfamiliar and unwelcome feeling of possessiveness would wane shortly.

"No—I don't. I'm not—I'm making a dictionary with the man, not tupping him." Harriet paused then. "Do women tup men? Or is it only men who tup?"

Alexander could not form a single coherent thought at the moment, so he simply muttered, "Don't rightfully know."

"If I am to remove to your house, I require your word that I may continue my work on the dictionary undisturbed."

"Of course." That wasn't at all a concession, especially when compared to allowing her to swive the man.

"Any profits I receive from the dictionary—or any subsequent book I author—are my own to do with as I please." She held his gaze with a challenge in her eyes, as if she expected him to deny her this.

"Absolutely. I will inform Hawthorne, my man of business, as much. He can draw up some sort of contract. He will be giddy. Anything else?"

"Do you have a library?"

Alexander could not keep the grin from his face.

"I do."

Chapter Seventeen

HARRIET LEFT WITH A PROMISE FROM CAROLINE AND FRANCES THAT they would write as soon as their father returned, or should they need anything at all. She had asked only thirty times or so while packing if they were certain they could spare her before Caroline gently reminded her that she was only going across Mayfair and that they'd done quite well when she was in Scotland.

Alexander looked both a little pleased with himself and a little nervous, Harriet observed on the carriage ride to his town house. Strange that he'd appealed to her so rationally about coming with him. He could have simply ordered her to, as was his husbandly right. Her father would have.

His town house in the daytime was far less imposing than she remembered, but Presley was just as kind as he'd been before.

"Wonderful to see you again, my lady," he said, bowing. Next to him was a tall, stern-looking woman, who had no doubt been a beauty in her youth.

"This is Mrs. Tanning," Alexander introduced. "Mrs. Tanning, Lady Alexander takes her tea with two sugars and a splash of milk. She should be allowed free rein to make any changes to the house or the menus or the staff as she sees fit." Harriet nearly swallowed her tongue at his announcement.

"Pleased to meet you, Mrs. Tanning, and, Presley, it's lovely to see you again as well. Thank you for your help that night."

"I am entirely and eternally at your service, my lady. It's not much, but marrying Lord Alexander must come with *some* benefit."

"Presley!" Alexander warned, playfully. "You're becoming entirely too impertinent."

"You'll have to dismiss me once again, won't you?" Presley rejoined, and then to Harriet, he continued, "It's become almost a quarterly occurrence. Almost a little ritual of ours." Alexander ignored this.

"Mrs. Tanning will show you your rooms, and perhaps later, to the library. It has recently undergone some . . . reorganization. I think you will find it ripe for your influence. I've instructed my cook to prepare chicken fricassee and asparagus tonight, but please inform Mrs. Tanning if you'd like something else. If you'd rather take dinner in your room, you may do that as well. Of course you can. It's your home. There is a maid for you as well, I believe? Mrs. Tanning will introduce you, I'm sure. And then to the rest of the staff tomorrow, perhaps? And I can have a bath brought up for you, if you would like, or if you—" He was rambling, which was not at all something she'd seen from him before. It was almost sweet.

"Thank you," Harriet interrupted, stopping herself from laying her hand on his arm in reassurance. "A bath would be lovely, the menu sounds perfect, and I will take my dinner in the dining room with you tonight." She turned to Mrs. Tanning and smiled, then followed the woman up the wide, elaborately carved staircase into a beautifully appointed bedchamber.

It required effort for Harriet not to gasp upon entry. She'd never had her own room before. And this? The bed alone would have taken up half of her room at her father's house. And one of the chairs would have likely paid his debts. There was a fireplace on one wall, and the ceilings must have been the height of two men, with windows that looked out over the square and thick drapes to prevent daylight from disturbing the mistress of the house.

Which was her.

"Oh my," Harriet let out as she took a turn about the room.

"Marvelous, isn't it?" Mrs. Tanning asked with a shy smile. It transformed her face entirely and Harriet couldn't help but like the woman.

"Unbelievable," Harriet answered, her eyes trained on the ornate ceiling. Then they fell to the bedside table, where a small stack of books sat. She crossed over to them immediately. On top was a small card that said simply:

For you.

—A

"I'll send Anne up to you, my lady, and a bath. Ring the bell for anything else you need," Mrs. Tanning said from behind her, and with that, she disappeared.

Had she known this room awaited her, she would have put up far less resistance to moving in. Harriet suspected she was going to get the best sleep of her life that evening.

∽

Alexander had gotten the worst sleep of his life that evening. He woke the next morning, gripped with fear. He'd dreamt a most concerning dream the night before: a dream of her, beneath him. That part hadn't been anything less than glorious. It was the rest of the dream—the emotions he'd felt for her that lingered in the morning—that frightened him.

In turn she was, it seemed, entirely uncharmed by him, if yesterday's confrontation was anything to go by. He'd had to practically beg her to even entertain living here. It was a most unusual occurrence, he mused. One which only made her more tantalizing. Of course, women had *performed* indifference before for him, hoping to beguile. But Harriet's disinterest seemed genuine.

He'd felt it in the library the night they met. She hadn't been rapturous or flattering. He couldn't remember a woman so unmoved by his presence. Well, he could remember one. But that had been ages ago and didn't signify.

She wanted to be *friends*. If she could only see the dream he'd had the night before, she would dispose of the notion entirely.

Perhaps he might convince her of the foolishness of her vow of chastity. One didn't want to be immodest, but Alexander was certain she would enjoy his company. The pleasure she was leaving on the table was significant. Of course, it wasn't entirely an unselfish line of thinking. Having her—even once—would be worth almost any effort. If anyone in the *ton* could win a woman over, surely it was him.

No. *No.*

Alexander had never had to persuade a woman of his appeal. It ought to be evident.

This was not that sort of marriage. She was not that sort of lady. Lord. One night with her in his house and he was starting to go mad.

He rose and dressed and packed himself into a carriage to be delivered to White's posthaste. His previous habits needed to be attended to.

He stalked inside the club, nerves raw.

Unfortunately, his dark mood was not to be ameliorated. His father sat in a corner, smoking a cheroot and holding court, at least seven young bucks hanging on his every word. It was pathetic the way the duke soaked up admiration; baseless fawning seemed to be the only thing that fueled the old man outside of snatching up properties from vulnerable parties. Miserable man. Lifting two fingers, his father summoned him. Alexander braced himself, ordered a drink from a passing footman, and headed over. Meetings with his father were never pleasant, but perhaps the public venue would forestall the duke's worst impulses.

"You must excuse us, gentlemen. I need a word with my son," the Duke of Belhaven instructed his admirers. "Come, let's find a room," he commanded Alexander.

Never mind about the audience then. This was to be a true confrontation. He should have known; his father cared far too much for appearances to set down his son in the middle of White's. And far too much *not* to set him down in a private room of the club. The blessed footman discreetly handed Alexander a scotch as he followed his father like a man sent to the gallows.

They reached a small private room, similarly appointed as the rest of the club in dark, comfortable leather, ideal for spending time away from one's wife, opulent curtains to hide the time of day, and wood-paneled walls to maintain the power within. Something about the forced masculinity of the room struck Alexander at that moment. It was a room—a whole club—designed to assure men like his father of their virility, their belonging and influence. It was an odd observation to come to after years of membership, and one he had the urge to share with someone, though he imagined his father might strike him if he did.

The duke gestured toward a chair across from him, as if he were "allowing" Alexander to sit before him. In his own club. That he paid his own dues to be a member of. Alexander fought to keep from rolling his eyes. Everything his father did irked him. Whether the duke drank scotch or brandy, smoked or refrained, crossed his legs or his arms, Alexander was determined to loathe the choice. And to do the opposite.

"I understand you've married." No preamble. The duke often seemed to go out of his way to avoid addressing Alexander, as if doing so would lend legitimacy to his birth.

"I have." Two could play the game of withholding. One wasn't raised as the Duke of Belhaven's son without learning that information was an asset to be guarded.

"I must admit some *surprise* at your choice," the duke sneered. He had a flair for eking out sentences like a snake. *Me too*, Alexander thought, but remained silent; his father wasn't waiting on his words anyhow. "No doubt this was meant to punish me for something."

"*I* must admit, Father," Alexander began, the term of address meant as both an insult and a reminder, "you didn't enter into the decision at all."

"You compromise a mopsy wallflower and we're all to believe...? What? That it's a love match?" The man's face was turning an even deeper shade of red than normal. Most unpleasant.

"I didn't compromise her." Alexander shrugged. The rest of his father's sentence wasn't worth addressing, since the one proper response would have ended with him in Newgate.

The duke's eyes nearly popped out of his head at the suggestion that the marriage had not been strictly required. Another shade of vermilion was achieved. Alexander normally would delight in rousing so much ire, but he found himself strikingly bored. "We were simply in the wrong place at the wrong time."

"I'm expected to believe that bitch just happened upon a duke's heir in Lady Dunley's library?" Alexander flinched at the slur, at the casual dismissal of his brother's existence, at the amount his father knew about the situation, at the unfeeling laugh the man let out.

Despite years of practice in not reacting to his father's outbursts, this moment tested him.

"What you do or do not believe doesn't signify. If it did, I would assure you that Lady Alexander has an uncommon disinterest in my wealth and, in fact, in marrying me in general."

"Perhaps she's heard the truth of your parentage and worries for her own offspring."

Alexander would have loved to see the look on his father's face when he found out the marriage hadn't been consummated and never would be. Instead, he sat in silence, clenching and unclenching his fists. It had been almost a decade since he'd let his father dictate his mood. He felt all the worse for giving in now.

The duke had no need for Alexander's input in the conversation, which was really more of a lecture, strictly speaking. "I have hope that this marriage marks a new epoch for you. I was growing ever so fatigued by your attempts to confound me. Your rakehell reputation was starting to wear thin. Lord knows you meant to taunt me with your strumpets and your birds of paradise. An embarrassing display all around, and a rather unsuccessful one, wouldn't you agree?"

"I encourage you to disabuse yourself of the notion that I factor your opinion into any of my actions. Past, present, or future. Not once in the thousands of hours I've spent in the company of women have I given even a passing thought to you. It would have been entirely antithetical to anyone's arousal."

"Either way," the duke continued, revealing no hint of displeasure at Alexander's words, "marrying the girl was for the best. Being my heir can only buttress your reputation so much. It's past time you make a gesture at respectability, even if it doesn't come naturally to one such as you. You may play at a disdain for aristocracy all you'd like, but *you* are the stain, not them. You know as much. I'm glad you've chosen the mature path. I can't pretend to be happy you're my heir, but I can decide what sort of dukedom you are left with. Be careful."

His father was correct that the marriage would smooth over some men's—men like Lord Holden—fears of engaging with Alexander. It was uncouth enough being a bastard, one didn't have to be so indecorous as to also be a debauchee. Lord Holden was a shrewd businessman, but remarkably devout, and a great champion of the institution of marriage. He answered to his wife first and God second. Harriet's existence would go far.

Alexander said none of this to his father, who was instructing a footman on how precisely to pour his brandy, as if there was a method required. It was as good a time as any to attempt escape. The meeting could have no purpose other than criticism, which had been given already. Alexander tossed back the rest of his scotch and stood.

"Your Grace," he said with a stiff nod, declining to give a reason for his departure.

The trip to White's had done nothing to ease his stress. His father had only sunk his mood lower. Alexander waved off his driver and began walking.

The bracing chill of the early March weather cleared his mind as he wandered through the busy streets, nodding at acquaintances, smiling at shop women. When his fingers finally protested the temperature even through his gloves, it became clear that he was going to have to return home.

Even if she was there.

Chapter Eighteen

Living in Alexander's house was proving deleterious to Harriet's mind. For all the wonders it had done for her sleep, having a room to herself had led embarrassingly to temptation. Or perhaps that was a product of being in such proximity to Alexander, knowing he was only a few yards away.

Yesterday, she'd been left alone in the bath only to find her hand dipping under the water and diving between her legs to try to sate the ache there. It hadn't worked. It had felt nice, of course, to touch herself. But it hadn't slaked her need. She hadn't reached her peak. If anything, she'd gone down to dinner even more bothered than before.

As with the previous night, tonight's meal had been pleasant, their conversation amiable. Nothing had occurred that might inspire anything other than friendship. Unfortunately, spending two hours in Alexander's company was unduly arousing. The wine they drank with dinner didn't help matters; it—along with his ungloved hands— had warmed Harriet's insides and conjured all kinds of unseemly thoughts. She had done her level best to tamp down any reaction that might betray the immodest direction of her mind.

She tried to meet his playful banter with a staid politeness and endeavored to remember that any flirtation from him was done unthinkingly. It came naturally for him to be charming, to ask questions, to watch a woman's mouth as she talked. Those were little habits he had cultivated long ago, ones she would do well to inoculate herself against, lest she end up in a puddle on the floor, begging for his touch. Or worse, his affection.

If he insisted upon wearing such finely cut clothing, on leaving books at her bedside, on knowing she took two sugars and a splash of milk, on smelling so divine, she was in grave danger of reneging on her personal marital vow—the one she made to *not* consummate their union. Better to dissemble a bit.

Tonight her behavior had bordered on coarseness. At least a dozen times, she had prevented herself from speaking, answering only when he asked direct questions of her. He must think her churlish and ungrateful, only she feared allowing herself to enjoy his company overmuch.

Now, having bid him good evening, Harriet lay in her bed, the copy of *Thérèse Philosophe* he'd left on her nightstand abandoned spine-up next to her—she had a terrible habit of leaving books splayed out like dead birds. The book was famously erotic, wicked even. She found herself blushing through passages. Why had he chosen it for her? Had he read it before? She scolded herself for her lack of focus and went back to reading. At this rate, if she allowed her mind to wander so, it would take an entire year to finish a book.

Evidently, being near the man was degrading her intellect.

Harriet picked the book up once more; as she turned the pages, something thrilled within her. Blood rushed through her and pooled between her legs. Her breasts felt heavy, and sensitive. Her entire body was throbbing. She had the oddest desire to lick something. Anything. *Him.* She did her best *not* to touch herself as long as possible. There hadn't been enough of a preamble in the bath yesterday, she decided. That was the problem. If she could tease herself, deny herself, perhaps she could get there.

Her mental image of The Count in the book bore an uncanny resemblance to Alexander. But really, who else was she supposed to use as a male model for her yearning? Roman statues?

Until last month, if she ever allowed herself to imagine a husband, she envisioned a man like Mr. Dawkins. Someone staid, rational, and academic. The opposite of her father. She had pictured sweet, simple kisses, the sort you might see at an altar; intellectual discussions; nights in a warm, unassuming house with children gathered around.

Her fantasies had been decidedly less . . . carnal . . . in nature.

She refocused and tried again, picking up where she left off: The Count was in his beloved's chamber only a short distance down the hall from her intended. The plot scandalized and aroused Harriet, even as it failed to distract her from Alexander. She scolded herself. The entire point of the exercise was to move on from her hunger for him. *Focus, Harriet!* She set her mind to the task, redoubling her efforts.

She imagined—or perhaps remembered—Alexander's hands on her. The way every single cell in her body seemed to burn under his touch. The way he'd seemed excited too. She wondered what it would be like to touch *him*. Her hand found its way back to her center and she rubbed herself leisurely, steadily, building a rhythm as Alexander had. It felt exquisite. Her fingertips traveled farther up, brushing across her sex. She repeated the movement, trying to replicate what he'd done. Harriet was diligent. Methodical.

A sound startled her.

Harriet's heart stopped and then, worse, beat madly. Someone was next door. Well, not someone. There was only *one* person who would be in the adjoining room at this hour. The thought of him overhearing what she was doing—although the act was virtually soundless—made her entire body burn. Unbidden, an image flashed in her mind of him somehow catching her in the act. Of him watching her. She felt more frantic than ever. Knowing that he was nearby, in his dressing room, perhaps *undressed* himself, made her crazed. She needed release; she was both farther away and nearer to it than she'd ever been.

The answer to her problems was so close. And friends did favors for one another, did they not? Who else was she supposed to ask? He *was* her husband.

Harriet threw the covers off and stood. She nodded once, as if affirming her own courage, threw back her shoulders, and stalked across her bedchamber to the door of his dressing room.

She wrenched the door open with rather too much force, sending it flying back into the wall with a loud *thump*. Embarrassed, she grabbed at the door to still it, and only then looked up to find, as she'd guessed—imagined? Dearly, dearly hoped?—Alexander shirtless and removing his boots. She sent up a small prayer of thanks that his valet hadn't been there, an outcome she hadn't even remembered was possible until that moment.

He looked up at her, apparently unmoved by her clamorous entrance, as if he'd been waiting calmly for her to burst into his dressing room.

"Good evening, dear wife," he said, with an ironic twist of his mouth. He said nothing more, waiting for her to speak.

Under normal circumstances, the idea of conveying any of the necessary information to him would have been mortifying. As it was, she hadn't the time nor inclination for embarrassment.

"I require your help," she said, her hands firmly grasping the doorframe to give them something to do now that they were no longer between her legs.

"Is there a spider in your room? Has your fire gone out? Is your bell pull no longer working?"

"I cannot reach my peak," she blurted.

Alexander went entirely still, his nostrils flared dangerously, and his pupils, already large in the dim light, seemed to swallow his eyes.

"I want to make certain I have heard you correctly," he ventured, carefully.

"I need your help. Again."

He rose to his feet immediately and gestured toward her room. "After you, my lady."

Harriet had expected reluctance or further inquiry, or at least for him to need time to get used to the idea. He behaved as if he'd been waiting years for someone to ask this favor. She hurried back through the door into her room, overcome with nerves in the face of his calmness. It was always easier to remain levelheaded when someone else was nervous, Harriet found, and she was used to being on the other side of the equation. When Frances had fallen out of a tree and badly broken her arm Caroline had fainted, Philippa shrieked, and Harriet was virtually unfazed. *Why was she thinking of broken arms at a time like this?* This was about another broken body part.

The nerves bubbled up her throat into words that she tossed over her shoulder. "I am sorry to ask, it's only that I think I might be doing something wrong. I can't make it work."

"I see we're friends again," he remarked wryly. "Can't make what work?"

"My quim. I think it's—"

∾

Alexander would have readily paid every cent in his possession, given away every property not entailed, to hear the rest of the sentence.

"Broken," she finished.

He would always regret the crack of laughter that escaped his mouth after that. In his defense, he could have been given forty thousand chances and he never would have guessed that was the word she was going to use.

Hurt flashed across her face. *Hell and damnation.* What was it about his wife that made him a fool in the bedroom?

He reached out to stop her from fleeing the room. She tried to wrench her arm away, but he stayed her. "I assure you, your quim isn't broken."

She seemed slightly soothed by either his declaration or his demeanor. At least she quit trying to flee. He gingerly unhanded her, watching closely for signs of escape.

"How do you know? I can't seem to . . ." Harriet said, attempting unsuccessfully to match his unaffected tone. If only she knew how much he *was* affected by this talk. The difference was that he wasn't embarrassed by his arousal. ". . . arrive at my crisis," she finished, blushing madly.

"It's not broken. A woman's commodity can't break. At least not that I know of and—" Alexander stopped himself.

"And you've had lots of experience with them?" she filled in, with a slight eye roll. "Yes, we're all aware of the prodigious amorous history of the venerable Lord Alexander Stirling." Alexander held his tongue—he was loath to let any of his smugness over her poorly disguised jealousy seep out.

"I can prove it to you, if you'd like."

"Prove what?"

"That your quim works perfectly well."

"Oh. Well." Harriet was fiddling with a ribbon on her night rail now and avoiding his eyes. He had assumed stupidly that a modest night rail that fit her correctly would be less erotic than that borrowed chemise.

"I'm sorry to have bothered you," she continued, finally looking up at him. He dearly wished she'd abandon her reservations; he could not take standing and talking much longer. "If you assure me that it's working. I suppose—I suppose that's sufficient. I really needn't have disturbed your evening with such a silly concern. I'm sure you're thinking—"

Alexander stepped closer to her, backing her up against her ludicrously large bed, the advance silencing her just as he'd hoped.

"I assure you, you have no idea what I'm thinking," he replied, tracing his fingertips slowly up her arm.

"I don't?" she asked, licking her lips; her gaze was glassy, and she seemed to have lost the conversation. Alexander shook his head slowly, then reached out and lifted her onto the bed. She sat stiffly, unsure of herself. He knelt, grateful to whoever had designed this bed at this particular height. A man with a proclivity for tasting his lovers, no doubt. Alexander grazed his hands up her legs, slowly pushing her night rail up. Her breath hitched, which he would have enjoyed more if his own were steadier. Sometime in the past forty seconds he'd lost the ability to appear unmoved.

The prospect of being with her again was frightening in its appeal. He'd tipped rather far over the line of wanting his wife, and into need. The sight of Harriet's exposed thighs pushed the concern aside.

Slowly, starting with her calves, Alexander availed himself of her, stopping to trace the backs of her knees. At his light caress, Harriet jumped. Her responsiveness to his touch ignited something. Well, his cock; it ignited his cock. Had he any thought she might be ready for such an act, he would have roughly spread her legs, licked her to her crisis, and then turned her around and fucked her against the bed without speaking a word.

At least he could do the first part—it seemed the most reliable way to assure Harriet that her quim was most certainly in working order. Reassurance was what she'd asked for, was it not?

Even the most delicate kisses trailed up her bare thighs made her squirm. He used his hands to slowly spread her legs wider, finally giving him an unobstructed view of the part of her which had consumed most of his thoughts for the past week. He hadn't been able to look last time, between the darkness of the inn and the positions they were in. But now he was treated to the full glory of her cunt, hot and wet with need. A need matched by his own to taste her, to show her just how good she could feel. Perhaps, in some small way, to show her what she could have if she gave up her resolution to never consummate their vows.

Alexander leaned in and slowly licked along her center, just once. Harriet let out a moan that the entire household probably heard, the fact of which thrilled him.

"You—? I didn't know!" she gasped, clenching her legs together in shock as Alexander looked up and met her eyes. Her surprise at the act wasn't unexpected; still, he relished it.

Instead of answering, he simply spread her legs once more and licked her again. And then again. He wrapped his hands behind her legs and brought her closer to his mouth as she moaned and whined, gripping the coverlet, her knuckles turning white, her legs shaking. He unhooked one arm and brought it to his mouth, wetting his fingers before bringing them to her core and opening her. His mouth returned to its task, and she let out an incoherent scream, grasping at his shoulder and his hair, pushing him away and pulling him close, unsure of what she needed. But he knew.

Breathlessly, she watched from above as he thrust his finger slowly in and out in time with the speed her hips moved against his mouth. Her shouts turned eventually to pleas, begging him to keep going, begging him not to stop, begging him for things she didn't have the words for. He was so far beyond arousal he wasn't even aware of his own needs, only hers. Only the sounds she was making and her uneven breath and the way she pulled his hair too hard.

And then she came apart against his mouth with a string of incoherent words and curses. Only after she stopped writhing against him did he rise and collapse onto the bed beside her.

For a few moments they lay next to each other, each grateful the other hadn't said a word yet. Happy to simply exist in silence together after that.

As they came down off the high, Harriet decided to speak up. Alexander felt the corner of his mouth tilt up; she could hardly leave words unspoken, could she?

"Do you ever need help with this?" His smile collapsed immediately, so busy was his mouth with groaning. "I should like to help, if ever you need it."

"Harriet," he growled, tossing an arm over his eyes.

"Does it work the same way for you? That sometimes you cannot achieve *it* on your own?"

"God, I wish I felt no compunction about lying to you." He turned his head slightly and watched out of the corner of his eye as understanding dawned on her face. "It's different for men, I think. Easier. Why, a poorly sprung carriage can get a schoolboy stiff."

"A *carriage* can make you . . ." Harriet moved her hand to indicate the rest of the sentence.

"Come? No, no. Just hard. At least, when you're a randy lad of fourteen. Eventually, it requires more, although not much. Especially recently." He should not have said that, but thankfully Harriet's curiosity overtook her.

"Hard?"

"Cocks get hard when they're . . . ready. Damned inconvenient at times."

Harriet rolled over to observe him, and he felt his gut clench. He should know better than to talk with her about these things. Harriet liked talking about intercourse a bit too much for his poor prick's taste.

"Is it ready now?" she asked, looking unabashedly at his breeches.

Alexander let out what was some mixture of a laugh and a guffaw and a groan of agony. "Quite, Harriet."

"I see." She chewed on that information for a moment, biting her lip in a way that Alexander felt must have been designed to make his condition more difficult to endure. "So helping me didn't bother you?"

"I couldn't be further from bothered." More precisely, he was an entirely different type of bothered, but he didn't want to debate Harriet on semantics now. Or ever really. That was a losing battle.

"But you didn't . . . come? Did you?"

"No, you would know if I had."

"How?"

"Harriet!" He groaned again, sitting upright. She looked chastised and he felt rather horrid, but distance was paramount to her chastity. "It's just, all this talk makes it harder—more difficult—for me not to come."

"You can if you want to. I don't mind! I find I'm rather interested."

"I'm to be a clinical specimen for you, then?"

"I'm simply curious, and surely it would feel nice for you! So, I could help; we're friends after all! You did say it felt better with others." At his hesitation, Harriet filled in the discomfort with what else? Words.

"Oh, no, of course not," she continued. "You must think me rather foolish." She looked sheepish again. He enjoyed her blushing innocence, but not her lack of faith in her own desirability. It was so at odds with the confidence she displayed in every other part of her life. "I'm sure you're used to much more experienced partners, aren't you? And I have no rightful idea what I'm doing."

"I assure you any ignorance on your part has proven to be quite the boon for me. I will not complain about your lack of schooling in these matters when it has benefited me most wondrously." He leaned over and placed a kiss on the top of her head. What possessed him to do so, he had no idea. The act was not how he ended things with bedfellows. Or anyone. Had he ever kissed someone's forehead? It was startling.

He was quite in danger around Harriet. They'd agreed this marriage was a false one; he couldn't be a true husband, one she deserved. Thus, he certainly couldn't let her take him in her mouth. He swung his legs down from her bed and stood, adjusting himself in his breeches, which did not escape her gaze. The first order of business upon returning to his rooms was taking care of himself.

"I do thank you for your help," Harriet said, almost primly, from the bed, "although I would still like to learn for my own sake. I can't just call on you every time I need relief."

"On the contrary, I'm hoping you do precisely that."

"What if you were indisposed?"

"I vow I am never too busy to help with that. Please bother me day or night."

"What if you were traveling for business? Or sick? What about when you die?"

"Killing me off already? Not to worry, I'm sure you'll find many willing volunteers after this tragic death you have planned for me," he jested. They were friends after all; friends jested.

"I will wait the proper mourning period, I promise."

"Before you take an ad out in the paper about getting your quim licked?"

"Seeking: Someone to replace dearly departed husband. Quim licking only. Position not paid, unfortunately. Living on widow's portion."

He laughed heartily. Alexander found himself wanting to stay in her room longer. Only there was nothing left to do. Or say. His duty was done. Perhaps it was this pathetic desire for more of her company that led him to ask: "Would you go to the Henderson ball with me next week?"

Harriet looked startled at the prospect. "You know I can't—I can't dance."

"I'm intimately aware."

"And you want me to go with you? As your wife?"

"It would look rather odd if you went with me as anything else."

She smiled up at him. "All right, then. I'll go." But her face fell almost immediately.

"Regretting your decision already?" he teased lightly, even as he held his breath for her response.

"Oh no, it's just . . . well, I have nothing to wear to a ball. Nothing that would be suitable for your . . . wife." She swallowed the word, as if she was embarrassed to say it. "Regrettably, Philippa's dress is quite the worse for wear. In fact, I'm not certain where my lady's maid has it. She is attempting some alterations."

If that lady's maid valued her job, she would be *very* careful not to alter that dress too much. Alexander would make sure of that. After a distracted moment, he pulled himself together enough to respond. "I will make arrangements for a dress."

"You will?" She seemed dubious. He wasn't used to people doubting his abilities.

"I will."

She looked quite satisfied, and he had the feeling, self-aggrandizing though it may be, that *he'd* made her feel that way. That *he'd* pleased her. The idea alone made him feel lighter than he had in ages. He was almost at the door of his dressing room when she called out to him.

"Thank you again. I'm glad we're friends."

He laughed lightly. *Friends, indeed.* He'd never wanted to bite the buttons off his friends' clothing.

"Me too, Harriet."

Back in his own room, Alexander spent the night tossing and turning. Well, first he took care of the urgent matter of his own pleasure—an act which usually lulled him into a restful sleep. This time, however, he felt unsated. It wasn't enough to imagine her, fully nude, hair splayed, lips parted, panting under him. His mind wished to imagine *every* possible scenario before he reached his peak, which was quite impossible as the whole endeavor lasted barely a minute, so eager was he.

When it was over, he felt even more frustrated than before, knowing he wasn't going to be allowed to reenact any of what he'd envisioned. Unless she needed help again. Lord, he dearly hoped she did. Although Harriet did seem rather put out by having to ask.

He shouldn't keep helping her.

He couldn't.

If they kept on like this, they'd both want more. He already did.

Less than a fortnight ago the woman had thought she might go her whole life without being kissed. Now she was begging for release in his mouth. When she discovered *more*—when she discovered how much she liked *more*—she would find someone to give it to her. He hadn't lied when he said any man would line up to help her. When she discovered how much *more* there was, his hands wouldn't be enough. His mouth wouldn't be enough.

He wouldn't be enough.

He sat up in bed, wide awake despite the hour. He was irritable and unsatiated and he knew what he needed to do. Whom he needed to see. He dressed hastily, forgoing his valet's help yet again. Coleson was probably already looking for a new employer. But there was no need to wake anyone. Besides, Alexander didn't exactly relish someone else witnessing what he was about to do. His own conscience itched enough as it was.

Not even three quarters of an hour later, his carriage pulled up to Giuliana's town house. He dearly hoped she was still awake. He wasn't one of those men who felt a mistress ought to be at his beck and call all hours of the day and night; he usually sent word well before their assignations. This did feel rather urgent, however.

Alexander knocked at the door and, after waiting a few moments, produced the key and entered. It was, after all, his home in a certain sense. No doubt her butler was asleep, even though the hall lights remained lit. He called out quietly for Giuliana and set forth into the house.

He eventually found her butler, Sanderson, in a rather advanced state of undress in the library, across from Giuliana who was halfway through a dreadful portrait of the man. Giuliana being inept at something—anything—tickled Alexander, who, like most people who'd met the woman, had assumed her to be infallible.

"Darling," Giuliana drawled, not looking up from her mediocre work. Both men present inclined their heads. "Won't you give us a moment?" Neither man knew whom she required privacy with and thus neither moved.

"Sanderson," she said, his name a caress, "do you mind if I meet with Lord Alexander here and we can conclude our undertaking another day?"

At the use of his name, the butler seemed to remember his station. He blushed deeply and stood, gathering a too-small scrap of silk that had been elegantly draped over his body and waddling out of the room.

Giuliana shared a smile with Alexander and chewed on the end of her paintbrush. "A dear, isn't he?" she asked, eyes twinkling.

"And so dedicated to his employment," Alexander replied, choosing the divan that Sanderson had not been occupying.

Giuliana stood, revealing that her own state of undress was rather more considerable than it appeared at first glance. She wore an entirely transparent robe, so delicate as to be impractical for anything other than raising the heart rate of a lover.

She put her paintbrush down and crossed to her sideboard for two glasses of Alexander's favorite brandy. The sight was, Alexander could admit, alluring. But not in the way he'd hoped. He'd wanted, desperately, to arrive here and be just as overwhelmed with the reality of Giuliana as he had been with the fantasy of Harriet.

"How is your lovely wife?" she asked, slyly, handing Alexander his drink as she sipped her own.

"Asleep," he replied, unnerved by her ability to read his thoughts.

"I must admit," she began, her voice smoky and alluring, "I wasn't expecting you to come back. Unless you've come to end our arrangement and reclaim your house?" Alexander choked a bit on the brandy. He hadn't even considered doing so.

"No, no. I'm not—You're welcome here. I came—" He paused then, tilting his head in confusion. "Why did you think I wouldn't be back?"

"You never struck me as the type to keep a mistress once married," she said gingerly, as if she didn't want to alarm him.

"But I never meant to marry. Besides, I'm a rake." The plain-spoken pronouncement made her laugh—a laugh that Alexander *knew* used to make him want her. Which now, though charming, didn't. The activities of the night must have confused his poor mind.

"Alexander, you are *not* a rake," she said. At his incredulous look, she laughed again. "Oh, I know you intend to be. You try at it most ardently. You are . . ." She searched for another word. "You are a lover," she continued, cutting off whatever argument he was going to wage. "You are amiable, forbearing, and quite generous. I have never felt used, humiliated, or neglected by you. You take other lovers only when the opportunity is easy and pleasant for everyone involved, not out of an insatiable need for adoration or possession. You simply seem to like women."

"I am quite certain my reputation comes from more than me *liking* women."

"All right. You like swiving them. You're occasionally good at it too," she teased. "Now," she continued, and Alexander was reminded of his wife. Was he damned somehow to be surrounded by women who never let him get a word in? His mouth lifted into an involuntary smile at the thought of Harriet. "I am quite happy to fuck you senseless tonight if you should like. It has never been a chore to bed you. But I'd like you to be certain of what you want."

Even as she said this, she slipped off her dress, which, though transparent to begin with, was still exciting: Seeing a naked woman *was* seeing a naked woman, after all.

She waited a moment, watching him, likely expecting him to take charge as he usually did. When he didn't, she knelt between his legs and reached for the buttons of his shirt, his cravat already scandalously absent. Before she could undo a third button, he asked, almost distractedly, "How do you make yourself come?"

Giuliana sat back on her heels and waited until he met her eyes. There was flirtation in them, which oddly felt unwelcome. She was misinterpreting his purpose for being there this evening. Or perhaps he was.

"Would you like me to show you?" she replied, coyly.

No man in their right mind would refuse such a demonstration. But Alexander had not been in his right mind for weeks.

"I don't want a display. I mean, of course I do, in a sense. Anyone would. Only that isn't my aim. I hope you won't take offense. I just . . . I wondered how you actually do it." Alexander's mind felt frantic and muddled.

"Ah, you're not able to make the lady reach her peak? Is that it?"

"No!" Alexander responded too quickly and too loudly. Giuliana's laugh dripped out again.

"You sound certain."

"I am," Alexander gritted out. "Forget I asked."

"I don't think I'll be able to forget for the rest of my days. Unfortunately, you've piqued my curiosity. What is it you're really after? You've seen me touch myself many times, Alexander."

"Yes, but is that the way you do it alone? Or is it more for viewing pleasure?"

Giuliana stood, realizing the evening was not going to turn sexual. At least not in deed. She draped her sheer dressing gown over her shoulders again and sat across from Alexander on the sofa.

"Alexander. It will be so much easier for us both if you ask me what you actually want to ask me."

"I don't want to speak out of turn—"

"Yes, one always strives to avoid that with their mistress," Giuliana replied sardonically.

He rolled his eyes and continued. Somehow, her teasing returned him to himself. His confident, assured self. Not the boyish, stilted wreck he'd arrived as.

"I have a companion who cannot make herself come alone." He studiously ignored Giuliana's raised eyebrow. "She is *perfectly* capable of it with my assistance," he bit out. Giuliana smiled and he continued. "I wondered, as it were, if there were other techniques she could employ that I might not know of, as a mere spectator and occasional lieutenant in the process."

There. He'd done it.

Giuliana's eyes sparked with glee, which was always either dangerous or expensive for him. She clasped her hands together, fingers intertwined, and sat back in her armchair, one part Duke of Wellington, one part Aphrodite. "I'm assuming, although I normally try to avoid doing so, that your exposure to the act has only involved women lying on their backs. For 'viewing pleasure,' as you so aptly put it?"

"Yes," Alexander answered, clearly trying to puzzle out the corollary to her assumption.

"Don't misunderstand me, there are plenty of women who can come that way. But a great deal of women need to actually be on their stomachs. Or sitting. Or riding."

"Riding?"

"Well, rubbing. Against something. Perhaps their hand, sure, but a pillow does the job remarkably well for some. A cushion. A lover's leg. The arm of a settee can feel quite marvelous," she said, gesturing to where his own arm rested. He reflexively withdrew his arm and crossed it over himself. Giuliana smirked and continued, spurred on by knowing more than he did about a sexual topic.

"I've had a woman ride me before, Giuliana. I'm not green." She shot him an arch look to quiet him.

"Truly, it's about the hips. Tell your 'companion' to try facing down on the bed. Or to try out some furniture. Let *her* guide the movements with her body rather than with her hand on herself."

Alexander, full of knowledge and images that would make sitting on a settee in the near future rather difficult, stood and inclined his head toward Giuliana. "Thank you, you've been incredibly helpful."

"Of course. Give my best to Lady Alexander in her endeavor." Giuliana winked at him.

"Ours is a marriage in name only. We have no plans to consummate the nuptials." He cleared his throat, unsure why he was explaining himself. And what point he was trying to make.

"My mistake. Pass my regards on to your mysterious companion then." She was still smiling as if she didn't believe him, which irked him to no end. When had he ceased to have control of conversations with women? Or control of himself? Had they all always seen through him? Had they merely been allowing him to play at being charming?

His mind swam with these existentially threatening questions the entire ride home. They ruined the good mood he'd achieved upon collecting useful information for Harriet. He stalked back up to his room, undressed in a state nearing anger, and then crawled back into his bed as if he were upset with the bed itself. Then he lay there again, tossing and turning, his station quite the same as it had been hours before.

Only with new positions to imagine Harriet in.

Chapter Nineteen

In the next week, Harriet fell into a routine. During the day, she met with Mr. Dawkins in the library. After he left in the late afternoon, she'd spend an hour or two gleefully organizing the books there. Truly, it looked as if the room had been ransacked by someone.

Most evenings, she and Alexander ate dinner together in the dining room. Harriet had a reputation in her family for being overly garrulous, but he never betrayed any boredom or disinterest. If anything, he encouraged her topics of conversation, odd though she knew they were. One evening, she'd found herself explaining the origin of the word *bastard* to him, how it had likely come from the French *fils de bast*, meaning a "packsaddle son," as saddles were sometimes used as beds, with the implication that the son had been born outside of the marital bed. Only after she'd spoken on the subject for a while did she stop herself in horror. She hadn't given any thought to either the propriety of the topic or to the personal connection Alexander had with it. He'd waved off her concern and asked more questions.

Twice that week, Alexander hadn't returned home until past dinnertime, and she had taken her meal in her room. She did not ask where he had been. And if she missed his presence, she dismissed the thought as silly.

She hadn't gone to him again for help with her quim, nor had he offered—not that she expected him to. Embarrassingly, she knew that had he done so, she would have readily accepted; she had still been unable to reach her peak on her own. The more time she spent around Alexander, the more pleasant his company, the worse the ache became between her legs.

Perhaps that was why, appallingly, Harriet found herself watching Mr. Dawkins's hands during their meeting today. She had entirely lost track of what he was saying about *balum* . . . something . . .

Mr. Dawkins's hands were not like Alexander's. They were ordinary and ink-stained. They didn't seem strong and capable. When he put his gloves on at the end of their meetings, she hardly felt it a tragic loss. She could not imagine them cradling her face as they kissed. She couldn't imagine him kissing at all, in fact. Indeed, it was a wonder she'd ever been able to picture herself as his wife. Her mind did something incredibly wicked to her then. It asked a dreadful question. What would Mr. Dawkins be like in the bedroom?

Harriet overturned her teacup into her lap.

Alexander had stayed out of the house most days, as was the normal order of things for him. He had business to attend to and properties to manage. And a wife to avoid. He was not going to become one of those dull men who married and suddenly proved incapable of living an independent life. When business proved insufficient to fill his hours, he rode his horse around Hyde Park until he was too exhausted to think.

At night he ought to have been resuming his social habits—balls, operas, routs, musicales. If not for the sake of normality, then to display their union to the *ton*. Yet he could not find within him a desire to share Harriet; he felt sorry he'd invited her to the Henderson ball. He'd spent one evening that week at White's, after a pointed observation from Presley, if only to prove to both himself and his meddling butler that he was not entirely changed. He had not returned to Giuliana's and had sent a note of weak excuse on the day of their normally scheduled appointment. She never minded an extra free evening, and it wasn't as if she wasn't being paid.

After five full days of activities, something dreadful occurred: rain. Worse, Hawthorne had left to see some land near Swindon. Being at home for a day wasn't so terrible, he decided. He had spent days inside before marriage. It was not, he assured himself, a sign of atrophy.

It took only a singular hour in his study for him to grow restless and decide to go look for Harriet. While he inquired after her days at dinner, she usually ended up talking about things like how the word *clue* had come from the Greek myth about the minotaur or interrogating him about other terms for a vagina. He was minorly surprised, therefore, to happen upon her in the library with Mr. Dawkins. Sure, he knew she'd been meeting with him, but she hadn't specified when or where. Alexander had, until that point, yet to encounter him.

Alexander ducked out of the library before he could be seen only to find himself in the embarrassing position of hovering outside the door. At least she had left it open. That was . . . well, he supposed it was unnecessary, wasn't it? She was a married woman. Besides, he had always believed that if you couldn't seduce someone with a door open, you weren't a very good lover.

Knowing he ought to feel more shame than he did, Alexander lingered, listening in to their conversation.

"I have never heard of a Hertfordshire kindness before," she said. "That is rather a sweet term, isn't it?"

"I suppose." The man did not sound inclined to talk with Harriet, despite her efforts. It made Alexander unduly distrustful of Mr. Dawkins—who wouldn't want to speak to Harriet? Presley passed Alexander in the hall and shot him a disapproving look. He tried to shoo the butler, but Presley was intent on traveling as slowly as possible down the corridor. Awful, impertinent man. Alexander turned back to listen in some more.

"I think you might ask your husband about this one," Mr. Dawkins suggested, rather prudishly. Alexander shook his head; withholding a word from Harriet would go over as well as the Peninsular War.

"It's quite all right," Harriet said, laughing politely. "This is an educational project. My husband understands what that entails. You may tell me."

"Well, it's a dance, you see."

"Yes, that makes sense. *Balum*—as in *ballare* in Latin."

"And *rancum*?"

"Hmmm, I don't know the origin of that." *Balum rancum?* They were speaking of *balum rancum?* Where had either of them encountered the phrase? What sort of man *was* Mr. Dawkins? There was a long pause then, with only the sound of flicking pages and the clink of a tea cup on its saucer. Then a quiet thump and a small gasp.

"Oh dear, I'm quite wet," Harriet said. *Quite wet?!* Alexander charged back into the library only to see both of them standing, Harriet blotting at her dress with a handkerchief, her teacup sitting in a saucerful of tea.

"Good day, pardon my interruption," he nodded, schooling his face into something resembling a normal countenance, "I have not been introduced."

"My lord," Harriet said, the title a surprise, although it should not have been. "May I introduce Mr. Dawkins? Mr. Dawkins, as you likely surmise, this is Lord Alexander." The man nodded and sniffed, seeming a little perturbed by Alexander's presence. *This* was the esteemed Mr. Dawkins? What a prig. What right had he to explain filthy words to Alexander's wife?

"I thought I might spend some time reshelving some of these books, if you two won't be disturbed." Alexander was being an ass and he knew it. He only hoped Harriet didn't.

"Oh, I had come up with an order of things, in fact," Harriet said, biting her lip, a concerned look in her eyes. It was utterly adorable to see how much she cared for the library. Though now Alexander could hardly hover around the pair under the guise of reshelving. *Bollocks.*

"I won't disturb it. I—" Alexander scrambled to find a reason to stay in his own damned library when Mr. Dawkins did something truly commendable.

"Actually, my lady, I must be going. I have an appointment with the publisher." Harriet looked a bit dejected, which pinched something in Alexander's chest. She was sad to see him go?

"Until tomorrow then!" Harriet singsonged. Why was her voice so high-pitched when talking to the man? She didn't speak to Alexander that way. Christ, he was being a fool. With the removal of Mr. Dawkins, Harriet turned to him, and Alexander grew light-headed. Her tea-soaked dress had become rather transparent in her lap. Nothing in particular was showing. But one only had to imagine . . .

Hell and damnation.

Harriet was looking at him oddly, no doubt confused by his perusal of her. He shook himself.

"It's a dance, by the way, that prostitutes do. In the nude," he said, to distract her. Her eyebrows pinched in further confusion before rising in excitement.

"Oh, how lovely!" *Lovely?* She crossed over to the paper she'd been writing on and scratched a note to herself. "I wonder how Mr. Dawkins knows of such things," she tittered.

Alexander had wondered the same, though he did not like the thought to be in Harriet's head. And since when did Harriet *titter*?

He was going fully mad. The rain must have waterlogged his brain. He left the library without excuse and retreated to his study.

Perhaps there was a piece of paper there he could read again. Or a column of sums to go over.

∽

On the night of the Henderson ball, Harriet stood in the entryway feeling rather like a little girl waiting for her parents. Alexander *had* told her to wait at half past eight. It was now nearly nine. Her gloves were on, she had a small reticule with a pencil and paper inside, and she had donned her pelisse a quarter of an hour ago. All she was missing was her escort. Alexander had indeed taken care of her gown for the evening. If one was so generous as to consider the fabric she wore a gown. Clearly, he employed the same modiste as Philippa.

Issues of immodesty aside, the dress was the most exquisite piece of clothing Harriet had ever laid eyes on, let alone been allowed to wear. It was a light-green dress, heavy and beaded, with puffed, diaphanous sleeves and only the suggestion of a bodice. He had also procured new dancing slippers and a reticule to match.

Anne had delivered all these gifts, as Alexander had been away from home all day. He had, according to Presley—who was standing sentinel with Harriet in the entryway—returned shortly before and was dressing now. Harriet did her best not to fidget; all this waiting was only inflaming her nerves. Perhaps she better claim a megrim and cry off. How did she expect to face a ballroom of peers on *his* arm?

Right as she was cresting the hill of anxiety, Alexander appeared at the top of the staircase. Every thought she had of spending her evening anywhere but next to him fled. He was—he—

In a fit of madness, she spoke: "Oh my, you are the most handsome man I've ever seen."

The smile that cracked open his face was almost worth her embarrassment at having let the words escape her mouth.

"I'm inclined to agree," Presley said, and Harriet had no idea how serious he was. It sent her into a fit of giggles, which she tried desperately to cover.

"Thank you both," Alexander said, taking his hat and gloves from Presley. "Harriet, I must sincerely apologize for making you wait. It was most ungentlemanly of me. I will endeavor to prevent such a delay in the future."

"You were worth the wait." Oh, heavens above! What was she saying? Alexander looked down at her as he donned his cloak and raised an eyebrow.

"I had no idea formal wear excited you so," he whispered in her ear, as they left the house. "I would have worn it ages ago."

She nearly swallowed her tongue as Alexander helped her into the carriage.

Tonight would be her first ball with him. Her first ball as a wife. Their first time in public. Tonight would be different.

∾

Despite her change in status and station, Harriet felt, if anything, more invisible than ever.

Well, there had been one moment when she hadn't. When she'd removed her pelisse at the top of the stairs and Alexander had finally laid eyes on the dress he'd had made for her. That had felt the exact opposite of invisibility. His eyes had swept over her, and his pupils widened in awe. He seemed, unless he was performing, truly overcome.

"I am not entirely certain we need to attend this ball," he said, his gaze not leaving her body. There was much to be said for a gentleman meeting one's eye when he spoke, but there was even more, Harriet found, to be said for one's husband's gaze not being able to make it to one's eyes.

Unfortunately, he seemed the only member of the *ton* who noticed her at all.

Had someone approached her and said, "Did you hear? Lord Alexander married, and he's brought his wife with him," she would have looked around the room for the woman in question. She was a stand-in, an understudy for some other woman in everyone's mind, whether they knew it or not. On some level everyone, herself included, seemed to assume that another more suitable match would present itself either this season or the next or even five years from now, and that woman, the eventual duchess—if rumors about the elder son were true—would so seamlessly replace Harriet that no one would ever remember she'd been there at all.

This was reinforced by two separate gentlemen congratulating other nearby women upon their nuptials to Lord Alexander, before turning in confusion to Harriet. One woman, upon introduction, simply said, "I'm surprised," and offered no further elaboration. Another lady, both drunker and kinder than the first, whispered,

"Enjoy yourself. He's marvelous, isn't he?" in Harriet's ear before she stumbled off. Alexander didn't seem to notice the slights, or the fact that no one actually spoke with her. After the fifth conversation in which she was clearly not desired, Harriet decided mentally tallying the number of women wearing ostrich feathers was a better use of her mind.

In fact, she was so engaged in the Great Ostrich Accounting that she only registered Alexander's absence from her side when she noticed him dancing with feather-wearer number 27. Harriet didn't know the woman and tried her best not to concern herself with their pairing. Better to refocus on her tally.

She tried, she really did, only she'd nearly run out of ladies and feathers anyway, and it was difficult not to study the way the lady was looking at Alexander as if she wanted to devour him. What did ostriches even eat? Harriet would have to look it up when she went home.

Her reverie was broken with a glass of cold lemonade pressed against the back of her arm matched almost instantly with the deep, throaty laugh of her beloved sister.

"You look parched. Or perhaps ill?" Philippa said, almost gleefully. "Perhaps a sign of a successful honeymoon?"

Harriet gripped her sister tightly, as if Philippa were a raft that had appeared after days lost at sea. It had been too long. Philippa handed over the lemonade, sipping on champagne herself.

"Is he that bad?" Philippa asked, in a voice that was light with humor but eyes that searched out the truth. When Harriet didn't answer, she looked around for Alexander and found him on the dance floor and then let out a soft "Hmmm."

"What? Who is she?" Harriet asked, unable to keep the desperation out of her tone.

"Lady Delonge. She's a widow. She's . . . well. You see," Philippa said, gesturing toward the woman with her champagne. Harriet did see. Lady Delonge was practically draping herself across Alexander, laughing a little *too* hard. The dance had ended—surely they didn't still need to be touching?

"Perhaps we ought to take a turn about the room?" Harriet suggested, needing distance from him. Distraction. Sisterhood.

As they walked, Harriet mostly asked after Caroline and Frances to see if her sister knew any more than she did. Unfortunately, Philippa was similarly isolated from their sisters by the presence of their father.

"I've only had one letter from them. Caro says everything is fine. But I know him to be desperate for money. He's come around a few times, although Matthews runs him off, the dear," she said, referring to her beloved stable master. After a slight pause, she admitted with uncharacteristic solemnity, "I haven't any money anyway."

Harriet stopped short. "You haven't?"

Philippa's sly smile had already reappeared, which would have reassured anyone who knew her less well. It frightened Harriet more than anything.

"The estate, you know. Oh, it's all tied up after Reginald's third cousin, you know the one who was in the Indies? Apparently, he went and died last month on the way over. Awful inconvenient.

It's reverting to the crown. Likely to be divvied up among Prinny's friends, or given to some war hero. Perhaps they'll leave me a small plot. No one quite knows what to do with me. Or if they do, they won't tell me. I'm a bit stuck at the moment. None of it is mine, but nor is it anyone else's." Philippa thrust her champagne—never lemonade—up in an ironic cheer.

"Philippa, what can I do? I'm sure Lord Alexander can help." And the odd thing was, she *was* sure of it.

"Oh, there's nothing to be done. I wouldn't let you anyway. One of those god-awful situations where the only action one can take is a bath." Philippa smiled at her and then looked across the room at a particularly handsome man. Turning to Harriet she winked once again. "Or a lover."

At that, Philippa unlinked her arm and set off, swanning across the crush of people, parting the crowd with her presence. When Harriet looked up to seek out Alexander, she found him hanging on every word that came out of a quite severe-looking woman's mouth. Harriet winced. She hardly needed more proof of how much he enjoyed ladies' company.

Unfortunately, he looked up then and met her gaze, and with a full lemonade glass and no dancing prospects, she had no reason not to reunite with her husband. Thus, she dutifully did.

As she arrived in the circle, she happened upon something almost miraculous in its rarity: a woman Alexander could not charm. It only took a moment's observation to recognize the signs, but here she was, an immune party.

Barely able to suppress her excitement at meeting such a woman, Harriet sidled up to the small group, her lips twitching in excitement.

"Lady Holden, Lord Holden, here she is! May I introduce my wife, Lady Alexander?" He sounded like an anxious schoolboy. Who *were* these people who had him on his best behavior?

"Lovely to meet you," Harriet said, dipping into a curtsy in front of the couple. Alexander's behavior was only dwarfed in peculiarity by the idea of these two people being married to one another. The man was not unattractive for an older gentleman, and he had an easy, open face, dominated by a mustache Harriet would have requested he shave off had she been his wife. Lady Holden appeared to be at least his age if not a touch older, and she seemed even more severe up close. If her husband had the appearance of an affable sheepdog, she brought to mind a raven.

"My dear," Alexander began, an endearment he'd never used before, "Lord Holden is a business partner of mine. We've been looking at some land together. I was just telling Lady Holden about you." His eyes held a plea, although for what, she could only guess. Fortunately, Harriet was quite practiced at playing along.

"You've said so much about Lord and Lady Holden, what a pleasure to finally make your acquaintance," Harriet said, hoping she wasn't too far off the mark.

"I was telling them, my dear, how sorry we were not to be married in a church here in London." Alexander's eyes widened and his head nodded along, as if Harriet needed clues that she was meant to corroborate his story.

"Oh yes," Harriet said, adopting his tone of deep regret, without missing a beat, "Lord Alexander had had his heart set on St. James; however . . . well. I don't wish to speak out of turn—I do hope you'll forgive me—but my father was rather ill earlier this month and we weren't certain he would make it much longer. Thus, we made the horrid decision to elope. It was his dearest wish to see us wed before he passed."

"Oh my," Lord Holden said, clearly affected by the tale.

"I hadn't heard your father had died," Lady Holden said, rather snootily.

Bloody hell.

"By the grace of Our Lord he recovered, actually," Harriet said, solemnly. "Some say our marriage was what gave him the hope to continue on." She hoped the detail hadn't gone too far overboard, although if they were as devotional as she suspected, she didn't think they'd find it unlikely. Besides, what good was an absent father for if not to use in a lie occasionally? It was not like he'd encounter the Holdens in some grand ballroom and contradict her.

"We were so fortunate, grace be to God. It had been so soon after the passing of Lady Alexander's beloved spaniel," Alexander added, gazing at her over Lady Holden's head with a hint of mischief in his eyes. "I didn't know if she could take another loss."

"Oh no," Lady Holden cried, losing all her previous iciness. "I just lost my beloved Alvin last spring. It's the greatest loss imaginable. They really do become part of the family, don't they? Lord Holden can attest. I barely got out of bed for months after my Alvie died. What was her name?"

"Lexicon," Harriet said. Noticing the quizzical look on the Holdens' faces, she added, "Lexi for short. I was ever so fond of her. You see, Alexander gave her to me years ago when we began courting."

"Oh, Lawrence!" Lady Holden gushed, overcome with enough emotion to use her husband's first name. "Isn't that just the sweetest story you've ever heard?"

The man, like his wife, seemed to be genuinely moved by the tale. Harriet couldn't imagine why, but perhaps that was because she knew there was no dog and no courting and no loving father.

"You know, I'll admit I had my concerns when my husband began conducting business with Lord Alexander," Lady Holden shared with Harriet, as if Alexander were not also present in the conversation. "With all his philandering."

"Lucille!" Lord Holden admonished.

"Oh hush, you can see they're perfectly respectable people. God-fearing, in love, and they like dogs, dear. No one can have a rotten soul if they like dogs. Clearly the rumors have been exaggerated."

"Whoever conceals hatred with lying lips and spreads slander is a fool," Harriet quoted, knowing that most rumors about her husband were true. In fact, perhaps the only false story Lady Holden had heard about him had come from her own mouth just moments ago. Though undoubtedly people had cited the Bible to justify worse.

"I couldn't agree more," Lady Holden said, as if gossip was suddenly beneath her. "It was lovely to make your acquaintance, Lady Alexander, I hope you get another doggy soon. That's the only cure, really. Lawrence, I'm ready to go."

With that, the couple stalked off. Alexander tugged Harriet along with him behind a large potted fern where they both dissolved into laughter.

"Doggy? Doggy!" Alexander repeated, in wonder. "I've never seen her like that. The woman positively *loathes* me, ordinarily."

"I simply had to lie about every single thing about you."

"Come now, that's not fair. I miss Lexi acutely," he deadpanned. Harriet let out a loud cackle of laughter and he clapped his hand over her mouth to stifle the sound.

Both of them jumped at the touch, as if struck by a thunderbolt. Alexander removed his hand slowly, but it was too late; Harriet's entire body was ablaze. He broke eye contact first, clearing his throat and looking out at the crowd. It was a grounding reminder that they were in public.

"Is everything all right with your sister?" he asked.

Harriet's heart began racing as she peeked around the potted plant to search the ball for Philippa's chestnut hair, the mirror of her own. What the devil had she done now?

Alexander put a gentle hand on her arm, stilling her. "I saw you talking with her earlier and you seemed upset." Harriet looked up, somewhat surprised to see genuine concern in his expression. She realized with a start that the surprise came entirely from her own experience of life and *not* from her experience with him.

"She's well enough, I think. Her estate . . ." Harriet wasn't entirely sure if Alexander was supposed to know about the whole affair. Besides, that land had been her precious bargaining chip in getting him to marry her. Was it something she might need in the future?

"Reverted to the crown, I heard." He knew? How long had he known? "Please do offer her my support if she needs anything. You should invite her to dine with us sometime; the company would be good."

"I'm sure she has plenty of plans. She's always occupied with someone or other; she won't be lonely."

"I meant for you," he said matter-of-factly. "You miss her."

Unfortunately, at that moment, they were interrupted by the first notes of a waltz. Alexander cursed and then stepped away from her.

"Excuse me, I have to—I promised—I apologize. I'll be right back."

With that, Alexander left her again, only to end up back on the dance floor with another woman. This one was young and fresh-faced; she had the poise of a ballerina. Apparently, the man had no preferences whatsoever when it came to women.

"What kind of husband leaves his new wife all alone?" came an unfamiliar voice near her ear. So near that Harriet had to fight the unladylike urge to screech and jump away. Instead, she froze for a moment and then turned slowly to face an impeccably dressed older man. The dressing didn't save his appearance. His face was florid and most of his hair had left his head, the rest being overworked in its absence. Worst of all, Harriet mused, was that his eyes were entirely blank. Her mind flashed to a cod dinner she'd had once, the way the fish stared up at her. Neither Harriet nor the man seemed to expect her to actually answer his opening salvo, so he simply began the conversation again.

"We haven't been introduced—to Lord Stirling's discredit. I figured a small break in propriety wouldn't be undue; I'm the Duke of Belhaven." Harriet could tell her father-in-law was put out by the fact she hadn't recognized him. She bowed deeply and suggested it was an honor to make his acquaintance.

Harriet didn't know much about the man other than that he was Alexander's father. Alexander hadn't mentioned him with any fondness, but Harriet had been trained well enough when it came to miserable fathers to turn her brightest personality on. Men loved it when you smiled up at them.

"I must say, I wasn't apprised of my son's intention to marry you," the duke sneered. Harriet was shocked at his rudeness—although, with his fish-eyes, she shouldn't have been. No one with that type of cold, blank expression ever turned out to be secretly friendly.

"I'm rather not the type of woman he usually goes for, am I?" Harriet demurred. And though she'd had the thought herself many times, she felt a sting of betrayal to share it with this man.

"Indeed, you are not," the duke said, almost thoughtfully. As if it had just occurred to him. "I rather thought he might end up with someone more like"—he pretended to scan the room and then his gaze landed on Philippa, and her phalanx of fawning men—"your sister." He cleared his throat in a grotesque way that gave Harriet the urge to clear her own, and then continued. "If he ended up with someone at all, that is. He was so determined not to marry. He meant to anger me, which is why I suppose he chose you." The duke cracked what, on a normal person, would be a friendly smile, but on him looked strained and snakelike. Harriet had thought herself somewhat immune to men's ill-opinion of her, but his asperity was jarring.

Perhaps she had let her emotions show, because the duke continued: "I don't mean to insult you—you're quite clever, I concede. How *does* such a girl end up in line to be a duchess? You must admit it's rather remarkable of you. A coup."

"I assure you, Your Grace, I have no desire to be a duchess."

He laughed, a brittle, unpleasant sound. "Oh, but you will! Not to fret, I'm not upset. Alexander has quite pigheaded ideas about what will anger me. Could he have made a better match? Perhaps. But with the proper tutors, we can shape you into an appropriate wife for him. You seem rather . . . malleable," the duke hissed out, making it clear that he meant something entirely more insulting with the word. "Never fear, he has plenty of income; there will still be enough left over for a generous allowance." He patted Harriet's arm then, and she began to feel ill.

"Would you like to dance, Lady Alexander?" He once again employed his serpentine smile, not removing his hand from her arm. Never before had Harriet been so grateful for her inability to quadrille.

"I'm afraid I cannot dance, Your Grace, although I appreciate the invitation."

"You cannot dance?" The duke was affronted. An ugly daughter-in-law was insult enough, but the inability to dance? It was beyond the pale.

"The instructor had his hands quite full with my sisters; my lack of innate talent was simply too much for him to undertake." Harriet shored herself with a deep breath and then continued. She wouldn't let this man cow her, no matter his rank or relation to her. "I couldn't agree more with your assessment of my unsuitability for your son, Your Grace. I'm a wallflower. I had five unsuccessful seasons. My father is poor, which is about the kindest thing you can say about him." She said all this in a treacly, biddable voice, the kind one used to present horrible men with the type of information they wanted to agree with. And if some of that information was false? Well. Harriet had learned the usefulness of dishonesty with violent men and felt no compunction about the lie she was about to tell.

"However, I can assure you that my sister, Lady Ellerton, has been very generous. My sisters and I aren't at all in need, despite my father's unfortunate situation. I know it's unbecoming of a lady to speak of money, and I'm reluctant to do so, but I do want to assuage your concerns. The late Baron Ellerton left her quite a lot of land and other holdings. I'll endeavor to keep out of your son's coffers as much as possible. Although we might have to dip into them to find a dance instructor with enough patience and expertise." And then she *did* borrow something from Philippa. She winked at him.

Harriet felt quite satisfied with herself. She had hit all the points she needed to for this type of man—self-deprecation, demureness, recognition of etiquette, a general awareness of her own inferiority. The oily smile on the duke's face suggested she hadn't made a single misstep. Upon reflection, she might have brought up the bit about not speaking of money a little sooner in the speech. Or maybe even thrown in something flattering about the duke to stroke his ego. Ah, well, next time.

It was just then that Alexander arrived at her side. Had she been focused on anything other than calming her heart rate, she might have noticed how he'd rushed over immediately after his dance with the beautiful woman ended. Or that that exact woman had ended up on his father's arm. As it was, she noticed neither.

"Congratulations, my son. I think you'll be able to bring her to heel quite nicely," the duke said by way of greeting. To Harriet he added, "Please let me know if you need help finding any tutors. We should like to represent the Belhaven line well at all times, no matter the cost. All one has is one's good name and good breeding." The dig at Alexander's birth was rather obvious. "I'm sure you'll agree."

"Of course." Harriet nodded with her widest smile yet, grinding her heel into Alexander's boot to keep him from adding something that might undo all her simpering. "It was a true honor to make your acquaintance, Your Grace."

Chapter Twenty

"Wʜᴀᴛ ᴛʜᴇ ᴅᴇᴠɪʟ ᴡᴀs ᴛʜᴀᴛ ᴀʙᴏᴜᴛ?!" Aʟᴇxᴀɴᴅᴇʀ ᴅᴇᴍᴀɴᴅᴇᴅ ᴀs soon as his father sauntered off, pulling his boot out from under her foot. "Good Lord, I thought to spare my toes by not dancing with you, yet you still managed to find a way."

"I met your father," Harriet said, as if that weren't obvious.

"My condolences," Alexander said, offhandedly. Though his eyes were searching her face for *something*. She felt quite . . . examined. Harriet turned away, put her back up against the wall, and began watching the dancers again; it felt safer than looking at him. For some reason, she felt like she might cry, although she had no idea why.

"Are you all right?" he said, bending a bit to try to meet her eyes.

Lord, how she wished he'd asked any question but that. It was so much easier to pretend to be all right if no one inquired. She avoided his gaze, focusing instead on the buttons of his waistcoat.

"Was he rude to you? No, never mind, of course he was," Alexander said, obviously frustrated. He dragged a hand through his hair and sighed, growing silent.

Alexander's eyes were scanning the ballroom, probably hoping to find the company of anyone else. Harriet couldn't even blame him, since she was being uncharacteristically irritable. She felt chastised and forgotten and useless. Tired. She felt tired.

He was clearly already bored standing with her. She wished he'd go and find another dance partner. Some small, sick part of her enjoyed how happy he looked while dancing, even if it wasn't with her.

"Hell and damnation," Alexander muttered at a sight across the ballroom, seeming for a moment to forget whose company he was in because he then quickly apologized for his language. Harriet followed his line of sight to see what had caused the oath.

Alexander had already taken off, tossing an "If you'll excuse me" behind him. He was heading right for Philippa, who was, much to Harriet's dismay, fawning over the Duke of Belhaven. Alexander cut in between his father and Philippa and then leaned low to whisper something in her ear. Philippa leaned back a bit and gazed up at Alexander a moment before answering; the pair seemed to be communicating with their eyes alone. Harriet watched as Alexander bowed to his father, reached for Philippa's hand, and then steered her sister onto the dance floor. Of course he'd rescue Philippa from his loathsome father. God forbid *she* endure a moment's unpleasantness with the man.

It was one thing to watch a more beautiful woman dance with your husband; it was quite another to watch your more beautiful sister do so. Surely, Philippa meant nothing by it. You couldn't quite decline a gentleman's invitation to dance—at least, if you actually *could* dance.

Harriet couldn't decide which was more painful: watching or not watching. Not watching did appear to have its advantages, except an active mind could fill in intimacies where none were. But watching? Watching was surely worse. In the end, Harriet decided that another glass of lemonade and imagined tenderness were preferable to whatever she might actually observe between her sister and Alexander. Plus, it gave her hands something to do. How she wished Caroline were here, or Frances. Or even Mr. Dawkins.

She'd never been so ready for a ball to end, and they had hours to go.

∽

Alexander had never been so glad to leave a ball. He had no desire to watch the sun rise in the Hendersons' ballroom. He'd been unsurprised by how agreeable Harriet had been about leaving; she hadn't seemed to be enjoying herself.

For the first time in memory, he hadn't either.

He'd danced half the evening with some of the most beautiful ladies of the *ton*. The dances had been fine enough. Earlier this month, they would have amounted to a perfect evening. Instead, he couldn't stop thinking about him and Harriet laughing behind a potted fern. Or, worse, about the look in Harriet's eyes when he'd returned after dancing with her sister. He couldn't shake the feeling that he'd caused her pain somehow. Asking about it seemed out of the question. How did one *do* that? *"Oh, have I hurt your feelings? Jolly sorry, dear."* He wanted to bang his head against the squab. These very emotions were why he'd so studiously avoided matrimony. That, and his duty to John.

Guilt shot through him. He'd barely thought of his brother in weeks, and he'd written to him even less. He didn't know what to say. How did you write about your new, beautiful wife, the balls you were going to, life in the city—how did you tell someone that you were living the life they were meant to live? It was as if Alexander were biding the time until John died, just like everyone else in the *ton* was. Time should have stopped when John fell ill.

Alexander felt sick to his stomach.

Suddenly, he felt a hand on his. Her touch was temperate and reassuring. It wasn't erotic or romantic, she had simply reached out to . . . comfort him. Alexander felt something like shock. He looked down at their hands and then up to her. She shrugged weakly and smiled a small, almost sad smile, as if she'd given in to something.

Harriet leaned across his lap to open the window slightly. "Carriage sickness?" she asked, knowingly. Although, of course, she did *not* know. Sickness had nothing to do with why riding in carriages with her was ordinarily so intolerable. This time, it was his sentimental mood causing the problem. The gesture from her, the care, it only made things worse. She held his hand the entire ride home, which felt so kind it verged on punishment.

Alexander didn't deserve someone who noticed his discomfort—even if they misattributed it to a swaying carriage—he didn't deserve someone who held his hand. He didn't deserve *her*.

She'd been right to avoid consummating the marriage. It would only make him want more. For the first time in memory, he felt like there *was* something more—some bigger, better, unnamed thing that went beyond charm, beyond dance floors, beyond fucking. With that frightening realization came another: Neither of them would ever have it.

Perhaps it was the warmth of her hand and the comfort of the gesture. Or her ease with the Holdens earlier in the evening. Or the fact that she didn't seem cowed by his father. Certainly, at least one third of what he did next could be blamed on how beautiful she looked. All night, he'd felt certain that ordering those gowns had been the gravest mistake of his life, though now, as he sat inches away from her in the carriage, covered though she was by her pelisse, he *knew* it had been among his wisest decisions. As for what he did next, it would not be.

Removing the distance between them, he cupped her face, capturing her lips in a kiss he was doing his best to keep polite. She remained stone-still for a moment, a moment which felt at least as long as any opera he'd ever sat through. Finally, when Alexander began to pull back, she moved. It was slight at first, just the inclination of her head to give him better access to those wicked lips of hers. Thank God she talked so much; it gave him the perfect cover for watching her mouth. Had he known from the start how delicious her mouth was, he might never have let her speak a word for keeping it busy. He licked the seam of her lips, and she opened up for him. A groan escaped him. He wrapped his arms around her back, drawing her in closer. From her mouth, he moved his way down, kissing her throat before traveling eastward. He brushed his lips in the hollow where her neck met her shoulder, producing from her the most delightful sound he'd ever heard. Alexander meant to do everything in his power to hear it again as soon as possible. He went back to the spot to attempt an encore, but he was suddenly being pushed away from Harriet.

Panic set in immediately. Had he gone too far? Too fast? Was she upset? Only upon their disentanglement did he notice the carriage was slowing.

"We're home," she whispered. It probably said something embarrassing about his mental state that he found her calling his town house "home" erotic. He shook off the thought and opened the carriage door himself. The crisp night air should have cleared his amorous thoughts, but instead it reinvigorated him.

Grabbing the carriage blanket, he jumped out of the vehicle. He reached for Harriet's waist and helped her down, steps and footman be damned. Waving off the man, he took up her hand and hurried Harriet up the steps. If he acted expediently enough, perhaps they might continue what was happening in the carriage; perhaps the spell they'd been under wouldn't break and the evening wouldn't end.

He took off down the hall toward the closest, most comfortable room he could think of. Though "thinking" was a generous term for what his mind was doing.

He wished there'd been a fire in the grate burning, ready for them, but even *he* wasn't so rich as to leave a fire burning when no one was in the house. He closed the door behind him, and then, for good measure, locked it. He turned around to a blushing, delectable Harriet.

They were in the library, of course.

Chapter Twenty-One

Harriet knew—somewhere in the back of her mind, she *knew*—this was a terrible idea. Libraries led to liberties, in her experience with him, and she could ill afford to further muddy her sentiments regarding the man. She understood his actions could be chalked up to availability—she was the only lady in residence—but nothing about his demeanor suggested this was an act of convenience.

"May I?" Alexander asked, stepping closer, tossing the blanket over a nearby armchair.

Harriet had no earthly idea what he was asking permission for and every confidence she'd enjoy it. So she nodded.

Alexander bent and cradled her face in his hands before claiming her mouth again. Tasting her, nipping at her. Each kiss of his made her *want*. She felt in grave danger of melting. His entire body felt hard and hot against hers. Were kisses supposed to make one feel heavy?

Then he pulled away and she almost whimpered with need.

"You can touch me back, you know?" he teased, tucking an errant lock of hair behind her ear. Mortification suffused through her at having to be informed. He was no doubt accustomed to women who didn't need to be instructed in the act of seduction. Harriet froze in place.

Without appearing to give it a second thought, Alexander bent and scooped her into his arms as if she weighed as much as an embroidery hoop. No one had lifted her since she was a child. Alexander might be used to tossing women around his bedroom—or library as it were—but undoubtedly, they were not her size.

"Alexander!" she screeched, the noise unpleasant even to her own ears. She was getting this all wrong, although he seemed not to be noticing.

He set her down on a divan as if she weighed naught and stood, grinning. "So you *do* know my name?" he jested, shrugging out of his tailcoat and beginning to unfasten his waistcoat, a sight which Harriet would never tire of. Should they ever be short on funds, they could no doubt sell admission to the display.

"I believe I've used it before," she replied, biting into her lip, hoping to stay fully attentive to both the conversation and the show before her.

"Only thrice," he said, simply.

"You've been counting?"

"Fantasizing," he corrected.

He undid his cravat and removed his cufflinks and then sat on the edge of a nearby armchair to remove his boots. Transfixed, Harriet watched for a moment; then, realizing what she was meant to do, began to take off her gloves. She reached down to remove her own shoes. The gown would require his assistance.

"Not that I don't adore what you're doing, but you can stop there." Before Harriet could be hurt by the words, Alexander held up a hand. "Don't fret, we *will* get there. If you'd like. First, however, I thought we might try something."

The suggestion brought no small amount of panic; if someone with his expertise was going to "try" something, she was certain to be out of her depth. A lump of nerves appeared in her throat, which she swallowed to ask, "You haven't done this before?"

"Well, no, not exactly . . ." he said, continuing to undress himself, removing his breeches and then returning to sit.

"Marvelous," Harriet trilled, sitting up next to him on the divan and placing her hands on her thighs to signal that she was ready. For . . . whatever came next.

Harriet was proud that her voice sounded relatively even. He smiled broadly at her and sank to his knees. Some of her nerves disappeared at the act. Or perhaps just rearranged themselves. He'd known quite well what to do with his face in that area last week.

Instead of rucking up her skirts and diving in, he watched her intently—a little *too* intently. He traced a finger up her now bare arm until he reached the sleeve of her gown. He skipped over the fabric and continued his ministrations on her collarbone.

"I had thought *you* might touch *me*," he explained, though he didn't stop his caresses.

Nodding, she reached out cautiously. "Right, yes. Of course." Alexander grabbed her hand before it could land on his impressive chest. A sigh of relief escaped her lips; she had no idea what he meant for her to be doing. He stood again and then held out a hand to her. She rose, still mystified.

"I thought I might lie down and let you have your way with me."

Upon reflection, Harriet would always be proud that she didn't choke or sputter or cough at the suggestion. Other than her insides rupturing and her mind dissolving, she remained unchanged—a portrait of stoicism and maturity as he crossed, almost entirely nude, to where he'd left the blanket. Then spread it down over the Axminster. He tossed a few cushions on the pile for good measure, then glanced back, noticing she had yet to move.

"You don't have to, if you don't want to," Alexander said, no doubt in response to the trepidation written on her face. Despite the nonchalance of his words, he himself looked apprehensive.

"It's not that I don't want to," Harriet rushed to assure him. "It's only—I have no idea what I'm meant to do."

"Come here," he instructed. So she did. He reached out a hand and gathered her close.

"Now what?" They were still standing; was she meant to sit? Was this to be like a picnic in the park?

"That's the beauty of the enterprise. You're meant to do precisely as you'd like."

"But I—I don't know what will feel good for you."

"Virtually anything you do will be enjoyable, I swear it."

"Yes, but . . ."

"As long as you don't knee me in the bollocks, we'll be remarkably far ahead of our last experience in a library." As he teased her, he took a step back and removed his shirt; he was now fully nude in front of her. More molten heat flooded Harriet's core. A fire wasn't necessary at all, as it were.

"Where would you like to touch?" he asked, simply. His lack of clothing didn't seem to bother him at all. It hadn't changed his composure or his comportment. Harriet couldn't fathom ever being so at ease, even with her clothing on.

She kept her eyes trained tightly on his face and the upper half of his body. Scandalous as those areas felt to ogle, she had at least seen his chest before. A chest was survivable.

She reached a tentative hand out to his forearm. It seemed like a relatively safe starting point. One could touch a gentleman's arm without impropriety. Although one was usually being escorted into dinner or around the perimeter of a ballroom. And the gentleman was ordinarily clothed.

Focus, Harriet, she chastised herself, willing her mind to stay present for this monumental event. This could be the last time she ever touched a man, after all. That thought spurred her on.

She picked her hand up and then moved over to his chest. Gaining confidence, she let her fingers trail down the hard muscles, enjoying the unfamiliar feeling of his hair there. He let out a groan of pleasure. She smiled and bit her lip, though she didn't lift her gaze. How different they were underneath their clothing, and yet, so much the same. She trailed one daring finger lower, following the path of hair.

"Enjoying yourself?" he asked, although his voice was strained. He let out a hiss as she continued down.

She snatched her hand back. "Sorry. Is that painful?"

He chuckled. "The opposite, in fact."

"Oh. Well then," she said, feeling bold. She returned her hand to where she'd left off only to discover that she was in the vicinity of his . . . She almost laughed at her reluctance to even think the word.

"Something amusing?"

"I find myself rather reticent, which is unusual."

"Quite," he answered. "I think this is the least you've spoken since we met."

"I'm not used to these words, is all."

"Which words?" he asked.

"Er, you call it your"—Harriet swallowed—"cock? Yes?" Alexander groaned at both her use of the word and likely how close she was getting to touching the appendage in question.

"I do."

"Cock," Harriet repeated, surer of herself this time. "Cock," she said again. "It's only a word."

"Come now, it's a bit more than that," he teased.

"It's only that I'm so used to saying words. I mean, obviously I am. And normally, I have no compunction about saying the 'bad' ones—though I'm loath to call any word bad. *Bloody. Damn. Hell.* See? I can say those just fine. I just haven't really had any experience saying *cock* in this context. I suppose it's simply a matter of time before you become comfortable. Perhaps one day, I'll have no compunction about saying it. I'll simply need to practice."

The rambling had either calmed her or emboldened her, or both. Harriet finally allowed herself a good look at all of Alexander. From his strong thighs, down to his feet, back up to his broad chest. She could admit that her gaze snagged a bit at his truly impressive cock.

"You can say *cock* to me as often as you'd like."

"How generous of you, my lord," she teased back.

"Only trying to assist my wife in her . . . practice."

"Is there another word for it?"

"For . . . ?" And then Alexander did something truly wicked and made it move on its own. Harriet let out a small yelp of surprise or delight or something in between. Then she laughed, fully and loudly, the sound bouncing off the high walls of the library.

"I had no idea it could do that! That *you* could do that! Can every man do that?"

"I would imagine. We haven't discussed it at White's, but I can't see why not."

"Intriguing. But you haven't answered my question. Is there another word for *cock* like there is with *quim*? A lack of synonyms often becomes repetitive."

"One wouldn't want that," he replied, trying to stay serious. "You could call it a 'penis,' although that feels rather . . . medical. Or 'member,' but that's rather bland. 'Prick' is fairly common. And then there are the less than appropriate names."

"Less appropriate than 'cock'?" Harriet asked eagerly, removing her hand from him, the body part in front of her forgotten in exchange for its synonyms. "Oh, you must tell me!"

"Harriet." Alexander sounded somehow rather desperate.

"Please," Harriet begged. This was precisely the type of information she needed.

"'Whore-pipe, frigger, hair splitter, wedding tackle, bush-beater.'" Harriet's eyes widened and she turned away from him.

"Where the devil are you going?" he growled, coming up behind her and grabbing her to him, preventing her movement.

"I have to write these down!"

He was encircling her, surrounding her. It was the most overwhelming sensation she'd ever experienced. More even than when he'd licked her quim.

"Harriet, I swear to you, I will remember every single one of them tomorrow. Perhaps even more. *Please*," he bargained, his voice a desperate whisper in her ear. It was, she could admit, quite a heady experience to have Lord Alexander begging.

Harriet considered his offer, then nodded. In that moment she realized she was being held by a very naked man. She rested her hands on his thick forearms, arms which were still embracing her most deliciously. She looked down, and the sight of her skirts bracketed by his bare legs was, for reasons she couldn't articulate, unbearably erotic. He was breathing just as heavily as she was, she was happy to note.

Alexander planted a kiss on the back of her neck, which shot a frisson down her spine; then he released her and lowered himself to the nest he'd made on the floor. She turned to face him, and it was a miracle she didn't collapse.

Harriet sincerely hoped he *would* remember those words because she suddenly forgot almost every single one she knew. She couldn't stop staring at him. The heat in his midnight eyes made her feel as if they both might combust here together in his library. Leonine as ever, Alexander was lounging on his side, waiting for her. She was the prey.

"I guess we better return to your cock, then," she whispered, joining him on the blanket.

Alexander didn't believe in seeking out pain for the sake of personal growth; life was hard enough. So he couldn't rightfully say what had compelled him to devise this exercise, which could most accurately be described as an acute form of torture.

"Can I touch it?"

"You don't have to ask, Harriet. I'm yours." As soon as the words tumbled out, Alexander felt the need to hastily add, "To touch."

Harriet knelt on the blanket next to him, dragging her gaze over him once again. The position provoked too many fantasies. Though, really, what position wouldn't have? He was distracted from this—and any—line of thinking when Harriet reached out and traced a tentative finger down his cock. A groan he barely recognized as coming from his own mouth filled the room.

"Is that all right?" she asked, tentatively.

"Very much so," he gritted out, shutting his eyes tightly. Watching her explorations was too much to bear.

She did it again, lightly drawing up and down his shaft. Alexander was doing his best not to fly off the floor at her every touch. Harriet continued, sweeping her hands down his thighs, and then back up. Every touch was gentle and hesitant. Despite that, she let out a little hum of pleasure as she traced his hip bones and then traveled back down to his desperate, aching prick. The sounds she was making were going to kill him. Or make him spill his seed all over himself. He clenched his teeth and tried to breathe through the feeling.

Then her touch stopped, and he opened his eyes to see her sitting back on her heels, hands tented together under her chin, appraising him. She looked very much as if his body was a problem she'd like to solve; it made him feel like he'd been dipped in fire. He met her gaze, which seemed to remind her that he was actually present in the room with her. She blushed furiously.

"Can one . . . well . . . ?"

"I've already decided I'm going to love this question."

Harriet reached out a hand and swatted his thigh as punishment for the teasing, though it didn't feel like punishment at all.

"Come now," he goaded, "don't be shy about it. It's only a body. We've all got them. Just ask."

"I suppose I *am* being a bit of a ninny," she said, dropping her hands to her thighs. She took a deep breath and straightened her posture, as if to resettle herself. "All right. I'm just going to say things."

"You usually do," Alexander said wryly, earning him another flirtatious swat from Harriet.

"Fine. You used your mouth on me. On my quim. I'm wondering if I might—that is, do people do that for cocks?"

Alexander's heart had either stopped or was beating so fast that it was going to explode; he wasn't sure, but something was wrong.

"They do," he said in a rush, completely unable to appear uneager. Harriet laughed at him for it, which was quite a small price to pay for her to even consider the deed. She could laugh at his avidity all she wanted; he *did* want her mouth on his cock rather desperately. Was it so bad if she knew?

"How do I do that?"

"What?" Alexander asked, pulled out of his reverie.

"With my mouth? How do I . . . what do I do?"

"Quite literally anything," Alexander practically begged, and then amended, "Well, no teeth. No biting." Harriet smiled before leaning in. It was Alexander's lungs that ceased to function next. But then she pulled back once more.

"I'm sorry, I just—will you at least tell me *something*? Explain it a bit?"

God, he'd have thought describing fellatio to a woman would have been an arousing task, but now he simply felt out of his depth. Forming cogent thoughts, let alone instruction, was proving to be rather difficult.

"Have you eaten an ice before?"

"No," Harriet said, sadly.

"God, we'll have to rectify that later. For now, just, well . . ." Alexander sat up on his elbows and tried to think of how to explain. And quickly. "Put your finger in your mouth."

Harriet looked like she was about to question this, but at Alexander's look, she did as he bid. "Now suck on it for a moment, and then remove it slowly from your mouth." Jesus, he needed to end this lesson. Alexander watched and wished he'd had her use his finger instead. After a dazed moment of silence, he returned to the lesson.

"Wonderful. Now do that with my cock. You can use your hand to guide it."

"But! It's huge!"

"You don't have to get the whole thing in! Or you can just kiss it or lick it. At this point, I'd spend about ninety thousand pounds for you to go back to touching it." Harriet grinned, reaching her hand out slowly to hover above him.

"Ninety thousand, huh?" She licked her lips then, the minx.

"Harriet," Alexander growled, "if you don't touch me in the next three seconds, I'm going to do it myself."

"I bet you didn't imagine having to instruct me so," she said ruefully, leaning back over him.

"On the contrary, I imagined it quite a lot."

"Alexander!"

"Using my name twice in one—" he began, only to have all thoughts cease when her tongue darted out of her mouth and licked the tip of him. He moaned with delight.

Harriet took him into her mouth and then his mind and heart and lungs and every other part of his body ceased to exist. He was in heaven. She kissed and licked him, not expertly by any means, but enthusiastically. Gleefully, almost. Knowing Harriet, she was probably more excited by learning something new than by the activity itself, but his cock couldn't tell the difference.

He was so close to coming in her mouth before he realized he ought not do that. "Harriet. Harriet, stop. Sorry," he said, pulling her up and off him.

"Did I do something wrong?"

"No, it's only I was about to spend, and I didn't think you'd want that in your mouth."

"Why?"

Alexander closed his eyes for a moment; this was too much lust for a man to bear in one evening.

"Some women don't enjoy it. It's not particularly . . . pleasant, I don't think."

"But some women do?"

"I think so. Or they're exquisite actresses. Hard to say."

Harriet dipped her head back down, as if to continue, but he stayed her. "We can try another time. It's my turn."

In one fluid movement, he switched their positions, Harriet beneath him as he knelt over her. He kissed his way down her body, lifting her damned gown to see her perfect, perfect quim. Had he not been as close as he was to coming, he would have taken more time, perhaps even undressed her entirely. As it was, he hoped that he could last through at least one climax of hers without spending.

He pushed up her skirts and began. She tasted heavenly; he could have lived here in his library between her legs. They could ring for tea and supper when needed. His estates might fall into ruin, and his investments might decline without oversight, but there was enough money for twenty or thirty years.

Harriet was writhing beneath him, clutching at his hair and cursing like a sailor. Smiling against her, he added a finger, pushing into her and stroking in time with what his mouth was doing to her. Harriet grabbed a small pillow from their nest on the floor and screamed into it, coming against his tongue. He almost felt sad it had taken so little time, though he wasn't sure how much longer he himself could last.

Alexander climbed up and lay down next to her, both of them breathing heavily—her in satisfaction, him with the lack of it.

Harriet came down from her orgasm and he felt her gaze travel down his body, lingering quite audaciously on his abandoned cock. Apparently, she wasn't the sort to spectate; she reached down and touched him. Her eagerness was so lewd that Alexander's eyes rolled back, and he gave up any attempt at keeping himself under control. It took an embarrassingly few strokes before he choked out, "I'm going to—" and then he spilled all over her hand and his stomach, yelling out a rather obscene curse as he did so.

As soon as his heart returned to a more normal cadence, he lifted his head to look at Harriet, expecting to find her disgusted or perhaps embarrassed. One did not spill one's seed into one's wife's hands. At least Alexander didn't think one did.

Instead, he found her beaming with pride.

"That was extremely edifying," she said, tittering with excitement, as Alexander reached to his discarded breeches for a handkerchief so she could clean herself. She nodded her thanks and wiped her hands. He'd already lain back on the blanket, quite incapable of moving for at least the next seventy-two hours.

"You look pleased with yourself," he teased a few minutes later, his finger drawing lazy circles on her exposed hip. They were lying on their sides, facing one another, her dress still half hiked up.

"Of course I am. Tonight we discovered the cure to your carriage sickness."

Alexander let out a loud, deep laugh, one that at first delighted Harriet, and then with its endurance befuddled her. She hadn't thought the joke *quite* that humorous.

One look at her face, and Alexander turned sheepish, which only made him more handsome, unfortunately.

"I fear I must confess something to you," he said, swallowing thickly. Harriet watched his Adam's apple, a sight which *almost* distracted from his forthcoming admission. With her newfound comfort around him, she reached out to trace a line down his throat.

"I am . . . That is, I don't . . . Perhaps you might remove your hand from my neck when I tell you this?" She smiled, confident enough now to know he was teasing her rather than critiquing her.

"We'll see" was all she answered, trailing her hand to his collarbone, his throat still within reach.

"I don't get sick in carriages," he blurted. It happened so fast that she barely registered the words until she replayed them in her mind. Even then, the sentence made no sense. She dropped her hand and sat up, as if that would help ease her confusion.

"You . . ." Her eyebrows drew together. She felt her head cocking like a dog. "You don't? But I thought—But you rode out." He sat up then too, still looking guilty.

"It was only that . . . well, I simply couldn't stand to be in a carriage with you"—as Harriet's jaw dropped in offense, he hurried to finish the sentence—"in that dress any longer."

"I beg your pardon!"

"That dress you were wearing—the white one?"

"Oh yes, I'm familiar with it. I thought you liked it! You made me a dozen copies of it!"

"*Liked* it? I couldn't possibly be a more ardent supporter of that dress. They should erect monuments to the modiste who came up with that neckline. It was driving me *mad*." Alexander leaned in then and nipped lightly on her shoulder, making her squeal with delight, though the smile that lingered afterward was much more about his confession.

"So you had to ride out because . . . ?" Harriet asked, laughing, as he bit and licked a path up her neck. "I just want to make sure I *completely* understand."

"Because I was worried for my poor prick if I didn't, you little devil. You needn't tease this out of me, I'll happily detail precisely what I considered doing to you in that carriage that required me to leave." Harriet gasped as he moved his hand back between her legs again and his mouth returned to her neck. With his mouth pressed just under her ear, he let out a groan of frustration and said in a near-whisper, "God, I wish I could fuck you."

"You do?"

He laughed at her. "Harriet, of bloody course I do."

Harriet remained still for a moment, thinking. And then, eyes trained up at the ceiling, she squeaked out, "You could . . ."

Alexander moved his lips up to hers and gathered her in his arms, kissing her desperately and hungrily. As if he were asking for something or perhaps atoning for something. He pulled back and smoothed a hand over her hair.

"I can't now, but that is . . ." He kissed her forehead instead of finishing his sentence. "Besides, the first time for women is sometimes rather painful. I'm having too nice of a time here to do that."

Something rather prickly sat in Harriet's chest, and she wasn't sure she liked the feeling. She couldn't tell if she was sorry to not have had sex, or embarrassed to have offered and been turned down, or if the feeling was because of the care he was taking of her. His affections weren't hers alone, or hers forever, which made the moment rather bittersweet. "You *can't*?"

"Men, we can't . . . go . . . again right away. We need to, er, recover a bit."

"But women can?"

"Yes. Quite unfair."

"I do think women were owed at least *one* advantage over men."

"I can think of many, many advantages of women over men," he teased, kissing his way across the top of one breast to the other.

"I meant one *we* could enjoy ourselves."

"Ohhh," Alexander replied, pretending to have been enlightened by her.

"So . . . how many times can a woman . . . reach her peak?" Harriet asked, biting her lip. Alexander responded precisely how Harriet hoped he would.

"Shall we find out?"

Chapter Twenty-Two

Harriet woke later than usual and allowed herself to luxuriate in bed for nearly a quarter of an hour, replaying the evening before. She felt wicked and delighted and exposed, as if the whole of the house knew what she'd done. The whole of London, even. A knock sounded on the door and Harriet still jumped at the sound. Her lady's maid, Anne, slipped in and dropped a quick curtsy.

"Good morning, my lady. Lord Alexander is waiting for you in the breakfast room."

"He is?" Harriet couldn't help the besotted smile on her face. Anne must think her a twitterpated fool. And was she not?

Harriet tried not to rush to get ready, lest she seem even more pathetic than she already did. Her impatience couldn't be helped. Harriet and Alexander didn't ordinarily break their fasts together. They occasionally met over toast and eggs by chance, but they were not the sort of couple to moon at each other over rashers. If such a couple *did* exist.

Suddenly, it occurred to Harriet—and she felt quite embarrassed that it hadn't occurred to her sooner—that he might not be in precisely the same giddy mood she was from the events of last night.

Having female company was not novel to the man; he'd had plenty of mornings-after. Perhaps he was requesting her presence for something quotidian like her opinion on drapery, or to remind her to go over dinner menus with the housekeeper. Perhaps he wanted to get rid of her now that he'd had her, in a certain manner? She had *offered* for him to fuck her, even if they hadn't actually done that. Maybe he was summoning her to remind her that she shouldn't fall for him after a simple tumble on the carpet?

Harriet shook her head. Trying to guess a man's mind was like eating soup with a fork.

She finished dressing at a more regular speed, not having to temper herself artificially anymore, and then headed down to the breakfast room. Alexander was there, reading the paper, bathed in sunlight like God had chosen him specifically to bestow the gift of beauty upon. She rolled her eyes at her own inanity and headed to the spread of food, determined to appear unaffected. Placid. Normal. Calm. Perhaps thinking of more synonyms would help. Serene.

Undisturbed. Tranquil. Agitated. Inflamed.

Blast.

$\backsim$

Alexander had read the same sentence thrice since she walked in. For good measure he began it a fourth time. His brain had become a nonce—useful only for noticing *her*. Or thinking of her. Or reminiscing about how she tasted. Or imagining how she might feel riding his cock. His mind was quite averse to any other avenue of thought. He did his utmost to remain composed upon her arrival, despite his heartfelt desire to jump from his seat and ravish her on the breakfast table. It had been ages since he'd fucked anyone on a table. He felt sure she'd be delighted by the novel proposal. She was so deliciously eager.

A footman appeared with more coffee and Alexander cleared the temptation to ask Harriet what she thought of swiving on the breakfast table from his mind. She finished heaping her plate with food and turned to sit across from him.

"I thought you didn't like kippers."

Harriet looked at him as if he'd announced himself the next king. He gestured with his hand at her plate, which was half full of the fish. Then she looked back at him as if, somehow, *he'd* caused their presence.

"I . . . I thought I might try them again. One never knows when one's tastes have changed," Harriet said with unconvincing conviction.

"True enough," Alexander said, wickedly, wishing she might tell him more about her tastes. Harriet took the smallest possible share of a kipper and raised it to her mouth so slowly Alexander worried the fish would go bad before it got there. She wrinkled up her nose and forced herself to take a bite. He watched gleefully, not because it was nice to watch a woman eat kippers. They were perhaps the least arousing food on the planet. But because it was apparent that Harriet had been distracted enough to load her plate with them this morning, and he had the foolish hope that he might be responsible for that in some way.

Harriet chewed for a moment with disgust and then swallowed with disgust and then took a bite of buttered toast with a face full of relief.

"Are you, by chance, available today?" he asked. Harriet, glad for the distraction from pretending to like kippers, shoved her plate aside.

"I have no plans at all, in fact."

"Wonderful. Wear your worst day dress and most comfortable footwear and meet me in an hour."

"For what?" she asked, in the most unladylike manner. It reminded him of the comfortability he felt as a child with his brother. The lack of care at what someone might think of your words.

"A surprise, I'm afraid."

"For me?"

"Yes, I fear anyone else would be rather disappointed with our outing."

Harriet looked suddenly as if she'd swallowed the entire plate of kippers in one go.

"Are you all right? We don't have to go. If you have something—"

"I've never had a surprise," Harriet said, quietly.

"You haven't?"

"I suppose I've *been* surprised by lots of things. Meeting you in a library. That men have hair on their chests. The size of your . . ."

Glancing up at the footman present, Harriet swallowed and then continued: " . . . town house." She blushed deeply, no doubt realizing how liberal she'd been with her words. Why she'd spoken of chests in front of another man. A servant, yes, but a man nevertheless.

"It is rather large, isn't it?" Alexander asked, trying his best to keep from grinning. "And you've been learning to handle it so well."

Harriet nearly choked on the tea she'd sipped to wash down her toast and the lingering taste of fish. She flushed again, or perhaps it was a continuation of the first blush he'd seen that morning. Either way, her rosy cheeks brought back to mind the idea of clearing the table, excusing the footmen, and seeing if she'd like to repeat last night on a different surface.

She stood abruptly, obviously both anxious to flee the room and excited for the impending surprise.

"You don't want to finish your kippers?" Alexander called after her, barely containing his mirth.

∽

Harriet had never been to this part of London. So frequently did activities with Alexander underscore how small her life had been before him. She kept her nose almost pressed against the window, willing herself to soak up the enormity of the city, the moment. Pressuring herself to experience the excitement of novelty.

Instead, she saw close-ups of gray people and gray streets and gray buildings with dirty windows, everyone living virtually the same as what she'd experienced on the other side of the city.

"It's not the best view," Alexander said offhandedly. The comment made Harriet bristle in defense.

"It is if you haven't seen it before," Harriet replied, a little peevishly, even though she'd been thinking the same thing. She expected him to ignore her grumbling or perhaps concede her point. She did not expect him to join her at the window and look out with feigned wonder.

"Would you look there, Harriet! A town house! And farther down, there's a horse! And another horse!" Harriet made a face at him, barely stopping herself from sticking out her tongue at his teasing.

"Now *there's* a sight you don't see in the ballrooms of Belgravia," he said, somewhat more sincerely this time, as they passed a young couple wrapped in a passionate embrace, uncaring or unaware of the broad daylight and their ample audience.

Harriet was laughing now, embarrassed a bit by her disagreeable nature. He was surprising her, after all. "I apologize. It's only . . . well, I was thinking about how men are so . . ."

"Attractive? Complex? Intriguing? Handsome?"

"Handsome and attractive mean the same thing."

"Not always. Some of the most handsome men are quite repulsive."

Harriet smiled. "No, I was thinking that everywhere I've gone in my life has been dictated by a man. Allowed or disallowed by him. And any places I may go? They're all owned by men. The land, the houses, the *horses*. I've never been this far east in London simply because no man has ever taken me here. It's rather depressing, don't you think?"

"I think you're giving East London a bit too much credit."

"Again, you're only saying that because you've been! And you can go any time! You can go anywhere you want! I can only go if a man approves it!"

Alexander was quiet for a moment, contemplating this.

"All right, you may go anywhere you want." He waited and then added, "As long as you have a proper chaperone for protection."

Harriet rolled her eyes. "You're proving my point, you git! I'm only able to go places if I am allowed so by a man. Even then, you'll have me take a lady's maid and an armed footman."

"I *am* rather beastly for not wanting you to be mugged or knifed or attacked."

"By a *man*," Harriet intoned testily.

A slow smile spread across his face, an odd response to her statement. "Of the two of us, I'm the only one who's been kidnapped, actually. And . . . you might find this hard to believe . . . my abductor was a woman."

Harriet's face cracked open with laughter again, further easing her nerves. She hadn't known how it might be with him after last night, and the uncertainty had made her feel like she was wearing a too-small and too-itchy gown. Laughing with him in a carriage felt normal. Odd, that. She'd only known him a couple of weeks.

The carriage slowed and Harriet looked out to see . . . a fish market.

"You brought me to a fish market?" she asked, trying not to sound too disappointed. "I must warn you, I sadly didn't discover a latent love of kippers this morning."

Alexander alighted from the carriage and then held out a hand to her.

"I know," he said simply. He offered his arm and Harriet took it, trying to ignore the thrill she felt at the small touch. The smell of the river and rotting fish did a good deal to put romantic thoughts out of her head. She had her reservations about this surprise, but she followed him, his large stride proving a bit difficult to keep up with. Harriet glanced around again, waiting to see something . . . else. A regal ship they were to embark on. A hidden gem of a building. A bridge . . . to somewhere else. She opened her mouth to ask what they were doing, and without even glancing back, Alexander cut her off.

"Just be patient."

He was enjoying himself rather a bit too much.

"Is this payback for kidnapping you?" she asked.

"You've turned quite prim all of a sudden. Wouldn't have thought you a snob," Alexander teased.

Under her breath Harriet mumbled, "I just hate fish." She thought she heard him let out a snort of laughter, but she couldn't be sure. He was keeping a quick pace as they cut across the market and toward the river. When they got to the dirty, brown banks of the Thames, he cut to the right and led Harriet onto a swaying, creaky dock toward a small ship. Identical, in Harriet's eyes, to dozens of others. *Do men have special eyes that let them differentiate ships and horses better?* she wondered.

And then he led her right up to a delicately balanced wooden board, spanning the water between ship and safety. Harriet stopped short, jerking Alexander back.

"Is something wrong?"

"Are we meant to . . . walk on that?"

Alexander looked perplexed at the question. "You can skip or run if you'd like. Waltz if you prefer."

Harriet would have rolled her eyes if she wasn't so suddenly seized with fear. She looked down into the murky water below. A rather perilous drop.

"Is it safe?" she asked, swallowing as if that could make the lump of fear in her throat disappear.

"Not to worry, they have only a few deaths on this plank a year," he answered, tapping the board with his foot. Harriet wasn't keen on feeling like even more of a ninny than she already did, so she braced herself for a plunge into the Thames and followed him, teeth clenched in fear.

"I didn't realize your distaste for kippers went this far," Alexander joked after they arrived safely on the deck of the boat.

"I can't swim," Harriet gritted out. Alexander looked over the side of the boat.

"You can probably stand at this point. The real concern is the eels." Harriet almost shrieked. There were few things she felt delicate about; large dirty bodies of water apparently made the list. She'd had no reason to encounter one before, thank God.

"I don't know if . . ." Harriet began. "I'm so sorry . . . I don't know if I'm going to like this surprise."

Alexander ran his hands up and down her arms, which felt oddly comforting. "We aren't going anywhere. This is it." Harriet looked around. The view wasn't better than it had been on shore. And the smell was, somehow, worse, though in London the stench was pretty much constant.

From behind them came a loud shout: "Stirling! Good to see ya!" A jolly, ruddy-looking man with a weathered face and a full beard approached and reached out his hand to Alexander, the gesture so out of place with the city they'd just left that Harriet could only gawk. Alexander, however, took the breach of etiquette in stride and shook the man's hand.

"Harriet, this is Captain Williams. Captain Williams, may I present my wife, Lady Alexander?"

He nodded in a bow, clearly aware of some level of propriety, just unconcerned with it.

"Lovely to meet you," he replied, smiling openly. Harriet liked him immediately.

"And you, although I'm not quite certain of the purpose of my visit." Harriet glanced between the two men, hoping someone would explain to her what was happening.

"To talk to me. And the men," Captain Williams said simply, wiping his hand on a rag hanging from his pocket. Harriet noted wryly that he'd done it after shaking Alexander's hand, too, as if just being near toffs was dirty.

"Talk to you? . . . I'm sorry, but I don't know what I would speak on . . . I don't . . ."

"Nonsense, love, you'd find a way to fill the silence no matter what," Alexander teased.

Had Harriet been less confused about what was meant to happen, she might have gotten stuck on the endearment. Alexander and Captain Williams were smiling at her confusion, and Harriet felt a bit frustrated with being left out of the fun. This surprise was turning out to be not a very nice one so far.

At her no-doubt dour expression, Alexander sobered and laid a gentle hand on her arm. "I thought—well, this might be silly of me—but I thought sailors might be more useful to you than any book I have in the library. They know all the worst words."

Emotion rendered Harriet immobile. This was . . .

"God's teeth, I've done it! I've rendered her speechless," Alexander exclaimed to Captain Williams.

"I . . ." she started, but the sentence went nowhere.

"I know Captain Williams from some shipping business I have with him, and I thought he might be useful to you for the dictionary. Sailors have almost their own language." At Harriet's continued silence, which he must have read as doubt instead of disbelief, Alexander continued, "If that's not the sort of thing that would help, then no harm. I'll take you right back to—"

Rising on her toes, Harriet cut him off with a simple kiss on his cheek. Oh, she wanted to do more. She wanted to loop her arms around him and squeeze him with all the delight she felt, but that wasn't the sort of thing they did. The touches they shared were either accidental or instructional, and only occasionally encouraging. But never . . . that. She separated from him and schooled herself back into a more ladylike mien.

"When Stirling here offered to pay me to tell his rib the worst words I knew, I thought he was putting me on."

Still shocked at the treasure trove before her, Harriet barely had time to organize her thoughts enough to mutter, "I don't have . . . I have no paper and pen."

Alexander reached into his jacket and produced a pencil and a notebook for her. The gift was small and simple, probably of no significance to him. Harriet couldn't think of a more meaningful gesture in her entire life.

"Come then, let me introduce you to the men, we'll tell you every word we know. Which I'll warn ya, ain't many. And they're all filthy," Captain Williams said, turning and crossing the deck and not waiting for Harriet and Alexander.

Which was just as well, as Harriet was simply staring up at him in wonder.

"Alexander . . . I . . . thank you," she said, her hands brushing across the leather cover of the notebook.

He seemed almost embarrassed by her gratitude. He simply nodded toward the captain, instructing Harriet to follow the man.

She had the strongest urge to kiss him again. Only this time, not on his cheek. A real kiss.

A proper kiss. A kiss that might be able to say what words couldn't.

Words.

Right. Kissing could wait; this meeting would do wonders for the dictionary.

Chapter Twenty-Three

Hours later, Harriet and Alexander wished the men well, crossed back over the unsound plank, and climbed back into the carriage. Harriet flipped through her notebook, which had hardly been sufficient for all she'd wanted to write down. Offhandedly, she let out a breathless: "I can't wait to show this all to Mr. Dawkins."

Alexander frowned. Unavoidable though it was, he didn't relish Mr. Dawkins benefiting from *his* surprise. Something rotten twisted in his gut at the thought of Harriet gleefully spending hours with a man going over all the words for a prostitute or a prick that she'd just learned.

Moreover, here she was thinking of blasted Mr. Dawkins while he was mooning over her and calling her "love." How *had* that slipped out? And then there was the kiss she'd given him on the cheek—was it meant to be as pleasurable as it felt? To tease him all day long? Or was it intended to convey an almost sisterly affection for him? Had she been thinking of her dictionary and Mr. Dawkins when she'd done it? And why was he thinking so hard about a kiss on his cheek anyway? He'd had kisses in far more intimate places that he'd never thought of again.

He was stewing in his thoughts when Harriet looked up at him with her gorgeous sea-glass eyes, which were worryingly damp. Lord, he hoped she wasn't going to cry.

"Thank you ever so much for today. It really was the nicest thing anyone's ever done for me." She seemed so sincerely grateful that Alexander's heart pinched. But then she bit her lip, and any sensibility Alexander had abandoned him.

"Really?" he asked, crossing the carriage to crowd her bench. "Nicer even than this?" And with that he hauled her onto his lap and pulled her into a kiss. Even without his hardness pressing into her, there was no possible way to interpret this as anything other than selfish desire on his part. This wasn't a lesson for her in how to find or give pleasure; this was simply for the sake of having her. Impatient, he reached his hand down to lift her skirts; it had been hours since he'd seen her legs, after all.

"It's midday!" she shrieked, pulling back.

"Yes, well, I'm feeling ever so carriage sick. And only my wife knows the cure," he teased, pulling the curtains closed. Then he reached behind her and flicked open a button on the back of her gown, and followed with his mouth, brushing her hair back and placing kisses along her neck. His other hand reached to the front of her dress, tugging down the bodice to expose her breasts.

Fucking hell.

He dearly hoped the carriage never arrived home.

∽

Harriet woke up in her bed with Alexander snoring softly next to her. Late afternoon sun spilled through the curtains; she couldn't remember a time she'd slept in the middle of the day. Napping was Philippa's answer to almost any problem larger than a broken teacup, but Harriet wasn't ever able to fall asleep. In fact, now that Harriet thought about it, Philippa might have napped over a broken teacup too. "A nap won't clean up the shards, but at least *I'll* feel better," she could imagine her saying. She laughed lightly to herself.

"What's so amusing?" Alexander grumbled next to her. His low, sleepy voice sent shivers of arousal through her that she tried to ignore. She was already in bed naked in the middle of the day; surely that was enough wantonness for one day, Lord help her.

Alexander flipped over onto his back and rested a bare arm—a superbly muscled bare arm—over his eyes, his other hand rubbing up and down his sternum idly.

Harriet watched the movement, rather dazed, as she answered. "I was thinking of my sister. She loves napping. She told me once her goal in life was to be horizontal as often as possible."

Alexander choked out a laugh that turned into a cough and Harriet swatted at his arm. "She didn't mean like that!" Harriet protested. Alexander lifted his arm and quirked an eyebrow at her.

"All right, maybe she did," Harriet allowed, sitting back against the pillows. "But she really was always napping. She could fall asleep at the dining table. She swore she could sleep while riding a horse, although we never had the chance to test it after . . . after Mama died. Papa sold all the horses."

Harriet hadn't meant to bring up her mother, and she tried to trail off at the end of her sentence so as not to encourage more conversation. Alexander snaked his hand under the covers and found hers, giving it a light squeeze. Somehow, Harriet felt the squeeze in her heart instead.

"You miss her?"

"I miss all of my sisters."

"I meant your mother."

Harriet smiled weakly, trying her best not to cry. "I don't remember much about her. I was only six when she died. I remember she smelled good, and she had big hands. Or maybe we just thought they were big because we were so young. But we always teased her about them. Papa was happier then; he wasn't mean. He was never sweet like she was, and he wouldn't play with us. But he was . . . he was better."

Alexander smoothed his thumb over her hand, which was so kind it made Harriet want to cry even more, which was not at all what he'd signed up for when he'd brought her to bed after their excursion.

"Sorry," she said, dashing a tear from her cheek.

Alexander sat up against the headboard then, the covers slipping deliciously down his broad chest. Really, the man was obscene in his beauty. Harriet appraised him unabashedly, which made his lips quirk into a smile. He didn't know what to do with a crying woman, she supposed. Not at all the thing to do in Lord Alexander's bed.

He spread his legs wide and gestured between them, and Harriet glanced around, unsure of what came next. Surely her crying didn't make him . . . aroused? Did he mean for her to . . .

"Come here," he said, lifting her as if it was nothing, and settling her so her back was against him—against that stupidly broad chest.

He pulled the covers back up over the two of them, tucking them under Harriet's armpits, which made her smile. The man had no compunction about nudity—he probably could have strolled quite unaffected through Parliament with no shirt on; Harriet wasn't quite there yet.

Leaning against him felt heavenly, almost as good as what they'd done in bed before falling asleep. In fact, it may have been better. Harriet felt warm and content and—though she wouldn't have liked to admit her enjoyment of the feeling—protected. She was in grave danger of instructing the man to hang the rules—she'd give him her virginity any time he inquired after it. Alexander brushed his hand lightly through her hair, a surprisingly comforting gesture. Was the man truly good at everything?

"What about you?" Harriet ventured softly, her hand tracing absently along his thigh. They didn't normally talk about his family. She knew he had a brother, but only because of the rumors about him, not because he'd mentioned his sibling. "What is your family like?"

Harriet felt Alexander still behind her at the question, and she fought to keep her composure casual, as if he were an easily spooked horse and not a rich, handsome duke's son.

"You've met my father," he said dismissively. Harriet, for all the talking she'd done in her life, knew a little something about listening. Most people, if you gave them long enough, would fill a silence. So she waited, urging herself to breathe normally. She hoped he'd give her this. She was rewarded for her patience when he let out a deep breath and continued.

"My mother, well, she wasn't meant to be a mother. She was much younger than my father, and they hated each other from the beginning. But she gave him an heir—my brother John—and then he couldn't complain so much when she went on her long sojourns across the continent. Then she returned after a suspiciously long trip to Sardinia with a child who had suspiciously black hair and dark eyes," he described wryly, almost bitterly. Harriet tried to think of what to say.

"Is she—" Harriet had no idea how to ask her question delicately.

"Alive? Yes, actually. At least, as of a few years ago. She was in Calais then."

"You don't see her, then?"

"I've only seen her once since she brought me back to England. I was a few years old, and she had run out of money, so she had to return. The duke took one look at us and decided he wouldn't house us both. And a son, even a base-born bastard son, was worth more than a wife who would fuck everyone except him." Harriet knew somehow not to ask more. "So, there I was with a father who loathed me and an infallible older brother, my perfect foil."

"Was he cruel to you?"

"My father?"

"Your brother."

"Much worse. He was marvelous to me. He didn't care for my father's favor, which quickly turned into my father's poorly concealed contempt when he discovered that John liked reading and poetry more than fencing and riding. My father tried to beat it into him for many years. Literally. John just took it. Then he'd quote some poetic verse or a bit of philosophy about suffering to me. I had no idea what the hell he was ever on about." Alexander spoke of his brother with so much love and admiration it made Harriet's heart feel heavy.

"Did your father beat you too?" she asked, sorry that fathers were allowed to be like this.

"Occasionally, though he mostly ignored me. Until John got sick." Alexander said the sentence so matter-of-factly that Harriet could feel how sad it made him.

"Why . . . why don't you see him? *Do* you see him? Is he here in London?" Something about the situation aroused anxiety in her. What had happened to the golden son?

"He's in Chelmsford. The air's supposed to be better there for his lungs. I don't see him as often as I should."

"Why not?" Harriet expected him to offer up something about how busy he was with his business affairs or to bristle at the question.

Instead, he grew quiet for a bit, before speaking again in a near-whisper. "I . . . I have his life."

Harriet waited again, but her trick didn't work this time. "What do you mean by that?"

Alexander groaned, and she could tell her luck had run out. "Let's talk about something else!" he ordered, wending his arms around her waist. He spoke softly into her ear. "I've seduced my way into a gorgeous woman's bed in the middle of the day. How often does that happen to a man?" Alexander brushed the hair off her neck and began once again licking and then nipping at the delicate flesh there. As diversions went, this was quite effective in its simplicity, though Harriet wondered if it was always how he avoided unpleasant conversations. Her worry disappeared quickly as she felt his cock harden and press into her back.

"To you? I imagine quite frequently," she teased, joining him in the abandonment of heavier topics.

"Too true," he said, pulling back from her, as if he were finished.

"Alexander!"

"Although Lord strike me down if I ever fail to take advantage of such circumstances." He returned his attentions to her, for the second—or perhaps third?—time that day. Would she ever get tired of this? Would *he*?

∽

Alexander woke that night with a start, alone in his own bed. He hadn't known how to ask Harriet to join him only to sleep—or why he wanted her to so desperately. He'd been with her all day, all afternoon, and well into the evening and still he felt almost desperate for her company.

All the better, though, that she hadn't been next to him for the nightmare he'd had, his first in years. They started when John was

300

sent away to Eton and then got worse when he was sent away himself to a lesser school three years later. The other boys took a break from teasing him about his parentage to tease him for missing his mother; he refrained from correcting them that it was John he missed. Perhaps telling Harriet about his brother had shaken something loose in him.

He itched to have a groom ready his horse, to flee to John, to see him and apologize for his absence and tell him about Harriet. He wanted to ask his older brother what he should do and why it felt like there *was* something to do, when he'd so carefully arranged from the beginning for this to be a marriage in name only. He and Harriet both knew the rules, and they were—for the most part—following them. If one was incredibly strict about what counted as consummation.

Why then, when she'd sat in his lap, had he felt as if he needed to confess something to her? As if he was pushing a terrible, fetid secret down in his chest that might spill forth at any moment?

He wanted to ask his brother what was happening to him. Why was he planning surprises for his bluestocking wife, why did he no longer think of other women, why did the thought of Harriet's smiles drive him to distraction and the thought of kippers make him laugh?

Alexander could imagine how John would answer. He'd be silent at first, deep in thought, and then he'd walk over to a specific book in his expansive library, open to a dog-eared page, and point to a verse, which to John encapsulated everything about the scenario. Alexander never felt he fully comprehended John's poems, even with great effort. But there was a certain comfort in the assurance that someone out there had felt this way before. At least, he assumed that's what John's aim was in sharing them.

But riding an hour outside of London at midnight to wake a sick man was foolish for all kinds of reasons. And for what? To brag to the man that he was living the life meant for him? To tell him that he had everything John could possibly hope for—and would never get—and that still he was mucking it up anyway? That he had a lovely wife, whose company he enjoyed above anyone else's, who wanted simply to be friends?

And it was entirely his fault. Because he didn't intend to be a real husband. He couldn't.

It was not as if he could actually love her one day. Could he? No. Certainly not for the rest of his life. He hadn't ever loved someone. Not like that. Even for a short amount of time.

Harriet had not expressed any desire for theirs to be a love match, he reminded himself. *He* was the one following her around like a lovesick fool, forcing her to move into his home, setting books aside for her, hanging on her every word, telling her about his mother, wanting her in his bed *to sleep next to.*

Oh, bloody hell.

He had feelings for her.

Which was incredibly inconvenient. Thank God above he hadn't gone to John. John would have seen right through him before Alexander even crossed the threshold.

What was he meant to do?

Alexander knew only three ways to rid oneself of unwanted feelings. It was too late for fencing, and he was intelligent enough to know that fucking another woman would simply complicate the matter. Which left him with one choice: White's.

Brandy-soaking his emotions was not going as well as he'd hoped. He was on his second glass and the knot of panic in his chest hadn't eased. How was he going to keep this truth from Harriet for the rest of their lives? How was he to ensure his affliction didn't worsen? Had she offered again for him to have her, he would have taken her, and then surely he'd be done for. He realized there was going to be no satiation. The idea of having her once and being inoculated was delusional.

What if he told her? He could say . . . What could he say? And what would she say in return? "You poor idiot," probably. If she were wise, she'd leave him now. She'd surely stop asking for help with her quim and suggesting friendship and giving him kisses on his cheek.

Hell. Hell. Hell.

Alexander was so engrossed in his line of thought that he hardly noticed a footman walking toward him, his brother John trailing close behind. He'd never seen John at White's. He hadn't seen John in London in years.

"Just the man I was trying to avoid!" Alexander let out, lifting his glass in a sardonic cheer.

"You've done exceedingly well at it so far," John volleyed back.

"You aren't supposed to be here."

"I paid my dues like all the other dissipated silk-stockings tarrying about."

"You pay dues here?"

"As of tonight," John explained off-handedly. He reached down and took the half-full glass of brandy Alexander had been sipping and handed it to the footman, then waved the man off without ordering anything.

"I meant you ought not to be in town. Not good for the lungs."

"Much harsher on the mind, I've found," John quipped, looking around the club with undisguised revulsion.

"You're meant to order a drink, West," Alexander explained, using the nickname of his brother's courtesy title.

"You've had quite enough for the both of us for the conversation I intend to have." Alexander huffed out a laugh. He wasn't *that* deep in his cups. Unfortunately.

"Oh dear, am I in trouble?"

"Routinely," John said, crossing one leg over the other and clasping his hands in his lap. "Now, when were you going to tell me about your marriage?"

He knew?

"Are you still corresponding with Presley? I told you to quit checking up on me! And I told *him* to stop being a snitch."

"They do deliver papers to my house, you know. And correspondence too, when people can be bothered to write," John said pointedly.

"I have been remiss as of late. I am sorry." He was. Truly, he was, but at the moment he was more concerned. "Why are you here in the middle of the night, West?"

"I tried your house first. I was informed I'd find you here." There was a tone of disappointment in John's voice, which made no sense. He'd been like this for ages now, and John had never once scolded him. "It's Mother. I received a letter."

Alexander's heart started pounding. Their mother did not write. Not even to ask for money. The last time he'd seen her, in Paris, she'd expressed confusion as to why Alexander had sought her out. When he'd suggested that they might form some type of amiable rapport, if not familial feelings for one another, she had summarily declined. *I'm not certain I see the point now*, she had said.

"Burn it. There's nothing that letter could possibly contain that could be of any significance. She has had no interest in us, and I will gladly return the favor."

"She's dead."

Alexander stilled for a moment.

"How did . . . ?"

"A solicitor from France wrote to me; she left me a small inheritance," John explained, softly, carefully. As if Alexander might fly into a fit of rage. "I believe it was written up before you were born."

"I wouldn't take a penny from her," Alexander spat. "I'm hardly hurt."

"I didn't come to boast about my wealth, you paper-skull. I came to warn you; Father can remarry now, which is a weapon he will wield. Indeed, I believe his target is one of your new wife's sisters. A widow with land he wants. That you wanted too."

"How on earth do you know such things?"

"People have a peculiar habit of underestimating invalids," John said, testily. "I don't just laze around waiting to die like you and Father prefer to imagine."

"I don't prefer that at all!" Alexander shot back, trying to keep his voice below a shout. "I want you hale and hearty and happy! I want you well!"

"Too bad. I'm not going to be. Ever. You need to accept that."

"I do." Alexander knew John was not going to magically become well again. He may not be as smart as John, but he understood basic truths.

"Then why do you behave as if you aren't the heir?"

"Because I'm not. You are. You could very well be the next duke. Since you've been in Chelmsford, you've improved greatly. Who can say when Father will die? I myself have thought of hushing him many times, if you catch my meaning. I can't be alone in that."

John tilted his head and narrowed his gaze, as if assessing Alexander. It was damned uncomfortable to be scrutinized by a man who saw so much. Alexander wanted to fidget, to shift in his seat.

"You do know, don't you, that even if I were healthy, even if I became the duke tomorrow, I don't"—John was almost never at a loss for words—"I won't marry, Alexander. I won't have children. I never wanted to, even before I was sick. I'm not that sort."

"No man *wants* to marry," Alexander jested, trying to move away from the direction of this conversation. "That's the very thing that makes it so appealing for women."

"Alexander, I'm only going to say this once. Mostly because repeating myself to you has never worked. I know you think rather highly of yourself, but I am not envious of you. I'd like more time of course. I regret not going to Paris before I was sick, and there are so many books left to read. But I'm not sitting around my house wishing I were in a lady's bed, I can promise you that. I am more thrilled to be free of the duty of siring heirs than I can say." John laughed softly, although Alexander didn't know why. "You cannot steal my fate, even if you wanted to—you don't dress half as well as I do. Besides, have you read none of the Greek myths? I want you to marry. And to have children I can dote on for seven minutes at a time on quarter days and birthdays. I'm *glad* it's your fate, not mine. You will make a much better duke than anyone actually related to that man ever could." With that, John patted his hand and stood. "Keep an eye on our father. And give your wife my fondest regards. I can hardly wait to meet the woman who's done this to you."

He left before Alexander could ask what *this* was.

Chapter Twenty-Four

HARRIET HAD NEVER SLEPT BETTER. BEING TAKEN CARE OF BY Alexander was doing wonders for her sleep. She sat up in bed, with no plans for the day until her afternoon appointment with Mr. Dawkins. As Harriet wound the day before through her mind, her maid, Anne, entered with a tray holding drinking chocolate and, bizarrely, a letter.

Not the sort to leave important matters for later, Harriet ripped into the letter immediately. It was short and to the point.

I do not mean to bother your newlywed life, but you told me to write. He's back.

C

Harriet rang for Anne to return, asked for a brougham to be readied, and dressed in haste. The entire ride to her father's house tied her stomach in knots. Caroline would not have written if things were not so bad.

Blast. Blast. Blast.

∽

The feelings didn't wear off in the morning. Or at least, the brandy didn't. It roiled in his stomach, robbing his mouth of moisture and pounding through his head. He dressed anyway, albeit later than usual, and headed downstairs, skipping breakfast even though it might have helped his condition. The mere idea of food was sickening. He needed to see Lady Ellerton and warn her about his father.

Upon arrival at Philippa's house, Alexander was shown to a lavishly appointed sitting room. The woman's tastes—assuming it was her doing—were sumptuous indeed. Had she run through all her late husband's money buying trinkets for this room?

Philippa came in shortly after his arrival, as his eyes were still darting from the thick drapes to the lush potted plants. He stood to greet her and she began talking immediately. A Bancroft sister trait, perhaps.

"I find I'm a bit immoderate when it comes to furnishings."

"It's a well-appointed room, I only wondered that your style was so different from Harriet's. Or perhaps, her taste runs similarly, and I have not given her enough opportunity."

"Oh no, I can't imagine Harriet would care to design a room. Even if she did, I don't think it would resemble this one very much at all." Philippa rang for tea and sat across from Alexander. She had the kind of natural social grace that made one feel entirely at ease, even when one called on her unexpectedly.

"I do apologize for—" Alexander couldn't even finish his sentence before she waved him off.

"None of that. We're family. Tell me why you are here. Is Harriet all right?" Alexander's brows pinched in concern.

"Why wouldn't she be?"

"Well, you are here calling on me in the morning. It seemed rather grave."

"What I came here to tell you doesn't concern Harriet. It's you I came for." Philippa's gaze narrowed. "Not in that sense. I'm not—I'm sorry—I don't—" Oh dear, he was bungling this. Philippa let out a sharp crack of laughter, one similar to Harriet's in her unguarded moments.

"Nothing could have persuaded me further of your feelings for my sister than you stumbling over an apology about not wanting to bed me. How precious." Philippa's cheeks were stuck in a smile. "You have feelings for her," Philippa pronounced. There was no question in her words whatsoever. Alexander didn't think he needed to agree. Philippa had made up her mind, and he had the sense that when Philippa made up her mind, it was usually the final word on matters.

"I came here because of my father. I received word that my mother has died." Alexander hurried through the sentence, hoping that would convey his lack of emotion about the matter. "That means that my father is free to remarry, finally. I have no doubt he intends to. And he knows you're in a precarious position with your late husband's estate reverting to the crown. A position that he can make even more dire with the sway he has. Your estate, and particularly some of the lands held up north, are valuable. I myself wanted to purchase them before you discovered what they held."

"What do they hold?" Philippa asked, betraying nothing more than a casual interest in the topic.

"Graphite. You're sitting on a massive graphite deposit, and with England producing the only pure graphite sticks in the world, you stand to make quite a bit of money. Germany is using graphite powders, but they cannot come close to what we have." Philippa raised an eyebrow. "That's unimportant. What is important is that my father will do anything—try anything—to get his hands on your estate. Marrying you is the easiest way in, I believe, and his path is clear now."

Philippa was quiet for a moment.

"I appreciate your coming here, Lord Stirling. It is a credit to you that you are so concerned about my well-being. I do not want to insult your father . . ."

"Do not hold your tongue on my account." Philippa laughed lightly.

"I assure you that nothing on this earth, not gold or diamonds or the promise of eternal life, could induce me to marry him. I would happily become destitute instead."

"I assure you, I will not allow that to happen. I will speak to my man of business and inform him that he is to help you should you need anything at all. Money or otherwise. I'll leave his card for you."

Philippa looked close to tears. "Thank you ever so much. I don't know what to say." He should have done this earlier. Had he known she needed it so, he would have. The money meant nothing to him. He took his leave then and bid her farewell. That taken care of, he could return home to Harriet. And if that infernal Mr. Dawkins wasn't there, perhaps he could persuade her to spend the day in bed with him again.

∽

Harriet steeled herself for her father's ire the entire carriage ride there. She expected him to be shouting and throwing dishes—a favorite pastime of his, and a rather expensive one. She did not expect him to be unconscious, slumped over his desk, drunk as a wheelbarrow.

Caroline and Frances, used to his ways, seemed relatively unbothered.

"You told us to write you, so I did," Caroline said apologetically.

"He hasn't been so bad. He's spent most of the time in his study drinking," Frances added, although the bruise forming across her cheek belied her words.

"I'm glad you wrote."

"What do you intend to do?" Frances asked, blunt as ever. Harriet didn't know yet, but she had some time to think before he sobered.

"Wait, I suppose." And she did. Harriet sat at the kitchen table, twirling her wedding ring in nervousness, trying to think of something. She still hadn't spoken to Mr. Dawkins about when she might receive her portion of the dictionary. *Oh blast!* Mr. Dawkins was meant to call on her today to work on the dictionary. Oh well, Presley would send him on his way with apologies.

While they waited, Harriet prepared a small meal for them, as respite from Caroline's horrid cooking.

A few hours later, a loud *thump* came from the study, followed by a few curses. Harriet's heart raced, but she tried not to betray that to her sisters. It was always easiest to perform bravery in front of younger siblings.

"Go to your room. I'll speak to him," Harriet said. Her tone brooked no argument. They scampered upstairs quickly, and Harriet stood, smoothing her skirt. She knocked on the door of his study and swallowed her nerves.

"What the hell could you want?!" her father roared from within. That was close enough to an invitation. She opened the door and entered carefully.

"I'm here to—"

"You're back," he spat, not standing from his desk.

"I am."

"Have you got more coin from your duke to give me? We've got quite an arrangement going, don't we? Next time, I'll come directly to your house," he slurred.

"There will not be a next time," Harriet bluffed. She knew her father would run out of money over and over again for as long as he lived. And as long as her sisters remained unmarried, they would be at risk. But she had one card left to play. "I am going to give you something. Something that should last you quite a while. If I give it to you, you are not to return. You must leave, and leave for good. Do you understand?"

"You cannot drive me out of my own home," he laughed.

"I cannot. But I can offer to take over expenses." Harriet had no idea if her dictionary could cover the cost of the house. That issue could be solved later. She could ask Alexander for an allowance if she needed to, perhaps. Either way, her father didn't need to know that. "And I can offer you this."

She slid the ring off her finger, reluctantly. She loved the ring. Loved having something from Alexander, even if she couldn't have him. Had her sisters been in any less danger, Harriet could not have parted with it.

Her father watched with rheumy, unfocused eyes as she handed it over.

"This should last you many, many months if you sell it to the right person. It's not Rundell Bridge and Rundell, but the stones are real."

He looked down at the ring, inspecting his loot. Harriet hated seeing it in his hands. She itched to snatch it back. Instead, she closed her eyes and breathed deeply.

"You will leave now. You have a half hour." Her father's nostrils flared, as if he was set to argue. "If you do not, I will call my husband here and he will handle you as he sees fit. I do not suspect it will be pleasant."

Her father sniffed, closed his fist around the ring, and dropped it into his pocket. He took a bracing swill of gin—he'd either found the hidden bottles or, more likely, replaced them—and stood, unsteady on his feet.

He swayed and lurched around the room, gathering his things without word. When he got close to the door, and therefore Harriet, he leaned in close, his hot breath fanning over her. "You are the worst sort of woman—an evil one. You mean to force me out of my house yet again, but one day your pretty little husband will force you from yours. I've heard talk at the clubs. He'll be through with you soon. And then your threats will mean nothing. I will return here, and you—you'll have nowhere to go." He laughed at the idea, which made him wobble a bit.

Harriet remained rooted to the spot until he made it out the front door. As soon as he did, she ran over and bolted it behind him, not that it meant anything. Then she turned and sagged against the door.

She was still leaning against it a few minutes later when it started to pound. Her heart rate matched the banging. He was back.

"I know you're in there, Father!" came a voice from the other side. Philippa! *Philippa?* Harriet rushed to open the door and came face to face with her sister, each of them equally surprised to see the other.

"He's gone," Harriet explained.

"Oh," Philippa answered, following her in. Philippa was looking around curiously. She hadn't been back in ages. Maybe since before she'd gotten married. She'd hated the house, and with good reason. Harriet yelled up the stairs for Caroline and Frances and then set off for the kitchen. Philippa followed her.

"Why did he leave?"

"I gave him my ring," Harriet said, not wanting it to be true.

"Harriet! You didn't have to do that!"

"I had nothing else!"

"Lord Stirling would have given you money! Hell, he offered *me* money this morning!"

"He did?"

"Yes, he told me I could go to his man of business at any time should I need anything." Harriet felt like someone had hit her over the head with an andiron.

"You saw him this morning?"

"Yes, he came to my house—you didn't know?" Before Harriet could answer, or indeed ask any more questions about her husband's whereabouts, Caroline and Frances descended upon them. And then any hope of communication was over.

Harriet sat in a daze. Why had Alexander gone to her sister to offer her money? He'd never offered Harriet an allowance of any kind. In faith, she hadn't needed one. What did she have to buy? Surely, Philippa was not doing anything untoward with him. Philippa would never. But was he attempting it? She had *told* him that the estate was reverting to the crown, that Philippa could not agree to a sale. If he wasn't there about land, what was he there for? There were only so many things a man could want from Philippa's company. Harriet tried to assure herself there was some other reason Alexander had been there.

What an embarrassment. Harriet had offered herself to him, and not only had he turned her down, he hadn't brought it back up again. Instead, he was out there begging for favors from her sister. Her sisters' chatter grew quiet as they noticed her lack of participation in the conversation.

"Harriet?" Caroline asked. "Are you quite all right?"

Harriet shook off the expression on her face and put a smile back on. She was not going to tell her sisters about her humiliating ordeal. Philippa knew enough and was clearly trying to prevent her from feeling pain. Which was kind of her, although she wasn't sure why Philippa hadn't simply lied about the entire encounter.

Harriet nodded and stood. "I must be off. I'm supposed to be meeting with Mr. Dawkins. Father should be gone for a while, but I'll send more money to you soon. I'll return shortly."

She dreaded returning home and confronting Alexander about money. And Philippa.

Alexander returned home from Philippa's, still not feeling altogether himself. Upon his arrival, he asked after Harriet, and when he was informed she was out, he decided to skip breakfast. If there was no hope of her presence in the breakfast room, then there was no point in trying to choke down rashers.

He ought to go to Hawthorne and see what they could do to help Philippa. He'd been quite neglectful of all his business as of late. Perhaps a day of work would do him good.

Alexander stopped short in the entryway at the most unwelcome sight of Mr. Dawkins. Something about the man made him angry, and it wasn't just his wife's admiration.

"Mr. Dawkins," Alexander greeted him, not meaning for it to come out so gruffly. The man sketched a bow, the manner of which also bothered Alexander, as everything Mr. Dawkins did always would.

"Lord Alexander."

"Are you here to meet Lady Alexander then?" Alexander asked, gathering his hat and gloves.

"I am."

"I'm afraid she's out."

"Yes, your butler informed me. I was just leaving."

"You've been here quite often these past weeks."

"The dictionary is almost finished; it's due to the publisher at the end of the week."

"How is it coming along?" Alexander was not one to make idle conversation with men, and he couldn't be sure why it was that he was doing so now, other than the thought of Harriet spending her days with the man. And the way she had saved the man's letters. And the portrait of him.

"Well enough. Lady Alexander has been quite a help to me. Very organized, although I find ladies usually are, aren't they? Well suited for this kind of work." Mr. Dawkins laughed a little uncomfortably, clearly trying to figure out where the conversation was going.

"She's quite wonderful, indeed," Alexander replied, not trying all that hard to keep the threat out of his voice. The man hadn't done anything—at least that he knew of.

"She has proven quite capable of carrying out all the little tasks I give her," Mr. Dawkins agreed, offhandedly.

"I would like to remind you that she is my wife, Mr. Dawkins. I won't have you trying anything untoward under my roof. Or under any roof." Then he added, rather stupidly, "Or out of doors!" Alexander couldn't help himself. "I don't care that you two thought to marry. She is mine."

To Alexander's eternal shock, Mr. Dawkins let out a sharp bark of laughter. "Marry? You believe I thought to marry her?!" Something twisted inside Alexander, embarrassment perhaps, or defensiveness.

"Don't do me the discredit of acting as if I'm stupid. I have seen how many letters were sent between the two of you; she told me of your intention to become engaged after the Dunleys' ball. I'm not so worried as to disallow her to be in your company, but I will command you to watch yourself around my wife." *There.* Alexander felt rather satisfied with himself.

"Letters? Between us?" Mr. Dawkins let out that annoyingly sharp laugh again and his face settled into something snider. Something altogether more natural for the man. "Evidently, you don't know your wife as well as you think. Throughout our *heft* of correspondence," he mocked, "I thought her a man."

At Alexander's stunned silence, he continued: "I assure you, your wife holds no interest for me romantically and never would have—even if I had known her identity." The idiotic man laughed again, as if Harriet were beneath him. "I'm sorry she operated under such delusion for any amount of time, though I hardly encouraged it."

Though he was glad to hear it, that most manifestly *was* insulting. His hands curled into fists and some part of him longed desperately to push the man against the stone entryway wall and pummel him mercilessly. Who *wouldn't* want to marry Harriet? This man was supposed to be intelligent?

"You utter blackguard," Alexander growled, trying his best not to hit the man. Only, Dawkins clearly mistook his meaning.

"Honest. I didn't even answer her missives at first, but she started sending so many words that I worried she'd write her own dictionary if I didn't answer. Of course, come to find out, not only is she a woman, but a peer. I assumed it would be worse to insult a lady than to allow her to believe she's helping. If you'd rather, my lord, I'm happier than I can say to sever ties with your wife."

The miscreant. Alexander couldn't stop himself then. He grabbed the miserable caitiff by the lapels and hauled him up against the entryway wall. He pulled his fist back only for Presley to choose that precise moment to clear his throat. Alexander had the sneaking suspicion his butler had been watching the entire exchange.

"My lord? Your appointment," Presley intoned. Alexander reluctantly released Dawkins.

"Get out of my house. Do not come back," Alexander spat at him. "You will not contact my wife again. If you so much as think of her in passing, I will ruin you. And I will make that ruination an exceedingly *painful* process."

"Very well, Lord Alexander. I wish you luck informing your wife of this." The man donned his hat and strolled out of the house so carelessly that Alexander had to fight the urge to run after him and punch him squarely in the jaw for being so cavalier about losing Harriet's help.

Alexander slammed the door behind the awful man and tried to get his breathing to return to normal. He pinched the bridge of his nose in frustration. "Don't say anything, Presley. Don't you dare."

"I was only going to thank you. I've wanted to strike that milksop for weeks. Never liked him. He never listened to her when she spoke." Alexander let out a resigned, overwhelmed huff of laughter, and Presley wandered off again, humming to himself.

Alexander was left in the front hall, lost. He couldn't remember what he'd been setting off to do before Mr. Dawkins waylaid him. All he could think was that the man was correct about one thing: Harriet wouldn't be happy.

Chapter Twenty-Five

HARRIET RETURNED HOME. SHE NEEDED TO WRITE A MISSIVE TO MR. Dawkins and apologize for today. And then she needed to make a plan. She couldn't think of Alexander, and his visit to Philippa, or the fact that he'd granted her free use of his wealth, when he hadn't offered the same to Harriet. He hadn't offered anything, really. He'd only asked her to come live with him for a short while for the sake of appearances. Well, they'd appeared. The *ton* had seen them. Not as much as he may have liked, although that was why one didn't marry a wallflower, wasn't it?

After penning her note, she rang for Anne and then went to her wardrobe. She'd stay with her sisters for a while, at least until she felt certain her father was gone and she had the money from the dictionary. She began packing a few simple day dresses into her valise; she would hardly need the ball gowns Alexander had ordered for her. The door opened behind her as she continued packing.

"The letter on the desk—will you post it, please?"

"Are you packing?"

Alexander? Harriet whipped around to see him leaning against the doorframe. He looked haggard and tired. As if he'd been awake all night. Lord knew where he'd been before he arrived at Philippa's that morning. For all she knew he was tired because he'd been out all night tupping the entire cast of *Le Nozze di Figaro*.

"I am. My—" Alexander had picked up her letter addressed to Mr. Dawkins and was examining it with an odd expression. "My sisters need me."

"I've told you, I will provide them with anything they might require."

Harriet tilted her head. "I think you may have the wrong sister," she bit out, wishing she didn't sound as waspish as she knew she did. He'd made the offer to *Philippa*. Could he really not keep them apart?

His eyes shot to her. "What does that mean?"

"Never mind." She continued dumping items into her valise, only now she was paying little attention to what they were.

"Harriet, I'm afraid I have to admit something to you." He set down the letter and came closer to her. She stiffened and scolded her stomach for fluttering with excitement.

"I believe I already know, my lord." He flinched at the honorific, which wasn't as gratifying as Harriet had hoped. "You need not confess."

"Harriet, I'm so sorry. I didn't mean to hurt you. I couldn't help myself—I—"

"I believe you," she said, cutting him off. The odd part was: She did. She believed he was sorry. Still, she couldn't continue to live like this. Watching him bed other women, offering nothing to her.

It might make her a ninny and a fool, and it unquestionably would make her lonely, but she wanted to be chosen. "I simply think we've run our course. We wanted to keep up appearances for the sake of reputation, and we have. If there is any other event you've a need for me to attend, please write to me at my father's and I will happily acquiesce. I see no reason for us to live as husband and wife. I believe we'd both be happier returning to our old lives."

"Do you really think that?" He looked hurt, which surprised her, although she knew he was used to having every single woman available to him. Perhaps he'd convinced himself that he had won her over, that she had fallen under his spell. He was correct, in a way; she *had* offered herself to him. He probably had assumed he had longer to avail himself. It was good she was leaving now.

"Yes," Harriet said, sadly. "I'm sure it's a relief to hear."

Alexander scrubbed a hand over his face, not looking at all relieved. He glanced down at the letter once more. "I know you don't want to hear any more on the topic, so I'll only say this, Harriet: that man—Mr. Dawkins—he doesn't care for you."

What an odd thing to say!

"And you do?" she challenged, her packing arrested. For a moment it looked like he might admit that he did, in some way, care for her.

"Did you want me to?" Harriet wanted to let out a deep and loud and *long* guttural yell at the man. *Now?* Now he was asking her if he ought to have tried to care for her? "I seem to remember you repeating many times that you did not want to marry me."

"And *I* seem to remember that you had to be kidnapped to offer for me. Not to worry, my lord. I am not holding out for some display of affection or promise of fidelity. We both know how constancy chafes you."

"We agreed—Harriet . . . I didn't . . . you know. I never wanted—"

"I know you didn't," Harriet said, rather sadly. She did not need to hear him explain yet again that he didn't want a wife. They both were silent for a moment, until an odd emotion crossed his face. Harriet followed his gaze down to her hands.

"Your ring" was all he said.

"Oh, yes," Harriet gulped. She hadn't for a second considered he might notice or care. Although it was, she supposed, his property. She winced before admitting, "I sold it."

It was close to the truth and she didn't relish admitting she'd given it to her father. The fewer people entangled with the Earl of Tidewell the better.

"It wasn't to your tastes?"

Harriet lied then. The first lie she'd ever told him. If you didn't count all the times she'd neglected to tell him precisely how much she wanted him to kiss her. Those were lies of omission. "Not exactly. And I suppose I'll no longer be needing it." Harriet felt tears stinging the back of her eyes. "I can . . . I can repay you." If she had to figure out how to recoup the cost of the ring, she could. She hoped.

"Don't trouble yourself over it. You can keep the money from the sale," he bit out, sounding almost . . . angry. Presumably he thought her careless with his funds. Or thieving. Still, she thought it a bit crass that *he* seemed so upset about a symbol of their vows.

Harriet finally tore her gaze from her hand to meet his eyes, and the emotion there almost knocked her over. He seemed to be as much in pain as she was, although she couldn't muddle through why. *She'd* had to watch him with other women. *She'd* agreed they wouldn't have children. *She'd* moved in for the sake of appearances and fallen in love with him.

Oh, bloody hell.

She needed to leave before she did something idiotic like telling him as much. She threw more things into her valise at random and clasped it, then turned to see Alexander still waiting. Waiting for . . . something. His jaw clenched and unclenched in apparent frustration. She didn't want to think about his emotions; she was too exhausted.

"If you permit me, I'll take a carriage to my father's and then have the driver return here." He looked like he was about to say something; instead, he nodded and turned out of the room. Only, a moment later he returned.

"Since you'll be going, I thought I might tell you something," he offered. Harriet looked around the room to avoid eye contact with him, which she felt certain would lead to tears on her part. "If you'd like to make yourself come, Giuliana recommended you being on top of something and rubbing your . . . self on it. A pillow. A blanket. The arm of a chair, even"—he cleared his throat uncomfortably—"is what she said."

"I—Thank you," Harriet choked out. It dawned on her then that this confirmed her assumption that he'd still been seeing his mistress. It also dawned on her that he was telling her this because he was no longer going to be helping her with that matter. "Give her my best," Harriet added, meaning it.

Neither of them seemed to know what to do with that. A disconcerting silence settled between them. He nodded and left, blessedly.

Harriet walked out of the house on the verge of tears. She was entirely unsure of what she'd packed in her valise. She wouldn't be surprised to find a bar of soap and a single slipper when she opened it. The rest could be sent for later. At least she didn't have to suffer Alexander's company any longer, and with it the reminders of all the women whose company he preferred.

Harriet was halfway to her father's house when she remembered she hadn't posted the letter to Mr. Dawkins apologizing for missing their appointment today. She tapped on the roof of the vehicle and requested the driver take her to Bond Street. She was going to need the dictionary income now more than ever. She could have—should have—asked Alexander for an allowance before she left. Only, he'd offered money to Philippa, so perhaps that would be enough. Or would he revoke that offer now that she'd gone? *Bugger*.

Once again, Harriet was shown into the sitting room to wait. She didn't relish having to move their work to the lodging house, but needs must. When Mr. Dawkins appeared this time, he looked even more disoriented than the first time she'd been here. Peculiar.

"Mr. Dawkins, good day. I am here because—"

"Because of your husband, I presume?" *What does he know? How?*

"It's only that, well . . . I thought we might work here now."

"Lady Alexander, I have no intention of working with you anywhere in this city. In this country. I have no intention of you being anywhere near my dictionary. Your husband made clear, in no uncertain terms, that you and I are not to work together."

Harriet couldn't breathe. There was not enough air in all of England.

"He did?" she eked out. Mr. Dawkins responded with a harsh, bitter laugh.

"He hasn't told you, then? Yes, I met your husband, and he was quite unequivocal. I am not to utilize your services anymore. Which is quite all right, as the book was sent to the publisher two weeks ago."

"Two weeks ago? But we've been . . . I've been working with you." Harriet felt the world spinning off its axis.

"On the second edition, yes. Should the book sell well enough, the publisher would like to release an updated version next year. That is what you have been assisting me with. Although, no longer."

"Please, Mr. Dawkins, I need this dictionary. I am no longer in residence with my husband, thus his opinion no longer signifies. Please, I beg you. I need the money. I know it's unseemly to speak of such things, but it's all I have."

"To what money do you refer?" Harriet's eyebrows snapped together in confusion.

The only practice Harriet had talking about money was with the bill collectors who came to her father's residence. She'd always been the one who owed someone, never the one asking to be paid. She swallowed and reminded herself of Caroline and Frances. "The money you promised me for the first dictionary. Twenty-five percent of the profits is what we agreed upon. The same ought to hold true for the second edition as well, if I have been contributing to it, which I will gladly continue. I vow there will be no interference from my husband."

Mr. Dawkins looked down at her unkindly. As if she were a puddle he was trying not to step in. "Even if I had promised such a sum—which I assure you I did not—I entered into that arrangement with the understanding I was exchanging letters with a man. You are not a man, therefore the agreement is null. And *after* I discovered you were a woman, you were married and thus unable to enter into a contract with me of any kind. I have no agreement with you. I have never had any agreement with you."

"No, no, that's not—that's not . . ."

"Lady Alexander, I have no further business here, so I must ask you to leave. I hardly wish to spend my day comforting someone else's sniveling wife."

Harriet's eyes grew wide with shock at the insult. He turned and absented the room, leaving her feeling entirely . . . Well, in fact she felt almost nothing at all. She felt as if someone had scooped out all her insides with a big soup spoon. In lieu of anything better to do or say, she quietly whispered, "I wasn't sniveling, you clodpate."

She left the lodging house in a daze and continued to her father's. Her entire life had collapsed, and it had only taken a single day. By the time Alexander's carriage reached her father's house, Harriet *was* sniveling. She hadn't cried so hard in ages, and she did her best to stop before her sisters saw her. To halt the tears, Harriet bit her tongue and dug her fingernails into her palms, trying to breathe only through her nose for the last few minutes of the ride.

Her plan worked, her tears gone when she entered her father's house, valise in hand. Unfortunately, that lasted only about seven seconds before Caroline took one look at her and asked, "Oh, Harriet, what has happened?" At which point, Harriet fell to pieces.

Chapter Twenty-Six

WHAT COULD ONE SAY WHEN CONFRONTED WITH ONE'S WIFE packing up and leaving? "Please, don't go! I beg you?" Or perhaps: "I'm a fool. Stay with me always." Alexander had somehow done far worse than either of those admittedly pathetic options: He'd instructed Harriet how to reach her peak without him. The only thing she'd ever needed from him. The only use he'd had in her life. And he'd given it away.

For the second time in his life, a woman had left him for good. He had no intention of going after her and begging for affection as he had with his mother.

He needed to move on. Forward movement was the only cure.

Throwing himself into business hadn't worked as well as he'd planned. A meeting with Lord Holden had proven particularly unproductive, as the man had spent a good half the time congratulating him on marrying such an agreeable woman, praising him for settling down, and threatening him not to "muck things up" with Harriet. He refrained from telling the man that he already had.

Alexander was miserable, wretched. His insides were made of either fire and glass or the cold damp of a remote cave, shifting back and forth between the two constantly. He was irritable at best and irate more often. Nothing tasted good, sounded good, felt good. He was livid and bored and couldn't see an end to these emotions, which frustrated him even more.

He went for a bracing swim in Peerless Pool. He rode his favorite mare across Hyde Park to their mutual exhaustion. He drank at White's. He fenced at Angelo's School of Arms, which ended with him yelling at an opponent for not trying hard enough to kill him, really kill him. He attended three balls in one week—rather a lot, even for him—simply for the sake of doing something that wasn't prowling around his house.

It didn't do a damned thing for him, not the dancing or the many beautiful ladies.

Nothing did.

∽

Harriet had spent a week at her father's house, and the pain had not abated. She'd expected to be quite over the man. As it happened, she thought of him between every breath and twice as often when she was falling asleep. One thing that she was morbidly thankful for was that she was too upset for lustful thoughts to visit her at those hours.

She'd taken to sleeping in her father's study, not because she liked the room, but so her crying didn't keep Caroline and Frances awake. After a week, which Harriet filled mostly with sulking and sniffling, Philippa showed up at the door, far earlier than she normally paid a call.

"Philippa, good morning, is something wrong?" Despite her insistence that tea tasted better at someone else's house, Philippa did not visit unless something was dire.

"Apparently," Philippa grumbled. Mornings were not her preferred time of day unless they were carried over from the previous night. She pushed her way inside the house and into the kitchen.

"What is it?" Harriet asked as she dutifully started making tea.

"Frances wrote to me about your weeping."

"I have hardly been weeping!"

"Why are you still here, Harriet?" Philippa asked, pointedly. Then she leveled Harriet with the type of stare only an older sister can give.

"My marriage has . . . reached its natural limits. We will maintain appearances in public, should we encounter one another, for the sake of Caroline and Frances's reputations. I can chaperone Caro this season. Well, maybe not the entire season. But on occasion. Perhaps my proximity to the duke might even help. Crass as that is to say. Regardless, I thought it best to stay here instead of . . . with Lord Alexander."

"Oh dear, bring that tea to me in the sitting room. I'm far too vertical for this conversation."

Harriet smiled and did as she was told. Minutes later, Philippa was recumbent upon the stiff divan that they never used and Harriet brought in her tea. No cream, no sugar for her, which did not seem to match Philippa's ordinary inclination toward extravagance.

Philippa sat to take a bracing swig of tea and then leaned back. "All right, now tell me the truth about why you've left his home. If you lie to me, I shall know it." That was probably true.

Harriet cleared her throat.

"You're going to think I'm a fool."

"I vow I shan't."

"I haven't actually . . . shared his bed. Not entirely. Not—We haven't precisely . . ." Philippa sat halfway up. "*Consummated* our vows." Harriet winced.

"Harriet Eugenia Bancroft."

"Do you truly not know my middle name?" Philippa waved the question off without answer.

"I daresay I must break my vow. I now think you're the silliest girl I've ever heard of, being here and not in that man's bed."

"Philippa!"

"There's no denying his . . . positive attributes." Harriet did not want to be reminded of this.

"I'm aware of how enticing you two find one another." Philippa made a face—the same face Harriet made when tasting kippers. "Oh, don't look at me like that! I know how much he'd like to *meet* with you."

"What moonshine!" Philippa shouted, startling Harriet. "Here I thought you were the cleverest of my sisters."

"He's made it clear that he wanted to return to his old life." Harriet kept her eyes trained away from Philippa at the embarrassing admission. "His life *before* me. His life of carousing and philandering."

"He said that? I haven't seen him so much as glance at another woman since he's been with you."

Harriet felt her entire body flush with heat.

"He *just* confirmed to me that he's been seeing his mistress, Philippa, and he would gladly take you to bed if you were amenable."

"Harriet!" Philippa was sitting straight up now. "You can't think—"

"Oh, I know you would never entertain such a thing. I didn't mean to accuse you."

"Harriet, what precisely do you think has happened between your husband and me?"

"He's . . . well . . . hasn't he . . . visited you? And settled some money on you? And of course, he danced with you at the Henderson ball. I must admit we have an agreement that he can . . . do those things. Which is why we haven't consummated our vows. Only, we have done . . . *some* things. I'm sure you can imagine. But I fear I had started to want more from him. More than he's capable of offering. So, yes, I know about his attempts with you. I know he wants to be with other women; I only wish it weren't my sister."

Philippa let out a sharp, ironic crack of laughter.

"Your dear husband has *less than* zero interest in me." Harriet opened her mouth to contradict this, but Philippa held up a finger. "Perhaps he did at one point, but I assure you he's lost any desire he once had for me. If I had to hazard a guess, that change happened in Lady Dunley's library. Since he's married you, he has only spoken to me of two things. One: his father, who is going after my estate quite aggressively. His Grace is convinced I'm being left some property up north. Alexander has been warning me away from the man—not that I could be induced to marry that gout-ridden old goat. That's what he spoke to me about at the ball. And last week when he paid me a call."

"What was the other thing?" Harriet asked, meekly, rather embarrassed by her assumptions.

"Other thing? Oh. You. You are the only other topic of conversation the man cares to entertain. In faith, I can't believe the man *allowed* you to decamp here. He seemed the sort who would have delighted in the intimacy of you running him over with a carriage."

Harriet stood then and started pacing back and forth across the small room. She wasn't quite sure what to think.

"You're making me positively nauseous," Philippa groaned after a few minutes.

"Nauseated," Harriet corrected, reflexively. "*I* am nauseous as I am causing you to feel nausea."

"Stop saying that word in any form and sit down," Philippa pleaded. Harriet sat, mostly because the pacing wasn't fixing anything.

"I am glad to hear that you two aren't . . . That he didn't attempt anything with you. Although, you are only one woman. He still has a mistress. And any number of opera singers and actresses and *other* widows that he might visit. I could have lived with that—I planned to live with that, with sharing him—only, I'm afraid I've grown to care for him, which is quite inconvenient as he won't ever love me."

"Whyever not?" Philippa asked, and the immediate affront in her voice warmed Harriet more than almost anything ever had. As if it were so natural to love her, so easy and obvious. As if their father hadn't spent a lifetime trying to convince them otherwise.

"Perhaps because I'm an unfashionably plump wallflower who'd rather be writing a dictionary than training to be a future duchess," Harriet offered.

"I don't think being duchess-like is high up on Lord Stirling's list of requirements."

"I feel certain I don't possess any of the other qualities on the list either," Harriet said, irritably.

"I find myself fascinated to discover what else is on this list."

"There isn't really a list! I'm only saying I'm not the sort of woman he wants."

"I'm aware. I hardly think it's a prerequisite of his love that you be able to put your leg behind your head."

"Is . . . is that . . . beneficial somehow? To lovemaking? How would that even increase pleasure?"

"Never mind the leg thing! That is not what he is looking for in love."

- "He isn't looking for love at all! He doesn't want love! In fact, he *promised* me he wouldn't love me. And I promised to be all right with that! So that's what I'm doing, Philippa!"

"I think it's because he doesn't know how."

"Hogwash. Who doesn't know how to love?"

"Someone whose father is cruel and whose mother is gone."

"What a coincidence. Mine are too," Harriet said, knowing she was being petulant.

"Yes, but you have *us*," Philippa reminded her.

"What does that signify?"

"You already know how to love someone. And how to be loved. Does he?"

"I don't—"

"If you insist you don't love him, I will scream at you."

"I—" Harriet chewed her lip, trying to think of something else to say. "I don't know if he has anyone, actually. Well, there's his brother."

"The sick one? Are they close?"

"You know, I haven't a clue. All I know is he reads poetry and lives outside of London, for the air. I don't think Alexander sees him much."

"That seems lonely. They both seem lonely." Philippa said it off-handedly, but the thought made Harriet's heart seize.

"I'm not sure he's ever suffered from a lack of company," she said, trying to match Philippa's flippant tone.

"Harriet," Philippa said then, her tone oddly serious, "I'm only telling you this because you seem in rather a desperate state. But as someone who also enjoys the presence of the opposite sex, I can tell you—and I'll deny it should you ever remind me of this moment—it isn't without loneliness. In fact, it's usually because of it."

Philippa stood then and brushed off her skirt, as if the moment of vulnerability had sullied her. Without another word, she left the house. And Harriet was left wondering: *Was* Alexander lonely?

Chapter Twenty-Seven

"Alexander," Giuliana purred upon his arrival at her door, "you're back."

"Do you practice that voice or is it natural?" he asked, unsure why this was his first question. But then it made her laugh one of her throaty laughs and he was glad to have said it. The sound dampened the anger he'd been desperately trying to hold on to. He collapsed into a chair, back yet again because of his troubles with Harriet.

"It's more or less effortless now," she answered, ringing a bell and asking for a bottle of champagne. "But that's not what you came here to discuss."

"Champagne?"

"We're toasting to the end of my service." She grinned at him.

"The end . . . of . . . what? You're leaving?"

"Aren't you letting me go?" she asked, without a hint of confusion. Her questions were always posed in a way that made the other person certain *they* had misunderstood.

"No. One would think you were looking forward to the end of our arrangement with how often you bring it up."

"Oh dear, it seems I've once again overestimated the male intellect. Regardless, champagne is good for you every now and then, and I like to err on the side of now." As if Giuliana commanded the world—and Alexander wasn't sure she *didn't*—a footman arrived then with the bottle and poured them each a glass.

"I'm certainly not going to let you go now. She's . . . Harriet . . . she left." Alexander decided Giuliana was correct about the champagne. He drained his glass and refilled it immediately.

"So, would you like me to tell you what an idiot you're being now, or shall we wait until we're done fucking and you're even more tormented?"

"I'm not—You're quite brazen, aren't you?"

"I'm positive it's why you chose me." She winked at him and took a delicate sip of champagne, acting as if she were somehow three steps ahead of him.

She likely was. Any feeling Alexander had of understanding women had vanished right about the time he'd entered the Dunleys' library.

"You're . . . you're being . . ."

"Brilliant? Correct? Wise?"

"Exasperating."

Giuliana nodded at his champagne glass. "Drink up and then tell me what you did," she said with an irritated sigh, as if Alexander were the one not performing his usual role in this scene.

"Why do you presume it was *me*?"

"I never take a man's side if I can help it."

"She sold her wedding ring, took the money, and moved to her father's house. I suppose that's all the use she had for me. Better that she left now, before we formed an attachment or something. It wasn't a true marriage anyway, so it's no bother really. A little irksome that my father was correct about her being a fortune hunter, though."

At Giuliana's harsh, narrowed gaze, Alexander shifted in his seat and amended his answer: "*Fine. Fine!* I *may* have gotten her removed from the dictionary project that she'd been working on, which she'd made me promise she could continue after we married. She also insinuated I've been visiting other women, which I have not." Giuliana sent another shriveling look his way. "Not in the way she's imagining! I haven't been with anyone since she . . . since we . . . since her."

"Hmmm" was all Giuliana said, pinching her lips together.

"Oh god, just say what you want to say, don't make me beg for it."

"Oh, but you begging is one of my most favorite sights."

"Giuliana," he growled, and something within him seared with pain. It was the tone he usually used with Harriet. *She* was the one whose name he wanted to say like that, whom he wanted driving him mad.

"All right, I'll tell you what I think."

"Your generosity does you credit."

"I don't think anyone with half a brain could meet Lady Alexander and assume she's a fortune hunter; I don't even think *you* believe that. Though anyone willing to wed and bed you deserves some coin tossed their way. You're a dolt for getting her removed from her project, not that I have any idea what that is, but one can assume you were doltish. Furthermore, regardless of your actions, the fact of the matter is that you *asked* to be allowed to still meet with other women, did you not?" The question was apparently rhetorical, as she didn't pause for him to answer. "Most importantly, I think you'd have to have *less* than half a brain not to realize you're madly in love with the woman."

"I am not!" Alexander roared, so used to denying the fact to himself that it didn't even occur to him to answer otherwise. Of course, it also didn't occur to him to examine *why* he'd had to deny the fact to himself so often.

"Oh, certainly. It's quite often a man who *isn't in love* visits his mistress for the first time after his wedding to ask her how to help his wife come. Even more often he stops seeing his mistress altogether, even though he's arranged otherwise with his wife. This sort of thing is always happening."

"Your sarcasm is not appreciated."

"Your obtuseness isn't either."

"It doesn't signify. Even if I *did* love her—which I don't"—Alexander could hear the lack of conviction in his own voice—"she's gone, and I have still ruined her dictionary. And even if she did forgive me and return, and we went back to how things were before, I'm sure to break her heart when I end up wanting someone else."

"*Do* you want someone else? *Have* you wanted anyone else?"

"No! That's not the point!" Then, realizing whom he was with, he added, "I don't mean to offend."

"Alexander, I've been here tupping Richard and taking hours-long baths in a house you bought for me, wearing only jewels you gifted me. I shed nary a tear. But let me ask you this: What if you do someday want the company of another woman? Are you not strong enough to turn that down? If not for the sanctity of marriage, then for the sake of Harriet?"

Alexander felt suddenly, embarrassedly, like crying, and he couldn't say why. He waited for the lump in his throat to disappear and then he decided, perhaps influenced by the champagne or the friendship, to say what he really wanted to say: "What if I make a mess of it?"

Giuliana laughed, which was both comforting and insulting in equal measure. "Oh, Alexander, of course you will! You already have!"

Alexander thought about that for a moment, scrubbed his hand down his face, and let out a simple "Fuck."

"Perhaps you might try actually demonstrating to your wife that you're in love with her?"

"Again, I am not."

"Yes, you've thoroughly convinced me," she deadpanned.

"Regardless, *she* is not."

"Did she tell you that?" Giuliana volleyed, sarcastically.

"No," Alexander gritted out. On the one hand, the visit was proving quite painful; on the other, Alexander was certain he deserved to feel wretched, and he did no matter where he was or what company he kept, so he didn't think leaving was in order.

He tried to win out and stay silent longer, hoping Giuliana would find another avenue of conversation. He gave in instead; truthfully, some sick part of him liked talking about Harriet, even if it was about why she didn't love him.

"I'm not sure what she'd"—Alexander cleared his throat and then continued—"love about me. I won't give her children, I took away her dictionary, she thinks I'm trying to seduce her sister apparently. On top of that, I'm a bastard."

"Alexander, I refuse to sit here and catalog things she might love about you. You don't pay me nearly enough for that. However, might I suggest that people fall in love not for *reasons*, but because that's simply what we do? We fall in love with improbable people at inconvenient times. Although falling for one's spouse is rather quaint of you two." Giuliana paused then, and after a thoughtful moment continued. "All right, I said I wouldn't do it, but, Alexander, you do happen to be quite handsome and rich and skillful at swiving. And pretending you're unaware of those truths is dashed annoying of you."

"Is that enough, you think?" Alexander asked, pathetically.

"God, no."

Alexander threw his hands in the air. "So, what do I offer her? Other than my money and my cock?"

"Let's not disregard such things outright."

Alexander *almost* smiled at that.

"She said you were my friend." Giuliana tilted her head in confusion at the non sequitur. "Harriet," he tried again, feeling a little shy. "She insisted that you were my friend. And, well, she was right. Thank you."

Giuliana scooted closer to him and nudged him with her shoulder.

"That's not going to make me list any more of your good attributes," she said, her tone not at all matching her teasing words. He could hear the emotion in her voice. She leaned up and gave him a kiss on the cheek. "You're a rather good friend to have, Alexander. And not just because you're a duke's legal son. As your friend, I must tell you that you're being a horse's arse and that you simply *must* fix things with this woman. If only so that you aren't such insufferable company."

"Yes, you've said as much. But how?"

"Oh, I don't know, give her everything she's ever wanted and then beg on your knees for forgiveness? That would work for me."

"I don't know what she wants."

"Think *hard*."

Chapter Twenty-Eight

Upon her arrival at a shockingly well-kept manor an hour's ride outside of the city, Harriet was shown into a small sitting room to wait. Her hands twisted in her lap at the prospect of meeting Alexander's brother. Of being here. She didn't know who else resided in the home, if anyone. Would he be willing to meet her? Was he mobile? What was she to call him? Certainly, *John* was *far* too intimate, even for someone who was nearly one's brother, but Harriet had no idea of the man's title. She had hastily looked up his name in Debrett's the night before, only to find out that her father's copy was woefully out of date. Harriet wasn't even certain precisely what her aim was in visiting him. She hoped she wasn't making a mistake coming here. But she wanted to understand.

Finding the residence wasn't as difficult as she'd expected; she simply wrote to Hawthorne and inquired about the house and hoped he wouldn't inform Alexander that she was asking after it. Or, if he did, that Alexander would assume, based on his low opinion of her, that she was simply taking stock of properties that one day might become hers.

Her worry, as it turned out, was for naught. The door to the sitting room opened with a flourish and a lean and impeccably dressed man waltzed in. He smiled broadly and bowed deeply to her, which was not what propriety asked for. One had the immediate impression, although Harriet couldn't say precisely why, of him being uncommonly striking and rather unusual. Like the peacock she'd seen once as a child at the Royal Menagerie. That trip was one of the last memories she had of her mother. The caged animals made her cry for some reason. Philippa had rolled her eyes and called her a ninny, and their mother had nearly cried herself at the trouble she'd gone to taking her three young daughters out of the house. It always made Harriet's chest ache to think of that day.

Something about this man made her chest ache too. Perhaps it was that he was dressed too warmly for the balmy weather. Or that he seemed to be exerting a bit too much effort to simply be standing. Or the sadness in his eyes, which nevertheless crinkled with kindness when they met hers.

"You must be Lady Alexander. I am ever so happy to make your acquaintance." He dropped a soft kiss on her hand and gestured for her to sit. "Tea will arrive shortly."

Harriet relaxed immediately in his presence, which was just as warm as his dress. "I—I don't know your title. I beg your pardon—"

"Oh, I hardly have any use of it, but the Marquess of Weston. Although I beg of you, call me West if you must, and John if you will. You are my sister now, after all."

Tea arrived and John poured her a cup and sat back on the divan, legs crossed, eyes still twinkling.

"Alexander couldn't make it, he is—"

"A bit of an arse? Yes. Well, we won't hold that against him, will we? No one else does!" Harriet's eyes widened at his candor. She sipped her tea, not sure what to say, and blessedly, he continued. "He doesn't like coming here."

"Why not?" Harriet asked; then, realizing her words, she demurred. "I apologize for being so forward. Please ignore the question."

"I refuse! It's the best one I've gotten in ages! Alexander . . ." He became contemplative, cautious. She could tell when someone shared an affinity or care for words. It endeared her even further to him, which she hadn't thought possible. "Alexander is afraid."

"Of you?" she asked, rather incredulous. "Not to imply that you aren't fearsome," she teased, hoping her familiarity matched his, made him feel as he had made her feel. His easy smile was her reward.

"Of himself."

Harriet dearly wished he would elaborate, but it seemed incredibly démodé to ask someone to explain your husband to you.

"I'm sure he wishes to come. He's rather busy," she supplied weakly, knowing it was a poor excuse and one John would see through easily. But in the case he wanted to make use of it, she offered it.

"You don't have to protect me from him. I know he loves me, in his own bullheaded, emotionally impoverished way."

"He is rather unlearned in that department, isn't he? In fact, it's part of why I came."

"Oh dear, are you here to do his bidding? Is there a painting he wants off my walls? A piece of Mother's jewelry he's under the impression I have? He has loads more money than I do, so it can't be that." He was jesting, but Harriet thought she heard a hint of pain in his words, as if some of the sadness in his eyes had seeped into them.

"He doesn't know I'm here."

"How chic of you! A wife off on her own—is there anything more enticing? You've come to the wrong place for trouble, I fear. It's quite dull here."

"Yes, I had . . . I'd noticed." John laughed.

"It's rather glaring, isn't it? I'm locked away in this tower to wait out my days," he said, waving a biscuit around with one hand. "Don't make a face of horror at me. It suits me quite fine most of the time. I've got a fully stocked library and a divine chef. What more could a man want?"

"Company," Harriet answered, a little too pointedly.

"Yes, well, my father gave up on me as soon as I got sick. Mighty inconvenient when your heir won't outlive you, eh? Rather defeats the entire purpose of my existence."

"And Alexander?" John's mouth twitched and Harriet could tell he was weighing how honest to be with her, so she interrupted his considerations. "I should tell you, I guess, that Alexander and I—we didn't have a . . . real . . . marriage. We don't. That is . . . we were caught in a library."

"Which one?"

"Lady Dunley's, I'm afraid."

"How dreadful, no wonder you took to kissing him. Terrible collection."

"Actually, quite embarrassingly, *nothing* happened," Harriet confessed, reluctantly.

"What a black mark on his character! I shan't forgive him." Harriet laughed then, enjoying herself for the first time in ages.

"Lady Neddlesby caught us. Or thought she did."

"And so he offered for you?" John said, a little skeptically.

"I rather forced his hand."

"Good girl," John affirmed, pouring them each another cup of tea.

"He made clear from the beginning that he couldn't offer me his . . . sole affection. Or any affection really."

"The blighter!"

"Oh, no, it was quite all right with me. I'm rather . . ."

"Too good for him?" Harriet laughed at their unspoken but shared understanding that while she probably *was* too good for Alexander, no one else would see it that way. At least no one outside of this room or her family.

"I suppose I came here . . . to understand him better. It sounds awful silly when said out loud. Especially after telling you our marriage is false. Truly, it's more pathetic than that because, well, we had quite a confrontation. But I find myself . . ."

"Loving him despite his poor behavior? Happens to the best of us."

"I'm afraid so," she said, admitting for the first time to herself or anyone that she might just love Alexander.

"I can't fault you. Well, I can but 'twouldn't do anyone any good. He's rather lovable even when he isn't likable."

"It's odd, isn't it, that everyone else sees it the other way around?" She shared then with John a deep look, an intimacy that she had heretofore only shared with her sisters.

"Then I will tell you—and only because you've admitted you love him, and I adore finding someone whose flaws line up so preternaturally with mine—all my secrets about him."

"I'm all ears."

"To start with why Alexander is the way he is, you must look where one always must look: the parents. My father is—"

"I've met the man."

"Brilliant; that saves us time. Rather embarrassing of me to be actually related to him. I was always envious that Alexander wasn't."

"Truly?"

"Oh, I wouldn't be so callous as to wish to be a bastard. He was quite mistreated by my father until I became . . . unviable. But knowing you have that man's blood in you in some way is rather like knowing the wine you drank with dinner was poisoned. Our mother was . . . well, she was stunning. No one had better taste—her only blind spot was men, I'm afraid. She did her duty and married my father, and they made each other miserable until she provided an heir, and then she left. Then, as you know, she returned with a spare. And then she left again."

"Have you seen her?"

"No, but I wrote to her. And her solicitor wrote back on her behalf on occasion. Once or twice I'd receive a letter asking for money, which I sent. I didn't mind who she turned out to be as much as Alexander did."

"How do you mean?"

"She was so young when she had me, and trapped in a marriage with an older man. I felt for her, even if I didn't understand her. I saw my parents together—it was hell. Alexander never really did. I felt happy when she left the first time; it meant a more peaceful house. And then she returned and gave me the best present I've ever received: Alexander. I was happy when she left the second time too. Only Alexander was miserable. He was three or four and he howled through the night. Eventually, I let him into my bed just to shut him up long enough to sleep." Harriet felt a bit like weeping at the thought of it.

"He said he saw her once."

"He did. He discovered she was in Calais, so he took a boat over. I warned him not to. That he might not like what he found. But by then, he was a young buck who'd charmed every single woman he'd ever encountered and he never imagined she might be immune to him."

"What did she do?"

"Nothing, rather. I think they were alike in so many ways. They knew how to get what they wanted from the opposite sex when it came to romance, but neither of them knew how to go any deeper. In truth, she never had any use for a son, but one never outgrows their need for a mother. Privately, I've always held the opinion that that visit is what shipwrecked him. The first abandonment stung, but at least he could imagine that she was avoiding our father. This time, it was *him*."

Harriet didn't know what to say to any of this. It was precisely the sort of information she'd been seeking and yet it hurt like the devil to hear. Furthermore, she wasn't sure what she was supposed to do about it now that she had it. Feel badly for him? Understand why he couldn't love her?

"Pardon my saying this, but how did you get to be so . . ."

"So much more astute than the rest of my family? I dare say it's a surprise *I'm* not the by-blow!" He laughed at himself, which resulted in an unfortunate coughing fit. John looked immediately older after it happened, subdued almost at the reminder of his frailty. Harriet's first inclination was to pretend as if nothing had happened, assuming that was the kindest way forward. But something stopped her.

"You really must stop sneaking so much brandy into your tea," she teased when the coughing stopped. She saw no spirits of any kind in the room, but she hoped dearly the jest read as such.

The joy on his face afterward was worth the risk. "You know, you're the first person to tease me about it. My disease." He said it happily, his eyes twinkling again.

"I am?"

"Well, I don't have much company, as you so *kindly* pointed out." She opened her mouth to defend herself and he waved her off with a grin. "But you know, everyone else is either counting down the days till I die—my father—or in total denial—my brother."

"He doesn't believe you to be ill?"

"He believes it on some level, otherwise he wouldn't insist on keeping me here. But he doesn't accept it. He stays away because, and perhaps this is the poet in me—I am prone to being quite generous in my assessments of my brother—because he thinks he's stolen my life. And he's ashamed."

"Stolen your—"

"He thinks he's living out the life I was supposed to have. Hence why he didn't want to marry and why once he *did*, he's been careful to avoid me."

"But that's—"

"Absurd? Yes. But such is grief," John said with a shrug, his tone belying the casualness of the gesture.

"Oh, John, that's awful."

"Most things are," he said again, growing more flippant the more emotional he became.

"I'm ever so sorry."

"You're the true victim of his lug-headedness too. He promised me once, when I was very ill and he was a blubbering mess at my bedside—he assumed, as many do, that because I was sick, I couldn't hear—that he'd never take my place. That he'd never marry, or have children, that the line would die with him if I never got to be duke. Which of course has the dual benefit of enraging our father. God only knows how Alexander thought he could manage to escape matrimony, handsome devil that he is."

"He—*That?* That's his reason for—?"

"My father had no use for him, and so Alexander spent his childhood making sure that *he* had no need for my father. He left me to be the heir, and avoided anything to do with the dukedom. Then I got sick, and my father had no use for *me*, and that *really* bothered Alexander, so he took up every vice he could find and made every investment he could afford to distance himself from the family name. Which actually worked rather well for everyone, not the least the women of London. And now neither of them knows what to do with me, so they keep me here."

"*Keep* you here?"

"My father to wait out my death, and Alexander to magically prevent it with fresh air. Of course, I'm an adult, I could leave any time, I suppose. But to do what?"

"What do you want to do?" The question rose out of Harriet's throat on instinct alone, and she was quite grateful for it. She'd learned too much about Alexander to feel anything other than indignant, both toward him and on his behalf. But before she could sort out her feelings on the matter of her husband, she wanted to do something for John. "I hope I'm not overstepping. I often do. But it seems a shame to me that you've been stuck here when you aren't dying."

"I *am* dying, I assure you. Just not quite so quickly as my family thinks."

"Well, what is it that you'd like to do? I'm availing myself of anything you might want. I have little power and not as much money as you might think at my disposal, but I'm rather good at talking people into agreeing with me."

"Perfect, I've got plenty of money and I'm still a duke's son. Together we might just be unstoppable."

"Yes, now we only need to think of what it is we want."

"I know what I want. I want to go to a ball."

"You haven't been?" Harriet asked, shocked.

"I got sick when I was nineteen, and before then I hadn't seen any reason to go. I wasn't interested in finding a wife."

"Not even a public ball?"

"Don't sound so horrified."

"Oh no, if anything, I'm envious. I find balls dreadful. Of course, you must go and experience that for yourself. I know just the one."

"You'll have to teach me how to dance. It's been *years* since I've learned. I'm sure they don't even dance the minuet anymore."

"Oh dear, I fear . . . well . . ."

"Bad news about the minuet, then?"

"It's only . . . I'm glad you say you have a lot of money. We're going to need it for the dance instructor."

Chapter Twenty-Nine

ALEXANDER STOOD INSIDE TEMPLE OF THE MUSES LATER THAT WEEK, watching people bustle in and out, their arms full of books. He'd been in a few times before, but now he came almost daily, waiting for the stacks to arrive. And now it was here: Harriet's dictionary. Not that any purchaser might know she was behind it. No, he'd ruined that for her. Or Mr. Dawkins had. They both had.

Without a single mention of Harriet—he'd checked—here sat a proud, fat stack of *Dictionary of Modern Cant and Vulgarities*. Privately, he thought the book might have done better with a different title. Although the word *vulgarities* might entice.

For over an hour, he'd been hovering over the books, almost daring anyone to purchase a copy. After the fourth bookseller of the day asked him if they could help him find what he was looking for, Alexander decided a more leonine method of circling and stalking might work better. So he pretended to browse all the thousands of offerings the bookshop boasted, hardly processing a single title as he kept watch over his paper flock.

He was drawing his fingers along a section of German plays, feigning interest as best as possible—but not so much as to get another shop attendant over to offer their services—when he glanced up.

The wind was knocked out of his chest. There, frowning over the stack of *Vulgarities*, was Harriet. In a drab, unadorned day dress, with her chestnut hair in a simple bun. Had he not known her, he likely would have overlooked her. But he *did* know her. He knew precisely how her hair felt running through his hands; he knew the soft skin and lush curves hidden under that plain dress. He knew how she tasted. He knew her sighs and her smiles and her laughs. Not that she was going to be sharing any of those with him again. Certainly not now. Indeed, she looked . . . defeated. Worn down.

The observation gutted him.

She reached out tentatively to flip open the cover of a copy of the dictionary, then swung the cover almost shut, then fanned it open again. It was as if she couldn't decide whether she ought to look inside or not. He hoped she wouldn't; he knew well what she'd find: a lack of herself.

Harriet thumbed quickly through the pages, and then, having arrived at her destination, dragged her pointer finger down a page three quarters of the way, scanning for something. Her finger stopped and she tapped it once, as if to demonstrate to someone what she'd discovered. Alexander rushed over to be that someone.

He sidled up next to her, nervously, and then cleared his throat. "My lady," he said simply, to announce his presence without startling her.

Startling her should not have been his concern, as it turned out. Harriet remained still as a pillar of salt. She didn't betray any surprise at him being next to her; she didn't even look up. Only her finger moved, to tap at the word again.

"Just wanted to see . . . if . . ."

"If he included your words?"

"I suppose. Although they aren't *my* words. I know that." He could hear the lump of sadness in her voice.

"It *is* your work, however." She shrugged, to imply she wasn't bothered. Or shouldn't be.

"It was foolish to expect otherwise," she said, though he knew she didn't really believe that.

"No, Harriet, it wasn't." He reached a hand out, tempted for some reason to meet hers on the page. He pulled back instead. Watching her was painful enough, and he was certain his touch would not be appreciated.

After a moment, she pulled herself together and glanced up at him. Her eyes were wet with tears. Her nose adorably red—and yes, not to worry, he chastised himself immediately for finding it adorable. She'd clearly been crying. Though he'd hardly missed an opportunity for self-recrimination in the past few weeks, the evidence of the pain he'd caused made him feel impossibly worse.

"What are you doing here?" she asked, and clearly they were to be done talking about the dictionary. She looked over to where he'd been standing before and his foolish heart told him this was a good sign—she'd known of his presence and she hadn't fled!

"Looking for . . . Lessing," he lied, glancing over at the shelf he'd been perusing for a name.

"You speak German?"

"No. But perhaps this might improve it." He was a fool, and more to the point, he was ruining their interaction with his bizarre desperation for conversation.

"I won't keep you." The shortness of the sentence saddened him.

"*I* approached *you*."

Harriet looked back up at him, as if surprised he was still there. "Oh yes, you did, didn't you?" She returned her eyes to the book. "Still, you needn't dwell on my account." The stiffness and formality of her tone felt like someone had taken a sharp sword and sliced through his sternum. It was the pain that gave him the push he needed to say what he did next.

"I'm sorry, Harriet, for ruining your dictionary." She betrayed no astonishment or appreciation for his contrition. In fact, she appeared indifferent.

"You didn't," she offered, gesturing toward the pile of books.

"I *did*. I am so sorry Harriet. *So* deeply sorry. I should never have confronted Mr. Dawkins. Only he—Well, no. It is all my doing. I won't make an excuse. I regret immensely that you are not in the book."

Harriet didn't say anything for a moment, which was deuced awkward, and he thought he'd better take his leave. As he was about to, she bit her lip. The first sign of Harriet-ness he'd witnessed in this meeting.

"What did you confront him about?" she asked, not looking up from her reading. Surely she knew? Surely that was the reason she had left, no? Had he done something *else*?

"He—" Alexander was about to say *He didn't want to marry you.* Except Alexander hadn't wanted to marry her either. But now . . . now everything was different. Besides, she had no need for that information. "He was beneath you."

She let out a small sigh that he couldn't read, as her gaze was still locked on the dictionary.

"He was never going to credit me," she whispered, the words sticking in her throat. "It wasn't your fault."

"Oh, I assure you, it was." Yet again, he wanted to reach for her. He felt overcome with the desire to gather her in his arms. To comfort her.

"Not entirely," she said, finally looking up at him. His heart lurched, and he attempted to remain as still as possible, as if movement might break the moment. "He'd already submitted the manuscript to the publisher a while back. That's why it's out so soon. My name wasn't ever going to be mentioned, though my contributions are . . . present." Alexander's thoughts were too fixed on her eyes to work out precisely what this information meant for him. For her. For *them*. He knew he shouldn't let his gaze wander down to her lips—he had been good about it for the duration of this meeting. But then the remaining threads of his discipline snapped, and he looked. A grave mistake indeed.

Though, had he not been watching her mouth form the words, he would have missed what she said entirely.

"By chance, do you plan to attend the Courtenays' ball next Thursday?"

He had not considered going even for a second. "Yes, I do," he said, hoping he didn't sound overeager but knowing he had.

"Perhaps I will see you there," she said simply.

Alexander swallowed, unsure what to say or do next. He tried to stop his heart from leaping giddily around his chest. She hadn't asked to attend *with* him, only if he was attending. But he would see her again. In eight days' time.

Perhaps.

He had arrangements to make. He might not be able to make matters with the dictionary right—he dearly regretted not killing Mr. Dawkins when he had the chance—but he could do *something*.

He excused himself, bowing his head.

Once outside, he glanced back into the window and saw her still there, still flipping through the dictionary, so solitary, so subdued. Despite her suggestion to the contrary, this *was* his fault. He may not have taken the dictionary from her, but he certainly had not given her enough to stay with him. He needed to fix this. He needed to do as Giuliana instructed.

Alexander crossed the street, found a tea shop, and waited until he saw her leave the store—two books in hand, neither the dictionary—and then he settled his bill and headed back to the bookstore.

Both the draw of and the problem with Temple of the Muses was that books could not be purchased on credit. One had to pay upfront. It kept the claims of being "the cheapest bookstore in the world" true enough for Londoners. It also meant that with the money he had on him, Alexander could only purchase twelve copies of *Dictionary of Modern Cant and Vulgarities*. It was a start. He'd come back for the rest.

And he did.

The next day he came back with his carriage and had a footman cart the rest of the books out for him. It was only on his return home from this frivolous journey that he realized the error in his thinking: the book seller would surely now buy *more*. Alexander sat in his study, surrounded by thirty-seven copies of the stupid book, trying to figure out what to do. He lit a cheroot and hoped it would help. It did not. He drank a brandy, and it did. A little. He was supposed to be offering Harriet everything she wanted. Wasn't that Giuliana's instruction?

He flipped open a copy of the dictionary that was stacked next to him, as if it might give him the answer. And there, on the first page, he found it. At least it was a start.

Harriet left the Temple of the Muses in quite a state. Instead of rushing home, she walked all the way to Philippa's house, at a much faster pace than was necessary or ladylike.

"Philippa," Harriet panted, when she arrived, "do you remember the thing you said about the leg behind the head?"

"Of course."

"I need your help." Philippa grinned, looking as if she'd been waiting her entire life for this moment. She stood, and Harriet held up a hand. "Before you get too delighted. This is more metaphorical."

"Drat. It always is with you."

"I need to become undeniable. You must teach me everything you know."

Philippa's eyes narrowed.

"May I ask why you have suddenly taken interest in matters of seduction? Did you meet someone?" A footman arrived then with tea, and Philippa began pouring.

"I saw Alexander at Temple of the Muses. I asked if he planned to attend the Courtenays' ball, since I intend to bring John. And he said he did."

"That is only a few days away."

"Quite."

"Mr. Monroe has his work quite cut out for him if you're to dance by then."

"Yes, and I need to retrieve one of the ball gowns Alexander had made for me. And perhaps we'd better speak with Clothilde about my hair."

"As I said before, I don't think you need to do anything to make him fall in love with you. Certainly, you don't need to alter your appearance or learn a new skill."

"I don't intend to make him fall in love with me. I intend to spend the evening with him . . . if you understand my meaning. Just once. I thought I could live my life and not know what it was like with him. But I can't. I wonder all the time about how it would be. And I *loathe* not knowing things."

"Yes, I am quite aware."

"When I saw him today it was agony. I expected our separation not to be so painful after a while but seeing him hurt almost as much as not seeing him. Then it occurred to me: I had refrained from consummating our marriage because I suspected it might make me fall in love with him, only I'm already in love with him. So, there's no harm to be done."

Philippa gave her a dubious look, which Harriet ignored. She wasn't going to be talked out of this.

"Philippa, I'm going to ask you something deeply humiliating."

"I am positively aquiver with anticipation."

"Do you know what a *godemiche* is? More importantly, do you know how I might procure one?"

Chapter Thirty

Alexander had dressed for scores of balls in his lifetime. Some with indifference, most with at least a patina of excitement. Tonight, the emotion rioting through his body felt more like terror. He'd jumped off a cliff once into freezing sea waters on a dare from other boys at school. As he'd hit the icy water, he'd felt all the air leave his body in a single, deep *whoosh*. Now, as his valet adjusted his cravat, a similar sensation occurred, only over and over and over again.

And what if she didn't come? She had only said that she'd *perhaps* attend. A megrim might come on or she might have found a particularly good book; she might simply wish to avoid his company.

His valet cleared his throat, suggesting he was finished dressing him, and Alexander gathered himself and headed downstairs to his waiting carriage. He tried to regulate his breathing on the ride to the Courtenays' house, so that he might not sprint like a madman to Harriet's side upon seeing her.

By the time he arrived, he'd calmed himself to some degree. This wasn't the last time he'd ever see her again. At least, he hoped not. He also hoped he had arrived before she had. He didn't want to miss a moment of her. Alexander wasn't one for arriving early at a ball; he'd always found the practice gauche and overeager. Besides, the most interesting people arrived later. The prospect of his wife's company *was* making him gauche and overeager.

The ballroom was sparse when he entered and was subsequently announced. He scanned the room quickly, compulsively for Harriet. When he didn't see any sign of her, he headed to the refreshment table. A stronger drink was tempting, but he had sherry instead. He needed his wits about him for the evening.

The ballroom slowly filled, and Alexander circled gingerly, doing his best to avoid conversation. He felt too tightly wound for either pleasantries or business. Despite choosing sherry, his brain felt muddled with nerves. Normally, he'd be halfway through a dance with a woman or trying to extricate himself from talk of land with a stodgy marquess.

Unfortunately, being on his own made him an easy target for the person he wanted to see least: his father.

"Where is your wife?" the duke asked, disposing with anything that might resemble the beginning of a conversation. "Trouble already?" The satisfaction writ on his father's face turned Alexander's nerves quickly into ire. He tried to force himself to take a breath before responding. Not that his father deserved cordiality, but simply to make certain he didn't give the man more ammunition.

"She's arriving later." Alexander dearly hoped this was true.

"Oh, so the rumors aren't true, then? I heard she was no longer in residence with you." Alexander stiffened and tried to bite back the urge to curse or punch the man.

"I didn't know you followed gossip," Alexander bit out.

"I do when it might embarrass my name."

The man was truly insufferable. Did he want Harriet gone so he could gloat about another man's wife leaving him or did he want her there to keep the reputation of their family intact? Was she an unfit wallflower beneath his notice or the future of the ducal line? It was on the tip of his tongue to ask his father some version of that question when the duke looked up at the staircase where guests were arriving and smirked. "Ahh. She is here, then."

Alexander remained frozen in place. He could not turn and look in case his face betrayed the emotions he felt for Harriet. "I said as much, did I not?" he offered, affecting an air of composure he did not possess.

Suddenly, his father's face changed; his eyebrows snapped together and his cheeks became redder, a feat Alexander wouldn't have thought possible. "Why is she with *him*?"

Alexander desperately wanted to turn around now. Good God, had she brought Mr. Dawkins with her? But his father didn't know the man and he'd hurt Harriet gravely; she wouldn't have brought him to a ball. What man *would* she have brought? Why would she bring a man at all?

He turned slowly, his ears ringing as the majordomo announced Harriet and . . . John? His eyes confirmed the announcement, but his mind was adrift in a sea of confusion. His heart, however, was not confused at all. As soon as he saw her—in a dress so clearly meant to kill him—his heart stopped. Which was so obviously the aim of the modiste. He was surprised that the entire ballroom didn't grind to a halt. Until, looking around, he found that it sort of . . . had.

Every pair of eyes was either trained on Harriet and John or pretending not to be.

∽

They were staring at John, of course. Harriet allowed herself a private moment of enjoyment at the attention, before the stares quickly turned stifling. Perhaps being a nonpareil would be more uncomfortable than she'd imagined. She found herself blushing madly, unsure where to look or go. John, thankfully, offered her his arm and escorted her down the stairs. He leaned over to whisper in her ear, "Excellent dress choice, if I may be so bold." Harriet blushed even deeper, but somehow the nicety, the reminder that she wasn't alone in this, bolstered her enough for her to whisper back.

"On the contrary, it's what's on my arm that's making people envious."

"I may be the source of their attention, but it's not envy. It is curiosity. Half the room likely assumed I had done the polite thing and died a couple years back."

Harriet tried her best not to laugh at the jest, instead letting out a snort as they made their way down the stairs. The warmth she felt for him overwhelmed her, making her suddenly feel quite overcome with sincerity.

"John, I have to tell you—" She stopped herself, struck at his earnest attention to her words. "I'm so glad we're family. Even if—"

She almost sullied the sentiment with a mention of his brother and decided not to say anything further. She shook her head and continued walking. John simply squeezed her hand. To recover, she changed topics. "Shall we get a lemonade?"

"Certainly, and make mine a champagne," he teased.

As they made their way to the refreshment table, Harriet tried her best to keep her heart and steps steady, not to search the room for Alexander. She found it odd not to know if he was present. Odd that her body wasn't somehow *aware* of him. Indeed, she had no earthly idea what her uneven breathing said about his whereabouts. Shouldn't she be able to sense him? Or was that just the fluff of romantic novels?

She drank her lemonade down quickly, glad she hadn't switched to champagne in tandem with John. After setting her glass down on an errant footman's tray, she finally turned back toward the ballroom and its occupants. She watched the dance floor intensely, hoping both to see Alexander *and* not to see him there. Watching him dance with another woman might no longer shock her, but it would hurt.

She didn't see him. Longing and relief in equal measure rushed to fill the emptiness inside her. The music died down and dance partners left, returning to their mothers or their card games as new pairs filled the floor.

"Shall we show them how it's done?" came John's voice from behind her. She nodded and let him lead her to the floor at the start of the next song.

The dance began and Harriet did her best to hide the amount of effort she was putting in to merely keep up. Despite his insistence otherwise, John had been a quick study. He and their dance instructor seemed to speak a language Harriet barely understood. John led with a grace and ease that Harriet could never hope to achieve.

"If only Mr. Monroe could see you now," Harriet said, surprised to see John blush at the mention of him. "You do him great credit."

"You think so?" John asked. Harriet had the impression that it took effort to make the question sound offhanded, that John was keeping his desperation on a tight leash. An idea occurred to her, and she opened her mouth to ask a question, then shut it again, unsure.

"I know so. I'm positive he was elated to have you as a student, especially after the effort it took with me."

"Nonsense. You were a wonderful pupil. He said no other students of his had done so much reading beforehand." The admission confirmed Harriet's suspicion that the two of them had been talking privately. Harriet laughed lightly and let herself be spun away from John. When they rejoined one another, she saw an unfamiliar look on his face.

As the dance ended, John leaned over to her and, looking almost guilty of something, began, "Harriet, you know I—I'm—I don't like . . ." She'd never seen him anything other than fully confident in himself, in his words.

Harriet rested a hand on his arm. "I think *I* might be a lost cause, but you—you should continue your lessons with Mr. Monroe."

They both knew John had no more need for dance lessons than Harriet did reading instruction. His eyes shone with emotion.

They made their way off the dance floor, only to be halted by the imposing figure of the Duke of Belhaven. On his arm was the willowy and silent woman from the Hendersons' ball.

"Who is she?" Harriet whispered quickly to John, hoping to sound casual in her interest.

"Miss Cressida Holmes. Father's mistress. I imagine the poor dear thinks he'll marry her now."

Harriet felt a surge of alarm at the impending company, which she did her best to tamp down. She wasn't sure why she felt worried—the duke wouldn't harm her, not here. In fact, she felt silly thinking he would harm her anywhere. But when she saw his gaze fall disdainfully on John, she knew the true source of her terror. Men like the duke enjoyed inflicting harm with words as well as weapons, with facial expressions as easily as fists. She might be safe enough, but John wasn't.

"What are you doing here?" the duke spat out, as if even speaking to his son was beneath him.

"The same things as everyone else, I presume," John intoned with, Harriet thought, convincing enough casualness. "Dancing, drinking, enjoying the company of another man's wife."

"Shouldn't you be *resting*?" the duke asked, making it clear he would have liked to use the verb *dying*.

"You know, I found myself rather well *rested*. I thought I might take a quick break from *resting*. It was growing rather tiring."

"I don't know why you're insisting on—"

"Being seen in public?"

Harriet felt the tension between the two of them rising as a heat in her sternum. She felt an acute sense of guilt at having exposed John to the presence of his father and to the curiosity and censure of the *ton*. She needed to do something.

"Your Grace, you'll be pleased to know that I've been taking those dance lessons you prescribed. Unhappily, I am not as quick a study as Lord Weston here; he is elegance itself, which I'm sure Miss Holmes will attest to."

The maneuver bordered on crass. To even subtly suggest another couple dance together? She was certain the duke found it unseemly, which hardly fazed Harriet.

However, he wasn't so improper as to contradict her. Instead, he simply nodded and released his mistress's arm, offering her up to his son. Harriet smiled innocently at her father-in-law, waiting for him to understand that he ought to ask her to dance. Which he reluctantly did.

She wasn't looking forward to any time with the man, but a simple quadrille couldn't hurt much, and besides, he was the one who touted the importance of her learning to dance. It was a small price to pay for John's comfort. Or at least to keep his father at bay for a few minutes.

∽

How much more time could one spend in a garden? Alexander hadn't taken in a single rose or lilac or . . . well, he didn't know the names of the other flowers planted there. He wasn't in the garden for greenery anyway. He was there to avoid making a fool of himself. Watching Harriet fuss over his brother at the refreshment table had been survivable, even if—for the first time in his life—he found himself wishing to take his brother's place. Truly, seeing the two people he cared for most in the world together filled him with arrant joy.

No, the problem was once they made it on the dance floor. Harriet didn't dance. Not like that, at least. It had undone him. She was utterly captivating. Had she known what she was doing to him, to the entire crowd, she would have blushed from tip to toe. He wondered who'd had the good fortune and immeasurable patience to teach her. Yet, despite his admiration, he found himself longing for the Harriet who'd danced so poorly at the inn.

The last strains of the song came through the open balcony doors. Alexander waited for another five minutes for good measure and then headed back inside, determined to talk to his wife now that his arousal had sufficiently abated.

Dear God! Was she to dance with every member of his family?

The sight of Harriet in John's arms, their obvious closeness, had been heartwarming. Harriet dancing with his father was, on the contrary, bone-chilling. He couldn't help but feel that the duke's presence was sullying her. Alexander fought the urge to force his way into the dance, to replace his father, consequences be damned.

Instead, he hung along the wall, thinking wryly that their roles had been reversed. He, the wallflower, she, the nonpareil of the dance floor. Next to him, taking advantage of his unusually fixed position, a woman sidled up. Lady Throckmartin. She was married to a much older, gout-riddled man, who was known to be cruel when he bothered to be awake. Their time together last year was enjoyable if infrequent. She was staid and remote, as was fashionable, though he knew her tastes in the bedroom to be quite different from her public mien.

"Lord Alexander," she said, nodding simply and keeping herself facing the same direction.

"Lady Throckmartin," he replied, wishing desperately he'd timed his garden exit more carefully. How long were songs meant to last these days?

"I heard you married while I was away."

"I did," he answered, unfocused on making polite conversation, his eyes trained on Harriet and his father. He couldn't miss the end of the song. There was no telling who might claim Harriet's attention next.

"I would express disappointment, although I can't imagine this would alter your course." She leaned in then, whispering in his ear, "We've never let a spouse get in the way of a good time."

At that moment, Harriet looked across the room. Alexander watched in horror as her eyes slid over to his conversation partner. God, how he wished to see a flash of anger or jealousy. Her eyes didn't even register surprise.

He turned decisively then, and with an unprecedented lack of remorse, replied, "On the contrary, Lady Throckmartin. I find myself wholly uninterested in entertaining the company of anyone who isn't my wife, if you catch my meaning. Please excuse me." He only hoped she'd pass the information around widely.

With that, he strode across the ballroom, hoping to finally get what he'd so fervently wished for this past month: an audience with his wife.

Chapter Thirty-One

M R. M ONROE HAD FORGOTTEN TO TEACH H ARRIET PERHAPS THE most important part of dancing: how one behaved when it was over. She would have allowed instinct to guide her, except instinct would have had her fleeing the duke. Fleeing the ballroom. Fleeing the *ton*. Instead, she kept a smile pasted on her face, curtsied politely to Alexander's father and took his arm when it was offered as he led her off the dance floor.

"Well" was the only word the duke spoke; Harriet couldn't tell how short she'd come up in his estimation. After all the dancing and counting in her head, she was too exhausted to care. As they made their way back to the edges of the ballroom, her eyes landed—where else?—on Alexander, standing against the wall with a gloriously handsome woman idling next to him. Harriet trained her gaze on the floor, which admittedly had a pattern so garish as to be almost diverting. Only when she was hauled to a stop by the duke did she look up again. As if by magic, Alexander appeared in front of her.

Harriet startled and dropped the duke's arm. She wondered off-handedly what had happened to the stunning woman, although the proximity of her even-more-stunning husband wiped the inquiry from her mind.

Alexander looked so handsome in his evening finery that she felt the urge to, in front of his father, in front of the entire ballroom, run her hand down his broad chest. Her fingers twitched with the desire to trace his jaw and her eyes refused to leave his face, even as John and Miss Holmes joined their small party.

Fortunately, she was staring directly at his lips as they formed the words "Can I have this dance?" for she couldn't seem to hear over her heart pounding in her ears. She nodded her assent, her tongue too busy fantasizing about what it would do to Alexander to be useful in speaking. The duke, however, had no problem speaking up.

"A husband dancing with his wife? Highly uncouth. Dance with Miss Holmes instead. Give your wife a reprieve; she's clearly quite unused to so much dancing. Not entirely in shape yet, is she?" Harriet suspected the entire group heard the insult intended in his words, but she was finding the duke extraordinarily easy to ignore in favor of Alexander's deep brown eyes, which were trained only on her.

He didn't look away as he answered his father.

"If you ever attempt to insult my wife again, I will disembowel you and then spend the rest of my life gleefully rotting in Newgate for it. Miss Holmes, I must politely decline; however, while I have your ear, I feel compelled to warn you that my father will not marry you. Ever. He does not view you as a legitimate candidate; your hand doesn't come with any land he might like to possess. I advise you to spend your energies elsewhere. Now then. I intend to dance with Lady Stirling; no one would begrudge me a dance with the most beautiful woman in the room, even if she is my wife. If they do hold my poor manners against me, let's mark it up to my being a base-born bastard, shall we?"

Harriet took his proffered arm and did her best not to look back at the sputtering, cursing duke, who was no doubt even more red-faced than usual. As Alexander led them to the relative safety of the dance floor, her thrill at the display waned. She was now met with the uncomfortable reality of being alone with him. Well, as alone as one could be in a room full of hundreds of people.

As they got into position, the strains of a waltz started to play. Harriet felt certain he'd known which dance he'd asked of her.

He gathered her closely in his arms, the feeling both foreign and familiar. "Based on your distinct lack of blushing, you've taken my compliment to be insincere," he whispered, leaning rather too close even for a waltz. Of course, this achieved his desired effect and Harriet's cheeks heated madly. Her poor tongue was still useless, and Alexander was obviously delighted by having flustered her. "You don't believe me, do you? I am your husband and thus I must insist you defer to me—at least on the topic of your beauty."

The joke—or perhaps it was the feeling of being held by him, or how good he smelled, or how much she missed his smile—tripped her up. She couldn't count one-two-threes in her head when she wanted to simultaneously throttle and lick the man in front of her.

Alexander was a good enough dancer to hide her stumble; he seamlessly guided them back into the rhythm of the dance and blessedly stayed silent long enough for her mind to settle.

"I didn't think you the sort to insist on being husbandly," she said, hoping it wasn't too late to appear unaffected by him.

His face fell, which made her feel only a tiny bit guilty.

"Harriet," he answered rather somberly, still guiding them effortlessly around the floor; Harriet's counting proving to be quite unnecessary to the project. "How many more of your dances have been claimed?"

She had no idea what he was talking about. Certainly he didn't intend for them to dance together again, was he? Or was she so dismal a dancer that he aimed to prevent another man from enduring the experience?

"None," she admitted.

His eyes grew wide in shock. "None?! The combined brains of every man in this room wouldn't fill a cordial glass."

As he grew more impassioned on her behalf—which Harriet felt was sweet, if overdone—he led them deftly off to the side of the dance floor.

"Present company excluded?" she teased from behind him.

"No, in fact, I'm the worst of them." Alexander seemed unusually intense as he drew to a halt behind a potted ficus. A chill ran up her spine at the rather indecorous look in his eyes. She swallowed and tried to school her voice back into practiced nonchalance.

"Would you like a refreshment, my lord?" she asked. Harriet had already had enough lemonade to fill a small pond, but what else was there to do at a ball?

"No."

"Do you . . . want to see the gardens?" She still wasn't certain why their dance had been cut short and why his eyes were still boring into her. "I've heard they're quite tasteless."

"Vulgar beyond imagination," he said, without breaking his stare. Giving up on having discovered why they'd stopped dancing, Harriet finally grew silent. She briefly glanced down at her feet simply to escape his study. It was far too heating to endure for long periods of time; she felt certain she might incinerate.

"Will you come with me?" he asked, not at all clarifying his intentions.

"Are we leaving the ball? I didn't think my dancing was *that* bad," she joked.

That was the jest that finally got Alexander to loosen up a bit. His mask of fierce self-possession slipped.

"Harriet, I'm . . . I need to talk to you. I can't do it here. I can't . . . Frankly, I can barely think in the presence of that dress."

"I could remove it for you?"

Harriet would remember this moment as her greatest triumph. Lord Alexander, behind a potted plant in a crowded ballroom, *blushed.* Had a woman ever made him blush? She felt brazen. Alive. So far from the pathetic creature she'd worried she'd be in his presence.

His lips twitched in the beginning of a smile, but he seemed determined to keep himself together. Rather unfortunate, that. She was enjoying the idea of him coming undone.

"I am sorry to cut your evening short, but would you come with me? Please?"

"Is . . . John all right alone? With your father?"

"If you knew my brother as I do, you'd be far more worried about my father." Harriet chewed her lip, still unsure about abandoning him. "I'll have the footman deliver a message to him on our way out," he promised, eyes pleading.

"All right," Harriet relented, taking the arm he proffered. In truth, leaving the ballroom suited her purposes.

∽

Alexander would have paid an ungodly amount of money for his carriage to have been brought around faster. He understood how these things worked. He wasn't trying to be rude to his driver, but God above, he wanted to get away from this place. To get away from his father. To get her alone. To *go*.

He had approximately 497 things he needed to tell her, and he wasn't certain of the order. In another life, a life he'd been living only a few months ago, he was an expert persuader. The bulk of his fortune had come from knowing exactly what to say to convince someone to agree with him. The person who had negotiated those land deals felt like a distant relative. In fact, the concept of linear thinking felt outside his capabilities.

He'd been disoriented to begin with, but then seeing her in that gown and then her offering to *remove* said gown! Well, it was a wonder he was still standing, let alone forming coherent thoughts. Though in truth, he couldn't quite swear he was doing the latter.

Finally, his carriage was brought around, and he helped her in, glad to touch her hand, a moment as grounding as it was destabilizing. Alexander took the bench across from her for the sake of focus and because he couldn't be certain she wanted him sitting beside her. Though acquiescing to both a dance and a carriage ride suggested some amount of goodwill, did it not?

He was ruminating so much as the vehicle took off that he didn't notice Harriet reaching down to the hem of her skirt. It was only as she started to reveal her delicate ankles that he took notice. Truly, it took a lot for him to tear his eyes away from her breasts most days, but her legs pulled off the stunt easily.

"What are you——?" Alexander asked dumbly as Harriet continued to raise her skirts and then crossed the cramped carriage and settled across his lap, her knees resting on the carriage seat, bracketing his legs.

"With all of your experience, I would have thought you'd understand, my lord," she teased wickedly.

He'd only had one glass of sherry, but surely, he must be drunk. He had no idea what was happening or how he'd gotten to the point where she was talking to him, let alone straddling him. He hadn't even begun to apologize.

He hadn't said a word, but she continued, unabated: "I would have thought you'd know what it meant when a woman sat on your lap. How silly of me. And here I was going to show you what you'd taught me."

Alexander was stunned, which had a lot to do with her fantastic chest being precisely at eye level. Really only a small distance to mouth level. He was just able to get out a few syllables, the only intelligible portion of which was: "What I taught you?"

"Yes. You see, your parting advice proved to be quite . . . useful. I thought I might demonstrate for you." Alexander couldn't remember a single conversation he'd had in his entire life, let alone any advice he'd given her. Although he wasn't stupid enough to pass up any demonstration that Harriet might want to bestow upon him, especially one held on his lap.

She leaned in to kiss the side of his neck and he nearly shot off the seat. The effect was his cock rubbing even more closely against her, which served to drive him madder. He wanted so desperately to rock against her. Of course he wanted to be inside her; however, that desire had been so ubiquitous for so long that at this point, it was simply a quiet background hum to his life. The need to rock against her was more like cannon fire.

Then, suddenly, miraculously, his prayers were answered. *She* was rocking against him. He heard someone moan before realizing belatedly it was himself letting out such desperate sounds.

She moved her pretty, plump mouth to his ear and in a sultry voice she'd evidently discovered in their time apart, whispered, "This is why you brought me to your carriage, is it not?"

It was one of perhaps only six phrases that could have stopped him. He pulled back from her slowly, trapping her wandering hands—dear God, where had they been off to?—with his. His breathing was heavy when he begged, "Harriet, wait."

He, of course, did not want Harriet to wait at all. He wanted her to continue to *demonstrate* all sorts of things all over his lap. But if he let it happen now, he might never say what needed to be said. He might never get her back. Fully. As his.

Worse, he might never be hers.

She looked—well, she looked rather embarrassed and a little heartbroken. He had no idea how to explain himself fast enough to prevent the pain of rejection, so he brushed an errant curl out of her face and kissed her. Passionately. Desperately. Pleadingly. He hoped somehow that his lips could convey what his tongue could not, that his kiss could assuage her fear that he didn't want her. He was so tired of not having the right words. He broke off the kiss and leaned his forehead against hers, his breathing still not anywhere close to normal. Finally, in a fit of desperation, he found words. Perhaps not the best ones or the right ones. But something.

"I didn't bring you here for this at all. Please don't mistake me, I can think of few things I want more than I want you on my lap demonstrating whatever it is you mean to show me. However, first, I need you to understand how sorry I am. I know I've failed you from the moment I made you agree to a marriage in name only. Before that, really. I didn't offer for you in the library, when I should have been down on my knees begging you to deign to be my wife."

"Lady Neddlesby would have had an apoplexy if she'd found you on your knees."

"I'd always assumed I couldn't love anyone, and I certainly didn't think myself capable of being faithful. My mother didn't and couldn't. I have no idea who my father is. Maybe he's a prick or a dandy or a milksop."

"Those all seem unlikely."

"Regardless, it doesn't signify because ever since I met you I haven't *wanted* to be with anyone else. I haven't been. You might not believe this, but there hasn't been anyone since you. I don't mean that in a poetic sense. I haven't been with anyone since I met you. I only ever visited Giuliana to ask for help with you. She will vouch for that, if you're inclined to believe her. Either way, I've released her from my employ."

Harriet, who had been heroically quiet for more than two sentences, rushed to interrupt, "You didn't need to do that, Alexander! Honest!"

"I settled a large sum on her and I intend to remain friends with her in the future. Only not the sort of friends who fuck. You were right about that, by the way. She is my friend."

"It has only been two months. You will want someone again."

"I won't."

"I'm trying to tell you, you needn't fret about that. I have quite an embarrassing confession. I deeply wanted to be different from every other woman, when it came to you. I planned to be immune to your charms, to get to know you and realize you weren't so desirable after all. Only, the opposite happened. I got to know you and now I want you even more. I know you worry you can't be faithful, but it's quite all right. You don't have to be. I want whatever of you I can have, however I can have it. At least for tonight. That's why I asked you to come to the ball. I hoped I might tempt you, and that you might bed me. Whatever happens after that, however long you might stay interested, I'll take it. I promise not to get all moony. This won't change a thing."

Alexander was livid. He was furious. He could hardly catch his breath for his anger.

"Harriet, you are a horrible, horrible listener!" Harriet gasped in offense, but he didn't care at all. "You are! You are perhaps the world's most accomplished talker. And I can't wait to hear the tongue-lashing I'm about to get for this, but you haven't understood me at all. *I want you.*"

"Marvelous, I want you too! I've just said as much. Now why don't we return to your town house so you can swive me senseless."

"No."

"No . . . ?"

Alexander grabbed her by the waist, lifting and depositing her across the carriage from him to the other bench. Perhaps the distance would help both of them.

"Harriet. You are one of the smartest women I know, but you are being incredibly dense right now!"

"I beg your pardon!"

"I don't want our marriage to be in name only. Even if you offer up the absolute miracle of having you for a night. I don't want that. Well, I do. But I don't think I could stand to have you only for one night. I want more than that. I want *you* to have more than that. I want you to love me." She opened her mouth. "Harriet, if you interrupt me right now, so help me God!" She wisely closed her mouth. "I want you to love me because I treat you well. Because I'm faithful to you. Because I'm actually a good husband to you. I want you to love me because I give you what you deserve, which is unadulterated devotion. Harriet, I want you to love me because I love you."

And for the first time Harriet was absolutely speechless.

Chapter Thirty-Two

Their carriage slowed to a stop on a near-empty street; Harriet had no idea what part of town they were in. Frankly, if asked, she wasn't sure she could come up with what country they were in. There were so many thoughts and emotions running through her that, when put together, amounted to a grand sum of nothing. She could say nothing. Think nothing. Feel nothing.

"Could I perhaps show you something? And before you ask, it's not my cock or any other sordid idea your newly filthy mind has come up with. It's the rest of my apology."

Harriet still couldn't form words, although when Alexander held out his hand to assist her in getting out of the carriage, she took it. He took them around the vehicle to a simple, unmarked door, produced a key from his pocket, and led them inside.

The sight that awaited Harriet was . . . nothing. It was pitch-black in the small room, assuming that the room actually was small. Very little light from the outside filtered in.

Alexander shuffled around, knocking into something. "Damn."

She smiled, as if it broke the spell of her shock. She'd never witnessed Alexander being anything less than graceful.

Finally, a small spark flashed as he lit a lamp. It illuminated only the two of them, but at least they could see in front of them. They were in a small, unadorned vestibule.

"I forgot we'd be here at night. I imagined this all rather differently," he said sheepishly.

She reached out and put a comforting hand on his arm. "I'm quite charmed already."

"Nothing has happened."

"Not yet," she said, grinning, "but I can't wait."

"What if there were . . . I don't know! . . . a rabid dog behind this door?"

"I hardly think that would make a good apology." Her excitement was unabated.

He produced another key then and opened the second door, gesturing for her to enter first. The dim light of the lamp showed rows and rows of heavy, complex machinery.

Which was nice, she supposed.

"This," he said gravely, waving the hand with the key in it, "is yours."

"Oh, thank you," she said, smiling kindly, "you bought me a business." Clearly it meant a lot to him.

Alexander laughed at her guess, and she blushed, which he tried not to find unbearably attractive before remembering that he didn't have to keep himself from wanting her anymore. At least, he didn't think so.

"Sort of," he said, setting the lamp down on a nearby desk. Perhaps the plan hadn't been as romantic as he'd thought.

"What sort of company is it?" she inquired with false curiosity. She was clearly trying to appease what she believed was his excitement over business ownership.

"It's a publisher. A book publisher. Specifically, it's the publisher of a dictionary called *Dictionary of Modern Cant and Vulgarities*, a book written by a woman I know."

"I don't—I didn't—I don't understand."

"Harriet, I'm so sorry I ruined your dictionary, your work. I kept thinking I'd do anything to take it back, and then I realized I could do precisely that. What other use have I for the gobs of money I've got? I bought every copy of that damned book I could find and then I bought this publisher, and I thought . . . well, I thought we could reissue the dictionary with your name on it too. I'm not precisely sure how these things work, but I'm sure with enough money we can convince Mr. Dawkins."

"How enterprising of you," she teased. He hoped she was teasing. Her eyes wandered around the dim room, catching finally on the stacks of books and the piles of periodicals. He could see the pleasure she was taking in being in such a place, but she was still holding back. He expected her to be rifling through the volumes, clutching copies to her chest in wonder, pilfering through the pages of unpublished gems.

"If you don't want it, that's perfectly all right. I can sell it again."

She let out a light, easy laugh, and set a gentle hand on his arm. The weight of her touch tore through him.

"It's . . . it's exquisite, Alexander." His heart pinched at the sound of his name on her tongue. "Truly, thank you."

"I hope I didn't overstep. Or give you something else you didn't want."

"Something else?"

"Your ring. I'm sorry I didn't consult you about this. And I'm sorry you didn't like your ring." Harriet's smile fell a bit, then, much to the concern of Alexander. Why had he reminded her of that?

"Oh, I feel horrid. I . . . Alexander, I *loved* my ring. It was my favorite thing I've ever owned. Until now."

"You did? Then why?"

"I needed my father to leave to keep my sisters safe, and it was all I had that was worth anything. He pawned it no doubt for gambling funds."

"Harriet! You could have asked me for money! I would have given you—I would have given you anything. Even if I—" A horrible thought occurred to him. A frightful, excruciating thought. "You don't need me for this, Harriet. It's in your name. I want you to know that it is not a precondition of this publishing house that you are . . . with me. It's yours. I mean, my name is on some of the contracts, but we can fix that. The money will be yours. And you needn't worry that I'll interfere. I don't know the first thing about books—"

But Harriet cut him off with a deep, aching kiss. Tasting her again was heaven. Beyond heaven. It was pure bliss. And then Harriet teased his bottom lip with her tongue and bliss cracked into mad, desperate desire. He backed her up against the nearest wall and reached down to start dragging her skirts up.

Christ, but he couldn't wait to be inside of her. If she still wanted that. It might make him the greediest man in all of England, but he desperately hoped she still wanted that. Alexander reached down and began undoing his fall.

Suddenly, her hands stopped him.

∾

"Don't you want to, err . . . engage . . . a device?" Harriet asked, unsure of how to phrase such a thing.

"Please, Harriet, just say what you mean, I can't think right now," he choked out next to her ear.

"French letters, sponges, I don't remember the rest. Something to prevent getting with child!" she said, pulling back and putting a few inches of distance between them. His face grew serious then, or more serious. Truly, the man became so sincere when aroused, it was rather comical. She did her best to suppress the giggle that rose in her throat, suspecting it wouldn't go over well at this moment.

"I don't think I made myself clear."

"Oh dear," she teased at his severe tone. She couldn't hold back—she laughed then.

"I'm serious," he growled, grabbing onto her wrists and pinning them to the walls behind her.

"Yes, quite!" she said, her eyes wide in sarcastic reverence.

"You really must be punished for your poor behavior, you little minx," he warned. His thumbs rubbed up and down her wrists where he held them. "I don't want a marriage in name. I want a real, full marriage with you. I want . . . Harriet, I *want* children with you. I don't care if they become dukes in this cursed line someday. I just want them to be yours."

The desire to giggle had long since disappeared, replaced with the urge to cry. He searched her face, clearly anxious that he'd said the wrong thing. His grip relaxed and she snaked a hand up to cup his cheek.

"Well, ours," she corrected.

He kissed her again, tenderly, which was lovely, but it wasn't going to get them any closer to solving the problem between her legs.

She pushed lightly on his chest, ending the kiss to ask: "Do you think we might fuck now?"

The brazen question cracked him open. He laughed deeply, his eyes crinkling in the corners, something Harriet bet the ladies of London didn't realize was actually his most attractive feature.

Second most attractive feature.

Still smiling, he nodded, then dipped his head again to return to her mouth, but Harriet stopped him.

"I thought I actually might return to my demonstration that was so rudely interrupted."

He grinned again, unable to wipe the joy from his face. "I do apologize for that. Rather unkind of me to declare my love."

"Apology accepted; now sit," she said, directing him to a wooden chair that looked as if it might not be able to bear his weight, let alone both of theirs. Oh well. It was her publishing house now. If she wanted to break a chair, she could break a chair.

He sat, obediently, apparently unconcerned with the chair's constitution. She drew up her skirts again and returned to straddling his lap.

"You see, the idea you gave me, about, well, rubbing myself on top of something. It proved quite helpful."

"Did it now?" he asked, already distracted. He reached between them and started tracing his hands down her sternum and across her cleavage, dipping closer to the edge of her bodice.

"I've been practicing quite a bit. I've tried all kinds of things. I wanted to make sure I could come without you."

"I would love to hear every single thing you attempted," he said, laying kisses across her chest. "In detail."

"The problem was, however, I couldn't stop imagining coming with you. *From* you." The filthy words made him come up off his chair, the hard ridge of his cock pressing right against the core of her. She let out a lusty moan, so glad to have him here, for him to understand just how much she wanted him. "But I did find it educational," she said, and he laughed. Harriet could feel his smile against the skin of her neck.

"You *do* love learning."

"One thing I learned about myself, for example, is that I simply love to ride things." Alexander sat back then and swallowed thickly. He was finally paying full attention to her words.

"You do?"

"Yes," she replied, grinding herself lewdly against his cock. "In fact, I believe I can reach my peak simply by doing this. Shall I demonstrate?"

Alexander's eyes were wide and dazed and he simply nodded his head. "Hmmm," he managed to get out as he reached up and pulled down the bodice of her dress, exposing both of her glorious breasts. She had to admit, now that she understood them better, they *were* one of her best features.

He leaned down, taking one nipple into his mouth, the other in his hand. He sucked lightly and then bit gently. Harriet let out a scream of pleasure.

He leaned back with a cocky smile. "You like that, then?"

She grabbed the back of his head and brought his mouth back to her.

"Keep going," she panted, oddly not embarrassed by her desperation. She simply was too aroused to entertain shame. She rubbed along his breeches back and forth, rocking along his cockstand until she felt her entire body begin to clench; she kept going, rocking against him as he laved and licked her breasts, mad with desire. Finally, she came against him with another shout and then collapsed atop him.

Against his ear, she breathed, "I am ever so sorry about those breeches. I may have ruined them."

"I had actually been meaning to remove them."

"Let me," she said, unbuttoning his fall and taking his cock in hand. Frustrated with the lack of ease at stroking him, she reached up and licked her hand—a sight which Alexander loved for some reason, if his wide pupils and flared nostrils were to be trusted.

She returned her hand to his cock and stroked him, reveling in the feel of his hot skin, of the power she had over him, of the joy of being his. *He loved her.* He'd said he loved her. She was about to speak when he cut her off, covering her hand with his own, stopping her strokes.

"Harriet, I'm going to spend."

"Didn't you say men could only do that once?"

"Yes," he gritted out, clearly on edge.

"Wouldn't you rather do it inside of me?"

He groaned and then helped her rise up on her toes, before holding his cock at her entrance.

"This might hurt a bit," he warned.

"It shouldn't," she answered gleefully, lowering herself slowly onto him. "Remember how you told me about *godemiches*? Well, I procured one."

"Harriet! Christ!" he hissed out, and she wasn't certain if that was in response to her admission or him entering her.

"Yes?" she asked, coquettishly. Such a shame she'd been forced to wait so long to flirt with men. It was some of the most fun one could have.

"You're going to kill me, Harriet."

"Not until you've made me come again, Alexander."

He groaned and thrust up into her, making her whimper with pleasure. God, this was so much better than anything she could do or had done on her own. It was heaven. His hands on her hips guiding her, his lips on her neck, his taste in her mouth.

As she rode him, he reached down between them and brushed his hand over her most sensitive spot, the place she'd become intimately familiar with in his absence. She cried out in desperation, simultaneously needing more and not being able to bear what he was doing to her.

"Harriet, come for me, please. You must. You ha—" She cut him off with her cries of ecstasy, her spine tingling, toes curling, legs shaking with the surfeit of pleasure.

As she came down from her peak, her heart slowed and she leaned into him to whisper, "See? I can be a good listener" into his ear.

He barked out something that might have been a laugh under any circumstances where his cock was not inside of her. Knowing he was close, she raked her nails across his back and then up into his hair, pulling his mouth back to hers with a moan they both shared. Almost as soon as their tongues met, he thrust into her with one last groan and came apart, spending inside of her. Filling her up.

Harriet's body felt weightless, and her breath was still coming in pants. "What is it about rooms full of books that makes you so amorous, my lord? It's becoming quite a pattern."

"That's nearly always where you are," he said, dipping his head to continue his kisses down the side of her neck and across her collarbone.

"Do you think there might be any books on your bedside table, by chance?" She inquired, as he passed his thumb over the stiff peaks of her breasts, "I find myself quite desperate to visit your room."

His eyes snapped up to her face. Without another word, he stood, deposited her on the ground, let her skirts drop to the floor, buttoned his fall, replaced his jacket, led them out of the publishing house, extinguished the lamp and hurried Harriet into the carriage, with a gruff note to the driver to make all possible haste in returning home.

Of course, seven minutes is quite a long journey. Especially when one is prone to carriage sickness.

Luckily, Harriet knew precisely the cure for that affliction.

The next morning, Harriet awoke, serene and sated next to Alexander. Surrounded, actually. Surrounded by Alexander. One wants to be specific with words. She scooted back, farther into his embrace, hoping not to disturb him, but still marveling at the feel of his arms around her.

She hadn't ever thought she'd have this. Not with him, and truly, until recently not with anyone. Sure, as a young girl she'd thought of marrying a prince, but even before her first disastrous season that fantasy had washed away. Later, she'd thought perhaps she might have a comfortable life with a fictitious version of Mr. Dawkins. But she hadn't imagined *this*. Waking up with someone, the warmth of them, the weight of them. She wouldn't have known how to. The reality of it was so much better than anything she'd known to dream of.

"What is it, Harriet?" he whispered groggily against her ear. The sound of his voice in the morning did something wild to her.

"I didn't say anything."

"Yes, love; and the effort of that was louder than cannon fire." As he said it, he tightened his grip around her waist, stopping her from pulling away.

"I forgot to tell you something. Last night."

To his credit, Alexander didn't pull back, but when he replied with a simple "Yes?" she detected a hint of concern. She bit her lip to keep from smiling—not at his worry, but at the fact that she knew him so well she could hear the emotions in his voice.

"I love you."

"Oh dear, how bad is this going to be if that's the preface? Have you lost thousands of pounds in a gambling scheme? Are you carrying Dawkins's child? Are you dying of the plague? I *will* still love you, but I hope it's not the second."

Harriet twisted out of his embrace and flipped over to face him. "Those are your top concerns? In that order?"

"I don't know! You seemed rather dire about the whole thing!"

"Alexander!"

"Well! Are you going to tell me?"

"I did, you oaf! I forgot, yesterday, to tell you that I love you. I love you. I love you. There!"

"Is that all?" he said, drawing her back to him, his voice hitching with emotion. "I rather assumed."

"You did, huh?" Harriet teased.

"I knew you'd come around," he continued, taking her mouth in his again. After all, it had been hours since they'd kissed.

And they had only a lifetime left.

Acknowledgments

Firstly, thank you for reading this book! *The Very Definition of Love* was the most fun I ever had writing; I hope you loved Harriet and Alexander as much as I do.

All the gratitude in the world to my exquisite agent, Jessica Felleman, who didn't blink when I wanted to write a book in an entirely different genre, who offered such wonderful guidance and tons of reassuring emails and phone calls.

A huge thank you to my brilliant editor Nicole Otto, who loved Harriet from the very beginning and who saw what this book could be. Thank you to everyone at Zando who helped make this book so much better, and who made it real. In design and production, Christopher King, Jennifer Freilach, Kayla White, Marina Padakis, and Patrick Leger. In publicity, marketing, and sales, Julia McGarry, Sam Mitchell, Nathalie Ramirez, Nancy Trypuc, Andrew Rein, and Ashley Alberico. And to the Slowburn team: Hayley Wagreich, Sierra Stovall, Ava Shaffer, and TJ Ohler.

Thank you to the early readers, especially my sister Lena, who—like Harriet and me—loves words. Lean Bean, if you like this book, the job is done.

Thank you to all the writers and romance-lovers who encouraged me and inspired me, especially Sarah MacLean, Jennifer Prokop, Hannah Orenstein, and Joss Richard. Thank you to the booksellers and librarians and the people who post about and promote romance novels.

I am embarrassingly rich in the friendship arena, but a special thank you to Tamara Yajia, the most dazzling woman alive, for always being down to have a bottle of wine and talk about writing and parents and salami. And to Emilee Kearney and Kelsey June Jensen, who have given me so much support, not just through writing a book, but through life. (They are also down to have a bottle of wine.) It's a dream and a half to be your friend.

Thank you to my whole massive family, but especially my parents, who are so insanely supportive and loving—it's borderline sick of you. Thank you for reading to us every single night before bed and for always buying more books. Sorry I moved so far away; you're with me every single moment. Really, really hoping you guys didn't read this one, but I know you did. Please don't mention it.

My dog Party cannot read and impedes my writing greatly, but she still deserves a thank-you for how much better she makes my life.

Lastly, thank you Dave, who had to bribe me to let him read this book because I was too shy even though we had been together for nine years at the time. Thank you for something beyond encouragement and support, just an unwavering belief in me and my capabilities. Thank you for being hot. I can't believe I get to be with you.

Author's Note

While I endeavored to make this book historically accurate, to a degree that perhaps wasn't required—please ask me about all the research I did into throw blankets and graphite mines—there are a few things I allowed into this world that may not have been perfectly accurate. (See the birth control situation below and the word "crisis.")

As much as I could, I tried to use words and phrases that Harriet would have had possible access to. Which was more difficult than you might think. For example, the word "escalate" didn't exist—it comes from escalators—and neither did the word "hello," which came about in 1826, and which wasn't popularized until Thomas Edison started saying it on the phone. People said, "Good day," or "Good morning/afternoon/evening," which is still much more common in other languages.

Sexual words were even more difficult to trace the use and nuance of because people are a lot less likely to put these things in print. While the word "sex" has been around since the fourteenth century, "having sex" as a phrase is relatively new (twentieth century).

During my research, I relied heavily on Francis Grose's 1811 edition of *The Dictionary of the Vulgar Tongue*. In fact, it's partially what I modeled Harriet's dictionary on. The book is commonly and heavily cited; however, some people suggest that not *all* of Grose's words were real, and that he may have included false words to see if other people were copying his work, since copyright didn't exist then. Other beloved phrases come from Georgette Heyer, who helped create and popularize the sub-genre of Regency romance in the 1920s, and who also enjoyed putting original (false) turns of phrase in her books.

Since this book is so much about words and Harriet's love for them, I strove to use words she'd actually use as much as I possibly could, but I also tried to balance that with writing a book that was enjoyable to read.

Glossary

Many of these words I'm sure you gleaned either from context clues, or because they're explicitly defined in the book. However, I thought I'd collect them all in one place for you—a small taste of Harriet's vulgar dictionary.

CHAPTER 1:

Globes: Breasts.

Apples: Breasts.

Paps: Breasts or nipples, although the word was also used for animals … yikes.

Peer: Someone who is a "peer of the realm" or part of the "peerage," which means members of the British nobility who held hereditary titles: dukes, marquesses, earls, viscounts, and barons.

Crush: A very popular, crowded event.

Fashion plates: Illustrations of fashionable dresses found in magazines that upper-class women could then bring to their dressmakers, or that middle- and lower-class women might attempt to copy themselves.

Davenport desk: A small, inclined writing desk.

Cyprian: A high-class sex-worker, often well kept by a gentleman.

Short stays: Stays and corsets were both structuring undergarments worn during the Regency era. The word *stays* was older, and around the turn of the century, the word *corset* started to be used. This is not, however, the Victorian corset you're imagining. The corset which Harriet borrows from Philippa is longer and supportive, but still flexible. Empire-waisted diaphanous dresses were in, so no one needed to have a tiny waist, but they did need boob support and good posture.

CHAPTER 2:

Muttonhead[1]: A stupid or dull person. This is an American phrase, first recorded in 1803, so hopefully it made it to London by 1816.

Wallflower: A shy or overlooked woman, often standing along the wall at a dance.

Ratafia: A sweet wine seen as appropriate for ladies to drink.

Buck[2]: A young pleasure-seeking man. (Notice the lack of judgment in this term versus those used for women.)

Rout: A large, fashionable party.

Flummery: Originally a light, soft gelatinous dessert, which came to be known for being bland and unsatisfying, later a term for empty praise or flattery.

Dolt/doltish: A stupid or foolish person.

Deuced: A word used for emphasis, often in place of a curse word like *damned*. A lot of Regency slang is people trying not to use naughty words.

Dirty puzzle: A promiscuous woman. This one comes right from Grose, whose definition is the rather judgy "A nasty slut."

Quim: A vagina. Unknown origin. Grose suggests it might be from the Spanish word *quemar*, to burn, which is romantic, but unsupported. Other sources suggest it might be from the obsolete Middle English word *queme*, which meant "to please" or "agreeable."

Monosyllable: Also a vagina, although the monosyllable referred to here is "cunt."

Milksop[3]**:** A male loser, basically. A weak, cowardly man. We need to bring this word back.

Namby-pamby[4]**:** More commonly an adjective, but also a noun meaning someone who lacks courage.

Banknote: A banknote wasn't legal tender, but rather a promissory note, meaning someone's bank owed you. Paper money wasn't really a thing; this was more like a check. It's not the same as regular paper money because the government isn't issuing it, a bank is.

Cry off: To back out of something or fail to keep a promise.

Ton: Short for the French phrase *le bon ton*. *Ton* referred both to the upper class of British society, and to the behavior required of that class. Something could be good *ton*, which meant, essentially, good manners.

Reticule: A small purse, usually closed with drawstrings, which held the absolutely necessary handkerchief, sometimes small change, maybe smelling salts, maybe a letter, etc.

Quadrille: A fashionable square dance that usually was performed by four couples. It came to England in 1816 via Lady Jersey and people went nuts for it. The waltz was introduced in 1813 and was given an endorsement from Dorothea Lieven, the wife of the Russian ambassador, although it was considered shocking and even indecent by some well into the 1820s.

John Julius Angerstein: An insurance broker who had a famous art collection you could privately tour. Private art collections were very popular during the Regency period, and his was particularly popular. His collection went on to become the National Gallery.

CHAPTER 3:
Bollocks: Testicles.

Innocent: As a noun: a young, unmarried woman who had no sexual experience (who was expected to eventually marry).

Assignation: A meeting, especially a secret one between lovers. We need to bring this word back.

Commodity: Vagina. As Grose crudely puts it, "The private parts of a modest woman, and the public parts of a prostitute."

Money: Vagina, although a more "polite" slang term, one someone might use with children even. (These last two terms are a little on the nose with correlating women's body parts to mercenary terms.)

Hothouse: A heated greenhouse for growing and keeping exotic or out-of-season flowers that wouldn't normally grow in England.

Squab: The cushions of a carriage.

CHAPTER 4:

Ruin: To taint the reputation of. To be ruined was to lose social standing and possibly be ostracized. While unmarried ladies could be ruined by being in a room with a closed door with a man, being ruined was more difficult for a man and usually meant financial ruin.

Swive: To have sex with someone. To fuck.

Rake/rakehell: A libertine, an immoral man. Often used for a dissolute man who "wasted" his fortune on women and drink and gambling.

Parson's mousetrap: Marriage.

Divan: A long, low sofa, usually without a back or arms.

Settee: A medium-sized low, upholstered bench. Similar to a couch today, though less comfortable.

Dowry: Also known as a marriage settlement, a dowry is the money brought into a marriage by the bride, provided usually by the bride's father or relatives. It was often essentially an advance on money the bride would have inherited from her father. Elopements came with no dowry, which is part of the reason they were so scandalous. Marriage settlements were occasionally drawn up by lawyers, although that was expensive. Those documents would decide how much pin money (allowance) a woman would get and what would happen financially should her husband die.

Entailed: A property that is entailed is connected to the title and cannot be sold or willed away. So if a duke has an entailed country estate every future duke will have that property; even if he wanted to leave it to his second son or mistress or daughter, he could not as it "belongs" to the title, not to him.

CHAPTER 5:

Hack chaise: A carriage for hire; basically, a taxi.

Shilling: Money conversions across time are difficult for a lot of reasons, not only because our economy is entirely different now from 1816. But: £1 in 1816 is about £125 today, and there are 20 shillings in a pound, which means that would be about £6.25, which as of writing is a little over $8. Again, none of this is perfect math.

Bloody hell: A strong curse in the Regency era. Very vulgar, especially uncommon for women and those of the upper classes to say in someone else's presence.

Cravat: Elaborately tied neckties men wore during the Regency era. Well-tied cravats were a point of pride among Regency gentlemen, although you could apparently also buy neck-stocks, which were kind of like pre-tied cravats, often used by military men.

Banns: A public announcement of an impending marriage. For three Sundays before the wedding, the church or chapel that the couple attended would read out the banns to see if anyone had a reason to object. The goal here was often to prevent bigamy. If you were under twenty-one, your parent or guardian could object to the reading of the banns.

Special license: This was one of the ways around banns being read. It was a license issued by His Grace, the Archbishop of Canterbury that allowed titled lords (and their families) to get married at any time (marriages had to take place between 8 am and noon in the Regency era) and any place, not just the church where the banns were read. These were very expensive and relatively rare.

Elopement: Another way around the banns being read was to simply elope to a country that was not subject to Hardwicke's Marriage Act of 1753. The normal destination, for many reasons (nearness, language, etc.), was Scotland, which had much looser marriage laws.

Gretna Green: Gretna Green was the site of many marriages because it was the first city across the England/Scotland border on one of the major toll roads, and at a junction where five coaching roads met. Marriage in Scotland did not require parental consent. All Scots law required at the time for an "irregular marriage" was two witnesses. Eloping English couples often still wanted some whiff of authority for their ceremonies, and eventually blacksmiths became popular officiants, with some performing thousands of marriages.

Bugger: Vulgar slang for anal sex, but also for a worthless man.

Sod: An unpleasant or obnoxious person, from—you will perhaps be unsurprised to learn—the shortening of the word *sodomite*. Lots of homophobic origins for slang.

Toothpowder: The Regency form of toothpaste. Toothbrushes had been fairly recently invented (1780) by William Addis while he was in prison, but even before then, people kept their teeth clean, or at least they tried to. Members of the upper class at this point would have used a toothbrush and toothpowder.

Night rail: A nightgown, usually very loose.

Chemise: An undergarment women wore under pretty much everything. Somewhat similar to how a man might wear an undershirt, women wore and washed their chemises rather than repeatedly laundering their dresses. They were very thin and made usually of cotton or silk, depending on how wealthy you were. It's the same thing as a shift. Some women wore them to bed.

CHAPTER 6:

Jilt: To reject or abandon, often unfeelingly. Often during this era the word was used to mean ending an engagement.

Cicisbeo/cavalier servente: A male companion to a married woman or a lover. Historically, the man would—with the full knowledge and permission of her husband—escort a woman around publicly, even to church. The origin of the word and the practice is from eighteenth-century Italy, where this practice flourished in the upper classes for a short period. There were elaborate rules of conduct, and not all cicisbei were lovers, although the word takes that meaning in English. Some were famously homosexual.

Paramour: A lover, especially one of a married person.

Gallant: Sometimes an illicit lover, but also a fashionable man or one who is chivalrous and particularly attentive to women.

Chit: A young woman, especially one who is ill-behaved.

Cast up one's accounts: To vomit.

Small clothes: A man's underwear, kind of like boxers.

Christian name: Your first name, so called because it is given at baptism. First names were very rarely used during the Regency era, except by family.

Fall: Men's pants, trousers, breeches, etc., were sewn with a flap in front called a fall front that buttoned up to the waistband. There were no zippers at the time, and men didn't wear belts, just tight, tight little pants.

CHAPTER 7:

Wanton: Lewd, lustful, sensuous, or promiscuous. Autocorrects to wonton a lot—be careful.

Carriage dress: A dress for traveling, easy to wear, easy to clean. Made of heavier fabric than a normal day dress or walking dress so that it didn't wrinkle as easily and gave better protection from dirt and dust. Often, they had less detail and ornamentation.

Missish[5]**:** Prim, demure, or squeamish.

Caprice[6]**:** A whim or inexplicable change in mood.

Bedevil: To bother or annoy, to cause trouble for.

Bluestocking[7]**:** A smart, learned woman who often enjoyed books.

Amorous congress: One of the more common euphemisms for

having sex, thought to be the most polite and appropriate way to refer to the act.

Tup: A vulgar term for having sex with someone. Regrettably for us all, the word originated with and generally referred to the act in relation to sheep, so it was very crass.

Coquetries[8]: Flirtations.

Kippers: A small, oily fish, usually pickled or smoked, commonly eaten for breakfast.

CHAPTER 8:

Slippers: Dancing shoes, usually without a heel, often made of silk, satin, or kid leather.

Coaching inn: An inn designed specifically to stop and change horses. This was not a comfortable hotel-like experience for most people. Often food was mediocre at best and rotten at worst. Rich travelers often sent ahead a servant to secure a good room. You were meant to bring your own bedsheets when traveling because nothing was guaranteed to be clean or provided. In the magical world of Harriet and Alexander, the sheets are clean and bedbug free. I promise.

Blighter: Someone people find annoying, pathetic, or pitiable.

Brainsick: Crazy, mad, or insane.

Breeches: Men's pants that stopped below the knee. Let's be honest, they're basically capris. Men wore them often during the Regency era, even as there was a transition to trousers starting. At balls, all men would be wearing breeches with their knee-length stockings. How cute, right? Personally, I don't find them hot; I tried to get Alexander into trousers, which did also exist at the time, as soon as possible.

Twitterpated: Infatuated or obsessed.

Birdbrain: Scatterbrain; a not very bright person.

Cork-brained: Foolish; someone without much substance.

Intended: Another word for someone's fiancé since, you know, you intend to marry them.

Louche: Indecent, but usually in a hot way.

Trousseau[9]: A bride's belongings that she brings to her marriage, like clothing, bed linen, etc.

Ladybird: A sex worker or mistress.

CHAPTER 9:

White's: A gentlemen's club which began, oddly enough, as a hot chocolate shop. The oldest private members' club in the world. Famous for gambling and known for some of the eccentric bets its high-society members placed, including on things like who would marry whom and when.

Tailcoat[10]: The coat a man wears for formal occasions. It's long in the back and split into tails.

Nineteen to the dozen: Speaking rapidly, with barely a pause for breath.

Blandishment[11]: Flattery used to persuade someone to do something.

CHAPTER 10:

Taking himself in hand: Masturbation, specifically in regard to men.

Woodenheaded: Stupid.

Greatcoat: An overcoat for men, designed for protection from the elements rather than just style.

Hellcat[12]: A foul-tempered, shrewish woman.

Droll: Amusing or odd, but in a humorous way.

Playacting: Pretending or acting.

CHAPTER 11:

Mayfair: The most fashionable residential neighborhood in London during the Regency era. *The* place to live if you were upper class.

Reel: A lively folk dance.

Curricle[13]: A carriage with two wheels pulled by two horses.

Cockstand: An erection. This is my favorite Regency slang word of all. It makes *so* much sense, I can't believe it fell out of fashion.

Tossing off: Masturbating.

Bringing oneself off: Masturbating.

Self-polluting: Also masturbating. This was a common phrase at the time as masturbation came with a lot of societal shame. The idea of course is that you are tainting or dirtying yourself with the act.

Crisis: An orgasm. Strictly speaking, it's difficult to find evidence of the word being used in this sense before the 1920s (very famously in D.H. Lawrence's *Lady Chatterley's Lover*). However, if you imagine that the word *crisis* also means a turning point, it makes sense. I let Harriet and Alexander get away with it.

CHAPTER 12:
Coverlet: A bedspread.

CHAPTER 13:
Daft: Crazy, addled, insane.

Godemiche: Another name for a dildo. A French loan word.

Gooseflesh: Goosebumps. This word was first used in 1810, hence the supposition that Harriet might not know it.

Foolscap: A piece of writing paper.

CHAPTER 14:

Valise: A small suitcase.

Gad about: To go from place to place seeking pleasure and enjoying oneself. You can also use it as one word, gadabout, to mean a person who goes from place to place seeking pleasure and enjoying themself.

CHAPTER 15:

Laudanum: A mixture of opium and alcohol that was used as a painkiller and sedative. Very common at the time. Concerningly common.

Cash book: A household book for keeping track of accounts, bills, what was owed, etc. Ladies of the house would be expected to take at least some part in the household accounting.

CHAPTER 16:

Leg shackled: Married. The jokes never change, do they?

Stuff and bother: An expression of annoyance.

Haven't a sixpence to scratch with: This one is likely not a real phrase used at the time, but rather comes from Georgette Heyer, as the only real records I find of it are from her book *Charity Girl*. Still, I felt it was a nice nod to Georgette and a good phrase, so it stayed.

Blunt: Money.

In a trice: Quickly.

Hack: Short for a hackney or a hackney carriage. A carriage for hire; basically a taxi.

Folding flintlock: A gun.

Crackbrained[14]: Stupid or crazy.

Cleaned out: Impoverished, lacking funds.

CHAPTER 17:

Cheroot: A filterless cylindrical cigar with both ends clipped during manufacture, commonly smoked during the Regency period. Really, though, people loved to get their tobacco in the form of snuff, which makes sense as friction matches didn't exist at the time, making it a little annoying to smoke.

Mopsy: While this came to be a term of endearment, it originally was used to describe a slovenly, untidy woman.

Strumpet[15]: A woman who partakes in casual sex; more often, a sex worker.

Bird of paradise: Alternatively called "birds of youth," this was slang for a sex worker or promiscuous woman.

Debauchee[16]**:** A person who loves sex and other sensual things. A fabulous word we ought to use more.

CHAPTER 18:

Widow's portion: The portion of an estate that a widow lived off of. Usually one-third of her husband's unentailed estate, known as her dower. There are some complicated math and legal rituals involved on this one, so sometimes a widow did end up destitute even when her husband had done okay for himself.

Green: Untried, inexperienced.

CHAPTER 19:

Hertfordshire kindness: A favor granted in return for another favor, *or* toasting twice to the same person.

Balum rancum: A dance performed by a company of sex workers, all naked. Grose dipped far back into the 1600s for this entry in his dictionary, and it seems like a bit of a stretch to imagine that people actually used this phrase in real life. He spells it *balum rancum*, others suggest *ballum rancum*.

Prig: Someone who is overly righteous and always believes they are correct.

Pelisse: A long, fitted coat worn over dresses.

Megrim: How people said *migraine* back then.

Reverting to the crown: Any property or title that, for one reason or another, went back to the crown (the monarch/government) to be absorbed by the government or redistributed as a monarch might see fit. Some reasons would include unpaid dues, treason, or even, sadly, suicide.

Coffer: Originally literally a box or chest for holding funds, but also a metaphorical place for holding money.

Bring to heel: To force someone to obey you, to control a person.

CHAPTER 20:

Fire in the grate: No new words for this chapter, but I do want to note that even the rich did not leave fires burning in unoccupied rooms, despite what other Regency-era stories might depict. It was far too costly to do so, and also dangerous.

CHAPTER 21:

Ice: Ice cream or any other frozen or cold dessert. A luxury, as ice itself was difficult and expensive to procure and transport. Some were water-based (think of snow cones) and some were cream- or custard-based.

Axminster: A popular type of carpet for the wealthy, named after a town in England famous for carpet making. Famous for bright colors and intricate designs that often were meant to evoke painted ceilings.

Whore-pipe: A penis.

Frigger: Also a penis.

Hair splitter: Again, a penis.

Wedding tackle: Penis. (This one gets points for creativity for me.)

Bush-beater: You guessed it: a penis.

Ninny: A foolish person.

Spend: To ejaculate.

CHAPTER 22:

God's teeth: An expression of surprise or amazement.

Rib: A wife.

Putting someone on: To deceive someone.

CHAPTER 23:

Base-born: Either born of low status or illegitimate.

Silk-stockings: An aristocratic or wealthy person.

Paper-skull: An idiot.

Hushing: To kill someone.

Quarter days: Four major holidays spread out throughout the year (Lady Day [March 25], Midsummer [June 24], Michaelmas [September 29], and Christmas [December 25]) that were widely celebrated in the UK and Ireland historically. They were also when rent was due and often when employment contracts began and ended.

CHAPTER 24:

Drinking chocolate: Kind of like the modern-day hot chocolate except far, far richer and thicker. Drinking chocolate was very labor-intensive to make and therefore typically a luxury of the upper class. Ladies often had drinking chocolate brought to their rooms before breakfast to hold them over until that meal. Mealtimes were weird back then; it's far too much to explain.

Brougham[17]: A carriage with a roof and four wheels.

Drunk as a wheelbarrow: Very drunk.

Rundell Bridge and Rundell: A famous London jewelry firm of the era. They were the Royal Goldsmiths of King George III, King George IV, King William IV, and Queen Victoria.

Blackguard[18]: A man who acts poorly, especially in a way that dishonors someone else.

Caitiff: Someone who is cowardly, craven, or wimpy.

CHAPTER 25:

Honorific[19]: A title or word used to convey respect, or to denote someone's station. A duke, for example, would be addressed as "Your Grace," which is his honorific.

Clodpate: A stupid person.

CHAPTER 26:

Peerless Pool: London's first outdoor public swimming pool.

Angelo's School of Arms: A legendary London fencing school founded by Domenico Angelo in 1758 and then taken over by his son, Henry Angelo, who made it into more of a social club. Eventually, Gentlemen Jackson's, the famous boxing club, was set up next door at Henry's encouragement.

Moonshine: Nonsense.

CHAPTER 27:

Dashed: A word used for emphasis.

CHAPTER 28:

Debrett's: A company that published both etiquette guides and *The New Peerage,* which listed peers (persons with titles) and their families and ranks and titles. The company still exists; it tracks peerages and puts out etiquette guides online.

Démodé: Out of style, outdated.

By-blow: An impolite term for an illegitimate child; a bastard.

Lughead: A stupid person.

CHAPTER 29:

Temple of the Muses: A real bookstore with a very interesting history. Owned by James Lackington, who wanted everyone of every class to have access to books. He was one of the first booksellers to not allow people to purchase books on credit in order to keep the cost low. Temple of the Muses was known for having a very extensive inventory—apparently over a million books at one point. The store was also very large, with lounging rooms and multiple stories and a famous, massive circular counter in the center. Unfortunately, she (the store) burned down in 1841.

CHAPTER 30:

Nonpareil[20]: Someone without an equal. A superior individual.

CHAPTER 31:

Newgate: A large, overcrowded prison in London notorious for its horrible conditions.

Dandy[21]: A man who is very into how he dresses; often mildly negative to mean a man who fusses over his style.

CHAPTER 32:

French letters: Condoms. Although there's debate about when people started calling them French letters, condoms *did* exist during the Regency era. They were usually seen as more for disease prevention for those who frequented houses of ill-repute than for the upper class to prevent pregnancy. Of all people, Casanova helped popularize them after being a critic earlier in his life.

Sponges: Sea sponges were sometimes soaked in vinegar or lemon juice and then put inside a woman, which was thought to kill sperm. It did not; it was not effective at all. While sponge use was at its height later in the 1800s, the idea of putting a sponge inside a woman to prevent pregnancy is fairly ancient—it was apparently mentioned in the Talmud.

Endnotes

1   "Muttonhead." Merriam-Webster.com Dictionary, Merriam-Webster, https://www.merriam-webster.com/dictionary/muttonhead. Accessed 26 Aug. 2025.

2   "Regency Lingo." *Regency Reader*, 29 May 2023, regrom.com/regency-lingo/.

3   "Milksop." Merriam-Webster.com Dictionary, Merriam-Webster, https://www.merriam-webster.com/dictionary/milksop. Accessed 26 Aug. 2025.

4   "Namby-pamby." Merriam-Webster.com Dictionary, Merriam-Webster, https://www.merriam-webster.com/dictionary/namby-pamby. Accessed 26 Aug. 2025.

5   "Missish, Adj." Oxford English Dictionary, Oxford UP, July 2023, https://doi.org/10.1093/OED/6477098678.

6   "Caprice, N." Oxford English Dictionary, Oxford UP, September 2024, https://doi.org/10.1093/OED/2961831264.

7   "Bluestocking, Adj. & N." Oxford English Dictionary, Oxford UP, September 2024, https://doi.org/10.1093/OED/7108945562.

8   "Coquetry, N." Oxford English Dictionary, Oxford UP, July 2023, https://doi.org/10.1093/OED/3240159512.

9   "Trousseau, N. (1)." Oxford English Dictionary, Oxford UP, June 2024, https://doi.org/10.1093/OED/7515804319.

10 "Tail-coat, N." Oxford English Dictionary, Oxford UP, June 2025, https://doi.org/10.1093/OED/6311335703.

11 "Blandishment, N." Oxford English Dictionary, Oxford UP, December 2024, https://doi.org/10.1093/OED/4743696370.

12 "Collins English Dictionary — Complete & Unabridged" 2012 Digital Edition © William Collins Sons & Co. Ltd. 1979, 1986 © HarperCollins Publishers 1998, 2000, 2003, 2005, 2006, 2007, 2009, 2012

13 "Curricle, N." Oxford English Dictionary, Oxford UP, December 2024, https://doi.org/10.1093/OED/3687817279.

14 "Collins English Dictionary — Complete & Unabridged" 2012 Digital Edition © William Collins Sons & Co. Ltd. 1979, 1986 © HarperCollins Publishers 1998, 2000, 2003, 2005, 2006, 2007, 2009, 2012

15 "Strumpet, N. & Adj." Oxford English Dictionary, Oxford UP, December 2024, https://doi.org/10.1093/OED/1190367146.

16 "Debauchee, N." Oxford English Dictionary, Oxford UP, December 2024, https://doi.org/10.1093/OED/1095209975.

17 "Brougham, N." Oxford English Dictionary, Oxford UP, December 2024, https://doi.org/10.1093/OED/4643086395.

18 "Blackguard, N. & Adj." Oxford English Dictionary, Oxford UP, March 2025, https://doi.org/10.1093/OED/4053604378.

19 "Honorific, Adj. & N." Oxford English Dictionary, Oxford UP, July 2023, https://doi.org/10.1093/OED/8557213404.

20 "Nonpareil." Merriam-Webster.com Dictionary, Merriam-Webster, https://www.merriam-webster.com/dictionary/nonpareil. Accessed 26 Aug. 2025.

21 "Dandy, N. (1), Adj., & Adv." Oxford English Dictionary, Oxford UP, March 2025, https://doi.org/10.1093/OED/6349277528.

Do you love historical fiction?

Want the chance to hear news about your favourite
authors (and the chance to win free books)?

Suzanne Allain
Mary Balogh
Lenora Bell
Charlotte Betts
Manda Collins
Joanna Courtney
Grace Burrowes
Evie Dunmore
Lynne Francis
Pamela Hart
Elizabeth Hoyt
Eloisa James
Lisa Kleypas
Jayne Ann Krentz
Sarah MacLean
Terri Nixon
Julia Quinn

Then visit the Piatkus website
www.yourswithlove.co.uk

And follow us on Facebook and Instagram
www.facebook.com/yourswithlovex | @yourswithlovex

PIATKUS